JASE & THE DEADLIEST HUNT

JOHN LUKE ROBERTSON

WITH TRAVIS THRASHER

 TYNDALE HOUSE PUBLISHERS, INC., CAROL STREAM, IL

For manufacturing information regarding this product, please call 1-800-323-9400.

Library of Congress Cataloging-in-Publication Data

Robertson, John Luke.
  Jase & the deadliest hunt / John Luke Robertson ; with Travis Thrasher.
     pages cm. — ([Be your own Duck Commander ; 4])
    ISBN 978-1-4143-9816-7 (sc)
    I. Thrasher, Travis, 1971- II. Duck dynasty (Television program) III. Title. IV. Title: Jase and the deadliest hunt.
  PZ7.R5465Jas 2014
  [Fic]—dc23   2014023383

Printed in the United States of America

20	19	18	17	16	15	14
7	6	5	4	3	2	1

This book is dedicated to my uncle Jase.

Jase, first of all, thanks for the dating advice!

Most important, thank you for never being afraid to share

the gospel message with others. It's something I have witnessed

my whole life, and it has helped shape me as a Christian man.

Keep calling ducks and people to the water!

WARNING!

DON'T READ THIS BOOK STRAIGHT THROUGH!

You'll miss out on all the fun if you do.

Instead, start at the beginning and decide where to go at the end of each chapter. You will be given many options. Just like in life, some of the choices you make will be good ones. Some will be bad. Very, very bad. Like being-mauled-by-a-raging-beast bad. But that's okay. You can always try again.

If you reach the end of one story, go back and start over. There are multiple story lines and many endings. You get to decide what happens. So it's your own fault if things go terribly wrong. You will have nobody to blame but yourself (and Willie, of course).

So get ready for the grandest adventure of your life. Be careful about what lies in wait in that cave. Don't get too risky around the river. Don't let Mount Fear live up to its name.

Oh, and avoid the hogs. Seriously. Stay out of their chubby way.

Have fun. Make sure you bring your son and nephew back home.

But it's okay if you leave your brother behind on the island.

THIS IS WHO YOU ARE

Your name is Jason Silas Robertson. Jase for short.

Your parents are Phil and Kay Robertson. Your father started Duck Commander, where you currently hold the position of chief operating officer. That's right. You're the chief. Your responsibility (among many) is creating unique duck calls for the business. But come on—you're really the company mascot.

You have three brothers. One of them, Willie, claims to be your boss and talks about being the CEO of Duck Commander, but you know who really runs this ship. You married your beautiful high school sweetheart twenty years ago, and you have three amazing children.

You take after your father in being a strong hunter—you've been at it since the age of eight. You are a frog's worst nightmare since you love catching them and you love to eat them even more.

You are a man of faith. A man committed to his family. You also have a great love of the outdoors and the animals in it. You appreciate every creature God made, and you love examining their strengths and weaknesses. Your favorite animal happens to be whichever one you're currently hunting. So go ahead and get some!

THE ISLAND OF THE GREAT UNKNOWN

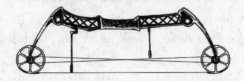

YOU ARE ABOUT TO EMBARK on the greatest hunting expedition man has ever seen, yet you have no idea where you'll be hunting, nor do you know what you'll be trying to track down.

There are four of you seated in a helicopter: you; your brother Willie; his eldest son, John Luke; and your middle son, Cole. You've gotten used to the rumbling of the chopper through your entire body, though you're also amazed at how smooth this trip has been. So far, all you've seen is water below. The helicopter took off from Fiji, where you arrived earlier this morning. Or maybe it was afternoon—your sense of time has disappeared since leaving West Monroe and flying to Los Angeles, then getting on a flight lasting over eleven hours.

You're ready to get there, wherever *there* might be.

"You ready to swim if this thing goes down?" Willie asks, sitting across from you.

You can tell he's bored.

"If this thing goes down, it's 'cause of you, big boy," you say.

"So you think this is going to be as good of a hunting trip as the wives promised?"

You shake your head. "Well, if it's not, then we better get another birthday present."

"Hey—it's *your* birthday month officially. I already had my present back in April."

"Mom says this counts for your present *next* year," John Luke says.

"Make sure you don't remind her," Willie says. "Got that?"

You gaze out over the Pacific. "Missy and Korie sure talked up this trip. The guy they met was either the real deal or some fraud who could've sold them a plot of land on the moon."

"Count VanderVelde," Willie reminds you. "He's the guy who bought the Duck Commander crossbow at the silent auction. Paid ten times the price. He's no joke."

"Every time I hear someone named Count anything, I think of Count Chocula," you say. "Do they still sell that?"

Cole, who's sitting next to you, just shrugs. Missy is the one who does the shopping, and Count Chocula isn't on the menu these days. It's not exactly a health food.

"Is that stuff any good?" John Luke asks.

"Of course it's good, John Luke," Willie says. "Come on."

2

Missy said the cost of this trip was a little high, but it would be a once-in-a-lifetime experience. You know that few things described that way actually turn out to be once-in-a-lifetime. But she promised it was going to be a hunting expedition like you'd never seen before. You reminded your wife that you've seen some pretty awesome things and hunted down some pretty wild things.

"Not like this," Missy said.

Now you're wondering what kind of island you're heading to. Obviously it's an island. It's gotta be an island. No way you're gonna be hunting for anything on an oil rig or an aircraft carrier.

"Did I tell you I got a call from Luke Bryan?" Willie asks. "He said he went on one of these expeditions."

"So what'd he say about it?"

"He's sworn to secrecy. That's part of the intrigue—not knowing what you're hunting for until you get there. Luke just said we couldn't pass on this opportunity."

"Oh yeah? Well, Lady Gaga called me and said she's been to this island," you joke. "Said not to order the veal. Bad idea."

Willie shakes his head while the boys laugh. You like to make fun of Hollywood Willie with all his famous buddies. Sure, country musician Luke Bryan is a part of Buck Commander. Maybe you can start Truck Commander and get some famous people to participate. Maybe someone like Darius Rucker. The musician. Yeah. That'd be cool.

"So we still have the wager going on?" Willie asks.

"You bet."

This wager will determine who wins the much-beloved family trophy that says *#1 Robertson Hunter*. The trophy's been passed back and forth between Phil and Uncle Si but now happens to be owned—horror of horrors—by Willie. He got it after nabbing a twenty-point buck on one of his Buck Commander hunts. That was pretty good, but you like to remind him that some teenager was reported on the news for bagging a twenty-four-point buck.

Thank goodness for the Internet and Google to show up fast-talking Willie.

"It's time to put the trophy in its proper place," you say.

"You know, one of the boys might get it," Willie says. "What do you say, Cole? Think you'll nab the biggest buck this weekend?"

"It might be something else," Cole says.

"The biggest catch. That's the deal. Whoever gets it."

You simply smile at your brother. Willie's all talk and no action. He'll get tired and try to convince someone to shoot the game for him.

Not this time. On this trip, it's every hunter for himself.

Then Willie points outside. "Looks like we've found the island from *Lost*."

You peer out the window and spot an island far below. It's covered with a thick jungle, a river cutting through it. A single

mountain towers over everything, and you can just make out the entrance to a cave on the mountain slope. You can't help but think of Tom Hanks in the movie *Cast Away*, but this island is much larger than that one.

As the helicopter rounds the steep mountain, you catch sight of a large resort/lodge complex at the base. A landing pad and a small runway with a private airplane on it stretches in front of the resort, right next to an endless beach.

"The ladies are gonna be jealous," Willie says.

"The ladies aren't gonna see a picture of that," you tell him. "Or else we'll *never* hear the end of it."

It's a rare moment when Willie immediately agrees with you, but in this case it's for certain that he does. All Missy said was that you'd be going somewhere rugged and dangerous and wild.

But this . . . this is a tropical paradise.

As the helicopter descends toward the landing pad, you look at Cole and John Luke. "So, you boys ready to become men?"

"I think that's, uh, technically called puberty," Willie points out.

You shake your head and ignore his comment. "Whatever's on this island doesn't stand a chance," you say. "They haven't met the Robertson clan yet."

After landing, you climb out of the chopper and are greeted by two military-looking men carrying

M16 rifles and dressed in camo. They take your bags but don't bother saying anything to you. The blades of the helicopter never shut off—as soon as you and your gear are unloaded, it takes off again.

"Check out this place!" Willie says.

"Looks like Fantasy Island to me," you tell him.

"See any animals while we were flying over the island?"

"Nope. There's a lot of terrain to cover."

"I want to fish," Cole says. "Maybe go on some deep-sea excursion."

"Last time you did that, you were puking over the side of the boat," you remind him.

"I want to know what kind of weapons we'll be able to use," John Luke says.

You follow the armed guards toward the multilevel lodge complex. It's sticky hot here, just like back home, but there's a cool breeze coming off the ocean. The sand looks so pure, and so does the water.

You're sweaty and probably stinky and could use a nice cool shower. "Man, I'd love to dive in there right around now."

A long flight of stairs at the front of the complex leads you to a spacious deck complete with a pool and lounge chairs. You're tempted to dive into the water here too, but you refrain for now. You want to be dry when you enter this building.

The guys with the rifles put down your bags. "Someone will be here to meet you soon," one of them says.

6

You're wondering if "someone" is that Count VanderVelde. Missy said he would be here. But his absence only adds to the mystique of this place.

An older man with a head of thick white hair and a long, slender face emerges from a nearby door, carrying a tray of fancy champagne glasses.

"Good day, gentlemen. I'm Winchester. I'll be guiding you to your accommodations. First, anybody care for some freshly squeezed orange juice?"

"My buns feel freshly squeezed after traveling all day," Willie says.

All of you take glasses and toast to the hunt. You realize you've never had orange juice this good in your whole life.

"Where's the count?" you ask Winchester.

"He will be with you shortly," Winchester says. "He has asked whether you would like to go to the weaponry room or whether you would prefer to see the operations room, which will give you an overview of the island."

Options already! *This is gonna be fun.*

Do you choose the weaponry room?
Go to page 33.

Do you choose the operations room?
Go to page 183.

GOLDFINGER

YOU ARE SITTING IN THE SHADE as the river flows by. It's not that wide, nor is it that deep. You've spent half a day walking upstream and crisscrossing the river to check for any animals. But you guys haven't seen anything. You've finished your lunch and are still waiting.

"Is there somewhere else we should go?" John Luke asks. You let him pick the crossbow this time, and he's itching to use it.

He's standing on top of a bank leading down to the sand at the riverside. Willie and Cole are behind him, sitting down like you.

"I think you should head out to the middle of the river and chill," Willie jokes. "Maybe some creature will show up then."

John Luke seems to decide, *Why not?* So he carefully walks down the bank, crossbow in hand. Next thing you know, he's standing in the center of the two-feet-deep water.

"Now stay there," Willie yells. "An hour or two. Something will show up."

Dense jungle foliage covers both sides of the river. You already feel like you've lost five pounds from sweating today.

"What do you think we're supposed to be looking for?" you ask.

"Bigfoot?" Willie says.

"I haven't seen anything moving."

You're staring at John Luke but not really paying attention when suddenly something bright falls from the sky and darts right onto John Luke's head. He drops his cross-bow, grabbing at whatever's attacking him.

The rest of you stand up as the flying beast heads into the sky again. You study it and realize it's a duck.

Except that's like no duck I've ever seen. In my life.

"Jase, did you see that?"

"Well, if you're talking about the gold thing that landed on John Luke's head and took off again, yeah, I saw that."

"What was that?" Cole asks.

"I think it was a duck," Willie says.

"Oh, that was a duck all right," you say. "But I think it's like the hog."

"How so?"

"It's . . . *special*."

You try to say the last word in Count VanderVelde's enigmatic tone.

As you follow Cole and Willie down to John Luke, who's out of the river now and seems to be okay, you glance at the Sphinx 300 crossbow in your hands and already know how useless it will be. Soon you're by the water with the other guys, laughing at John Luke.

"That thing was like a hawk or something! Did you see it?"

"It was a duck, John Luke," Willie says.

"*That* wasn't a duck."

"Yeah, I have to say it was," you tell him. "And I also have to say—we're out of luck, gentlemen."

"What do you mean?"

You give them a meaningful look. "That there was one of the fastest ducks I've ever seen in my life. Not to mention it's gold. *Gold.* I think if we were in a blind and had our shotguns, it might be difficult enough—"

"But we have crossbows," Willie says.

"Yep."

"John Luke, why'd you take the crossbow?"

"Told you I should've picked," Cole says.

You think for a minute. "Well, this will make for an interesting afternoon."

"I'm not giving up just yet," Willie says. "You got your duck call on you?"

You can't believe he asked you that question. Of course you have your duck call.

"I would think the CEO of Duck Commander would bring his duck call for a day of *hunting*, wouldn't you, boys?"

John Luke and Cole agree.

Willie mutters something about leaving it back at the lodge. Seems like a flimsy excuse to you.

"Are we going to have to build a duck blind?" John Luke asks. "Wait it out in there?"

You shake your head. "I don't think that's an ordinary duck, just like that boar wasn't any ordinary hog. I say we give the duck call a try. See what happens."

But it produces absolutely nothing. There's no sign of the duck at all. You try the duck call again and again for an hour, but it's no use.

"Maybe it's ashamed of hitting John Luke on the head," Willie suggests.

You're about ready to trek down the river when suddenly you spot the duck, floating as casual as can be on the surface of the water.

"You see that?" you ask Willie.

He nods and gets his crossbow ready.

All of you are standing on the edge of the river, watching the duck glide right past you. Willie shoots first and misses. Then you miss. Then John Luke and Cole miss.

The duck, still calm for some reason, is ten feet away from you now. But he's quickly passing by.

You fire more arrows. But none of them get close.

As the duck begins to fade from view, it flies into the sky, then lands upstream. It's floating down the river again, allowing you to take shots at it.

"He's mocking us," you say as the shiny duck comes close once more.

"What do you mean?" Willie doesn't get it.

"I mean the duck is obviously taunting us. It's as if he knows we're stupid enough to try to shoot him with a crossbow, and he wants us to know that he knows."

"John Luke picked it," Willie says.

"He's even watching us," you say. *"Look at that."*

Sure enough, the duck seems to be smiling and giggling at you. If, of course, ducks could smile and giggle. *And wait—did it just wave at us?*

You use up the rest of your arrows. Like the golden duck, they're all floating downstream.

Your ammunition is gone. So's your pride.

"That was the most embarrassing thing that's happened to me in my entire life," you say.

"Oh, come on. I've seen you do far worse." Willie's humor is not appreciated on the banks of this island river.

"I can't say I want a hog's head in my living room, but that duck sure would've looked nice."

The hunt is over. Score: One for the gold duck. Zero for the Duck Commanders.

Phil would be so ashamed of all of you. Which is why he's never, ever going to find out.

THE END

DINING WITH
THE COUNT

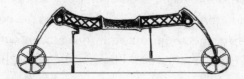

AS WINCHESTER FINISHES taking you on the tour, he tells you dinner is the next event on the schedule. He lets you go to the room you'll be staying in so you can take a shower and change clothes. You'd love a nap but know there's not time, so you opt to stay awake. You decide to splash on a little cologne that Willie gave you. It's called Duck Sweat—he calls it awful, but you rather like it.

When you meet the others in the dining room, you notice several people milling around, all dressed in white clothes. You're not sure if they're the cooks or the servers or both. All you know is they ask what you'd like for dinner, offer you various appetizers on plates, and bring you the beverage of your choice. They heavily encourage you to try the little pastries with hot dogs in them. So you happily have several.

You love this place and think you might stay here for a while. It could be a good spot to brainstorm ideas for Duck Commander. You are chief operating officer, after all. You need help getting ideas on how to operate. And this place seems to have some really good operations going on.

You stand around talking with Willie and the boys for half an hour before the count arrives. You've been wondering if he'll wear a cape or a beret and look really goofy, but the guy who shows up appears to be a professional businessman. He's tall and wears dress pants and a button-down, short-sleeved shirt. He has a dark tan and a clean-shaven head, and he greets each of you with a firm handshake, his bright eyes studying you from behind fancy designer glasses.

"I'm so glad to meet all of you," Count VanderVelde says. "After meeting your better halves, it's truly an honor to have you here in my home."

"So you live here?" Willie asks.

"Of course. Didn't Korie tell you?"

"There's a lot Korie neglects to tell me."

"Well, please blame me," the man says. "I encouraged them to be as tight-lipped as possible."

VanderVelde doesn't have a Transylvanian accent, so you'll have to rule out the possibility that this could be Count Dracula. Instead, he speaks with a Midwestern accent and seems very friendly.

16

"Our wives being quiet isn't something that normally happens," Willie jokes.

Count VanderVelde smiles. "Part of the fun of this expedition happens to be about the expectations you bring into the hunt. And about what happens when you're in the midst of battle."

"A battle consists of two sides," you say. "When I hunt, there's only one side that counts. It's whatever I'm aiming at."

"Please, let's all sit at the long table and dine. It may be the only time we get the chance to be together like this."

"Are you going somewhere?" Willie asks.

"Yes. I have certain obligations and places I need to be."

"So what exactly are you the count of?" you ask. "Not trying to be rude, but I've been wondering about that."

"It's an honorary title given to me by a small region of the Netherlands. My family is Dutch."

"Are they cheap?" you joke.

"Actually, yes, they are. My father likes to collect coupons and can never pass up a free meal. But as you may have already noticed, I didn't inherit that frugal gene."

After an outrageous meal of heavily seasoned steak and lobster and shrimp and chicken, you wonder if you're ever going to be able to stand again. Now you're *really* tired.

"I trust all of you have had enough time to think about the locations you'll be hunting in and the weapons you will choose," Count VanderVelde says.

"Well, this is a birthday gift for the old man over there," Willie says, "so we're gonna let him decide."

You realize Willie must be talking about you.

"Old man?" you say. "This old man could whip you any day."

"See?" Willie tells the count. "He's getting feisty in his old age."

"This is a birthday present for you too," you remind him.

"Uh-uh. As I said, I'm hoping Korie's gonna forget."

"I'm not gonna let her forget."

"There are a few ground rules," the count breaks in. "Just so you're aware before heading out."

"Rules?" Willie asks.

"Yes. There is a possibility that this whole trip will be completely free of charge. You could also win the coveted Hunter's Cup, made of pure gold."

"How do we get that?" you ask.

"By successfully fulfilling your mission each day," Count VanderVelde says. "And to do that, you will need to produce one—and only one—trophy from every day's hunt. Any more or any less than one will be invalid."

"You're talking about a dead animal, right?" you ask him, just to be clear.

"I'm talking about the wild game you've taken," he says with an air of mystery. This guy isn't a big fan of calling a spade a spade.

"Seems pretty easy," Willie says. "But what do you mean by *invalid*? What happens if we don't end up with this, uh, 'wild game' by the end of each day?"

"The hunting trip is over. The rest of the week is forfeited. All charges will go on the credit cards given."

"How can that be?"

"That was agreed to by your wonderful wives, who signed and paid for this excursion."

You shake your head. *Read the fine print, Missy. Always read the fine print.*

"So we end up empty-handed on one of the days, and what?" you say. "It's good-bye, good riddance? Game over?"

Count VanderVelde only smiles. "I wouldn't put it like that. I have faith in you four. You are the Duck Commandos, right?"

"That would be Duck Commanders," Willie says.

"So you head to your first destination, succeed there, and in theory, by the end of the week you will have managed to secure trophies from all six locations on the island."

"Do we pick which destination we go to first?" John Luke asks hopefully.

"No. We've done that for you. Each day gets a bit more . . . well, how should I put it—challenging?" Again he smiles.

"Will the animals we're hunting be different every day?" Cole wonders.

The count doesn't answer. Once more he simply smiles.

That smile is starting to annoy you.

"So the decision of which weapon you'll take on your first day is up to you, Jase," Count VanderVelde says. "What would you like?"

"Can we reuse weapons the next day?"

"Perhaps. If indeed there is another day on which you can choose."

He gives you a wink, and for the first time since meeting him, you get this ominous sort of feeling.

It kinda spooks you out a bit.

"Decision time," he says.

"Can you give me a *little* hint about the first place?"

"Fine, fine. You'll be hunting in the jungle."

Which weapon will you take into the jungle?

For the crossbow, go to page 59.

For the shotgun, go to page 193.

ROBERTSON AND THRASHER

For the rifle, go to page 89.

For the sword, go to page 161.

For the dagger, go to page 201.

For the cowbell, go to page 223.

EXPERIMENTS

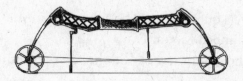

WINCHESTER IS RIDING IN THE HELICOPTER back to Fiji with the four of you. You're so glad to get away from Tabu Island, to finally be heading home. Ten minutes into the ride, Winchester decides to tell all of you a little more about the island. And about Count VanderVelde.

"The things you saw on the island . . . you didn't imagine them. They weren't in your heads. They were scientific experiments many years in the making. These were the count's life's work. But some of them went wrong, as you may have noticed. Terribly wrong."

You raise your eyebrows at Willie and keep listening.

"VanderVelde was a multimillionaire businessman. The fact that he uses his honorary title of count shows how arrogant he happens to be. He bought this island and dreamed of creating a Jurassic Park. A *real* Jurassic Park. Of course, he

was crazy enough and rich enough to find people who could assist him in performing the experiments. Oh, it wasn't like he managed to make dinosaurs or any new species. He never even got close—he only created messed-up versions of existing animals."

You have a question that's been burning in your brain ever since you climbed Mount Fear.

"Did the count ever—did he ever experiment with himself?"

Winchester gives you a very serious gaze, then shakes his head. "My honest answer is I don't know. But I've wondered. Sometimes he acted strange. Sometimes I saw unusual things. Things that gave me nightmares for days."

Yeah, I saw some strange things too.

"Well, I'm glad to be leaving the mad professor behind," Willie says.

"I am too," Winchester replies. "It's about time I left that place."

He pauses for a moment, then asks all of you a question. "Do you have any work for a seventy-year-old?"

You can imagine Winchester and Uncle Si hitting it off. And who knows? With a little practice, this guy might be able to make a duck call with the best of them.

"Maybe." You clap a hand on his shoulder. "There could be a job at Duck Commander for you. But you'll have to know some people to get it." You give him a smile.

Speaking of Duck Commander . . . you cannot *wait* to get back to West Monroe and the very normal animals you always took for granted. *What I wouldn't give to see an ordinary duck right now!*

THE END

FRIEND OR FOE?

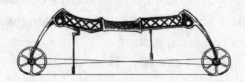

THE THUNDERSTORM MAKES YOU FEEL like the whole island lodge is going to blow down. The power has gone out, and now the inside is illuminated with candles. You've had dinner but are still waiting in the living room to see Count VanderVelde. If indeed he shows up.

Since he might have gotten *shot* today.

But just as a blast of lightning illuminates the darkness outside, the door swings open and the count enters the room where all of you are gathered. He's wearing a black turtleneck and walking slowly.

"Winchester tells me you have a bit of a dilemma," the count says.

"A bit of a dilemma?" you reply. "Nah. No dilemma. What kind of dilemma would we have?"

"We shot a mountain lion today," Willie tells him.

"It took an arrow right here," you say, pointing to your neck. "And then around here." You gesture toward your side.

The count nods but doesn't say anything. He looks suspicious and shady, but then again, he often seems that way.

"It is always interesting what the mountain produces, isn't it? Even I am constantly surprised."

"Meaning what?" you ask. "There are different animals up on Mount Fear?"

"This island is an unpredictable place."

"I can predict something," you say. "I predict we're going home tomorrow."

"Never predict what tomorrow will bring. That's a dangerous thing, my friend."

You want to tell him that you're not his friend. And that *you're* very dangerous. But you don't say either. At the moment, he seems to have the upper hand.

A boom of thunder shakes the windows.

"Every now and then we get these storms. It will pass."

You can't help staring at his turtleneck. "A bit warm for a turtleneck, isn't it?"

"I was chilly earlier, to be honest."

You narrow your eyes as you wonder if he's telling the truth.

"A bit earlier?" you ask. "Like earlier today?"

"Yes."

"Were you on the island today?"

Willie interrupts your line of questioning. "What Jase wants to know is when we will be able to head back home."

You're glad he didn't ask *if* you'll be able to head back home. That's the real question on your mind.

"Tomorrow. If all goes well."

"If all goes well?" you ask. "What's that mean? If the storm doesn't take us away tonight?"

The count looks pleasantly surprised by your statement. "Exactly, Mr. Robertson."

The way he says your name—so formal. Mr. Robertson. Nobody calls you that. You get goose bumps, and you're not a fan of geese.

"You never know what the night will bring, do you." He gives you that smile of his.

Suddenly a blast of wind rips open the main doors of the room, and all the candles go out. You and Willie rush to the doors, slam them, and try to find a way to relight the candles.

"Is everybody okay?" you ask as you blindly search the room. With all these candles, there has to be a lighter or matches around. And shouldn't the count already have them lit again? He's the one who knows this place.

"Yeah," John Luke's voice says.

"Cole, you there?"

"Yep."

"Count? Are you there?" Willie asks.

Silence.

"Count VanderVelde?"

More silence.

Oh, great. He must have disappeared like a vampire bat. "I think he's gone."

You locate some matches in the drawer of a side table and light a couple of the candles.

"Where'd he go?" Willie asks, squinting into the shadowy corners of the room.

"I don't think I want to know."

The boys look concerned. Well, you probably do too.

"What should we do now?" John Luke wonders.

Questions. All these questions. You wish someone else would answer them for you.

Do you go to your bedrooms and try to get some sleep?
Turn to page 229.

Do you stay in the living room and
wait for the count to return?
Turn to page 123.

Do you head to the weaponry
room to arm yourselves?
Turn to page 105.

ARMED AND READY

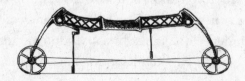

YOU'VE BEEN DYING TO FIND OUT what sort of weapons are available for this hunt. Missy said one of the few requirements Count VanderVelde made was that you couldn't bring any gear with you. Nothing, in fact. No handguns, no knives, no sights—absolutely nothing. (Of course, you each sneaked a duck call onto the island. No way were you guys going on a hunting expedition without those. Duck calls aren't "gear." They're essential.) Everything you could imagine and more would be here, according to your wife. And the weaponry room might be a clue to what you'll be hunting.

Winchester leads the four of you into an elevator. He punches in a security code to get the elevator moving, and you begin to descend. How far down, you're not sure. When the door opens, you realize this whole floor must be the weaponry room.

All of you get off the elevator and say a collective "Whoa." Willie seems more dumbfounded than anyone else, but that's not hard for him to do because most of the time he just looks dumb.

Every weapon you know of is here at your disposal, including a lot you've never laid eyes on before. It's incredible. Maybe "Count VanderVelde" is really a pseudonym for Batman. 'Cause it looks like this guy has got an arsenal the size of the superhero's own.

"Impressive, isn't it?" Winchester's looking at you. "You will select the weapons of your choice each day. You are permitted to have one large weapon—to the right over there, on the wall. Then you'll be allowed to choose a couple smaller items, which are straight ahead. Gear and clothing are on the racks and shelves to your left."

"Wait a minute," you say. "Do *each* of us get weapons of our choice?"

"You will each receive your own weapon, of course, but all of you will have the same type of device."

There's no question where you go first. Gear and clothing are nice, and smaller weapons are necessary, but you want to take a look at the goods. The real *good* stuff. So you and the rest of the gang head to the wall showcasing all the big weapons.

A massive crossbow catches your attention. It's a kind you've never seen.

"Can we take these off the wall?" you ask Winchester.

"Of course," he says. "There is a small ladder to climb for the items near the top."

This is like a showcase for some high-end weapons shop. There's only one of each piece on display, but Winchester reassures you that they actually have multiples of everything. You scan the row of prominent items before you.

"If you like, I'd be happy to name the items you see here, along with their particular highlights." It sounds like Winchester's talking about people instead of weapons.

"That'd be great."

"I see you're eyeing the crossbow," he says with a hand extended toward the black bow, which is covered with lots of gadgets and components. "This is a test model produced in Europe by a small company. Called the Sphinx 300. It's larger than most, but what makes it truly unique is how lightweight it happens to be."

Winchester takes the bow off the wall and gives it to John Luke. He seems to be in disbelief holding it. When it gets to you, you feel the same way. It's probably half the weight of your own crossbow.

"The stock resembles a sleek, military-style model," Winchester explains. "It has the highest-known feet-per-second shooting speed—almost twice that of the closest competitor out there. The draw weight is light, and it's quite comfortable to cock. But the real magic here, gentlemen, is the arrows."

He produces one of the arrows from the quiver. "You will have six of these. You won't want to fire off many of them. They are set to be able to cut through any living, breathing thing. Well, *almost* any."

You turn to Willie and see him laugh silently. You gotta give it to this Winchester fella—he takes his job *very seriously*.

You hand the crossbow back to Winchester, and he places it on the wall again before continuing on to the other weapons.

"Right here you have the RD-4000 shotgun. It's a fully automatic, low-recoil, gas-operated 12-gauge shotgun designed for the military. This currently doesn't exist, according to the government, because it's simply too lethal. It delivers over three hundred rounds a minute. Three hundred 12-gauge rounds."

"What are we supposed to hunt with *that*?" Willie asks.

Winchester simply shakes his head. "More on the game later, Mr. Robertson. When you see the count."

Willie mouths the word *Chocula* as Winchester hands the shotgun to Cole, then moves on.

"This is a Stettinga hunting rifle using specially built 6.55-millimeter ammunition that explodes upon impact."

You let out a chuckle. "Are we even *trying* to keep any parts of the animal intact?"

Winchester doesn't react but keeps talking about the sleek rifle in his hands. "You can hit a target over 2,500 yards away."

"Wait, what?" Willie asks. "That's like—a really long ways away."

"I've never even heard of that brand," you say. "Stettinga? Sounds like Stetson cologne."

Winchester hands you the lightweight rifle, and it feels really good in your hands.

On to the next weapon. He points upward. "This is a genuine katana sword made of a special metal that will not break. There is not a sharper blade on the planet, so right now I'm just going to leave that on the wall."

You look at the sleek, long silver blade with an ornate black handle.

"So an automatic shotgun or a samurai sword?" you ask.

"That is correct, Mr. Robertson. Along with the other options."

Become a hunter or a ninja. Hmmm.

"Sure would help to know what we'll be hunting," Willie mutters.

You nod and agree with him.

"There is not just *one* thing that you can hunt on the island of Tabu," Winchester says cryptically.

He takes a knife concealed in a black sheath off the wall, then slides the sheath off, revealing the black blade of a dagger. "This is a double-edged Black Widow dagger. It's nine inches of the strongest metal in the world. It's lightweight and easy to carry."

"That's all we'd get?" John Luke asks. "We can't have that along with the rifle?"

"Not these weapons. Each of you will be able to carry a handgun with you along with some of the other assorted gear. But those are more for precaution."

You can't see the final instrument until he picks it up off the floor. It's black and looks a lot like a . . .

Nah, it can't be that.

"This is a six-and-a-half-inch cowbell," Winchester says in all seriousness.

All of you burst out laughing.

"What's that gonna do?" Willie asks. "Round up the herd?"

Winchester holds a drumstick in the same hand as the cowbell. "This is an actual weapon," he says. "Hitting it is the equivalent of throwing a live grenade right in front of you."

"Let me try that out," you say.

But Winchester keeps the cowbell in his hand. "Not right here. No bomb blasts going off inside."

"That thing really works?" Willie asks.

"Yes, indeed. These are the six items you need to choose from. You must take one of them first thing tomorrow morning, when you set out on your expedition." He dusts his hands together. "Now for our next stop on this little tour."

If you haven't been to the operations room, go to page 183.

If you've been to the operations room, go to page 15.

A GRAND MYSTERY

WHEN YOU WAKE UP, you can feel the throbbing of your cheek. You can also tell it's bandaged up. You look around and realize you're back at the lodge in your own bed. You're really groggy.

"Ah, back to life."

Winchester is standing in the doorway.

"What happened?"

"Well, the good news is that you're still in the hunt. The bad news is your brother managed to take off a chunk of your beard—and your cheek too—when he shot the gopher."

Somehow you're not surprised. But you can deal with Willie later. Right now you have some questions, and you've got Winchester all to yourself.

"Tell me something, Winchester."

"Yes, sir?"

"This island," you begin. "Are there any normal animals?

Ones that aren't outrageously big or strangely colored or laughing at you—literally?"

"It is a strange island indeed."

"A gopher? I almost died because of a gopher."

"It would have been a pity," he says.

Would have been a pity? You shake your head.

"Well, Willie's gonna pay for this."

"He does feel bad," Winchester assures you.

"He *should* feel bad. He shot me!"

"If it's any comfort, you won't have any guns to choose from tomorrow. Only the crossbow and the sword."

You don't say anything, but you're pretty sure Willie could inflict a lot of damage with those too.

Willie is extremely and unusually apologetic when he comes into your room. You realize he not only feels guilty but was scared by what happened. So you play it off like it was nothing big. Yes, a bullet grazed your cheek. But hey, things happen. Gophers laugh. Bullets graze. Life is a grand mystery.

"So I guess tomorrow we'll be going to Mount Fear," Willie says when he visits again before bed.

"Can't be much worse than the beach," you joke.

Willie doesn't reply.

"Well, it *could* be worse, but it won't be," you add, trying to lighten the mood. "We still have the crossbow and the sword to choose from."

"I'll keep both away from you," he promises.

As you eat in the dining room that evening, you feel like the animal heads are watching you. You feel like the people in the paintings are staring down at you.

You feel sorta creeped out.

"I'm beginning to really miss home," you tell the guys.

John Luke and Cole agree.

The night is dark outside the windows, and the wilderness around you seems to be alive with noise.

"I'd hate to have to go out there now," you say. "I bet there are lots of creatures we have yet to see."

"I'm going to get that gopher stuffed so you can put it up at home." Willie actually seems to think this is a good idea.

"Thanks, but that's too much."

"I insist."

"I insist that you don't. I don't want a rodent in my house. Real or stuffed."

You wonder if you'll see the count tonight. But he doesn't appear, and nothing unusual happens. Maybe he's leaving you alone because of what happened.

Later on, as you're about to go to sleep in your bedroom, Willie comes in again and asks how you're feeling.

"Oh, I don't know," you say. "I sorta feel like I got shot by my brother."

"Man, I'm sorry!"

"You've already said that twenty times. I know. I'm kidding. I'm glad it's nothing worse."

"I don't like this island," Willie says.

"Yeah, me neither."

Willie looks around the room, then whispers, "No, I *really* don't like it. I want to get off it. ASAP."

You nod but don't say anything because you've begun to wonder if the room could be bugged.

"Two more days, right?" you finally say.

This doesn't seem to comfort Willie. "I got a bad feeling."

"That's not good. 'Cause I'm usually the one who gets those."

"Yeah."

You try to change the subject. "So which weapon are we choosing tomorrow?"

Willie shakes his head. "Whatever's gonna get us out of here."

Which one will it be?

If you pick the crossbow, go to page 215.

If you pick the sword, go to page 111.

INDIANA JASE

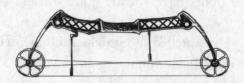

YOU STAND IN THE CENTER of a rope bridge hanging four or five stories above the river. This is where the river begins to form, just below the falls between Mount Fear and the jungle. You're holding your sword and begging those ducks to join you.

"Come on out," you shout. "Come on."

And one by one, they get on the bridge and start waddling toward you. From both directions.

I have you now.

You grab a part of the bridge in one hand and hold the sword steady in the other.

This might hurt.

• • •

Rewind six hours, and you're standing in the middle of the river, your katana at the ready but no animals in sight.

"Hey, Jase, you caught any fish yet?" Willie yells.

He and the boys are up the bank at the edge of the jungle. You're wading in the water.

No, make that waiting *in the water.*

A couple hours have already gone by, and you've seen nothing.

Yesterday you searched and searched and then a boar nearly bowled you over. Today you've got nothing.

Not much of a hunting expedition.

"You guys see any tracks or any trace of anything?"

"I smelled some bacon," Willie jokes.

"I'm a bit tired of the bacon humor," you say.

"Oh, I'm sorry. Yeah, it's getting old. Hey—want some pork and beans for lunch?"

Sometimes your younger brother can be funny and sometimes he can be annoying. Actually, he's annoying most of the time. Occasionally he can be funny *while* being annoying. No, he's not really that funny, but he's always annoying.

You came into the water just to cool yourself off. Your face and hair and beard and neck are still damp from where you doused them in the river. You look to the sky and hear a commotion from the hill above you.

John Luke is chasing after something. All of a sudden, a bright shape darts into the sky.

It's a duck. A golden duck.

Oh, I wish I had a shotgun right about now.

You rush to the edge of the bank and join the guys, who are all out of breath.

"Did you see it?" Willie asks.

"The flying duck that looks like a bar of gold?" you ask. "Nah, didn't see it."

"I *almost* had it," John Luke says.

Willie gives you a look that you don't have to ask about. You both realize it's going to be almost impossible to get a kill today. You have swords. *Swords*. Which is a problem for several reasons:

1. None of you are ninjas, even though Willie occasionally tries to act like one.
2. Ducks might not be the fastest animals in the world, but they can do something this duck just happened to do: *fly*.
3. You can't exactly use the sword for anything once the duck is flying. And it's always, *always* going to fly away.

So you're almost ready to call it a day.

"Who picked the sword again?" Willie asks, then turns to his son. "Oh yeah. Good call, John Luke."

"You said to be creative."

"Yeah. There's creative, and then there's duck hunting with a sword."

You're all standing there trying to figure out what to do when you see the same duck (or maybe an identical golden bird) land at the edge of the river where you left your bag.

"Hey, look at that thing," you tell the gang.

"It's peeking in your bag," Cole says.

"Think it wants your lunch."

The duck takes hold of your lunch container and begins picking at your peanut butter sandwich.

"Stop eating my lunch!"

It not only ignores you but seems to go into some kind of frenzy while eating the sandwich. Its head bobs up and down in a wild, jerky manner.

"It likes your sandwich," Willie says with a laugh.

The golden duck starts nipping and ripping at your lunch container once it's finished with the sandwich. You all run down there, assuming it'll fly off. But it doesn't. For a while it remains in this manic state, trying to find something else to eat.

"It might want more peanut butter," John Luke says.

"That's crazy," you say. "That thing's probably gonna get really ill eating that. Ducks aren't supposed to have high fat content. They're waterbirds."

"Dr. Jase, the duck nutritionist," Willie says.

"Whatever."

You unsheath your sword and get closer to the golden duck, but it finally flies off into the river. After examining the damage, you confirm that you won't be having lunch today.

"Thing ate my entire sandwich."

"I brought a whole jar of peanut butter," Cole says.

"You did?"

"Yeah. The big jar. I figured we might be hungry."

A crazy idea hits you a few minutes later, when the rest of the guys are eating their lunches in front of you. John Luke and Cole give you some parts of theirs. Willie, of course, decides to take some of their offerings for himself.

"If you were a kindhearted brother, you'd offer me your sandwich," you tell him.

"If I were a dumb brother, I would have left my bag next to the river for an animal to get into."

You open the jar of peanut butter Cole brought and scoop some out with your pocketknife. Then you smear it on a leaf and set it on a flat stone edging the river.

"What are you doing?"

"Let's watch."

You make sure everyone is a safe distance away from the peanut butter.

Sure enough, the duck floating on the water somehow ends up realizing the peanut butter is there.

"Wait—can ducks smell?" Willie asks.

You shake your head. "What kind of Duck Commander would ask that question?"

"I don't know if they smell or not. I just shoot them."

"They have a good sense of smell."

But this is a special duck you're talking about. A golden one—a kind you may never see again.

It circles above all of you for a while, then lands on the peanut butter. But interestingly enough, a couple other golden friends join it. Ducks who look exactly the same.

This time it's Willie who decides to attack. He runs after the ducks, and it's almost as if they're in slight disbelief at the sight of this big, bandanna-wearing dude running at them with a sword. They're like, *Really?*

Then they fly away.

"Wow, you showed them," you tell Willie.

"I wanted to see if they'd finish the peanut butter."

You all examine the leaf.

"Oh, they finished it, all right."

This gives you another idea. (Sometimes you wish you could get paid for the ideas in your head. You'd be the richest man in the world.)

Your idea ends up working too. Every now and then they turn out well. Who knew ducks liked this kind of food?

Slowly the afternoon sinks by as you keep luring more and more ducks with peanut butter. It's working, but the peanut butter in the jar is getting lower. And the minutes in the day are ticking away. Soon there won't be enough of either for you to work with.

"Okay, we have one last chance," you tell the boys.

And yes, you're including Willie in that description.

• • •

You're standing at the edge of a cliff on the mountain you've spent the last half hour climbing. The others are right behind you. They didn't want to miss out on any adventures. There's a rope bridge hanging between the cliff and the other side of the divide, a wobbly sort of bridge that could have been used in an Indiana Jones movie.

Hence idea number 454,201.

"What are you gonna do now?" Willie asks.

"Give me that jar of peanut butter," you tell Cole.

You open it and notice there's still enough left. You put one hand in the jar and begin smearing peanut butter over your face, your pants, and your T-shirt.

"Have you lost your mind?" Willie says.

"Maybe. But we're gonna catch one of those ducks."

Once you've used up the peanut butter, you stand in the middle of the rope bridge. They won't be able to resist this.

Sure enough, it works. One by one, the golden ducks start walking toward you, slowly but steadily. Willie, John Luke, and Cole all watch from the mountainside.

You lift your sword and think about Indiana Jones again.

The ducks get closer. Closer.

Almost here. Almost.

One of them is within reach. That's when you begin to attack.

And that's when things go terribly wrong.

You're lashing and swiping and swinging and slashing, and then . . .

You're falling.

You're swimming.

You're drowning.

You're out.

• • •

When you awake, you're in your bed at the lodge. You're wearing a bathrobe and have the world's worst headache. Willie's sitting in a chair next to you.

"What happened?"

He shakes his head. You can see a big ole grin underneath his big ole beard.

"You know what makes a rope bridge cool?" Willie asks.

"Oh no. Here we go."

"That it's rope. And you know what's cool about rope? You can cut into it. So you know—on a rope *bridge*, why in the world would you attack ducks with the sharpest sword in the known universe? Wouldn't you think—?"

"Yeah."

Willie laughs. "I mean, I would think that—"

"Uh-huh."

"Any logical man would know—"

"Absolutely," you say. "So are we done?"

52

"Oh yeah, we're done," Willie says. "'Hi, Korie. This is Willie. Yeah, we got ourselves a big, fat boar that we're bringing home. But no. We couldn't find anything else. Jase almost killed himself cutting down a rope bridge.'"

"Tell her I said hello."

"Oh, I will," Willie says as he leaves the room. "I will."

You lie still for a minute before you smell something familiar.

Peanut butter.

You realize you'll probably never eat peanut butter again for the rest of your life.

THE END

ROOMMATES

THERE'S NOTHING LIKE WILD ANIMALS ATTACKING to make you a little homesick. You have no idea what time it is back home, but if it's night there too, the kids are asleep. Missy is dreaming about finding the perfect outfit on sale. It's quiet.

And there are definitely no signs of spider monkeys bouncing and attacking in anyone's bedroom.

But this is what you encounter in Cole's room. The monkeys are black and white and red, and they're freaking out. Cole's trying to fend them off, but there are too many. They're on his shoulders and his head and his legs and his arms.

"Don't you wish you had a video recorder?" you whisper to John Luke.

"A little help here!" Cole shouts before a spider monkey punches him in the mouth.

You hold up your sword. A blast of thunder cracks outside. "Has everybody gone crazy tonight?"

"Yeah, I think so," John Luke says. "But at least Uncle Si isn't here to say something crazy."

"True."

Then you attack.

Spider monkeys are pretty active. And they're difficult to pin down.

So it takes the three of you a long time to get rid of the twenty or so monkeys in the room.

When you think you're done, you hear a sound from another room down the hall.

"That's gotta be Willie."

"I bet it's snakes," John Luke says.

"No, I bet it's some kind of bird," Cole says. "Like a bunch of owls."

The image of a roomful of owls attacking Willie is kinda funny.

You hear his howl and you laugh. It's not funny—but it's kinda funny.

John Luke and Cole are ready with their samurai swords.

"We look pretty tough," you say. "Like we're starring in an end-of-the-world movie."

Willie screams again.

"Should we help him?" John Luke asks.

You think about it for a minute. A *long* minute.

"Yeah. I guess."

You get there and find Willie crouched in the corner.

There's only one animal in his room. *How* it got there is a good question. *Why* he's screaming is another good question.

"Willie," you say.

He screams again until he realizes you guys are there.

The moose in the middle of the room is just standing still. It's not attacking him. It actually looks sorta bored.

"Willie, what are you doing?"

"That monster moose was attacking and gonna kill me, and I wasn't going to—"

"The thing looks half-asleep."

You extend a hand to Willie. Then you lift him up and lead him past the big ole moose.

"See?"

"That thing was going to kill me." Willie picks up his sword from the floor, his eyes wide.

"Uh-uh." You shake your head. "Just—just leave him in the room."

"This is madness."

"No. You should've seen the spider monkeys. This is—this is actually kinda funny."

You all head out of Willie's room and make sure to close the door.

Once you're back in the living room, you light a bunch of candles, lock the doors, and hunker down to wait out the storm and the long night.

No other animals show up.

Nor do any other humans.

Go to page 167.

JUNGLE LOVE

YOU'VE BEEN WALKING through the jungle for an hour on this hot and humid morning, and so far you've seen hardly anything. A lizard, some birds, a monkey's tail. But after standing still and looking and waiting for the monkey to reappear, you begin to think you were imagining it.

Maybe it was just a vine.

"What if we don't find anything?" Cole says to you as he maneuvers with the massive crossbow in his hands.

"We are here for an entire week," you remind him. "Or at least we will be if we shoot something today. And we will. Wouldn't you guys be a little disappointed if we came right out here and bagged something ten minutes later?"

"Not really," Willie says. "I could hang out by the pool."

You adjust the crossbow in your grip. It's remarkable how lightweight such a large weapon can be.

Like the others in your group, you're dressed in camouflage and carrying a pocketknife and a sidearm in a holster. You've already drained half the water in your canteen, for which you blame eating too much last night and not getting enough sleep. Having Willie in the room next door didn't help. The guy sure does snore!

Willie's been leading you guys through the dense trees and foliage, and it seems like you're already back where you started.

"Did you just guide us in a big circle?" you ask him from the end of the line.

"No." Willie's voice is defensive, like he's some little brother who got caught sneaking a cookie from the jar in the kitchen. He looks around and shakes his head. "Well, maybe. I swear, this looks like the exact spot where they dropped us off in the Jeeps," he says. "But there's no way we could've gotten back here. No way."

"If there's a Willie, there's often a way." You decide to take point for a while, whether he likes it or not. You guide the group down a path that cuts through the jungle, the very same route you already took earlier this morning. You do find it strange that you ended up at the exact place you began. How you could have gone in an entire circle in just an hour boggles your mind, but then again, lots of things Willie does make your brain hurt.

The less I think about Willie, the less head-scratching I gotta do.
There's a slight incline to this tropical path. You head up

the moderate hill, careful with your crossbow and also listening to every sound you can. As you near the top, you get the feeling that you're close to something. Exactly *what*, you don't know.

Then you hear it.

It sounds like . . . like some kind of tortured wild beast.

"You hear that?" John Luke asks.

"What'd you say?" Willie says. "Sorry—I can't hear you because of the *wild animal that just screamed*."

You tell them to be quiet. The sound continues for a moment.

"That's a wild boar or something," Cole says.

"Think that sounds more like Willie snoring," you reply.

There's a commotion in the woods in front of you. You can feel the ground shaking a bit. But why? There's no way one boar or even a group of them could make the ground tremble like this. At least not an ordinary boar.

The noise is getting louder and closer.

You raise your crossbow, one finger resting on the trigger while your other hand holds it as steady as possible. Then something dark, round, and waddling faster than you've ever seen rushes forward out of the bushes.

The arrow rips out of your crossbow but comes nowhere close to whatever's rushing at you.

The creature plows into you and keeps going just as you hear—no, make that feel—someone else's arrow whizzing by your ear.

What the—?

Another couple arrows fly off into the woods while the squealing, raging sound gets even louder.

It's gotta be a herd of wild pigs or boars. A dozen of them. More.

You hear one of the boys yell. You think about trying to reload the crossbow but realize there's no way. There's no time.

You regain your feet and reach for your pocketknife as Willie works on reloading his crossbow and John Luke unholsters his handgun.

Then you stare all around but don't see any of the dozens of boars that must have been right next to you.

"What in the world were those?" you ask.

"Those?" Willie says. "What are you talking about, 'those'?"

"The pack of wild boars that just came out of the woods."

"Pack?" Cole says.

"There was only one," John Luke adds.

"Biggest hog I've ever seen in my life. Looked like a cow."

You stare at Willie in disbelief. "No."

"That was one hog."

"That was *not* just one hog."

"Nothing like we got back in West Monroe, but that was a single hog."

"There's no way."

Willie only nods.

"You see how fast that thing ran?"

"I saw how fast it knocked you over," your brother jokes.

"I took one for the team."

"'Pack of wild boars,'" Willie mimics.

You roll your eyes.

For the next hour, you guys try to find the wild hog that ran you over, but you can't.

You keep trying for the rest of the day, but wherever he went to hide, he decided to stay put, and nothing else comes out of the forest either.

You wind up empty-handed.

When you arrive back at the island lodge, you can see your bags out on the deck, already packed.

Wait a minute—we paid for a whole week! I don't care about the fine print.

But the Count of Monte Cristo is nowhere to be found.

Winchester comes out to see if you need anything. Like milk or cookies before you head home.

"What kind of hunting trip is this?"

"The agreement clearly stated that you would need to make a kill in each location. Six different kills."

"So we try again tomorrow," Willie says.

He's fully in agreement that this is ludicrous.

"As the count told you, if you fail at any given part of the

hunt, the quest is over, Mr. Robertson. 'You take the good, you take the bad, you take them both, and there you have the facts of life.'"

You just stare at Willie.

Did he seriously just quote the theme song from that show?

"I'm really sorry," Winchester says. "The helicopter will be here in five minutes. Ciao."

Now Winchester's telling you good-bye in Italian.

What's up with this place?

"I can say one thing," Willie says after Winchester disappears into the lodge. "I am definitely having me some bacon the first chance I get."

THE END

DON'T DO IT!

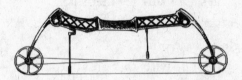

YOU WATCH EVERYBODY take food from their containers and begin poking at it hesitantly. But when you open your own dinner, it only resembles some chicken nuggets. Somehow you expected a more exotic meal.

"Are these some strange kind of nuggets?" you ask the count. "Like lizard-intestine nuggets? Or goat-brain nuggets?" *Or could they be something worse?*

"No. They're just fast-food chicken nuggets."

"What? Are they, like, old or something?" Maybe he's trying to get rid of his leftovers. But that wouldn't worry you. Plus, the count doesn't really seem like the leftovers type.

He shakes his head. So you try one. And yep, it tastes just like the chicken nuggets you're used to. Not too bad. Actually, pretty tasty. Maybe the count's trying to make you guys feel right at home with this meal.

The count gasps. His eyes widen as a hint of horror crosses his face.

"What? What's wrong with these?"

"Do you know what those do to you?"

"Nope," you say. "Can't say that I do."

"Fragments of them stay in your stomach. Forever."

You laugh. "Come on."

"No. It's true. The parts that aren't food."

"Parts that aren't food? Then what are they?"

He explains, and you almost throw up. It's so awful that it can't be written down.

It can't be true.

"That's impossible."

"It's the truth," the count says.

"And millions of kids are eating this stuff every day."

"It also has a known additive."

He tells you what that is. You shake your head and whip the chicken nuggets across the room. They hit the wall and floor with sickening thuds.

The other guys jerk their heads toward you, alarmed. You turn to the count again.

"It can't be."

"It's true," the count repeats.

"People need to be informed! This can't be legal. It's not even—it's just plain wrong."

"Yes. Chicken nuggets. Ordinary, simple chicken nuggets. There's more to them than meets the eye . . . or the taste buds."

You feel ill.

So very ill.

Go to page 197.

FOR YOUR EYES ONLY

"SHHHHHH."

You're hidden in the brush and overgrowth on the top of a bank overlooking the river. It's not much of a river, to be honest. It's probably only two feet deep and maybe twenty yards across. But you're aiming the rifle at the center of the river, where you can see the same creature you've been watching all afternoon.

A gold duck.

You look into the Stettinga hunting rifle with its massive scope. You can see the duck perfectly. And even as you examine it, you realize you've never seen anything like it before. It resembles a mallard or a wild duck, but you observe some unique features in addition to its surprising color.

First off, the beak looks longer. A *lot* longer than a typical duck beak. And there's something shiny, almost prickly, on its bright feathers. Like it's got scales on its wings.

Then there are the eyes. This duck's got *Mona Lisa* eyes. The kind that seem to be looking at you regardless of where you're standing.

I gotta sound crazy.

But that's okay. You're not crazy. And in about five seconds, those *Mona Lisa* eyes aren't gonna be staring at nothing.

You fire, but right before you do, it flies off.

Just like last time.

"Come on!"

"Shush," Willie says. He's lying on the edge of the hill, taking shots as well.

"Go ahead—shoot the duck in the sky," you tell him. You stand to get some circulation in your body.

"It's as if it knows when I'm about to shoot," he says.

You decide to take a break, heading into the jungle to use the bathroom. You leave the rifle propped up against a tree. Minutes later, as you're walking back to the edge of the river, you see the duck standing right next to your rifle.

Those eyes. They're looking at me. They're looking through *me.*

Even though you're walking straight toward it, the duck doesn't budge. It doesn't move. It just keeps staring directly at you.

You take out your handgun.

I killed a hog with a dagger. Maybe I can pop this duck with a pistol.

Six shots later, you feel like a complete loser.

"Hey, what are you doing shooting at a tree?" Willie asks.

"The duck. It was right there. You didn't see it fly away?"

"It's on the edge of the river. I've been watching it this whole time."

"Well, then there's more than one duck."

Either that or you're starting to lose your mind.

You settle down again and prepare yourself. This really should be easy, right? Sure, you're not in a duck blind and you don't have a shotgun. But this is target practice. The duck's on vacation. It's taking life far too easily. You should be able to pop it at least once. Shouldn't you?

But you steady yourself. You lock in the rifle, and as you aim and fire . . .

Nothing.

A big splash. That's all you get.

The duck flies up and circles above your head.

It's totally taunting me.

Then it heads back to the river.

You try again.

Nope.

"You using that scope?" Willie calls out from his spot.

You see his shot blast a small fountain of water.

"I'm getting closer than you are!"

The boys are having similar luck, and you hear their shouts of frustration each time they miss the target.

You're reloading once more when something waddles out of the bushes. The dark, unmoving eyes meet yours.

It's another duck. The same kind, with its weird golden feathers and extralong beak.

You try to swipe at it with the butt of your rifle, but it's no good.

The duck flies into the sky, then circles over you again.

"That's it! I'm done here." You've had enough taunting and teasing for now. Time to get back home, where the ducks know their place.

"Where are you going?" Willie calls out.

"I'm not going to be made a fool of all day long," you say. "Too bad we don't have the shotguns."

"Yeah, great choice on the rifle, John Luke," Willie says.

You start walking back toward the lodge, but you can hear the guys laughing at you. In a second you stop and turn around.

"*What* is so funny?"

They all keep laughing, but nobody says anything.

"What is it? I don't see any of you hitting the targets either." You continue walking, trying to ignore them.

"Hey, Jase," Willie says.

"Yeah?"

"Look down at your feet."

You stop midstride, with a bad feeling about what you'll see when you look down.

Sure enough, it's one of the ducks. It's staring up at you like some kind of lost puppy.

You're so frustrated, you try to lash out and kick it with your boot. But this only makes you stumble and lose your balance, landing on your back in the dirt.

More laughter from the gallery.

You stand and brush yourself off but can't seem to find the duck. It's flying again. Of course.

Soon enough, all of you will be flying too. Flying back to West Monroe empty-handed.

THE END

BROTHERLY LOVE

YOU'VE BEEN IN THE CABIN of the helicopter for about ten minutes, enjoying the sense of relief and joy that comes with leaving the island. But you're also melancholy for some reason that you can't pinpoint.

As you glance at John Luke and Willie across from you, and then at Cole sitting beside you and staring out the window, it suddenly comes to you.

I almost lost them.

So you decide to tell them something you've maybe never told them before.

"I just gotta say this. I'm not trying to get overly emotional or anything like that. But I gotta say it." You take a deep breath. "I love you guys."

Willie looks at you as if you've lost your mind.

"I know it's crazy, but I thought I might lose all of you back there on the island. And if I never get another chance to say it, I just want to let you know how much all of you mean to me. Each and every one of you."

Willie still seems to think you're crazy.

You keep talking. "I know I tease you a lot, but, Willie, I can't imagine this world—"

"Whoa, whoa. Hold on. Where did Jase go? What happened, and who is this guy?"

You wipe the tears lining your cheeks. "It's just—I never say these things, but I feel them." You decide to make it even more personal. "Cole, I want to be a better father. John Luke, I want to be a better uncle. And, Willie—"

He holds up a hand. "Just stop now."

"I can't stop. I love you, man."

"If you don't stop, I'm jumping out of this helicopter. Without a parachute. I'll swim back to Wacko Island. I'll snuggle up with a gopher."

You reach out for Willie's hand. "Take it."

"Take what?"

"Take my hand."

He folds his arms. "I'm not taking your hand."

"Take it."

"You are crazy. Bona fide nutso."

"I'm proud of you, Willie. And I always will be."

Suddenly some sweet orchestra music begins to play over

the helicopter's speakers. You couldn't have planned this moment better yourself.

Willie and the boys are glancing around, wondering what's happening.

"Take me back to the island!" Willie screams. "I gotta get out of here!"

You just smile and reach out for a hug.

THE END

GOING NOWHERE

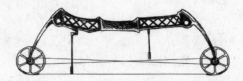

"I DEMAND TO SEE THE COUNT!"

You've been telling Winchester this all morning, but the older man doesn't seem to understand the gravity of your situation. He must have been here for so long that he's lost all perspective of what it's really like.

"You can demand all you want, Mr. Robertson. He is not currently on the island."

"I need to get out of here."

"You do realize that your wife signed an agreement saying the decision for you to stay or leave would be left up to the discretion of Count VanderVelde."

"Look. My wife might've signed an agreement giving away our firstborn," you shout in his face. "I don't know *what* she signed. All I know is I can't take this anymore. I'm leaving.

And if it's not by helicopter, then I swear I'll find a boat. I'll *make* a boat."

"That will be impossible," Winchester says.

You stomp out of the room and onto the porch.

I'll show them.

You walk down the hill toward the beach.

Nobody's keeping Jase prisoner.

Storming across the hot white sand, you search desperately for a boat. But after ten minutes, you don't find one. Not even a raft.

You do spot four armed soldiers marching toward you, Winchester close behind. The butler—or whatever he is— looks strange following them. Winchester resembles some nice grandfather while the other guys look like a bunch of commandos.

A couple of them aim M16s at you.

Winchester steps forward. "Jase, please."

"Am I a prisoner here?" you ask.

"Of course not."

"Well, call me crazy, but when someone aims a *gun* at my head, I don't feel so welcome. You know?"

"Absolutely. And I told the men that you were going to happily oblige them and come back to the lodge to get ready for today's hunt."

"What if I don't want to go hunting?"

"I think you can be persuaded to," Winchester says.

The two men aiming their rifles at you don't look like the types you should mess with. In fact, they look like the types you should try to get on your side at all costs. But you don't know how to do that.

"What if I just started swimming?"

It's not the best idea, but I'll try anything.

"You seem to be forgetting that your son Cole is still here. Right?"

"Yeah . . ."

Winchester just smiles. You don't like that smile. Reminds you of the count.

"We would hate for something to happen to him."

That's a threat if you've ever heard one.

They got me now.

"Okay, okay, fine. The hunt continues."

"Smart man. See, gentlemen? I told you Mr. Robertson would come to his senses."

So settle down and pick a weapon for your next day! Winchester reminds you of your three options this time. Which will it be?

If you pick the crossbow, go to page 95.

If you pick the shotgun, go to page 153.

If you pick the sword, go to page 171.

WHAC-A-MOLE

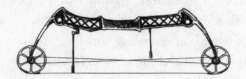

THIS RIFLE HAD BETTER BE the right choice. It hasn't done much for you yet today.

You sit there, sweating like a pig on a spit. Except you're a Robertson in the sand. Kinda the same thing, though, 'cause this soft sand is blistering hot. And you're letting the sun suck out every single drop of perspiration you have left inside.

Good thing I wore deodorant today.

Then again, if something goes wrong, like really wrong, the last thing you're gonna be worried about is smelling bad. Dead people already smell bad.

That's right. Dead men don't dance. But they sure might smell awful.

You stare toward the jungle.

Don't shoot unless you know you have a good shot, you remind yourself.

You're right next to one of the holes your target has made on the beach. After hours of watching it and being tormented by it, you've learned that it does indeed have a personality. It's like that one girl who always smiles and talks to all the guys but never has any intention of going out with them. Kind of like the golden duck earlier this week, come to think of it. Yeah. That's what you're dealing with.

Oh, and you're also dealing with a rodent.

A gopher, to be specific.

You've seen this gopher a dozen times. You've heard its laugh. And yes, it has a laugh. The thing might as well be wearing a shirt that says *Psych!* Because all it does is emerge now and then to check things out, but the moment it sees any kind of movement, it's gone.

Altogether, the four of you have probably fired fifty rounds at the creature. It hasn't worked.

So now you're the bait.

Now you're lying in wait, trying to get it to pop out of the hole. To see what you're doing. To taunt and tease you like it's been doing all morning.

And then . . .

Yep.

Its final mistake. Overconfidence.

After thirty minutes, however, you begin to think this is a terrible idea. You're just one big ball of sweat. Your head and face feel like they're in an oven.

That's what I get for having a full beard and long hair in this weather.

But the heat isn't what's bothering you the most.

It's the waiting.

The wondering.

You close your eyes for a minute. Or maybe for ten.

When you open them, it's there.

The round head and those big buck teeth. The whiskers.

The look that says, "Who let the dogs out?" and "What does the fox say?"

The face that appears to completely and totally mock you.

The gopher's glancing around nervously as if it doesn't trust the situation.

You don't move. You don't breathe.

Something's wrong with this scenario, but it takes you a second to pin down what it is. The gopher isn't in the hole you're staking out. This is another hole—and you don't have a clear shot at it.

You want to try sneaking closer, but it would hear you for sure.

Willie's not gonna try to—

But apparently he is. A shot is fired, quick and loud.

You hear a snap and a crack. Then something drops to the ground.

You also feel something burning on the side of your cheek. Maybe it's sunburn or some kind of bug bite.

Jumping up, you run to the hole where you last spotted the gopher. Sure enough, Willie got it.

"Yes!" you shout, but suddenly you feel dizzy.

Soon John Luke, Cole, and Willie are standing around you, expressions of concern on their faces.

"We got it," you say. "Willie, you did it."

"Yeah, I think I did it, all right." He seems most worried of all.

You feel woozy. Too much time in the sun. Too much time thinking about the slippery slidy Spider-Man sunshine drink of lemonade mama water that's so wonderful.

Wait a minute—I'm gettin' loopy.

You fall to your knees.

"Woo, I don't feel so great." You rub your cheek again. It burns even worse.

Then you raise your hand and see blood smeared across it.

"That don't look too good," you hear yourself say.

Willie grabs your shoulder. "No, it doesn't."

And that's the last thing you hear before passing out.

Go to page 41.

SMOOTHIE

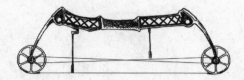

THE GREEN CONTAINER holds a large glass full of something thick and greenish-brown.

"This looks like some kind of shake."

Count VanderVelde nods. "Yes. It's very healthy."

"Can I ask what it consists of?"

"Yes. In the kitchen, we have a container—about the size of a bathtub—that we put vegetables in. All sorts. And we let them sit and mingle and come together for two weeks or so."

"Do you mix anything in with them?"

"No. They just morph into the dark liquid you see now."

"That's deeply disturbing," you say.

"It really cleans your system," the count explains. "Take a guess: How many glasses of your average health shake would it take to equal the fiber content of one island tropical treasure drink?"

"You're calling this an 'island tropical treasure'?" You take a whiff of the concoction. "What part of this is the treasure?"

"The way your body reacts to it. Of course, I'd stay close to a bathroom. All night long."

Go to page 197.

SOME KIND OF UGLY

YOU SQUINT THROUGH THE PERASIGHT QUANTUM 5 Thermal Imaging 42mm scope that's on your rifle. Even though you're only looking at the thick and endless trees and brush in front of you, you can tell the scope is a thing of beauty. You'd really just love to stay put and do target practice with this thing. But first off, you and the rest of the gang have to figure out *what* the target of this hunt will actually be.

A couple Jeeps dropped you off at the edge of this rainforest earlier this morning. Now the sun is hot and your legs are tired and you swear Willie has gotten all of you lost.

"Where *are* you going?" you ask Willie.

"Into the jungle," he replies from the point position at the front of your expedition of four.

John Luke takes a drink of water as Cole tries to figure out how to adjust the rifle scope.

"Stay alert, boys," Willie says.

You follow a trail that leads into the jungle and seems to stay adjacent to the river. But you come to a point where it splits in two.

"Go right," you tell Willie.

"How come?"

"Get away from the river a bit. Maybe we'll find what we're looking for if we get farther into the woods."

"Any of you seen any tree stands?" Willie asks, heading into the jungle.

"Are we hunting deer?" John Luke asks.

"That's the whole point—we don't know," you say. "But I haven't seen any duck blinds or tree stands."

"You'd think they'd give us a little more information," Cole complains.

"*That* is part of the experience," you say, being a bit sarcastic as usual.

But Cole has a point. If you were hunting deer, you wouldn't be walking through this island wilderness making noise and sending them away.

Something tells me we're not hunting deer.

"What if we find out we're hunting humans?" you say, just to mess around with the boys.

"This isn't a horror movie, Jase," Willie says.

"What if this is an island where they send the worst prisoners around to fend for themselves, and then they invite people like us to hunt them down?"

"Isn't that a movie?" Cole asks.

"I don't know," you say. "But maybe it should be. I could start writing the screenplay."

"Shhhh," Willie says, stopping at a massive tree that has to be a hundred years old.

You can hear the songs of birds along with other forms of life. But then you notice what Willie surely heard.

It sounds like someone in pain.

A *lot* of pain.

"What is *that*?" John Luke asks.

"Shhh," Willie repeats.

It reminds you of a squealing pig, except heavier and lower. Maybe it's some kind of wild boar.

That'd be cool—to bring back a boar's head to put in your house. *On the wall in our bedroom. Right before Missy kicks me out.*

The squealing gets louder.

"I think someone got up on the wrong side of the bed this morning," you say, aiming your gun into the trees.

"Hey, there. Right in there!" Willie aims his rifle to the left of where yours is pointed.

Suddenly you hear something to your right.

Wait a minute.

You turn and look into the scope and then—

It's coming too fast, too hard, too much.

Something plows into you like a running back, sweeping you off your feet.

You fire one shot, but it goes into the tops of the trees.

You hear another shot go off, then another. Meanwhile you're on your back, dizzy, gasping, and confused about what just happened.

"I got it; I got it!" Willie shouts. He heads into the woods to bag it but comes back empty-handed. "Couldn't find anything."

"That was a big, fat hog," Cole says.

"You saw it?" you ask.

"Yeah. When it mowed into you. Could've shot it too."

"Could've shot me too."

John Luke is still pointing his rifle into the jungle, where the hog that did this to you escaped. He fires off a couple rounds but doesn't hit anything.

"I saw it, but it's moving way too fast," he says.

"Did you see it?" Willie asks you. "It's like—it's like a hog that looks like a bull. Swear. Ugliest thing I've ever seen. And I've seen some things."

"Come on, let's go track it down," you say.

But it's almost like the giant hog got wise once it heard the gunshots. You spend the rest of the day hunting for it but don't find a thing. You do nearly pass out from the heat, and you

think the spicy food from last night might not be doing great things in your stomach. So by dusk you're ready to call it a day. Time to head back to the lodge and get packing.

"We got beaten by a hog," Willie says.

"Well, that's sorta how I feel every day," you say to him in your typical deadpan way. *"Boss."*

THE END

CAVEMEN

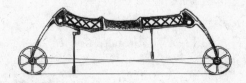

THE JEEPS ARE TAKING YOU GUYS up a winding mountain road that loops around and around and makes you a bit
nauseated. You're in the passenger seat, staring at the jungle
below and the ocean farther out. You make a few attempts to
talk to the driver, but he doesn't say a word.

He lets you out at the gaping mouth of the cave in the
mountain, then drives away. All of you stand still, peering into
the ominous cavern.

Willie laughs uncomfortably. "Think it's lit up inside there?"

"I think we'll be using our flashlights all day," you say.

"At least I didn't have to pick the weapon this time," John
Luke says.

Today's pick went to Cole, and he selected the crossbow.
Maybe a good choice for hunting inside a cave.

Unless it's pitch-dark and you're running from something and shooting at the same time.

It would really stink to go into this cave and get shot by your own brother or son or nephew. Imagine having to go home and explain *that.*

"Well, are we ready?" Willie asks.

You step behind him. "You take point."

"Oh, thanks."

The first thing you notice after entering the cave is how cool it is in here. You're thankful for your camouflage jacket and know it'll probably be staying on all day.

At first, the cave appears to have only one chamber to explore. It's wide and tall inside, with those cone-shaped formations sticking out of the ceiling.

"What are those spiky things called again?" you ask.

"Stalactites," John Luke says.

"Oooh, look at Brainiac here," Cole jokes.

"Stalactites," you repeat, examining them in the wide and powerful beam of your flashlight.

Willie holds his crossbow in his hands while the rest of you carry flashlights and illuminate the way, bows slung over your shoulders. Hopefully you won't have another boar situation on your hands with an animal that attacks out of nowhere and runs you over.

"Can you imagine being a cave person?" Willie says, clearly in awe of your surroundings.

"No, but I sure can imagine growing up with a bunch of them," you joke.

"Very funny."

The floor is sloping downward now, and you wonder just how far it goes. Eventually it breaks into a number of smaller chambers.

"Are we gonna get lost in these?" you ask, following Willie into the far right chamber. "I'm not leaving any kind of bread crumbs behind."

"It's not that complicated."

"Not yet. What if two passageways lead to four? And four lead to sixteen?"

"Not quite following your math there, Einstein. I think we got it."

Willie keeps taking right turns, so you come up with the idea that if things get bad and you have to start running, you'll just need to reverse your course and make sure you take lefts all the way out of here.

Or would we take rights? Let me think for a sec.

Willie begins to slow as the passageway you're walking down becomes narrower and narrower.

"Having some trouble there, Willie? Things getting too *tight* for you?" You always like giving your brother a hard time about being a little bigger than you.

"It looks like it dead-ends ahead," he says, either ignoring you or simply not getting your comment.

You lift up your flashlight, and the beam shows a wall of red straight ahead. "What is that?"

Willie nears the end of the chamber. "It's like there's some kind of growth everywhere." He touches the red stuff, which covers part of the floor as well. "It's soft. Like a lush carpet. Feel it."

Everywhere you look from top to bottom is this red, furry thing. When you touch it, you get this really weird vibe. It tells you stay away, to head on back, to leave ASAP.

"Hey, guys, I don't know—"

"Look," Willie says, plopping down and sitting back. "It's like shag carpet!"

"Willie, man, I think we should go."

You shine the light in his face, and he holds up a hand. "Man, you're blinding me."

John Luke jumps into the ground-and-wall covering. When he lands, all of you feel an abrupt and shaking growl.

The flashlight shows the *uh-oh*s on Willie's and John Luke's faces.

"Where'd that come from?" you ask.

Suddenly John Luke and Willie topple over. Cole takes a step back from where he stands next to you.

"Hey, what the—? John Luke!"

Willie grabs his crossbow and aims at the wall in front of him.

The wall that's currently moving.

That's no wall.

Another deep, rumbling roar seems to shake the entire cave.

"John Luke, Cole, run. Take off!" Willie says, gripping his crossbow and preparing to shoot.

The boys obey, and you're left there holding the light and trying to get your crossbow ready.

"Just hold steady, Jase. One minute," Willie says.

The wall continues to shift, and then you see the face.

The face of a giant red bear.

And it's angry. Oh, is it angry.

Willie fires an arrow straight at the bear's head. The creature simply bats it away and gives you a front-facing, ferocious yell.

"Uh, let's get out of here!"

Both of you bolt, the flashlight bobbling back and forth. You don't hear anything at first and actually have the stupidity to think, *We're gonna outrun this thing—it must be really slow. We're totally getting out of here.*

But you hear it running and realize it's not fat. It's just big-boned. And big-headed. And big-clawed.

Everything about it is *big*.

Including its teeth.

You manage to get out of the cave, and the bear doesn't follow you into the light. But there was no way you could've taken that thing down. *Come on! It was invincible.*

Guess it's back to West Monroe and *normal* hunting. Fine by you.

THE END

FLIGHT FROM
THE ISLAND

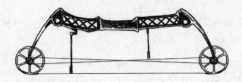

YOU ARE RUNNING WITH A SHOTGUN in your hands.

How'd I get here?

You're not sure. You take a look at your pants and notice bloodstains on them.

Are those mine, or do they belong to someone else?

No one else seems to be nearby, but something's following you. Something big. Something massive. But what is it? And where are you heading?

The jungle on the island. You're in the jungle, but you're running toward the water. Toward the beach. That's it. Yeah.

Your legs burn, but you don't think you have a wound of any kind.

Something whizzes by your head. Then something else flies past your arm. You recognize an object sticking out of the tree you're racing past.

A dart.

A poison arrow.

Is someone shooting at you?

It's not that kind of island.

Or is it?

You run faster and trip over a log. Several darts land right above you.

Good thing. *Maybe it is that kind of island.*

You keep going. The trees are getting thinner and thinner. Almost there.

Suddenly you break free.

The helicopter is waiting for you on the beach. Cole, Willie, and John Luke are already in it, waving you on and yelling.

You turn to fire back at whoever's chasing you and realize you're out of ammo. So you ditch the shotgun and keep running.

Why am I so out of shape? Note to self: start running again and go easy on the chips and guacamole.

You're nearly to the helicopter, running through the sand, when you turn back and finally see them. *Them* as in plural *them.* As in dozens of them. As in a whole tribe of angry men wearing only cloths around their waists. They're carrying blowguns and bows. Some of those darts and arrows are flying toward you.

One barely misses your heel. Another almost plugs into your brain.

You're still running when you notice something banging against your side. Something in a cloth bag. You take a quick peek—it's something golden.

It looks like an idol.

I've seen this before, haven't I?

You make it to the helicopter, and it takes off right as you jump in. Willie and Cole hold on to you. You hear arrows hitting the sides of the chopper.

"You made it," Willie says. "We're heading home."

Finally. You collapse on the floor of the helicopter.

You've reached the end.

But then again—how'd you get here in the first place?

Go to page 1 and start over.

THE BOYS ARE
BACK IN TOWN

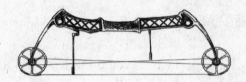

YOU'VE GOT A PLAN. Sort of a defensive plan. "Hey, guys. I think we need some weapons."

"What kind?" John Luke asks.

Cole smirks. "Well, we can have either a rifle or a shotgun or a crossbow—"

"Be quiet, Cole," you say. "I'll take anything at this point. We need something to protect ourselves. I'm not feeling very confident about tonight. Especially since the count has disappeared."

"Where'd Winchester go?" Willie wants to know.

"Who knows where that guy spends his time. He's probably in his room."

"Let's go get some weapons, then," he says.

You each carry a candle down the hallway to the elevator. But when you reach the elevator, you realize you won't be taking it down.

"What's wrong?" Willie asks from behind you.

"The power's out. And the elevator isn't battery operated, is it?"

The four of you stand still as echoes of thunder rumble through the hallway.

"Let's search the place," Willie suggests. "Maybe we'll find something."

After looking for a while, you do indeed find something.

The four katana swords are in a closet as if they're waiting for you to get them.

"Well, we only have one choice this time, right?" John Luke picks one up. "The sword."

You feel a little better now that the sword is in your hand.

It's a good thing too. 'Cause it's shaping up to be a long night.

● ● ●

When you return to your room, you discover a nutria under the bed. It's basically a giant rat. A swamp rat. Long tail. Fuzzy white whiskers.

Yeah. It puts up a good fight. But the nutria is very, very slow. No match for your very, very fast katana skills.

Just as you're finishing up, you hear a scream and run to John Luke's room. Somehow, someway—some weird, magical, crazy, wacky way—there are frogs in his room. Big, fat, bouncing frogs.

They're going berserk. Not jumping up and down but jumping *at* you.

Oh, these frogs don't know who they're messing with.

You are Jase Robertson, and you have the longest, sharpest sword you've ever seen.

"Let's do this" is all you have to say to John Luke.

The flickering candlelight is enough for you and your sword.

You're going to name this sword Tebow. Fast and unpredictable and bringing the pain.

That's right.

Frog legs for the whole island of Fiji!

This does take a while.

Soon the room is a big . . . well, it's a mess.

Let's not dwell on that.

And you can't, either, because you hear another scream.

It's Cole.

"Come on," you tell John Luke.

Turn to page 55.

HOT HOT HOT

YOU OPEN THE RED DISH, revealing numerous red and green peppers you've never seen before mixed with a broth that contains several kinds of seafood, like fish and shrimp.

"And what is this?" you ask Count VanderVelde.

"This is our variation on a wonderful clam boil."

You take a whiff and your eyes start to water. "It smells . . . spicy."

"Yes. We call it the Blister Boil."

You take a deep breath, then pick up your spoon.

"Men have been known to black out after eating that," the count says.

"Wonderful. Great."

The first bite feels like molten lava poured into your mouth.

The second bite and you lose all sensation below the waist.

"An adventurous spirit!" Count VanderVelde shouts. "I love it!"

The third bite contains a bit of lobster. That and a forest fire. Such a great combo.

You wipe your head and feel dizzy. "This is definitely—"

But you can't take any more. You jump up and run out of the room and out of the lodge, then dive into the pool just outside.

You swim underwater with your mouth open. For a long, long time.

Go to page 197.

MEOW

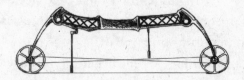

THE TWO JEEPS DRIVE YOU up the winding mountain road early the next morning. You pass the cave and remember the massive red bear John Luke managed to take down. After another ten minutes, you reach a closed gate blocking the path.

"Rest of the way is on foot," your driver says.

All of you get out and walk around the rusted gate.

"So we hike this to get farther up the mountain?" Cole asks.

You nod and shrug. "Only one way to go, and it's up. So yeah."

After you've been walking for ten minutes, drizzle starts coming down. It feels good because the weather is so warm and sticky.

"Is this one of those tropical storms?" you ask the guys.

"Comes in for an hour, and then it's sunshine for the rest of the day?"

"Those clouds don't look too sunny to me," Willie says.

His words seem to be an omen of sorts. The light sprinkle turns into a steady rain, which then becomes a downpour. Soon you forget how hot you were this morning as every inch of you becomes pruny and wet.

"Tell me something," Willie begins as you all keep slogging uphill on the dirt trail. "Has it rained a drop this whole week?"

"Not one," you say.

"This is making up for it," John Luke adds.

At one point you all try to seek shelter under a tall tree along the trail, but it offers little. The wind has picked up and the rain is shifting, blowing first in one direction and then the next.

"Maybe there's shelter closer to the top of the mountain," you suggest.

"Something tells me there's not." Willie's the one disagreeing, of course.

"So you want to stay here getting soaked?"

"Not really."

"At least if we move, we stay a little warmer."

Willie looks like a wet mess. So do John Luke and Cole. You can only imagine what a sight you are. At least you're wearing a cap that's blocking some of the rain. *Some* of the rain.

The farther up the winding dirt trail you go, the more you realize it's becoming less of an actual trail. Grass and brush cover more and more of it the higher you get.

"Hey, check this out," John Luke calls from the side of the path.

You walk over to see what he's pointing at—bones scattered on the grass.

"Looks like some kind of animal."

"After someone finished feasting on it," Willie says.

You adjust your cap as raindrops spill off the brim. Your cheek still aches and throbs, but thankfully you took some heavy pain medication earlier.

A few minutes later you see another set of bones. Then another soon after.

"I hope these aren't the animals we're supposed to be hunting," you say.

"I hope the animal we're supposed to be hunting isn't doing this."

Willie has a good point. And you have the sword you're carrying. You figure you have to use it eventually, right? But the swords might not be enough.

The higher you walk, the darker the sky becomes. The rain is starting to hurt because you're so cold and so wet.

"I think it'd be awesome if at the end of this we saw an allibeaver," John Luke says.

"You and your allibeavers." Willie shakes his head.

"They're real."

"Uh-huh."

"Ask Papaw what happened at Camp Ch-Yo-Ca."

"Yeah, right. I'm not making a fool of myself."

"Hey, you guys, hush for a minute." You hold up a hand. "Hear that?"

The sound comes from overhead somewhere and resembles a vicious scream.

"What was *that*?"

It sounded like a noise from a horror movie.

Then it rings out again, morphing into a higher-pitched mew this time.

"I think that's some kind of cat," John Luke says.

Willie snorts. "A cat can't make a sound like that."

You glance at your brother and have to laugh. "You're a sopping mess, you know that?"

"Be quiet," he says. "I forgot my hat at the lodge."

"I think that was a mountain lion," you say. "Or this island's version of a mountain lion."

"Well, we are on the *mountain*."

You keep walking, hopefully getting closer and closer to your objective. The path soon ends, and there's only a sharp, rocky incline left to climb. Trees and brush cover all of it but the very top, which consists of jagged stones.

Willie points up the slope. "Who wants to be king of the mountain?"

"I'm gathering that you don't," you say.

"You're gathering correct. That's a little too steep for me."

John Luke steps forward. "I'll head up there."

"I'll go too," Cole says, joining him.

"Keep your swords in their sheaths," you say. "We don't want any more *accidents*." You look at Willie when you say that.

It's still pouring as John Luke and Cole begin to head up the final stretch of mountain. They disappear into the trees, then reappear for a while as they hike up the rocky terrain.

The wild, high-pitched wailing sound rings out again. You shoot Willie a look. "Think we should go up there too?"

"They'll be fine."

The wildcat sound rips through the woods, closer now.

"Maybe we should go," you say.

Willie nods. "Yeah, maybe."

So you follow the boys' path.

As you ascend the slope, you hear some screams, then a commotion ahead of you. You rush forward, and as you do, here come John Luke and Cole, straight toward you. Falling, stumbling, running.

Their swords are nowhere to be seen.

"What's going on?" you shout, but soon John Luke and Cole are flying past you.

"Get out of here! It's coming!" John Luke yells.

You steady your sword and hold your ground. Willie does

the same next to you. You don't hear anything, but that doesn't matter.

Then you spot it. About twenty feet above you, crouching on the edge of a boulder, is a massive cougar. It's just . . . immense. Its fur is silver gray, its face round, its ears erect. The animal stares down at you before unleashing a wicked, ripping roar. Fierce and high and cackling.

"That's a big cat," Willie says, holding his katana with both hands.

"It's a cougar," you correct him.

"I think it's a mountain lion."

"Yeah, same thing."

"Or maybe it's a puma."

"Well, yeah," you say.

"Or maybe a catamount."

You give Willie a look. "Yeah, it's a big cat. I know."

"Maybe a panther."

"Would you be quiet?"

All of a sudden, the cougar leaps from the rock to the ground close by you, and that's when . . .

Wait a minute. It looks like Spider-Man.

The mountain lion doesn't jump with all four paws. It leaps the way a man would leap.

And now it's standing on *two* feet, right in front of you.

Now you notice what John Luke and Cole probably saw.

This is no ordinary mountain lion.

"That's a dude," Willie stammers.

It sounds crazy, but he's right. This is some kind of big mountain lion–meets–man hybrid.

I'm losing my mind. I gotta be losing my mind.

"Hello, gentlemen."

You look at Willie and know you've lost it.

"Did you say something?" you ask.

Willie shakes his head and points toward the creature. "He sounds exactly like the count."

"That mountain lion didn't just talk to us."

"Guess again," the voice says.

Then it rips out another ferocious roar.

You've seen and heard enough. Time to sheathe the sword and start running.

You think you hear Willie's footsteps behind you, but you're not sure. Brush and branches strike you in the face until you finally make it out of the trees and back onto the dirt path.

John Luke and Cole are standing there, waiting for you, arms hanging at their sides. The rain still pours.

"Did you see it?" John Luke asks.

"Yeah. But I don't know *what* I saw."

"It's like a human mountain lion," Cole says.

"No, it can't be."

"It's like an allibeaver," John Luke explains. "Half-alligator, half-beaver. Except this is half–mountain lion, half-human."

"Half–Count Chocula," Willie adds as he joins you, out of breath and doubled over.

"This is crazy," you say.

Rain falls steadily as you wait a few more minutes. You stare up the slope again and draw your sword, just in case. But nothing comes.

"Did you see how it jumped?" Willie asks you. "It was like some weird-looking thing from a comic book."

You nod. You'll leave the island but will be forever haunted by the cougar-man.

The weirdest animal you've ever encountered.

The one that thankfully got away . . . until something pounces on you from behind and you're knocked out cold.

Your story continues on page 151 in *Si in Space*.

CRAZY IDEAS

ON THIS NIGHT—your third evening on the island—none of you see Count VanderVelde. But he left you a short and cryptic note.

Congrats on bagging the golden duck. Testy little fellas, aren't they? I bet you've never brought home a duck that color, have you?

Tomorrow you will be hunting in the cave. To make your life (and mine) easier, you'll only have three weapons to pick from this time: the crossbow, shotgun, and sword. Choose wisely.

You live to see another day.

Sleep tight!

Count VanderVelde

You're just glad he didn't say anything about not letting the bedbugs bite. Who knows what kind of bedbugs this island would have.

Before heading to bed, you talk in private with Willie. The boys have already gone to their rooms.

"Is it just me, or does this trip feel a bit strange?"

"You mean the gigantic boars and golden ducks?" Willie asks. "Yeah, they were strange."

"Well, yeah. But weren't you expecting something even more . . . exotic?"

"I don't know. I just hope the count comes back to take us off this island. I'd hate to be stranded here." Willie laughs, but you're left with the thought, and it's not a good one.

What if that actually did happen?

What if you were all left alone on this island? You don't have any Internet or cell service. You haven't been in touch with your wife for the last few days.

Maybe this is a prison.

Maybe the world will never hear from you again.

"Hey, you got that look on your face," Willie says.

"What look?"

"The kind when you have all those ideas rumbling around in your head."

"No, I don't."

"Go get some sleep," Willie says.

You go to bed, but sleep doesn't come.

You try and try, but you keep hearing scratching sounds.
I'm imagining that.

They seem to be coming from everywhere. Your bed. The ceiling above you. The walls around you. The floor underneath you. You can't help thinking about bedbugs again.

Scratch, scratch, scratch.

Every time you get out of bed and turn on the lights, the noise stops. You examine your pillow and mattress, as well as the walls and floor, but nothing is there. The scratching starts again as soon as you flip the light switch.

Yeah, you don't sleep well. But tomorrow is a new day.

A brand-new day for a new hunt.

Heading to the cave.

Only one question remains: Which weapon will you choose this time?

If you pick the crossbow, go to page 95.

If you pick the shotgun, go to page 153.

If you pick the sword, go to page 171.

If you try to leave the island because
you're worried, go to page 79.

MWAHAHAHA

THE SECOND TIME the candles go out in the living room isn't because the wind blasts open the doors.

No. Something inside the room blows them out.

You've been waiting on the couch for the count to return. You're almost asleep when you hear the puff of air and everything goes dark.

"What's happening?" you ask, wiping your eyes. "Willie? Cole? John Luke?"

"Something's in here with us," Willie says in a low, soft tone.

"Where are you, Cole?"

"Over here."

"I'm here too," John Luke adds.

Your eyes are adjusting to the dark, but not fast enough. A streak of lightning glows through the window. The whole lodge seems to shake as the wind howls.

"Let me try to find the matches again," John Luke says.

You hear movement, then a jolting, breaking sound. Something crumples to the floor.

"John Luke?" Willie shouts.

There's more movement, more shuffling, more breaking.

Now you're up and trying to help somehow.

You find the matches and light a candle. It stays lit long enough for you to see what's happening.

There are cougars in the room. Except these cougars are standing.

Really? Come on.

Then one of them with white hair like Winchester's launches itself at you.

The candle goes out, and so does everything else.

The wind howls outside.

You can't see the moon above, but you're betting it's a full one.

THE END

THE HORROR

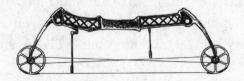

YOU STAND ON THE BEACH as rising waves crash onto shore. The wind picks up as the sun goes down. You hold your katana high and wait for the monster to raise its ugly head again.

You are the only one left.

It's taken your group out one by one.

The relentless, soul-sucking beast.

A creature of the dark, with a heart residing in the night.

First it forced John Luke to go back to the lodge, his ankle twisted after getting stuck in a two-foot-deep hole.

Then it bit Cole on not one ankle but both. Wretched, deep bites. He too needed to return to the lodge for treatment and pain medicine.

The sickly, terrible animal.

You don't even want to remember what it did to Willie. How it attached itself to his face, laughing all the while.

Oh yes, the brute laughs and laughs.

The possessed pariah protecting its turf on the beach.

Willie cried like a baby while screaming for you to get the thing off his beard. There was a point where you couldn't tell the difference between the thing and Willie's beard. It was a truly terrible sight.

You checked Willie out after you managed to knock the gopher away, and he simply had some scratches on his face. No big deal. He was being overdramatic.

But now it's only you and the monster.

You know it will be nighttime soon. The creature (and its foul stench) will go back to the hole it came from, and you'll miss your chance.

Hopefully you're not going to let that happen.

I've come seeking revenge.

I've come for payback.

I will avenge my family.

You stand still, peering here and there. The holes on the beach are clearly visible even in the twilight. You have all been busy today. Not only fighting the foul creature of the night but also digging and trying to find him.

"Come on out," you call.

It's time for the final showdown.

Then suddenly a head appears out of the ground, a whole fifty yards from you. Here it comes. The evil, awful thing. The horrific monster.

It's a gopher.

And it's approaching you.

It's running now.

Getting ready to attack.

You hold the sword, totally prepared, and then you think of Willie screaming as the thing launched itself at his face.

Closer now . . .

Your hands are shaking.

Your sword is poised to strike.

And then . . .

You ditch the sword and scram.

You're not about to have that thing chewing on your head.

I'm no Evander Holyfield, and that gopher's not Mike Tyson.

You're not taking any chunks.

I mean chances. *Not* chunks.

You run and don't look back. If you look back, the thing might sail through the air and start nibbling.

No.

No.

You were the last Robertson standing.

And you bolted.

But that's because this is no ordinary gopher.

This is no ordinary island.

And this is no story Willie will ever hear. *Jase running away from a gopher? Jase who?*

Tomorrow you'll be heading back home. Back to ordinary. Back to normal.

Thank goodness.

THE END

STRANGER THAN FICTION

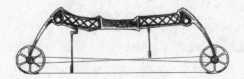

"CONGRATULATIONS, GENTLEMEN. The boar's head will make a terrific trophy once it's stuffed and mounted."

It's now evening, after the sun has slipped away and the wind has turned warm instead of hot. The table is set for another feast, and Count VanderVelde has made his entrance. You thought the count would probably be gone for the rest of the week, and you haven't decided if this is a pleasant surprise or not.

"I'm not sure I really want to see that thing again," you tell him. "I'd say it was already a bit overstuffed."

"What *was* that, anyway?" Willie asks.

"Feisty suckers, aren't they?" the count says.

"So explain this to me—*when* does an animal bleed purple?" You need to be clear on this point. "I mean—we're not color-blind, right? Is it something special for this island?"

The host picks up a piece of fruit from his plate and devours it. "You'll find lots of strange things on this island the longer you stay here. By the way—you have to try the strawberries. They're impeccable."

"Great," you say.

"How is purple blood possible?"

"John Luke, please," Willie says, shaking his head.

But you nod at your nephew with approval. The count never really answered the question. Willie obviously doesn't want to appear rude in front of the master of ceremonies. You, on the other hand, aren't so worried about that and continue John Luke's line of questioning.

"So when you grow the hogs to look like *that*, does it mean their blood turns a certain color? Is it some DNA thing? Is this island like Jurassic Park?"

"Everybody knows truth is stranger than fiction," Count VanderVelde says.

You're beginning to get used to how he doesn't answer a single question you ask.

"I bet you're not going to tell me where we're heading tomorrow, are you?"

The pork on your plate doesn't look particularly appetizing. You're not quite sure why.

"I will give you a clue. It involves water."

"Either the beach or the river," Cole says.

"Freshwater," the count adds. "You'll need to let me know which weapon you'd like to use."

"We can use any, right?" Willie asks. "Including the dagger again if we want?"

"Yes. I'm feeling generous tonight."

Which weapon will you take to the river tomorrow?

The crossbow? Go to page 9.

The shotgun? Go to page 145.

The rifle? Go to page 69.

The sword? Go to page 45.

The dagger? Go to page 191.

The cowbell? Go to page 177.

WOOF

YOU OPEN THE ROUND ORANGE DISH in front of you. Smoke rises from the top of it, but you can tell the smoke is cold—maybe it's actually mist. And whatever's inside is covered with a cloth.

"Chilled Chihuahua," the count says. "Quite the treat in these parts of the world."

You swallow hard and hope you didn't actually hear what you thought the count said. "Chilled *Chihuahua*? As in the dog Chihuahua?"

"Yes, sir."

"What part of the world thinks that eating a tiny dog is a good thing?"

"Have you ever eaten a burrito in a big city late at night?"

You shake your head, then glance at Willie.

"Yeah, he does have a point," Willie says.

"What?" Cole exclaims.

The count goes on. "It's chilled so you may fully taste the delicacy of the brain."

You jerk back from the dish. "Wait a minute—this is dog brain?" You've eaten what some might consider unusual food before, but nothing like this. *Where are the PETA police when you need them?*

"Yes, chilled Chihuahua," the count repeats in a matter-of-fact way.

When you get up the nerve to actually remove the cloth and see what's in the container, you have to search. It takes you a minute to locate the small item.

"This looks like an M&M."

"Have you ever seen a Chihuahua?" he asks.

"Well, yeah, of course."

"They're not very smart, you know."

Everyone is watching to see what you'll do. It takes everything you have to put the spoon in your mouth. And a funny thing happens when you do.

It's not *that* bad.

You swallow and shrug as the others wait for your reaction.

"What's it taste like?" John Luke asks.

You're still trying to figure out how to describe it.

"Well, you know those little hot dogs in SpaghettiOs? It's kind of like them. The flavor, texture, everything."

"Ew," Willie says.

"No, they're actually pretty good. Got any more in there?"

Go to page 197.

DOUBLE VISION

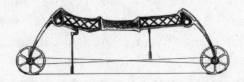

THE WEIRDEST THING HAPPENS. You feel like you just dropped in here from another world. No, make that another life. And in that life, you were Willie. Talking about nothing like he usually does and acting crazy.

You touch your face to make sure the confusion is over. Feels familiar.

Okay. I'm Jase, not Willie.

Still, this is strange. You were in the middle of some kind of wild story, and now . . .

What am I doing here? Oh yeah, that's right. Hunting in a cave on a mysterious island . . . for some kind of dangerous creature.

Cole, John Luke, and Willie are in here with you. You guys seem to be lost, and if you are, you know who's to blame.

"I swear we've already come this way," Willie says.

Yep, sure enough.

It's cold, and your footsteps echo through the cavern. You have a rifle slung over your shoulder, your flashlight illuminating the way. Everybody's walking around and making more noise than hunters should. It's like all of you doubt you'll find anything in here.

"I'm getting kinda hungry," you say as the passage begins to slope downward. "Hey, Cole, you hungry?"

You glance over your shoulder but don't see anything. Then you shine your flashlight behind you and see nothing but rock.

"Cole?"

"What's up?" Willie asks, a few paces ahead of you. "Hey, John Luke, stop for a minute."

"Cole was right there. Right behind me. Hey, Cole!"

But you hear and see nothing. Worry sets in. "He must've accidentally gone the wrong direction." You wave your flashlight frantically.

"How'd he do that? Wouldn't he just call after us?"

"I don't know. I'm gonna go look for him."

"No," Willie says. "We have to stay together."

"Okay, then. Come on." You double-time back the way you came without waiting to see if Willie and John Luke catch up.

You want to walk faster but have to be careful since the ground is so uneven. You're still calling Cole's name and hearing no response when you arrive at a three-way intersection.

"Didn't we come from the left?"

"I thought we came from the center," Willie says.

"No, didn't we come from the right?" John Luke asks.

Oh, this is great.

You call out for Cole. And you finally get a reply.

It's a sound, not a voice.

It's the sound of a duck call.

"Was that—?"

"Sure was," Willie says.

"You think it's Cole?"

"You think someone besides us is in these caves with a duck call?"

You head in the direction of the call. But a few moments later, another one sounds. This is a different duck call.

And it's *behind* you.

"What's going on?" Willie asks.

"Cole!"

Now you hear yet another duck call—a third kind. This one is directly in front of you.

"Okay, someone's messing with us," you mutter under your breath, hoping only Willie and John Luke can hear you, not any terrifying cave monsters.

You take the rifle off your shoulder and cradle it in your hands. Just in case.

"Hey, Cole?" you call out. "You around here?"

One more duck call. They seem to be coming from every

direction. "If you guys weren't hearing that, I might be a bit freaked out."

"I hear them, but they keep changing," Willie says. "And I don't know where they're coming from."

"We need to keep heading this direction," you say. "Shine your flashlight ahead, John Luke. It's getting dark."

No response from your nephew.

"Hey, John Luke, flash the—"

You turn around and see only Willie standing there, his back facing you.

"What's wrong?" Then you see what Willie's staring at.

Nothing.

"Where'd he go?"

"I don't know! He was literally *right* behind me. John Luke! John Luke, I swear, this isn't funny. Don't try to be funny now. Serious."

But there's no laughter coming out of the dark.

"What is this?" you say.

"Where'd he go?" Willie asks.

"You head that way—"

"No. Jase. We stay together."

"So where do you want to go?"

"John Luke! John Luke?"

You both wait for a few seconds. Then you hear the multiple duck calls going off, in unison this time.

"Someone's totally messin' with us."

"If it's the boys, they're so gonna get it," Willie says.

"Come on, this way. Straight ahead."

You point the flashlight with your left hand, which also holds the barrel of the rifle. Your right hand controls the grip and trigger.

The stone spears dripping down from the ceiling suddenly look ominous to you. The light bounces off of them and gets sucked into the darkness.

"Why duck calls?" you ask.

You don't hear anything from Willie, so you turn.

"Oh no," you say. "No, no way."

You aim the flashlight back where you were headed. Nothing but an empty, shadowy passageway.

"Willie! Come on. I know you're just messin' with me."

There are many places someone could easily hide. But disappear?

First Cole; then John Luke; now Willie.

You sigh and shine the light everywhere you possibly can.

"Hey, guys?"

You can hear water dripping. Then you hear something else. Something behind you in the darkness.

A shuffling sound.

They are so messin' with me.

You wait until it gets really close.

Then you spin around with both the light and the rifle aimed into the darkness.

It takes you about five seconds to understand what's in front of you. Then it registers. This is the biggest bear head you've *ever* seen.

Those five seconds happen to be the last moments of your life.

Or so you think.

A shot goes off. And another. Then several more.

The bear doesn't fall but rather darts away from you, down the passageway.

For a minute you want to chase after it. Then you look up and see John Luke and Willie standing there with . . . *Wait a minute!*

That's me.

You notice they're all wearing different clothes than they had on earlier today. Including you. Jase Robertson. The figure you're staring at.

"Look, you are *not* gonna believe this, so just come on out of the cave," Jase tells you.

I'm talking to myself. Literally, and not just in my head.

As you follow them out of the cave, you see Cole, Willie, and John Luke waiting.

"You guys are alive."

"*They* saved us," Willie says.

"We saved ourselves," Other Willie says.

You shake your head. You are totally lost.

"What's going on?" you ask.

"Look—we took a time machine to get here," Other Willie explains.

"You took a *what* to get here?" *Maybe it wasn't my imagination after all. . . .*

"They took a time machine," Regular Willie repeats. "They say it looks like an outhouse too."

You shake your head. "No way."

"It's okay," Other Jase says. "You're always confused. Because I am too. But we saved your lives. That's what counts."

"The bear got away," you tell them.

"Sure, but that means this trip is over. Don't you want to go home?" Other Willie asks.

"With you?"

"No," he answers. "You can't go home with us. Then things will get messed up."

"The world doesn't need *two* Willies," Other Jase says with a dramatic shiver.

You sit down on the dirt and shake your head. "I must be dreaming or something. I bet this is a dream within a dream . . . within a dream."

"Yeah, well, try going back to the Civil War," Other Jase mutters.

Soon enough, the doubles leave you guys alone. You wonder whether your mind will ever recover from the past few hours.

"I gotta admit," Willie begins.

"What?"

"I'm a lot more handsome in person than I thought."

You roll your eyes.

Sometimes Willie can make you truly speechless.

THE END

SHREDDED CHEESE

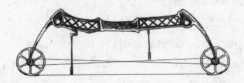

ONCE YOU FIND OUT *what* you're shooting, it's game on.

More like game over.

And you're laughing and waiting and loving it. This is right up your alley.

You're down by the river and nobody's fired a shot yet. But you've all seen the target.

A golden duck. Not superbright gold but medium gold. A bit bigger than a mallard, with an extra-long beak for some reason.

Maybe someone painted it. Maybe Count Chocula bred this variety and fed it only his morning cereal. Who knows. It doesn't matter one bit.

You're gonna shoot a duck. And so far, you've only seen this one.

But by the time it starts to fly off and you fire away with your shotgun—picked out this morning by John Luke—something unfortunate happens.

The gun works a little too well.

There's this wonderful word called *vaporization*. And that's exactly what happens.

As you pull the trigger, forgetting this is a high-powered automatic shotgun, the duck literally vanishes into thin air. *Is that even possible?*

It can't have disappeared. Can it?

"Ewwwww," Willie says.

You search for any part of the duck that's left, but there's nothing.

There's absolutely nothing.

Willie comes over. "Uh, Jase?"

"Yeah."

"Maybe next time don't make it into golden fertilizer."

"Funny."

"Too bad John Luke had to pick the shotgun," Willie says. "Great job there."

"It's a shotgun," John Luke says. "That's what you use for hunting ducks."

"I wouldn't call what Jase did hunting."

"I shot and killed that duck even if we can't bring back a piece of it," you say.

"Not sure if that counts."

"Oh, it counts," you say.

But later, after an entire day of searching for another duck, someone else disagrees.

Speaking of counts . . .

"No. You have to produce the trophy here," Count VanderVelde says once you're back at the lodge.

"Everybody can confirm that I shot it," you say.

"Yeah, he shot it all right," Willie says. "Blasted it like a string of firecrackers."

The count shakes his head. "I'm sorry, but in the fine print of the contract, it states—"

"Not the fine print again," you protest.

He spews some meaningless, random blah-blah-blah about the need to preserve the remains of the blah-blah-blah for evidence or proof or whatever.

"Was there only one gold duck out there?"

"No, Jase. There are more. Lots more, in fact."

"So where'd they all go?"

"Maybe they saw your shooting spree and all decided to hide in the cave," the count says. "Or maybe they're here, in one of the rooms."

You laugh, but the count doesn't laugh back.

Oh, well, that gold duck was annoying you anyway.

When you retrieve your bag before hopping on the helicopter to fly back to Fiji, you see something in your bed. Something you thought you'd never set eyes on again.

It's a duck. A duck the color of a king's crown.

It's alive, and it's watching you as if you killed its sister. When you move, its eyes move with you.

"You better watch out, or you're next," you warn it right before leaving quickly. Not that you're scared of it or anything. Of course not.

THE END

SOMETHING
IN THE WATER

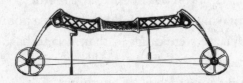

IT FEELS GOOD to see the island disappear. You're all in the helicopter, listening to the rumbling and gazing at the blue water below.

"Maybe none of that happened. Maybe we were drugged," John Luke says out of nowhere.

"What are you talking about?" Willie replies.

"Think about it. When we arrived, we were given orange juice. Maybe it was spiked with something strange. Something that caused us to start seeing weird things. And every day we ate food they made for us."

You wonder if he's right. "They did keep feeding us *strange* things."

"No, I don't think we were drugged," Willie says. "Why would they do that?"

"Explain the mountain lion that looked like it was half-human," you challenge him. "And *sounded* like the count. Are you saying that was a real thing? The count is a mountain lion version of a werewolf?"

Willie stares at you but doesn't say a word.

"I'm just saying that John Luke does have a point. It's easier to believe that we were drugged than it is to have absolutely no explanation."

For a while none of you say anything.

Cole breaks the silence. "I did think that fish tasted kinda funky."

"Drugged," John Luke repeats.

"Yeah, yeah." Willie rolls his eyes. "Well, none of us are gonna tell the moms what happened on Fantasy Island, got it? I don't care if it was real or some kind of hallu-cination. What happens on Tabu Island *stays* on Tabu Island."

"Easy enough for you to say. I'm among the walking wounded here. Do I have to remind you that you *shot* me? Literally shot me in the face? I mean, I am still wearing a bandage on the side of my head."

"You got nicked by a tree," Willie says.

"Oh, I'm telling Missy and Korie. No doubt about it."

Willie shakes his head.

You keep going. "I'm gonna give you a shirt that says *Got Milk?* Maybe a bandanna that says it too. 'Cause I'm gonna milk this for a very, very long time."

The helicopter flies on, and you keep wondering about the mysteries of Tabu Island.

THE END

THE BIG RED GLOB

DAYLIGHT BEGINS TO SLIP AWAY as you enter the cave and trek deeper and deeper into the unknown. A cloak of doom settles over your soul. Then again, maybe that's just you being a tad dramatic since you could simply be feeling bloated from the double-stacked pecan waffles you ate this morning.

"It's cold in here," John Luke says.

And the farther you get into the cave, the more you agree with him. You zip up your jacket and keep the powerful beam of the flashlight in your hand directed straight ahead. The shotgun is strapped around your shoulder.

You take a left down a wide passageway that dips lower and lower. As you pass a flat wall with water streaming down it, you notice markings on the stone.

"Look at these." You stop for a moment to examine them. They seem to be not just markings but a series of pictures.

"Are these, like, some kind of ancient cave art?" Willie asks.

The top picture shows a group of people clustered together. The one right underneath it depicts something big and round and red attacking the people. The third picture shows the big red thing just sitting there, with a caption that says, *Burp!*

"What's that say?" John Luke asks.

"'Burp.'"

"It doesn't say *burp*." Willie always has to argue.

"It says *burp*. You look. It's supposed to show that the big red glob *ate* the people above."

"That says *bug*."

"It's *burp*."

This goes on for about five minutes.

"Can we just go?" Cole says.

"So we're looking for a big red gob of goo?" Willie asks.

"If that thing wasn't red," you say, "I would've thought they were drawing you."

"Really funny. You are jealous of my manliness."

"The only manly thing about you is your odor. And it's the smell of a caveman."

The boys laugh. This only prompts Willie to keep going. "Look, why order a kid's meal when you can get a Big Mac?"

"That doesn't even make sense," you say. "I think you're missing Uncle Si, 'cause you're startin' to sound like him."

"Yeah, I think you're right."

When Willie says you're right, then you know you're in trouble. And that's exactly when you hear the deep, booming roar. It echoes all around you.

"Did you hear that?" Willie asks.

"Uh, yeah. It was the *loudest* bear roar I've ever heard in my life."

"I don't want to see what made that," John Luke says.

"Oh, we're gonna see it," you tell him. "And we're gonna haul it out of these caves."

It's easy to have confidence when you've got an automatic shotgun with a hundred rounds in its ammo magazine.

You reach an intersection that forks to the left and right.

Do you take the left fork and go—?

Oh, let's just keep going.

You head right and guide them in the direction of the big, bad, beary-scary roars you just heard.

"Be ready," you warn the guys behind you. "But don't shoot me in the back."

"I'm not making any promises," Willie says.

Another loud, deep sound booms past you. You feel it under your skin and deep in the caverns of your soul. But maybe that's being a bit dramatic again because you could be feeling those seven pieces of bacon you had with those waffles.

You slow down.

You stop.

You itch underneath your arms.

You check to see how bad you smell.

"Hey, what's up?" Willie asks. "Why are we stopping?"

You feel it. The eye of the beast. Or maybe just the eye of the tiger. You're not sure.

Something's ahead—I know I feel it.

"Shhhh."

"What'd you say?" Willie asks in a loud voice.

"I said please shut that yapper of yours. *Comprende?*"

"Oui, monsieur," Willie says.

"Dad, that's French."

"I know that, Mr. United Nations."

"Shhhh," you hiss again.

The flashlight you're holding illuminates twenty yards of passageway in front of you. The shadows play tricks in these caves, so you blink several times to make sure the dark and slow-moving something at the end of the chamber is real.

"Is that a-a—?" Cole stammers.

"Yep."

It's a bear. A bear that takes up most of the space in the cave tunnel ahead.

"I'm going to keep my flashlight on it." You gesture with the other hand. "Willie, come in front of me."

"For what?"

You shake your head. "To ask for an autograph. Or maybe just to do what we're out here to do."

Willie slips in front of you and fires off three rounds right away. The shotgun blasts drill your eardrums. The big beast screams and shuffles, sounding really, *really* angry, and then it roars full force.

"Uh, what now?" Willie asks.

"Let's get out of here!"

You all bolt back the way you came.

"I'm gonna fire a few shots, okay?" you say, out of breath and not sure if they can even hear you.

After running about a hundred yards more, you turn and unleash the shotgun's power. Maybe ten rounds.

The bear isn't running at the moment, but it's still slowly moving toward you. It roars at you as if saying, *"Is that the best you can do?"*

You catch up with the guys.

"John Luke, fire a bunch of rounds at him."

This might seem cruel, but the rounds aren't doing a thing to this animal. It's like some kind of zombie bear that just won't go down.

John Luke fires his shotgun and goes a little crazy. He fires about fifty rounds.

You don't think you'll ever be able to hear again. Plus, there's so much smoke from the blasts.

"Think you got it?" Willie asks.

"If I didn't, then we're all in big trouble."

"Let's check it out." Willie shoves you ahead.

"What?" you protest.

"Go check it out."

"How did '*Let's* check it out' become '*You* check it out'?"

"Life's hard," Willie says. "Just go."

Sure enough, John Luke got the big red bear.

Up close, you cannot believe how massive this thing is. "I didn't know bears could grow this big."

"I think Count VanderVelde is putting something in the animals' vitamins," Willie says.

All of you congregate around the bear.

This would be the moment for the thing to suddenly rise up and growl, scaring you all half to death.

But this is a kids' book, and we want happy endings where people smile, and flowers bloom, and . . .

The bear lifts its head and roars one last gasp.

Willie screams like a little boy. Cole and John Luke jump a foot in the air. You, of course, keep your cool—well, mostly.

The bear's head drops down again, this time for good.

Turn to page 187.

REDNECK NINJAS

"SO MY QUESTION IS, how exactly do we do this whole samurai sword thing?" you ask.

Willie is guiding you through the jungle, and with each yard, it seems to get a little steamier.

"You take the blade and you stick it in the animal," he says, trying to be clever.

The long, slightly curved sword is in its sheath, strapped to your side.

"Well, I keep trying to pull it out, and it takes *way* too long," you say.

You try again, and it still takes too long to slide the weapon out. Then it takes too long to wield it in front of you.

John Luke is holding the sword in its sheath like one might carry a rifle. Willie is swinging his in his right hand.

"Willie—what are you gonna do if something charges at you?" you ask him.

"What are you talking about?" He grabs the sheath with his left hand, slides the katana out with his right, and pretends to chop whatever thing is attacking him.

"I have *never* seen something so ridiculous in my life," you tell him. "A redneck handling a Japanese sword. I hope these animals aren't dangerous, because we might be in trouble."

"Hey, I'm not the one who picked the sword," Willie says. "You passed over an insane crossbow for *this*." He cuts the air with the sword.

"Variety is the spice of life," you tell him.

"Yeah, well, the only spice you got is *Old* Spice, and it doesn't smell pretty."

You ignore Willie 'cause you know this will go on practically all day. He does have a point with the sword, but if something's moving fast, this weapon just might help get it.

You can't help recalling Winchester's admonition to you after you chose the sword: *"Just remember—never pull it out of its sheath until you have control of the animal. Don't run with it unsheathed. And aim toward the dirt as you make your kill."*

All of you were cracking up because this implied you were going to have control of an animal in some way. You guys have problems catching *mice* back in West Monroe. So the thought of chasing down some wild animal and having the time to contain it before grabbing the sword seems a bit unlikely.

Then again, you're hunting with samurai swords on an island in the Pacific.

All of this is a bit unbelievable.

Willie stops and examines something on the ground. "What in the world . . . ?"

"What is it?" you ask, walking up to him.

In front of you is a big pile of poop. A *very* big pile.

"It looks like a dozen or so animals did this," Willie says.

"Let's hope."

"That's disgusting," John Luke says.

You glance at Willie, and the two of you share a knowing sort of hope-some-individual-animal-really-didn't-do-that look.

A sword might not necessarily do the trick on it.

Half an hour later, you hear a sound. A low grunting like something's got a stomachache and is in pain.

"Sounds like a hog," Willie says.

"Or a boar," John Luke says.

"Or a really, really angry woman left alone on this island," you joke.

Soon you're not laughing.

The squealing can be heard all around you. As you round a corner, you set eyes on one gargantuan hog that looks like it really needs to get acquainted with Weight Watchers. It's standing right on the trail you guys are walking along.

"There—see it?" Willie says, taking out his sword.

You nod and do the same.

The hog seems to realize what you're doing, and it comes running.

It's charging! At us!

Willie takes a swing at it, loses his balance, and falls to the ground. John Luke fumbles to get his sword out while Cole accidentally drops his, left with only its sheath.

It's up to you. The true hunter out here.

It's mano a mano time.

The thing is still rushing at you, snarling, and you can't help but notice the ugly welts on its face. It's squealing as if angry that it's so hideous to look at. You point the sword, ready to strike.

Then another hog comes out of the woods to your right and plows into you, knocking you down. As if that was part of the plan.

Your sword digs into the place you thought the first hog would be, but now you're on the ground, and the other hog is scooting around you.

Willie and the boys chase after them, but they're the fastest hogs you've ever seen.

They're the fastest *animals* you've ever seen.

You try to pull your sword out of the ground, but you stuck it in pretty deep.

Soon Willie and the boys return to where you're standing. They're out of breath and sweaty.

"Did you see how fast those things were moving?" Willie asks. "It's unbelievable."

You still can't get your sword out.

"Were you trying to set a new Olympic record for the sword plunge?" he says.

"Funny. You should've gotten that thing. It slid right by you."

"Yeah, well, it took you out," Willie says.

"Something's up with those things," you say. "Like—I've never seen hogs that big. That fast."

"That smart," John Luke says.

You all turn to John Luke and nod.

You take in your surroundings with fascination and horror. "Guys . . . ," you say, "what kind of place is this?"

Willie manages to jerk your sword out of the ground. "After that failure, I don't think we'll get the chance to find out."

THE END

THE MORNING AFTER

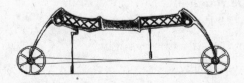

WHEN YOU OPEN YOUR EYES, the first thing you see is a giant bear growling at you.

Of course, this is just a stuffed head hanging on the wall. But it does give you a bit of a fright.

You glance around and spot Willie sleeping behind a chair. John Luke looks unconscious on the couch, and Cole is on the floor next to him.

You wonder if last night was real. With the swamp rat and the frogs and the spider monkeys and the moose. A *moose*. On a tropical island.

Right now it seems like you dreamed it.

It takes you a minute to sit up all the way. Even longer to stand. You fell asleep by the wall. You were keeping watch at first but must've passed out at some point.

Now sunlight is beaming through the windows, no signs of storms outside.

The familiar face of Winchester watches you from the open doorway.

"How are you doing, Mr. Robertson?"

You shrug. "I've been better."

"You survived the stormy night."

"If only you knew."

Then you think to yourself that maybe he does know.

"The helicopter leaves at noon," he informs you.

It could be six or it could be eleven. You have no idea.

"What time is it?"

Winchester smiles. "A little after eight."

"Tell me you have coffee somewhere."

"I do. In the dining room."

"There are no rats or monkeys in there, right?"

He looks a bit puzzled. "Not that I know of."

"Good."

Then you think about what he said before.

"So you're telling me we're leaving. Really? At noon?"

"Absolutely."

It's unbelievable. The idea that you're actually leaving. The idea that you've survived. The idea that you're going home.

And I'm gonna kill those women for signing us up for this nightmare.

But first things first. You need some coffee and you need it bad.

"Will we see the count today?"

He shakes his head. "No."

"Why not?"

"He's a sore loser."

"Loser? What did he lose?"

"Face," Winchester says. "He has a lot of pride. And to get this far—nobody's ever done that before."

"But what about—? Willie said he knew someone who had done this before."

"Someone who was selected to come to the island. Nobody's ever made it to the end."

"Well, we're Robertsons."

"I'm coming to realize that." He smiles again.

"So what about the prize? The Hunter's Cup made of pure gold."

"Yes, about that . . . That was completely made up."

You shake your head. "Can I at least get a T-shirt? *I Survived Tabu Island and Didn't Turn into a Mountain Lion*? Or something like that?"

Winchester only chuckles. "The helicopter will be leaving promptly at noon. I trust you won't be late."

You laugh. "I've never wanted to leave a place so bad in my *life*."

"Good thing you still have the option."

To pick your ending, choose from the following:

Go to page 149 for a logical ending.

Go to page 23 for a sci-fi ending.

Go to page 75 for a sweet ending.

YOU SHALL NOT PASS!

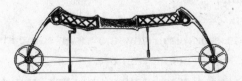

YOU CHOSE THE SAMURAI SWORD TODAY, but now you're beginning to regret it. What made you think this weapon would be a good idea? Cole suggested that maybe you could creep up on the animal from behind, but the creatures you've faced so far have been fast and sneaky.

You've been in the cave for at least an hour, maybe longer, when you catch sight of a large ball of fur from your position at the front of the line. You hold up a hand. "Guys! Be quiet," you hiss. "I think we can sneak up on whatever this is."

"Told you," Cole whispers.

The four of you take up positions around the back of the mysterious creature. "On the count of three . . . ," you begin.

Everyone strikes at once.

But this doesn't have the intended effect. The thing wakes up, swipes you all away, and gets mad. Really mad.

The thing.

It's actually a giant bear. Yes. A gigantic, bright-red, fluffy, furry bear. But when a bear brushes away samurai swords like it doesn't even notice them, well, that's when it goes from a bear to a thing.

"Did you see that?" Willie shouts.

It's like the world is in slow-mo for an entire minute.

Your life flashes before your eyes.

You see yourself frog hunting and duck hunting, and you see Phil and your wife and your kids, and then you see the largest set of teeth you've ever witnessed on *any* animal.

"Run!" That's all you can get out before you sprint back through the cave.

Your right boot lands in a small dip in the rocky floor, causing your foot to twist a bit, but you catch yourself with one hand and keep going. The growls behind you are as loud as ever—so far you haven't heard any racing, pounding bear footsteps, though.

John Luke's leading the group now. You follow him and the rest of the guys to the left, then straight for a while, then right. Soon you're stopping, gasping for air, and trying to figure out where that bear is. You and Willie extend your unsheathed swords in front of you. The boys wave their flashlights around.

"You see that thing flick away those swords?" Willie asks.

"Yeah, I saw it."

"Why are we even holding these, then?"

"I don't know, but I'm gonna keep mine right here." You clasp it more tightly. "Somehow it makes me feel a little safer."

The booming roar of the bear echoes through the cave again.

"A *little* safer."

"We have to get out of these caves," Willie says.

John Luke turns with a frustrated expression. "I was trying to take us that direction, but they just keep winding around and around."

You sigh. "I say we talk once we're outside."

"Then *you* figure out how to escape," Willie challenges.

So you take the lead through the maze of rock surrounding you. The deeper you go into the caves, the more chambers you discover. You spend half an hour trying to get anywhere you recognize, but everything looks the same.

"What if we can't get outta here?" Cole asks.

"We're gonna get outta here."

Then the bear howls again.

It sounds closer.

"Aren't we trying to get *away* from that?" Willie asks.

"Yeah, that's the plan."

You take a passageway that seems to be leading up. That's good because most of the way into the cave, you were heading downhill. So you have to be getting closer to the exit, right?

"Hey, you guys smell that?" John Luke says.

"What?"

"Hold on." He stops in the middle of the passage. "Yeah, that. Smell it."

You take a sniff, trying to see what he's talking about. Sure enough, you smell it too.

"That's strange," you say.

"It smells like Chick-fil-A," John Luke says.

"It smells *exactly* like Chick-fil-A," Willie confirms.

But you don't see any delicious fast-food restaurants around here. No drive-through windows and no waffle fries.

"I'd like to say let's find out where that smell is coming from, but let's don't." You start walking until you hear a roar that's closer than before.

No, it's not just closer. It's *right* in front of you.

You realize two things in that instant.

First off, you're all about to go down.

Second, somehow this massive red bear that can barely even squeeze through the cave smells like a chicken sandwich from one of your favorite restaurants. No joke.

I'm going to die thinking of chicken and waffle fries. That's just unfair.

"Boys, head the other way."

"What are you doing?" Willie asks.

You hold the sword up and face off with the bear. "You too, Willie. Go. Get the boys out of here."

"Are you crazy?"

"Absolutely," you say.

"Jase, I don't think—"

"Go!"

Your cry echoes all around these walls. The three of them take off, leaving you there with your katana, the bear, and the scent that's more delicious than ever.

"Just you and me now," you tell the hulking beast approaching you. You hold your ground, the sword tight in one hand, the flashlight in the other.

Perhaps you'll be able to do some damage before it defeats you.

Steady now. Steady.

The bear rips loose with another roar.

You stare at it for one more moment. Then you nod, take a deep breath . . .

And toss your sword at the bear before taking off. In the opposite direction.

Come on. You're no Gandalf the Grey.

No. You're Jase Robertson. And you're pretty fast when you want to be.

You run at top speed for what feels like hours, but finally light burns your eyes, and the mouth of the cave comes within sight.

You're out. The bear didn't follow. Maybe he was impressed with your courage and bravery. Or maybe he was insulted by your taking off and running.

Maybe he's just lazy and didn't want to come after me.

You're kneeling on the ground, exhausted, when you feel a hand grab your shoulder. You look up and see Cole.

Thank you, God.

"You made it," he says.

"I made it."

Willie and John Luke are safe too. Everybody looks sweaty and tired and in need of a long shower.

"Well, *that* was sure interesting," you tell them.

"Did you kill it with your bare hands?" Willie asks. "Or with the sword?"

You shake your head. "No. But it'll never forget me. I promise you that." You begin to lead them down the mountain toward the jungle and the lodge. No reason to wait for the Jeeps—you're ready to get out of here.

"Hey, guys, I have a question," John Luke asks.

"What?" Willie says.

"Why'd that bear smell like Chick-fil-A?"

"I don't know," you say. "But I sure am hungry."

THE END

TO KILL A MOCKINGDUCK

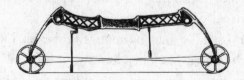

"SO YOU *HAD* TO GO WITH THE COWBELL, didn't you?"
Willie asks John Luke.

You let John Luke pick the weapon this time.

"It's just a hunch."

Willie shakes his head. "Sometimes you gotta know when
to say no to your hunches."

You've been walking along the river all morning when you
finally see an animal. An unexpected kind of animal. Right
there in the middle of the shallow water. Floating so happily
downstream. Glistening in the sun.

Willie squints toward the river. "Is that a duck?"

"Looks like a gold duck," Cole says.

"We're going duck hunting?" you ask. "With a cowbell that
explodes things?"

You realize right then that you're doomed. You might as well start packing your bags now.

Willie aims the cowbell toward the duck. "So can you set off these explosives underwater too?" He sets the device in the river and strikes it with the drumstick. A plume of water bursts out of the river. "Well, that answers that."

Sure, it missed the duck by about twenty feet, but at least it worked in the water. The duck looks your way, and you swear it does something you've never seen a duck do before. It opens its beak wide and blinks slowly.

"Did that duck just *yawn* at us?"

"No way," Willie says.

"I'm pretty sure it yawned. Sorta a taunting yawn."

"I think you've spent too many hours in the duck blind."

You get closer to the edge of the river, point your cowbell toward the duck, and tap it with the drumstick. Another explosion in the water—this time closer, but still nowhere near the target.

The duck flies into the sky, but it doesn't abandon you. It circles above, then lands on the bank across the river and strolls back and forth, totally at ease.

Willie seems to have a plan. "John Luke and Cole, cross the river—you can wade where it's shallow. Maybe we can try to trap the duck somehow."

"That thing's gonna keep flying away," you protest as the boys make their way across.

"We'll see."

Of course, an hour later, all you've done is blow up some parts of the riverbank and watch the golden duck fly back and forth. It's hanging around as if to drive you crazy. It doesn't ever fly *away*. No, that would be too logical. Instead it lands in the water in front of you every time, sometimes diving and splashing playfully.

It's definitely mocking you. And what's worse, it seems to be enjoying itself way too much.

You notice a dense but moderate-size tree beside the flowing water.

"I have an idea," you tell Willie.

"Oh no."

"Seriously. It could work."

Moments later, as the duck is preparing to land in the river again, you tell Willie where to stand.

"Every time, it floats about ten or fifteen feet away from us, right?"

"For some reason, yes," Willie says, obviously as annoyed with this bird as you are.

"Fire off the cowbell as close to the duck as you can. It'll head in the direction of that tree like it always does before flying away. And then I'll set my blast off."

"And that's going to do what?"

"Just watch."

Sure enough, after John Luke and Cole miss with their

cowbells, the golden duck coasts over to your area and stops in its usual spot. It's like the thing *wants* to die. A duck with a death wish. Maybe. But you believe that, just like the boar you encountered, this is a special kind of duck. It's got a personality, and that personality reminds you of a girl who plays hard to get. She ignores you but keeps coming around. Every time you ask her out, she turns you down. But she keeps letting you ask her.

And now I'm gonna blow her to bits.

Okay, sure, not all metaphors work very well.

"Whatever you're up to, are you ready?" Willie asks.

"Born ready."

He hits the cowbell with the drumstick, and the water in front of the duck shoots upward in an explosion. The duck isn't harmed, naturally, and it ends up right where you expect, splashing and preening.

You set off your own bomb blast. Except this time you do three in a row, and you point at the base of the tree.

BOOM!

BOOM!

BOOM!

The tree tears apart and begins to fall. Right in the direction of the flying duck.

Like a bunch of falling, flailing arms, the thick tree limbs claw at the duck and take her down with them.

You and Willie rush over to the duck. John Luke and Cole trail behind.

"Is the thing flattened?" Willie shouts.

But sure enough, the duck's still alive. It's pulling and tugging, trying to get out from underneath the massive tree branch that has it pinned. Willie pulls up the limb while you grab the duck.

It makes a strange sound, not much like a quack. Instead it sounds a bit like a smoker's cough, low and rumbling.

"Sounds like it has asthma problems," Willie says.

The golden duck has an exceptionally long beak. It keeps coughing and squirming in your hands, trying to get its beak in optimal pecking position. But you're not letting it go, and you're sure not letting it peck you.

"Can we bring it alive to the count?" Willie must be getting attached.

You glance at the duck, then back to Willie, shaking your head. "Sorry, Susie Q," you say.

"The duck's name is Susie?"

"Yeah. She was playing hard to get."

Willie stares at the duck in your hands. "Funny how it took a cowbell to capture a duck."

"Life is full of many great mysteries."

You look at the duck. She sure is pretty.

Oh, well . . .

Go to page 119.

TABU ISLAND

WINCHESTER GUIDES YOU to a large meeting room with a huge table in the middle holding a scale replica of the island. On the walls surrounding you are mounted animal heads. You see a massive deer with enormous antlers, then a tiger, then a full-size bear in the corner.

"These are some serious animals staring at us," you say.

The four of you approach the model island, probably about twenty feet tall and twenty feet wide.

"This, of course, is an exact replica of our island, Tabu," Winchester begins. "Here you will note the island's distinct features."

"Here's where we're at," Willie says, pointing to the building on the edge of the mountain.

"There are six places you may hunt in. You must hunt as a

group. Unless, of course, you accidentally become separated, which is bound to happen sometimes."

"Why's that?" you ask.

He seems not to have heard. "You will observe the six different sections here as I point to them. First of all, the largest section of the island is the jungle. You can see that right here."

Dense trees cover the vast majority of the model. It looks like a massive place to hunt.

"Right in the middle of the jungle, basically cutting the island in half, is a river that goes from here to here," Winchester says, indicating this with his hand. "On one of your days here, you will be hunting along the riverbank."

"What happens if we wander off and head into the woods?" Cole asks.

"Good question, young man. There will be no need for you to do that."

"But what if we do?"

"Let's just say it would be a bad idea."

That sounds a little ominous.

"Will we know what we're supposed to be hunting?" Willie asks. "I mean, what if I'm on the river, and suddenly a bear comes in view?"

"The creatures you end up hunting will gladly make themselves known. And if an animal from an area you didn't choose wanders into your zone, well, the more the merrier. Isn't that the saying?"

Willie still appears a bit perplexed, and you probably do too. *I just want to know what I'm hunting.*

But you can hear Missy's voice in your head: *"This is part of the fun, Jase. Come on and go with the flow. You wanted epic. This is epic."*

"So the jungle and the river are two of the locations," Winchester continues. "Then, on the side of the mountain, there's a cave—you'll be hunting in there too. And farther up, you have the mountain itself—Mount Fear."

"Mount *Fear*?" you ask. "Why is it called 'Fear'?"

"Mount Happy wouldn't sound like a particularly thrilling place for hunters to track down animals, would it?"

"I guess not," you say.

"The fifth area is the beach. Right along here, on the north and west sides of the island."

"Hunting on a beach?" you ask.

"Could be worse," John Luke points out. He looks pretty excited about the idea.

"Listen," Willie says.

You roll your eyes at him. "I'm just saying . . ."

"Shhh."

Winchester continues. "The final area is right here, a place you have already experienced." He is pointing at the lodge complex, the very same one you're currently standing in.

"Are you saying there's a hunt on the property?"

"That's right."

"What would we hunt for here?" John Luke asks.

"That's the point, John Luke," Willie answers. "To discover what we're hunting for. Right?"

Willie finally seems to get it. But you still have no idea how you're going to hunt for something in the place you're staying.

"You will have dinner with the count tonight, and afterward he will give you some more guidelines for the hunt. I hope you make wise decisions about it."

"So you're sayin' there are bad decisions we can make?" you ask.

"I never said the word *bad*," Winchester replies. Then he smiles. "Shall we continue?"

**If you haven't been to the weaponry room,
go to page 33.**

**If you've been to the weaponry room,
go to page 15.**

YUM-YUM

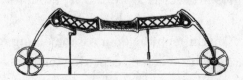

YOU ENTER THE ISLAND LODGE and come face-to-face with an animal head on the wall that you've never noticed before. It's a koala bear. *Yikes.*

The count is waiting for all of you right outside the dining room, and he gives you a strong handshake.

"Good job, gentlemen," he says, his bald head looking extra shiny tonight.

You point over your shoulder. "Did you shoot that one?"

"The koala? You know, most people think they're warm and cuddly. But they can be quite fiery."

"It looks really sweet from here."

"How did your bear look today?" the count asks, smirking.

"We didn't exactly have time to study his facial expressions, did we?" Willie says. "I gotta say—I've never seen a bear that big. And I haven't ever seen a bright-red bear either."

"The animals on this island are unique. That's the reason the hunting expedition can always be an unpredictable thing."

"Where do all these animals come from?" John Luke asks.

"I can't give my secrets away, can I?" Count VanderVelde wags a finger. "Is everyone ready for dinner?"

He leads you through the doors of the dining room. Place settings line the table. Each place setting includes a container, but no two containers are shaped the same. And each setting is a different color.

"I thought we'd have a bit of fun tonight," the count says. "Before tomorrow's hunt."

"Fun? Are we gonna shoot our dinner too?"

The count laughs. "You are a funny man, Jase Robertson."

"He's more funny when he's not even trying to be," Willie adds.

"Tonight I'm going to serve you an island delicacy. I trust you will enter this dinner with an open mind and an adventurous stomach."

"This can't be good," you whisper to Cole.

But you must have whispered kind of loud, because the count responds. "It's very good. It just depends on what culture you happen to be from."

"We've eaten some pretty exotic fare," Willie says.

"Yes, I imagine you have. Well, I'm letting you *choose* what you eat. Except, well, you won't know what you're choosing."

"Let me guess." Willie points to the table. "We have to pick a color."

"Yes."

"Red, orange, yellow, green, or blue."

"The rainbow," John Luke says.

"Yes. Makes it easier to remember."

Which color do you pick?

For red, go to page 109.

For orange, go to page 133.

For yellow, go to page 221.

For green, go to page 87.

For blue, go to page 65.

WILLIE AND JASE

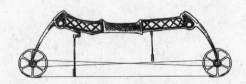

OH, SEE WILLIE AND JASE.

Oh, oh, oh.

See Willie and Jase run.

Oh, see Willie and Jase run with daggers in hand.

Funny, funny Willie and Jase.

Chasing a funny, funny golden duck.

Oh, see the golden duck.

See how it flies.

See the golden duck fly every time Willie and Jase come close by.

Funny, funny boys.

Come, Willie and Jase.

Come see.

Come, come, and see.

Come see the golden duck fly, fly away.

"Look," says Jase. "See it go. See it go up."
See Willie.
See Willie and Jase run.
See Willie and Jase run back home empty-handed.
Oh no.
See them go.

THE END

FOOT-AND-MOUTH DISEASE

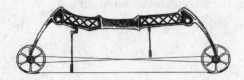

YOU TAKE A SIP from your camo-patterned canteen, which matches the pants and T-shirt you're wearing. The shotgun in your hands is lightweight, just like the pocketknife and .38 you're carrying as additional backup for the hunt. Willie is point man, and so far it seems he's gotten y'all lost.

"You need me to take over?" you ask.

"No. I got this."

"I swear I think we've gone in one big circle," you say.

"I swear I think you've already said that," Willie replies.

The sun is a scorcher today. It's one of those days when you feel like you're wearing a rug on your face. 'Cause, well, yeah, you sorta *are* wearing a rug on your face. But it's a handsome rug and makes the face all the more attractive.

"Hey, I think I spot some tracks," Willie says.

You and the boys come beside Willie and look down at the dirt he's staring at.

"You think *that's* an animal track?" you ask.

"Yep."

"It looks like a footprint," Cole says.

"That's right," you add. "It looks a lot like the back of my boot!"

"No, it doesn't."

"We're totally backtracking."

"No, we aren't."

"We're going to find nothing out here with you leading."

Right then you hear something that is either a wild animal having a bad case of the stomach flu or your own stomach about to give the good ole heave-ho.

"What's that?" Willie asks.

"Sounds like Uncle Si when he's angry," you say.

They all laugh, but the noise continues. It's getting louder.

"Whatever that thing is, it's absolutely the *worst* sound I've ever heard."

Willie is looking around, his shotgun pointed at the ground. You study the round barrel that's attached to it, containing the 12-gauge, double-ought shells.

A thought crosses your mind for a random, fleeting second. *The barrel of that thing's pretty close to my—*

Chaos comes stomping out of the trees in front of you.

Then the blasts start going off, and you feel the worst pain in the world in your right foot.

He shot my foot! Willie shot my foot!

You hear the automatic *boom-boom-boom-boom* right in your ear. Something low and thick and heavy and lightning fast barrels past you like some kind of lone ranger.

My foot is shot off—my foot—I can't feel my right foot!

You go to the ground as the automatic shotguns rip and tear up the trees and foliage around you. Yet you can still see the thing moving.

It's a gigantic hog.

The meanest, ugliest hog you've *ever* seen.

Its face looks like a bunch of intestines stuck together. Rolls and rolls of them on top of an ugly, goober-wet snout and ears that stick out.

It chases Willie for a minute as the boys fire their shotguns at random.

"Stop shooting!"

They finally run out of shotgun shells, and Willie finally finds a tree to run up. You manage to stand again and see the wide, ugly backside of the hog wiggling into the woods.

That thing moves like a cheetah.

Hunting for an oversize hog that runs as fast as a cheetah isn't *anything* like what you were expecting.

The hog disappears just like Willie did. You hobble over to the tree he's hanging from.

"You *shot* me!"

He peers down at you. "No, I didn't."

"*Yes*, you did. Look! You can see my boot. It's all cut up."

"Well, what was your foot doing there?" Willie asks.

You shake your head, then turn on the boys. "And what were you two shooting at? The birds and the bees?"

They glance at each other and shrug.

You realize that you probably need medical attention since you're starting to feel kind of light-headed. Oh, and yeah, there are little red-and-orange dots coming all around.

The hunt is over.

No fried pork tonight, gentlemen.

THE END

DOG OF THE HAIR
THAT BIT YOU

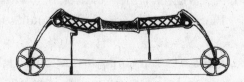

IT'S MORNING ON THE FOURTH DAY, and there's a tsunami going on inside your stomach. You're afraid to even see what's for breakfast, but thankfully it's only eggs, bacon, and toast. A piece of toast will be enough for you.

Winchester enters the dining room, greeting all of you. "How is everybody feeling after last night's dinner?"

"Awful," Willie moans.

"Not so good," Cole says.

John Luke shakes his head. "I had nightmares last night."

"My stomach's having nightmares now." You hope this toast will calm things down.

"The count likes to mess with the minds of his guests," Winchester says in his logical, levelheaded manner.

"Someone needs to show him the meaning of the words *Southern hospitality*," Willie mutters.

Winchester nods. "Today you will be heading to the beach."

You glance up hopefully. "A day to swim and surf?"

"Not quite."

"Let me guess," you say. "We get to pick which weapon we'd like to use. A toaster, a meat cleaver, or a whisk."

"Professor Plum in the library with the candlestick," Willie jokes.

Winchester doesn't even smile at that one. He continues on as if you Robertson brothers' banter is muted. "You will choose from three weapons today. The crossbow, the rifle, and the sword."

"I'm gonna miss that cowbell," Willie sighs.

"You will also want to put on sufficient sunblock. It's going to be hot outside."

You notice that Winchester is about as white as a person can get.

"I see you spend a lot of time in the sun." You grin.

He doesn't. "The count keeps me busy with *other* things."

Winchester leaves you four alone to finish breakfast.

"Is it just me, or do you get the feeling that those guys are in the back room doing weird scientific experiments on animals?" You glance around at the others. "Maybe people too."

"I think it's just you. I think it's always you."

You shake your head at Willie. He'd disagree with you on anything. *Anything.*

So which weapon will you select?

If you pick the crossbow, go to page 207.

If you pick the rifle, go to page 83.

If you pick the sword, go to page 125.

PURPLE HAZE

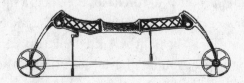

YOU'RE NOT SURE you've ever gone hunting with only a dagger and a handgun before. You've heard about notorious hunters showing off by using only a spear, for instance. Or a knife. No gun at all. But you're no Crocodile Dundee or Ernest Hemingway. (Wait, which one was the writer again?) You're used to carrying something big and strong and heavy. This dagger and little gun on the side of your hip simply make you feel like you're play-hunting. Like you used to do with Willie and Alan and Jep when you were all kids.

"Didn't we head over this hill like an hour ago?" you ask Willie, who's leading the group.

"Things look the same 'cause we're in a jungle."

"I remember that big tree," you tell him.

"They're all big! What are you talking about?"

You might as well be singing that Talking Heads song "Road to Nowhere" 'cause that's exactly where you're headed.

"Hey, you can take over, Christopher Columbus," he calls back.

You wipe sweat off your forehead, then take a sip from your canteen. For some reason, you've been thirstier today than ever before in your life. Maybe it was the long trip yesterday and the extra food you shouldn't have eaten (like those little hot dogs wrapped inside that doughy bread).

"Seen any trace of anything?" you ask the boys.

Both of them seem tired. You don't blame them. Coming all this way to trek through the steaming jungle with wimpy weapons and not an animal to be seen . . . well, that doesn't scream *excitement*.

Willie has his Black Widow dagger out, holding it forward in case some monkey or lizard or bear comes bursting through the brush. You put your canteen back and take your dagger out to examine it. It's sleek and long and could be really deadly to someone trying to attack you on a street corner. But out here . . .

Why'd I select this thing again?

All of you decide to rest for a moment, point man Willie drinking from his canteen. And that's when it happens. Like some kind of blurry, mad rushing dash right in front of you. Like a race you didn't even know was happening until you're in the middle of it.

Willie has his head tilted back for a drink when something low, bulky, and dark crashes into his legs, knocking him on top of John Luke. The fast-moving creature is like a runaway go-kart or something. That's what it looks like at first until you actually see its crinkled, ugly face glaring at you.

It's a hog. A really massive, hideous hog.

Another appears right next to it. And the two are racing like a pair of NASCAR drivers a lap away from winning the Daytona 500.

Before you can say or do anything, the first hog barrels right past you. The next one comes closer and closer and—

As it's about to plow into you, you thrust the blade of the Black Widow into its back. Somehow, someway, you manage to sidestep the animal while still holding on to the dagger.

Now you're running alongside it.

Forget runnin' with the bulls. I'm runnin' with a boar!

You're—you're still holding on—still holding on. . . . The thing's pulling you—it's so strong, stronger than a bull. . . . You're hanging on to the dagger with both hands—

Then you jump on the boar's back. It can't be a hog; the thing's too big.

You are riding a big wild boar.

Let's say that again.

You are riding a big wild boar.

For about two minutes. And it's squealing and breathing heavily and smelling bad and looking ugly.

Then you can't sit up anymore. You fall to the ground while the boar keeps plowing through the jungle.

It take a couple of minutes for the rest of the guys to join you.

"You let it go!" Willie says to you.

You still can't breathe very well since the fall took your breath away.

"Come on—did you at least stick it good?" he asks.

"This coming from the man who was tackled by a boar," you gasp. "Yeah, I got the entire blade into that thing. But it acted like it was just a toothpick."

"Hey, look at this," Cole says.

A dark, wet substance covers the leaves and branches along the route the boar carried you.

"Wait—is that . . . ?" you begin.

"I think it's blood," Cole says.

"It's purple," John Luke says.

That's what you were going to point out.

"Well, call me crazy, but isn't blood supposed to be red?" Willie says.

You can't help thinking about the hog that got away.

"Come on," you tell them. "Let's follow the purple trail. Whether or not it's blood, it's coming from that animal."

"If it's *not* blood, then what exactly do you think it would be?" your brother says.

Same little Willie, always having to nag you with questions. Just like when you were hunting together as boys or traveling

together on family trips or sitting together at the dinner table. Nitpick Willie.

"Listen, wise guy, let's just *find* it and then figure that out."

The purple drops and splatterings are easy to find. You could probably follow the rampaging boar even without those clues because of the trail it left behind. So for the next hour, you stay on the hunt.

John Luke is the one to finally locate it.

"It's over here," he calls from near a thick growth of bushes by a tree.

"Is it dead?"

"I sure hope so," he says. "'Cause this is the biggest boar I've ever seen."

Turns out the dagger did its trick. Guess it really was a Black Widow in the end.

Go to page 129.

MOCKERY

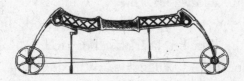

JOHN LUKE HAS HIS SHIRT OFF and his pants rolled up. He's lying on the beach with the shirt over his face to block the sun. Cole is next to him digging a hole in the sand. Willie is cleaning his crossbow for some unknown reason since he hasn't even used it yet.

You stare at them for a moment and shake your head. "I don't want to ruin anyone's spring break, but aren't we supposed to be *hunting*?"

Willie is the only one of the three to even look up at you. "It sure would help if we knew what we were hunting."

"But *that's* part of the fun, right? I mean, aren't you having fun?"

Willie just stares at you.

"I'm having fun," you say.

Of course, you're not having one ounce of fun. You're

sweating down your back and down your legs and all the way into your boots. You've been walking back and forth on the beach for hours, looking for anything. Anything. A bird. A frog. A shark or a fish. But nothing has appeared.

"We're just takin' a little break," Willie says.

"Here we are, hunting on some exotic island, and you three want to take a little break. It's a sad day to be a Robertson."

"Oh, pipe down," Willie says. "Why don't you sit and chill out for a minute. Maybe you're scaring off the animals with the scent of your manly testosterone."

You finally go ahead and do as Willie said, plopping down on the beach. The water looks so clear and the waves so gentle. You really want to pull off your boots and dive into the water. Maybe you will. But only *after* you shoot something today.

As you gaze into the bright ocean in front of you, it's easy to drift off a bit. Your eyes dip, but nobody will be able to tell since you have your shades on.

You're only taking a five-minute break.

Then you hear laughter.

"What's so funny?" you ask, opening your eyes.

"What?" Willie asks.

"What's so funny?"

"I didn't laugh."

"Well, who laughed?"

Cole and John Luke remain quiet. You think John Luke might actually be asleep.

You close your eyes again and hear the laughter once more.

"I heard it that time," Willie says. "But it's coming from over there." He points down the beach.

You both stand and head in the direction the high-pitched laugh came from. For a few minutes you walk in silence, sinking into the hot sand. You can see the lodge from where you're at—it's above you, in the distance. But no other landmarks are in sight.

"Check this out." Willie's examining a small hole, barely visible in the sand. "Looks like some little critter made it."

"Think that critter was just laughing too?"

"On this island?" Willie asks. "Sure."

You kneel beside the hole and put your hand in it.

"I wouldn't do that if I were you," Willie says.

The hole is too deep for you to reach the bottom. You're pretty sure it's attached to a tunnel.

The laughter sounds again. You jerk your hand out. "Where's that coming from?"

Willie's aiming his crossbow toward the border between beach and jungle. "Somewhere over there."

John Luke has his shirt on again, and Cole's got his cross-bow out. They're squinting in every direction.

"Did you guys hear that laughter?" you ask.

"Sounds like a little girl," Cole says.

John Luke nods. "Sounds like Sadie's laugh."

"Well, if you see Sadie, don't shoot," Willie says.

You walk over to the water and place a boot on the wet sand. Then you hear it again.

To your left.

You jerk your head around and hold your crossbow at the ready, and for a brief second you catch a glimpse of something. A round head with whiskers and two buckteeth.

Then it's gone.

Wait a minute.

"Hey, guys," you say as you begin to walk over to where you think you saw the animal.

"You see something?"

"I saw something, all right."

"What is it?" Willie asks.

"You're not going to like what I'm about to say."

"What?"

All of them are questioning you now.

You reach the hole—a second hole. You look over to where Willie's standing, close to the original hole. He's about fifty yards away from you.

"We're dealing with a gopher."

"A what?" John Luke asks.

"A gopher."

"No, we're not," Willie says. "We can't be hunting a gopher."

The laughter sounds again. Giddy, silly, sweet.

Suddenly you hear someone's crossbow firing. It's just a quick whoosh.

It's Cole's.

"What'd you see?"

He rushes over to yet another hole. "I saw him. Over here."

"You saw what?"

"The gopher."

"See, I told you," you shout to Willie.

Cole peers into the hole. "It was grayish colored. And ugly."

"Gophers are all ugly," you say.

"In the immortal words of Jean-Paul Sartre, 'Au revoir, gopher,'" Willie says with a funny accent.

"What are you talking about?" you ask him.

"*Caddyshack*. Come on, you remember that one, right?"

"Do you want to share movie lines or do you want to kill a rodent?"

You hear the click and snap of a crossbow firing again.

It's John Luke this time. He fired at the hole you were standing near a minute ago. "The thing is messin' with us."

"Too bad we already used the cowbell," Willie says. "We could've blown the thing up."

"How many holes are there?"

You count a total of four. So you assign everybody a hole. "We keep our crossbows aimed and ready at each designated hole."

"And the gopher's gonna magically appear at one of them?" Willie sounds skeptical.

"Of course it will."

"Somehow I imagined hunting wild deer and buffalo and zebras," Willie says as he camps out ten yards from his hole. "I flew to an island in the Pacific to hunt *gopher*."

"Don't forget our wonderful dinner last night," you tell him.

"I threw up afterward," John Luke says.

"Thanks for sharing that," Willie replies. "Anything else you want to tell us?"

"No."

"Good."

It's been about twenty minutes when you hear the laughter. And it sounds like the gopher's practically right behind you.

"You guys hear that?"

Willie stands. "It's coming from your spot."

You haven't stopped staring at the hole you're targeting. "It's not in my hole."

The laughter again. *Hee-hee-hee, ha-ha-ha.*

It sounds like someone's laughing right in your ear.

You finally decide to turn from your position, and sure

enough, you see Mr. Smiley Teeth sticking his head out of the sand from a brand-new hole.

You try to grab him, but there's no point. Head's buried in the sand again.

You let out a frustrated scream.

"That's gonna bring it back," Willie says, rolling his eyes.

This happens again. And again. Every time you think you know where the gopher's going to come up, it pops out somewhere totally different. It's as if the creature understands what you're trying to do and is laughing at you.

All the animals seem to be laughing at us.

The gopher appears a few more times, and your shots are always way too late. Each arrow drives into the sand of the beach.

Soon the sun begins to fade away.

"This is incredible," you say.

"I know," Willie replies. "Look at that view."

"No. It's incredible that we can't kill a gopher."

"They're tricky suckers."

"No, they're not. They're small and dumb. They dig holes with their big teeth."

"This one keeps laughing at us."

"Am I the only one here who thinks that's a little strange?" you ask.

"It's strange," John Luke confirms.

"Uncle Si is strange," Willie says. "Strange is the new normal."

"Is that your new tagline?"

"Maybe. Maybe we can brand the laughing gopher. It can be part of Duck Commander somehow."

You shake your head. "How can a gopher be part of Duck Commander?"

"We can have a whole line of laughing gophers. Trademark them."

You let out a sigh.

"I think you're onto something," John Luke says.

Cole nods. "Me too."

Maybe the food from last night has made them all delirious and crazy.

"Y'all are nuts," you tell them.

Suddenly you hear the laughter of the gopher. As if it's agreeing with you.

Taunted by a rodent.

Not a terrific way to end this expedition.

THE END

HE'S A BEAST

THERE ARE TIMES when the joke is over, and life has given you something hard and awful to deal with, and you have no idea how to handle it. At these points, all you can do is stand up and stay strong and pray for God's help.

That's exactly what you're doing.

You're wet and you're bleeding, but worse than that, you're completely bewildered.

You still don't know what you saw.

You still don't know *what* you're waiting for.

But as you crouch behind a boulder on the edge of Mount Fear, a jutting rocky cliff straight in front of you, you realize that you've never seen or heard anything like this before.

You breathe deeply.

It'll be okay. I'll be okay. The boys are fine, and Willie's hopefully fine.

The jokes are done. This is some serious crazy stuff.

You wipe your face as the rain gushes down.

It started a couple of hours ago as you hiked up the mountain. You all got soaked when it began to rain, but that wasn't a big deal.

The big deal started with the strange sounds. Loud, ferocious cat noises. Everyone assumed they belonged to a cougar. To some kind of mountain lion.

So you all searched the area around this cliff.

John Luke was the first to spot *it*.

He fired a shot with his crossbow and actually nicked it.

But then he was out of there.

When he reached you and Willie, he was screaming with terror. You couldn't understand what he was saying at first. It sounded like "The mountain lion talks—it talked to me."

Surely John Luke had a little too much fun in the sun the day before. Or maybe the strange food and stranger animals have gotten to him.

Then Cole came out of nowhere, screaming that the mountain lion had legs like a human.

At that point, you were beginning to think something was wrong with *both* of them.

But that was before you saw it.

That was before you *heard* it.

No, it wasn't mocking you. It wasn't laughing.

No. It sounded like . . .

That can't be. So don't even think that because there's no way.

But you know what you saw and heard.

You saw the mountain lion walking on its hind feet like some kind of weird *something*.

What do I call it? A mountain man? A coug-man? A man-cat?

At that moment, the mountain lion opened its mouth and said, "You act like you've never seen a cat walking on two legs before, *Mr. Robertson*."

The voice sounded *just* like Count VanderVelde's.

So he's secretly half-cougar, and I've secretly lost my mind?

The cougar raced up the mountain before you could respond.

You sent the boys down to the lodge after that. It's only you and Willie now.

Silently you wait with the crossbow aimed toward the flat field just past the steep incline. Willie has gone up to draw the lion out of hiding. He's the bait today.

So this time, maybe I'll accidentally take off a chunk of his side with my arrow.

But jokes aside, there is nothing to laugh at.

This is crazy, and you just want to get out of here.

You keep thinking, *Am I dreaming?* But the rain and the ache in your legs and the fear in your gut mean this is definitely *not* a dream.

Deep breath in, deeper breath out.

Stay focused, Jase. Focus.

Soon a sopping-wet, hideous creature emerges from the dark. Yes, he happens to be your brother, but that doesn't change the fact that Willie's running in complete and utter terror. You've never seen him so scared.

"It's comin'! It's comin'!"

He rushes up to you, stumbling on the way.

Then you see it. The massive, silver-gray mountain lion. This time it's running on all four legs. But as it steps onto the flat ground just past your position, it stands on its two hind legs, tall and menacing.

You don't hesitate.

You fire a shot that hits the creature in the neck. Then you reload fast and fire off another shot.

The hulking mountain lion goes down.

"Did you get it?" Willie asks, panting.

"I got it. Two shots."

He's got the crossbow in his hands once again. "Okay, come on. Let's go see what that thing is."

You reload your crossbow just in case, then head over to check it out.

But when you get to where the mountain lion should be, you don't see anything.

"Where is it?" Willie asks.

"It was right here."

"I'm not seeing anything."

"It was right there!"

You peer up at the rocky mountainside above you and all around, but you don't see a thing.

"I shot it," you insist. "It went down."

"Well, it didn't *stay* down."

For the next hour, the two of you search for it. You spot a little blood—it's a strange grayish-red color. The downpour has washed away all but a few traces of the bloody trail, and rain continues to fall.

Eventually you're forced to give up.

"I know I shot that thing," you tell Willie. "I definitely wounded it."

You don't want to ask Willie about the voice you heard. The fact that it looked like a human on its hind feet is one thing, but the voice . . .

And the fact that it sounded like Count VanderVelde?

That's just insanity.

But you know insanity. You know it quite well.

Go to page 27.

CHEESY

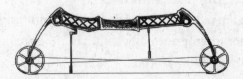

THE YELLOW PLATE in front of you contains melted cheese over . . . something. Melted cheese over lots of somethings.

"Ah yes, you have the melt," Count VanderVelde says.

"The melt?" you ask. "I know what a patty melt and a tuna melt are, but what kind of melt is this?"

"Well, this is the weekly melt. We collect various things in a pot over a week and then put melted cheese on them."

You start picking at the food. "This looks like a fly."

"Yes, that's possible. The pot can collect those over a week. We put it outside."

"You put a pot outside? For what possible reason?"

"It's a long-standing tradition that the island will feed you. That's what the natives think."

"The natives?" you ask. "Are these people who are still here on the island?"

He smiles without answering. Figures. You take a bite, and the flavor reminds you of cheddar cheese and . . .

"I swear this tastes like dirt."

"You are eating a portion of the island. You will forever have a part of this place within you."

"Maybe I'm okay with just having West Monroe inside me."

The others might normally laugh, but they're having issues with their own food.

Go to page 197.

MORE COWBELL

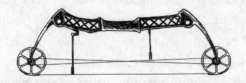

"WE LOOK LIKE A BUNCH OF FOOLS," you say as you glance forward at John Luke, Cole, and Willie, who's leading the pack as point man.

Each of them is carrying a cowbell in one hand and a drumstick in the other.

"Then you look no different from normal," Willie says.

"I'm holding a *cowbell*."

"You're the one who picked it!"

"What if it doesn't even work?" You've been second-guessing ever since leaving the complex.

Winchester told you to make sure the target is at least five feet in front of you before engaging the cowbell. You're more curious than anything to see if this really, truly is a weapon.

"Why don't we find out what this baby can do?" you ask.

If nothing else, you could throw it at the target. Or hit the animal over the head with it. Or ring it really loud as a diversionary tactic.

"Yeah, let's try it out," John Luke says.

You're sweating like a dog and seemingly have been walking in circles for the entire morning. You simply want to take a break and have some fun.

"Okay. Y'all stand behind me. I'm going to give it a try."

You're near a slight opening in the woods where the blue sky can be seen. You hold the cowbell out and strike it hard with the drumstick.

It doesn't make a noise at first, but then a sharp blast goes off right in front of you.

"That's like setting off an M-80!" Willie says.

"I think it fires in the direction you're holding the cowbell," you say. "My left arm was pointed this way, and that's where the blast went off."

Suddenly another blast sounds. Then another.

"Hey, knock it off!" you call out to John Luke and Cole. "You're going to scare everything away."

Cole smiles. "We're just testing it."

"Wonder how many rounds we have?" Willie asks.

"Guess we'll find out, won't we?"

Before continuing, you examine the damage. The cowbell left several six-inch-deep holes in the ground. Whatever and however the cowbell is firing, it sure does pack a punch.

You decide to lead for a while, but soon you get off the trail you've been following and head into dense growth. You're surrounded not only by towering, ancient trees but also by thick vines and brush.

"We should backtrack," Willie says. "I'm being eaten alive by mosquitoes."

"I think it gets a little clearer ahead," you reassure him.

After another few minutes, you're engulfed by weeds and branches and vegetation, so much so that you can hardly see your feet.

"Okay, this is ridiculous," you say.

John Luke and Cole hold their cowbells high as they wade through the mess.

Then you feel something jam up against your leg. Something moving.

You pull aside the brush only to see something dark and thick and ugly. Really, really ugly.

A hog.

The biggest hog you've ever seen.

For a second you're about to—wait. You have something that shoots off bomb blasts.

"Gentlemen, I think—"

"Right there! I got something, right there!" Willie is yelling and screaming, and the next thing you know, blasts are going off on all sides of you.

You see two—no, three, four, five—hogs bolting away. Not

waddling or scooting, but *darting* away. Meanwhile, the explosions all around you are tearing tree bark and vines and ripping through shrubs and leaves.

Soon everything quiets down.

Not one hog was touched. They've all disappeared.

You run in the direction they may have gone, but it's pointless. They're too fast.

You just got beat by a pack of massive island hogs in a footrace. What's that all about?

"See where they went?"

"No, I didn't," you yell, sucking in breaths. "Not with you guys blowing up the entire forest!"

You all stand there looking at the devastation around you. Cole hits his cowbell one more time. There's just a dull thud. "Guess I'm out of ammo."

You shake your head. "I've never heard of anything more ridiculous in my life."

Unfortunately you won't be able to use your cowbell anymore, even though you've still got several rounds left. The hogs, or whatever they were, are gone for the rest of the day. It's like they were never here in the first place.

You can't go on without game to bring to the count. Your mission is over.

The women are gonna wonder why you're back so soon.

"Don't tell anybody I picked the cowbell," you warn the rest of the guys. "Or that I got outrun by a hog."

"Oh, I'm telling them," Willie says. "The world's gonna know about this. Trust me."

Some grand hunting expedition *this* turned out to be.

THE END

NASTY

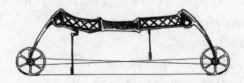

YOU'VE BEEN IN YOUR ROOM for thirty minutes *trying* to sleep when you first hear it. Not the thunder outside or the wild, wailing winds.

No. It's a scratching sound. Above you. Then to your side. Then underneath your bed.

You get out of bed and try the light switch. Nope, power's still out. You find a candle to light, but as soon as the light spills over your room, you know you have trouble. Trouble you hope you can handle, but on this island, who knows?

There's a long, dark-brown tail sticking out from under your bed.

Where's my gun?

But this isn't home. And you weren't allowed to bring your gun. Right now, you don't have any weapons in this room. Not even a pocketknife.

You wonder if there's any chance this is a friendly creature. Or maybe it's asleep and will leave you alone for the night. *Yeah. I'm sure that's really gonna happen.*

The tail slides under the bed. So much for being asleep. Then a head pops out. A face that looks a bit like a beaver's is staring at you. No, it's not a beaver. It's more like a big mouse. Actually, closer to a rat.

No, wait. It's a nutria. A swamp rat.

There are thousands of those in Louisiana. So many that it's actually become a problem.

This particular one looks larger than a typical nutria.

You tiptoe toward the door, but your motion disturbs the nutria. It fully emerges, from its long, white whiskers to its long, gross tail. It crouches in a strange hunched posture and makes eye contact with you, blinking slowly. You've probably shot a hundred of these in your lifetime, but you're not really in the mood for nutria hunting right now. Even if you did have a gun.

"Come on, buddy. I gotta sleep," you tell the thing.

The thing, however, is definitely *not* your buddy.

You learn this when it launches itself across the room at you. Jumping across the floor like some kind of turbo-powered kangaroo.

You scream, but the rain and thunder drown you out.

You don't think the nutria rats back home are this mean. Or this ugly.

But this isn't West Monroe.
Not even close.

THE END

A HAPPY EPILOGUE

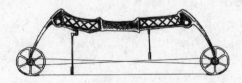

COME ON. CLAP.

You're still here, and you're celebrating life.

The credits are running and a groovy Pharrell Williams song is playing. You can dance. Even if you have a beard, you can dance.

Age? It doesn't matter.

You might be sixteen, but boy, do you have a future.

You might be sixty-eight, but boy, was that an amazing duck call you invented. That made a whole bunch of futures for lots of your family members.

But you can dance 'cause you know something bigger.

Roll the names and the credits.

Rugged, handsome hero—Jase Robertson
Whiny, out-of-shape younger brother—
    Willie Robertson

Heartthrob #1—John Luke Robertson

Heartthrob #2—Cole Robertson

Weapons provided by Mossberg & Sons

Music by Alan Silvestri

Wardrobe by Armani

Filmed on location on the island of Monuriki
   in the Pacific

Yes.

Time to dance now.

Come on, Willie. Show us how it's done.

Clap along and clap in stride.

Come on, Cole. Get jiggy with it.

Come on, John Luke. Show the girls that dimple.

You're the last one to come in view, Jase, and you're doing your low-crouching hip-shaking boogie dance.

It's a new kind of dance that's gonna be popular one day.

Celebrate today 'cause it's the only one you're gonna get right now.

Don't worry about tomorrow 'cause worrying won't change a thing.

Be thankful for yesterday 'cause God's given you every single one of your memories.

Be happy.

This world is full of sadness, so don't you want a little joy?

This crazy chaos can bring you down, but all you need is a crossbow loaded with a little happy.

Maybe you need a shotgun full of joy.

Spear the dark sadness with a dagger. Slice the hopelessness with a samurai sword.

Aim the rifle and fire and laugh.

And play the cowbell. We all need a little cowbell in our lives.

We all need some laughter.

The credits are almost over. So smile.

Happiness is a gift. So celebrate.

And please—stay away from those nasty nutria rats.

THE END

LET THE
GOOD TIMES ROLL

A Note from John Luke Robertson

EVER SINCE THE WORLD HAS GOTTEN TO KNOW the Robertson family, we've been providing lots of laughter. It's a great thing to know we're spreading a little joy and happiness in the world. As the Duck Commander motto goes, we're about faith, family, and ducks. And there's plenty of joy in all of that. Well, unless you're a duck.

Many times, this world can be the very opposite of joy. Everyone has opinions. Everybody takes sides. Sometimes we get angry and even defiant over the things we support and believe. There's a lot of hate out there.

Our family continues to choose love. To strive for joy.

I really like John 16:33:

"I have told you all this so that you may have peace in me. Here on earth you will

have many trials and sorrows. But take heart, because I have overcome the world."

Jesus is telling us to cheer up. To take heart.

This is the reason we Robertsons have so much joy inside us. We've put our faith in the same Jesus who spoke these words. He's not a made-up character in a book, nor is he just a historical person. Jesus Christ is God's Son, and he came to bring peace and joy. He came to die for us and to overcome death.

Like these fun books, life is about making decisions and choosing which direction to go. Many times we make bad decisions or wrong choices. But take heart. God knows that, and he still loves us in spite of it.

There's a Ben Rector song called "Let the Good Times Roll." I love to crank this song in my Jeep while I'm driving. And wherever you are and whatever you're doing, I hope you find some good times today—some true joy and happiness. Leave the shadows and worries in the dust.

Thanks for taking these crazy journeys with me and my family. We hope there are many more in the future that we can share with you!

There was a soft knock on the door . . .

When he called, "Entrada," the naked black girl came in, looking like she'd have been blushing, if she'd been able to.

He was stark naked, too. But what the hell, there was a lot of that going around. He nodded at her and asked, "Well?"

The girl licked her lips and said, "I am called Varginha. Dom Luis says I am to make you happy. . . ."

Books by Ramsay Thorne

Renegade #1
Renegade #2 Blood Runner
Renegade #3 The Fear Merchant
Renegade #4 Death Hunter
Renegade #5 Macumba Killer
Renegade #6 Panama Gunner
Renegade #7 Death In High Places
Renegade #8 Over The Andes To Hell

Published by
WARNER BOOKS

Renegade #8

OVER THE ANDES TO HELL

by
Ramsay Thorne

WARNER BOOKS

A Warner Communications Company

WARNER BOOKS EDITION

Copyright © 1981 by Lou Cameron

Cover designed by Gene Light
Cover art by M. Hooks

Warner Books, Inc., 75 Rockefeller Plaza, New York, N.Y. 10019

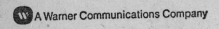 A Warner Communications Company

Printed in the United States of America

First Printing: April, 1981

10 9 8 7 6 5 4 3 2 1

Renegade #8

OVER THE ANDES TO HELL

1

It was raining in Buenaventura and General Reyes had won this year's revolution. So Captain Gringo was both wet and unemployed as he stood across from the railroad depot, trying to make up his mind. He was undecided, as well as on the dodge.

It didn't size up as an ambush. The tropic downpour had cleared the normally busy streets of the seaport. A couple of peons were sheltering in the arcade of the depot across the plaza. He didn't see the navy blue of the Colombian Military Police anywhere. A setup seemed pointless in any case. The old geezer who'd approached him that morning at the cantina had known who he was. They could have blown him away at his table if that had been the game. So the old man's yarn had at least a fifty-fifty chance of being on the level. It had sounded reasonable enough.

"You are waiting here, Señor, for your friend Gaston Verrier? I come for to warn you that you wait in vain. They are holding him at the presidio in the capital. They caught him right after the two of you split up during the fighting around Bogotá last month. If you do not leave Colombia *muy pronto*, they will catch you, too!"

And that had been it. The old geezer had lit out like spit on a hot stove before the surprised American soldier of fortune had been able to ask any questions. He still had no idea who'd sent the message. If it had been Gaston himself, there'd been no time, and no way, to send a message back.

Captain Gringo grimaced as smoke from his cigar curled up into the rain from under the wet brim of his straw

7

planter's sombrero. He had to make up his mind. The afternoon train would be leaving soon for the high country.

The message had told him to look out for his own ass. That part had made sense. Gaston would hardly expect him to be fool enough to break all the rules of the professional revolutionary. Gaston had taught them to him when they'd first met, as prisoners in a Mexican jail a while back. Old Gaston had been at this game a long time, and if there was any way to get him out of this latest mess, Gaston had already spotted it and was doubtless making plans of his own.

Like Captain Gringo, Gaston Verrier had accumulated a lot of Wanted posters in his travels. If the victorious Colombian junta hadn't shot him by now, they were almost certainly planning to turn him over to the French for that longstanding reward. Hell, by the time anyone could get from here up to Bogotá, the dapper little Frenchman figured to be well on his way down the far slope to Devil's Island on the east coast of South America!

"Dumb," Captain Gringo told himself again. He and Gaston had taken the money and run, or just run, in more than one revolution since they'd teamed up. This would be the very first time he ever turned around and walked right back into the jaws of the winners.

Gaston was a friend and comrade in arms, sort of, but loyalty stops short of suicide, and he knew damned well that if the shoe was on the other foot, Gaston would not, repeat not charge head down into any goddamned military presidio in the heart of enemy territory for his own mother!

Captain Gringo knew he'd be completely on his own. Those young rebels he'd been with a few weeks back wouldn't be there when he arrivéd in Bogotá for a rematch. If the winning side hadn't wiped them out, they'd have gone deep underground by now. So there was nobody in the highlands he could hide out with. They'd know him at any of the places he'd been before. And a tall blond Yanqui attracted attention down here, even when nobody was looking for him. He'd chanced staying in Buenaventura to wait for Gaston long past what common sense dictated. Moving one step closer to General Reyes's headquarters was just offering the other side two rebels for the price of one. The only smart move even Gaston would expect from him would be a sudden departure aboard the next boat out to anywhere.

Captain Gringo felt in his pocket for a coin. He decided that if he flipped it heads he'd go over there and board that train like an idiot. If it came up tails, he'd save his own ass.

He took out the fifty-peso piece and flipped it. It came up tails. He sighed and said, "Sorry, Gaston. I guess you're on your own."

Then he put the coin away, patted the holstered gun under the damp linen of his tropic jacket, and glanced each way to see if anyone seemed interested in him.

Nobody was. He took a drag of smoke, threw the cigar in a nearby puddle, and headed for the depot. As he squished across the plaza a little voice inside asked, "Why are you doing this, you maniac? We won! It came up tails!"

Captain Gringo didn't answer his common sense. As Gaston Verrier and others who'd fought beside him had observed in the past, Captain Gringo seldom listened to his common sense. That was one of the things that made him Captain Gringo.

2

It didn't really take a million years to reach Bogotá. It just seemed like it did to a man who spent the whole trip sweating bullets. General Reyes was a man who knew his business, and his business, these days, was putting the country back together after the egg had hit the fan. Reyes was neither a Conservative nor a Liberal, as the two sides who'd been fighting for control of Colombia had laughingly called themselves. General Reyes was the Man On A White Horse who'd waited until the fire-eating idealists had whittled themselves down like the Gingham Dog and Calico Cat. Then, with everybody very tired of the noise and wondering when in the hell it would be safe to walk the streets again, Reyes had simply moved in to "restore order" with plenty of machine guns and the usual firing squads.

Captain Gringo got to tense up every time he passed through another checkpoint, but apparently the forged passport and I.D. he carried wasn't on any of the lists they had. At one mountain station where they changed trains, a fellow passenger didn't make it. The sleepy-looking sergeant checking papers yawned at the guy, a middle-aged fat man, and said something to the *soldados* with him. They frog-marched the fat man down the track, around a bend, and one of the women passengers screamed when they heard the fusillade of shots. Then the sergeant smiled pleasantly and told the rest of them they were free to go on. Captain Gringo was glad he hadn't been seated near the guy they'd caught.

At another stop, some other soldiers took a woman from among them. It wasn't clear to anyone he was with whether the woman was a suspected rebel or just pretty. Considering

his size and Anglo features, they seemed even less interested in Captain Gringo than he'd expected them to be. He didn't get to use his cover story once on the trip. Apparently anyone on the ruling junta who remembered a tall blond soldier of fortune had assumed he'd be out of the country by this time. The suspects they were really worried about would of course be native Colombians who might be planning the next round.

So, as the last leg of his journey approached, Captain Gringo began to relax, as he was supposed to.

At military headquarters in Bogotá a certain Colonel Maldonado, alias El Araño, was watching his progress on an office map. Captain Gringo's pins were blue. There were others. Many others. The cool head of Colombian Military Intelligence was notorious for the webs he spun with those coded pins.

They didn't call Maldonado El Araño because he looked like a spider. He was a rather handsome man who didn't wear his military decorations or an expression anyone could read. He was coldly correct to other officers and as kind to enlisted men as military discipline allowed. His wife and kids adored him. Few newspaper reporters were aware he existed. He was the most dangerous man in the junta now ruling the country under General Reyes. Some of the wise money sometimes wondered whether General Reyes or Colonel Maldonado was really running the country. But, in truth, there was no rivalry. General Reyes needed El Araño's talents to keep him on his white horse, and Maldonado didn't care who rode the white horse, as long as they let him do his own job, his own way.

This wasn't always easy. Nobody in his right mind would knowingly cross El Araño, for the same reasons prudent men don't shove a finger into a hornet's nest. But the sardonic Maldonado's methods were often more subtle than anything a junior officer might have read in Machiavelli, so it was a good idea to check with the boss before you pulled anything as bush league as a triple cross. El Araño didn't set up double or triple crosses. He set up rows of domino treacheries.

And so an aide was cautious when he entered the colonel's office with a telegram to say, "That Americano, Captain Gringo, will arrive this evening at six-fifteen, my Colonel. I assume you do not wish for him to see any military police around the depot?"

El Araño turned away to stare at his map-web as he tried to remember the boy was young. When he spoke, his voice

11

was controlled and polite as he said, "On the contrary, Lieutenant. I have crossed blades with this Richard Walker before. He is good. Very good. A bit dramatic for my taste, but a man who thinks well on his feet. He will be expecting a police check at the main depot. Ergo, there should *be* one! Make certain the men understand they are to act reasonably suspicious, but that they are to let him through."

"Ah, I understand, my Colonel. We let him through so that our agents may follow him, eh?"

Maldonado sighed and murmured, "God give me strength." Then he said, "No. That big Yanqui will spot any tail we can put on him. I keep saying this over and over. I wish someone would listen. I want Richard Walker, alias Captain Gringo, to pass through our checkpoints unmolested. I want him to take the usual countermeasures and make certain he is not being followed. I want him to move about the city in complete freedom. I don't want any of our agents going anywhere near him! That big bastard is dangerous and I see no need to risk one of our people when we don't have to."

"Very well, my Colonel. Your orders shall be carried out to the letter."

The colonel turned from his map with a pleasant smile. He saw his junior was totally confused, despite his willingness. Maldonado said, "I know where Walker is going. I know what he is going to do. He is going to do exactly what I want him to do. Frankly, I find it rather amusing to be using the notorious Captain Gringo for my own pawn this time."

"A most dangerous pawn, if I may be allowed an opinion, my Colonel."

Maldonado's eyes flickered slightly, the way a shark turning in deep water roils the surface. Then he shrugged and said, "I seldom allow a junior officer to have an opinion, but I am in an indulgent mood and your father is an old friend of mine. I shall tell you something of this Yanqui, Captain Gringo. I want you to know he is good. I don't want you to think he's as good as they say he is. Nobody could be."

"My Colonel has had dealing with him before, no?"

"Yes, and I confess he made me look bad. I thought at first I was dealing with the usual soldier of fortune. Since then I have had time to study the man's background. He is not the usual lazy bully with a zest for violence. Until about a year ago he was a U.S. Army officer, a graduate of West

12

Point with a good record in the Yanqui's Indian Fighting Army. Before he started giving people down here a hard time, he was learning tricks from Apache and Mexican border raiders. Unfortunately, he has a very good memory. So what we are dealing with is a trained professional soldier with a rather alarming grasp of guerrilla tactics."

"They say he is very good with the new machine gun, too."

"That is unfortunately all too true. Walker is more than a good shot. He's an ordinance expert. The woods are filled with soldiers of fortune who know how to shoot. Captain Gringo, in a pinch, can repair or even *make* a gun. He can run almost any kind of machinery and seems to understand that new Marconi wireless business. He can navigate a vessel on the high seas. He once surprised some people alarmingly with a lighter-than-air balloon. I would not be at all surprised to see him at the tiller of one of those new horseless carriages, if there was one around here for him to steal. But, fortunately, there aren't many in Bogotá at the moment. One must think about things like that when Captain Gringo is in town!"

The aide blinked in surprise and blurted, "For why would he steal a horseless carriage in any case, my Colonel?" and Maldonado chuckled almost fondly before he replied, "To get away, of course. I assume he'll begin to suspect a trap as soon as he's been in town a few hours. We shall, of course, have a highly visible roadblock set up near the railway depot as soon as he leaves the vicinity. My plan won't work if he tries to backtrack for Buenaventura."

"He won't be able to get to the train again, my Colonel. May one ask just where you *want* for him to go? Forgive me, I do not understand your plan at all."

Maldonado said, "You're not supposed to. I forget who it was who said that two can keep a secret if one of them is dead, but he was right. Are there any new developments on Captain Gringo's little friend Gaston?"

The aide shook his head and said, "No, my Colonel. Frankly, I was afraid the Frenchman could have sent another message to his big friend after we intercepted the first one he put on the rebel underground telegraph."

Maldonado shrugged and said, "Impossible. Once we'd, ah, amended the original message and sent it via our own agent, Captain Gringo never went back to his old haunts.

13

Ergo, even if Gaston somehow got another through, Captain Gringo's had no chance to get it. He has been in my maze since he left the cantina down in Buenaventura. Now, all we have to do is keep him headed in the right direction with a minimum of danger to our own people. So this discussion is over, Lieutenant. I want you out on the street, keeping it cleared. I'm going to be very cross with you if there's a firefight I hadn't mapped out ahead of time."

"I'll do my best, sir. But what if *he* starts a fight with *us?*"

"Damnit, Lieutenant, Captain Gringo won't shoot our agents if they don't get near him. Get out there and make sure they don't!"

3

It wasn't raining in Bogotá that evening. It seldom did. The interior capital stood high and dry at 8,500 feet on an intermontane plain of the Andes. So, despite the latitude, it always seemed to be springtime there. That was why it was the capital.

But despite the benign atmosphere, Captain Gringo smelled a rat as he strolled out of the railroad depot. The police check inside had been a lark and the people on the street outside seemed relaxed, considering. There were still fresh bullet pocks on the walls up and down the street and you could see where they'd thrown a barricade across the pavement near the corner. But the more obvious signs of a recent revolution had been cleaned up and nobody seemed excited about anything. So what in the hell was wrong? Why were the hairs on the back of his neck tingling?

Returning to the scene of one's recent crimes against the state, while dumb, offered at least some advantages to a man on the dodge. Unlike most of the places he'd hit since jumping the Mexican border one jump ahead of the law, Bogotá was a place he knew his way around.

Captain Gringo hailed a horsedrawn cab and ordered the driver to take him to the hotel he and Gaston had stayed in the last time they were here. He had no intention of staying there, of course. A man trying to throw folks off his tail makes certain basic moves.

Any police informer around the station would have heard his shouted destination as he climbed in the back of the cab. As the vehicle left the neighborhood of the depot, Captain Gringo watched to see if they were being followed.

15

He couldn't spot any tail. So far, so good. It sure was beginning to look like nobody was expecting him in Bogotá.

"Bullshit," he muttered darkly to himself, as he lit a cigar with a frown. If they had Gaston locked up in the Presidio, they had to be expecting somebody to try and spring him. He and the little Frenchman were unfortunately well known in military mercenary circles and it wasn't as if a tall blond Anglo was hard to describe or keep an eye out for in this neck of the woods. Gaston tended to blend in. Captain Gringo knew he didn't.

The tall American studied the passing scenery, getting his bearings. It was early evening but, as always in the tropics, darkness fell fast with none of the gloaming afterglow he remembered from back home in the States. He took out a bill and placed it on the leather seat beside him. It was three times as much as the regular fare from the station to the hotel. He didn't want the driver bitching loudly later.

Captain Gringo waited until they were passing through a tunnel of shade trees he'd noticed the last time he'd made this trip. Then he cupped the smoke in his palm to hide the glow, silently opened the side door, and slid out to land, running in a catlike crouch that carried him silently away from the rumbling cab as the driver drove on, oblivious to the sneaky change of destination. Captain Gringo flattened out against the shaded bole of a massive pepper tree and waited until the cab rattled on out of sight. Then he grinned and started walking with the cigar at a jaunty angle. There wasn't another soul in sight. He was well clear of the depot and nowhere near the hotel where his face would be known. The driver would be puzzled, even annoyed, when he pulled up at the hotel entrance to find his passenger missing. But he wouldn't search too hard once he found the money in the back. If he ever saw the son of a bitch again, Captain Gringo intended to ask for his change.

He came to a corner and headed down a side street. First he'd put more distance between himself and any attempted tail. Then he'd figure where the hell he was and what he intended to do about it.

He knew where the military presidio was. Before he figured out how he'd ever get Gaston out of there, he had to have a place to take him. So a base of operations was indicated. Captain Gringo came to another corner and turned it automatically. He was in a middle-class residential area that

16

offered nothing but temporary cover. Like most Hispanic homes in this part of the world, the ones around him faced inward on their patio courts and offered little of interest to the narrow street. Captain Gringo walked casually, trying not to be any more interesting than the blank stucco walls and barred gates he passed. The neighborhood was dimly lit with an occasional streetlamp. When he saw a group of youths lounging under one, well down the way ahead, he turned another corner without having to think too hard about it. He passed one or two people in his travels and nodded politely. It was now too dark to see if they nodded back. Things were looking up. If he couldn't see them any better than that, they couldn't see him any better.

He was starting to feel safer now, but he knew he couldn't just roam the streets all night. He had to find a safe hideout before it got late enough for folks to wonder about footsteps outside their private little worlds. He knew that like most Latin American cities, Bogotá was surrounded by shantytown *favelas*. The one to the north between the main drag and those mine installations he'd blown up the last time he'd been here were out. The young rebels he'd worked with had enough on their plate right now, just trying to stay alive. A big gringo with a price on his head would not only be less welcome than the plague, somebody in the gang might opt for the reward.

He felt his groin tingle wistfully as he wrote off the rebels he knew in town. That one *muchacha* had served him a sweet enchilada indeed, and a couple of the other girls in the gang had looked interesting, too. But it was dumb enough to be back in town this soon. He couldn't risk looking up a single soul he knew here!

He swung a corner and found himself on a slightly wider street with some lights ahead down the block. As he passed a girl lounging in a doorway she murmured, *"A 'onde va, querido?"* in a lackluster voice. So he knew he was drifting back to the action part of town.

That was okay. He'd be less likely to attract attention in the parts of Bogotá a single man was expected to be interested in. Pulling his hat brim down a bit to shade his features, Captain Gringo strolled on, ignoring the casually lewd suggestions from some of the doorways he passed. He knew where he was now. He knew the street ahead. He'd passed through it more than once during his last adventures here.

17

More important, he hadn't made any friends or enemies within blocks.

He drifted to a closed shop on the corner and pretended to look at the shoes in the window as he got his bearings. There was a neighborhood cantina across the way. That was to be avoided. Strangers stood out in any local joint and the police in every city expected knock-around guys to show up in places like that.

There was an open *farmacía* a couple of doors past the cantina. Nobody cared who ducked into a drugstore early in the evening. So he headed that way. The druggist inside was waiting on a woman in a straw hat and shawl. Captain Gringo noticed the politely startled glance of the druggist but ignored it and waited politely until the woman had paid for her purchase and left. Captain Gringo went to the counter and bought a big bottle of quinine. He didn't need any quinine, but it was reasonably expensive. The druggist got even friendlier when he asked for some Havana Perfectos. As the druggist rang up the sale and made change, he asked, "El Señor is new in this *barrio*, no?"

Captain Gringo had been hoping for something like that. He smiled pleasantly and said, "Yes, I'm with the German legation, as you may have guessed."

"Ah? El Señor speaks Spanish very well for a German. Although, now that you mention it, I place the accent. Your consulate is that big pink building over on the avenue, no?"

Captain Gringo wondered what else was new, but he nodded and said, "Yes, I came over this way tonight to talk to some people I know about renting a furnished room. I understand there are a few around here, but the fellow I was supposed to meet wasn't in the cantina just now. I sure hope I didn't get the address wrong."

The druggist brightened and asked, "Ah, you are searching for a room?"

"Yes, I've been staying at a hotel near the depot since I was posted here, but it's costing me the earth, and I'm afraid it's not a very nice hotel. This Colombian fellow who works with me at the German consulate says he has an aunt around here who lets out rooms, but, like I said, he hasn't shown up yet. I guess I'll just have to hang around and hope he does."

You could see the little wheels spin around in the neighborhood druggist's eyes as he tried not to look at the

18

expensive purchases on the counter between them. He said, "Well, far be it from me to interfere, Señor. But if your friend can't find you a place for to stay, I have a regular customer who owns a small hotel just down the street. She is a most respected widow who keeps her rooms most clean. I can vouch for the fact she uses a formidable amount of soap. As to her rates, I cannot say. But I do not think her rooms are very expensive."

Captain Gringo resisted the impulse to nod. He frowned dubiously and said, "Well, I'm certainly tired of waiting around for that other guy, but . . ." and then all he had to do was relax and let himself be sold. It took the druggist less than fifteen minutes to close shop and almost drag him down the street to the hotel a relative *had* to be running.

Somebody had once told Captain Gringo that a true bargain was a transaction in which each party thought that he or she was getting the best deal. So the grim little hotel, run by a grim little woman in rusty black, was a better bargain than he'd hoped for. The landlady and the neighborhood wise guy who'd steered him to her doubtless thought he was a live one. He pretended he didn't know that he was being charged twice as much as the small furnished suite of rooms was worth. On the other hand, the place was reasonably clean and, more important, private. He paid a month in advance for the rooms tucked into a corner on the street side. The widow's doorway opened on the vestibule downstairs, but a guy could come and go by the stairway unobserved, when her door wasn't open. He could keep an eye on the street out front from between the slats of the jalousied shutters. There seemed to be a way out the back, too. He'd explore the upstairs hallways later.

Meanwhile, he'd established, should anybody ask, that the corner suite was occupied by a nice boy from the German legation, consulate, or something. They hadn't asked him what he did for *Der Kaiser*. Once he'd shown them the color of his money they hadn't appeared to care. He of course had no intention of staying a month, or even a week, if he could help it. But by paying well in advance he'd hopefully lulled her interest in him for a while. Anxious landladies ask questions. Contented ones didn't, as a rule.

The druggist left discreetly as the black-clad widow puttered about a bit to make sure he was going to stay. He made a point of saying he'd have his luggage delivered in the

19

morning. What would it cost to buy a couple of cheap suitcases?

So, having taken his money and given him his key, she left him to his own devices, too. He grimaced as he shut the door after her and snuffed the candle. He wondered if she'd pay off the druggist in cash or something more personal. He'd noticed the little druggist ogling her in the cracked mirror across the room. Some guys were like that. The poor old broad had a reasonable figure under that rusty black poplin, but the severe bunned-up hair had been streaked with gray and the lips had been as kissable as a steel trap.

Captain Gringo moved to the window in the darkness. As he'd expected, he had a clear view of the street below through the slats. He could see the sign of the *farmacia* but not as far as the cantina. Nobody down there seemed to be interested in the front entrance of the hotel. Except for an obvious whore in a doorway down the block, nobody was lounging around looking like they *weren't* interested, either.

Captain Gringo struck a match and relit the candlestick. Then he sat on the bed and took out his .38 to check it as he pondered his next move. It was early and he was edgy as hell, but his best move right now would be no move at all.

He'd let them get used to the idea that a "German" was staying in the neighborhood. He'd picked that nationality because he knew few Latins could tell a German from an English accent in Spanish and because the story fit. He'd remembered there was a German legation nearby and, of course, everyone knew Germans were big and blond. Later, when people asked the locals about him, they'd be assured he was "neighborhood." Meanwhile, he knew he'd never be able to approach the presidio where Gaston was being held this late at night without attracting attention, no matter who they thought he might be. He'd case that part out by daylight, when the streets were crowded and he had this "address" for any nosy cop.

He tossed his hat on a chair, put the gun in a fold of the mattress near the headboard, and started to undress. He didn't want to go to bed. It was early, he wasn't the least bit tired. He was edgy as hell, as a matter of fact. He'd eaten aboard the train, but he was starting to get hungry again and he was dying for a drink.

But that was tough shit. All too many guys on the dodge had been taken, just as they thought they were safe, by

20

dropping their guard as soon as the pressure seemed to be off them for the night. Billy the Kid had bought the farm about this same time at night when he'd left a safe hideout for a bedtime snack. Captain Gringo remembered that lawman he'd met during his hitch in Apache country. Mean-looking gent named Pat Something. He'd said he'd have never gunned the Kid if it hadn't been for the Kid's uncontrollable appetite, and that some owl-hoots just never learn. The Kid had been caught once already, when he'd succumbed to the smell of frying bacon and eggs. The night he'd died at the Maxwell Spread he'd been after a steak. Captain Gringo decided it wouldn't kill him to sleep on a growling gut.

He finished stripping and turned down the counterpane on the bed. The sheets were cool and scented with lavender. It seemed almost obscene as well as wasteful to slide a solo unwashed body between them. But he did. For some reason it gave him a hard-on.

That was another appetite he hadn't been able to satisfy lately. It had been a three-day journey from the coast, changing trains a lot and mule packing over some of the rough stretches.

He hadn't looked for any action, coming up from the lowlands. He'd seen some nice-looking stuff in the last few days. A guy could hardly go anywhere without seeing somebody worth laying, but he hadn't really considered anything along those lines until just now when, for the first time in days, he found himself alone in bed with nobody likely to point a gun at him in the next few minutes.

He willed himself to forget it. He hadn't come all this way to find a woman. He was risking his ass to save Gaston, and that was going to be a *real* problem. Bogotá was full of broads. There was one holding up a wall with her for-sale spine just across the goddamn street! It was time he got down to some serious planning about that goddamn military presidio on the far side of town.

But he'd been thinking about that for days. He hadn't come up with a sensible plan either. But, as a natural survivor and professional man of action, he'd learned to move on the guns and play it by ear until fate, or a mistake by the other side, offered an opening.

So far this trip, Lady Luck seemed amazingly benign, considering how the old bitch had been treating him since the day he found himself facing a U.S. Army court-martial on a

bum rap. He was almost certain nobody had trailed him to this lair, and the neighborhood offered a better base of operations than most. It was too transient for a stranger to draw all the gossip, and too quiet to draw the undivided interest of the law. In the morning, along with some cardboard luggage, he'd pick up a change of clothing. It was cool enough at this altitude to get away with a dark suit and felt hat.

Just in case some rat in Buenaventura had described him to the new government, a gringo was a gringo and they'd be looking for a big guy in a Panama suit.

"Then what?" the small voice asked from somewhere in the worried shadows of his mind. Captain Gringo told it to go to sleep. He knew the dangers as well as the discomforts of planning the unplannable alone in bed with a weary brain and a hard-on. A guy could squirrel-cage all night and never come up with an idea that made much sense in the cold reason of broad daylight. He'd done all he could for now. The rest depended on the measures the enemy had taken. He couldn't see them from here. Hell, he wasn't even sure who the enemy *was*.

The last time he and Gaston had passed through these parts they'd been fighting the government in power for people paying to see it overthrown. Then General Reyes had popped out of the woodwork and started mopping up both loyalists and rebels to "restore order." To give the devil his due, things seemed orderly as hell right now. Captain Gringo knew many of the erstwhile loyalists and rebels would have made peace with the new junta and, if useful to Reyes, were probably working for him. That was a good reason to avoid seeking help from his old rebel comrades here in Bogotá. If they had not yet changed sides, they were losers having enough trouble just trying to stay alive. The apparently loose security he'd noticed so far hinted that the Reyes government felt pretty smug in their new rug. So, okay; if they were running things so relaxed, why had they picked Gaston up? Like everyone else who'd fought the old government, Gaston had only asked for *out!*

Gaston and Captain Gringo had split up when the revolution went sour, not to oppose General Reyes but to get the hell out of his way. Gaston had led a party of innocent refugees out to the north while Captain Gringo had finished

22

their contract by blowing up a few loose ends and escaping via another route. If the fucking government now running things had just left them the hell alone they'd have met by now in Buenaventura and been out of the country. They said Reyes was smart. So what was this bullshit about arresting guys who'd never done all that much to him?

The reward? That sounded stupid-greedy. The little Frenchman wasn't worth that much to the Legion he'd deserted years ago. The two of them together were worth a sum a private citizen might find tempting. But for God's sake, General Reyes had a whole fucking country to loot at his pleasure if he needed cigarette money. They must have known Gaston had friends. They must have known that grabbing him would be asking for other soldiers of fortune too . . . That was it.

Gaston was bait. They were holding him to lure a rescue try and . . . then what? They hadn't even questioned him at the depot. The handful of military police had waved everyone through with a casual glance at their papers. He probably could have gotten through with a laundry list. They certainly had most definitely not trailed him from the depot and . . .

Captain Gringo slid out from between the now-warm sheets and over to the window. It was getting really cool now, and the effects on his hard-on were the same as a cold shower while he stood, covered with gooseflesh, peeking out through the slats of his shuttered window.

The whore who'd been standing in that doorway was gone. The street out front was deserted for the moment but somewhere in the night a piano tinkled a lively tune. It was funny what night and a little distance did to the sound of music. He knew that up close, in the smoke-filled cantina, the rinky-tink piano sounded cheerful and rowdy. From here in the lonely darkness it sounded wistful and homesick.

Captain Gringo spotted a moving light in a window across the way and watched with interest as he softly sang along with the distant piano. A woman in a short white shift was moving toward the window carrying a candle. It was too far to make out her looks, but he could see her legs from mid-thigh down and they looked yummy as hell in the soft candle glow. She put the candle down near the open window and started to pull the drapes of a fourposter bed open. She had her nicely shaped derriere to him as she bent to smooth

the sheets and fluff the pillows. Captain Gringo grinned and sang, "Up in a balloon, dear. Up in a balloon. Up among the little stars, beside the silvery moon . . ."

The girl, woman, whatever, stood up, satisfied, with her back to him. She seemed to be talking to someone in a corner he couldn't see in to. It had to be a guy. He wondered if she was that *puta* he'd seen in the doorway before. 'She started to pull the shift off over her head and as the hemline rose, he found himself singing, "Oh, there's something very daring, going up in my balloon."

It didn't matter what her face looked like. That hourglass of naked female flesh was giving him another hard-on. The customer, lover, whatever, came into view now. He was a heavyset guy in black pants and a white shirt. As Captain Gringo watched, he moved over to put his arms around the naked woman. The tall nude American wondered how much further they'd go with the candle lit. They were too deep in the room to be seen from the street level below, but they had to know that window faced others across the way. If she was a whore and he was the local Romeo, maybe they liked to show off?

Captain Gringo grimaced, feeling a little sheepish about his peeping tommery. He knew it was really stupid to torture himself like this and, what the hell, he wasn't even close enough for a good peep show. But he went on watching, even as the rest of us would have.

The guy over there tried to move the woman on to the mattress. But she suddenly pulled coyly away and turned from him, facing the window stark and spectacular for a moment as the candlelight illuminated her heroic breasts from below. And then the dirty teasing bitch leaned forward and snuffed out the light.

"You did that on purpose," Captain Gringo muttered with a wry grin. He knew the joke was on him and anyone else peeking out of other windows, and what the hell, it sure paid to advertise.

He was about to move back from the window when he heard heel clicks from below. He craned for a better view of the street. It was the whore he'd seen before. She was walking back to the doorway he'd last spotted her in. As she lit a cigarette and lounged against the jamb, he glanced over at the now-dark window across the way and thought, "No, nobody

is that fast." So the woman across the way was somebody else. He felt a wry satisfaction in having his wordly judgment confirmed. He'd *thought* the one across the way moved pretty slow for a streetwalker.

He tried to judge the time the one down there in the doorway had been gone. He gave it up as a pointless exercise. At the most optimistic, it had been maybe ten minutes from the moment some poor hard-up bastard had spoken to her in the doorway until she was fully dressed and back there waiting for the next. It didn't matter what she looked like. A gal in that much of a hurry wasn't selling mock romance. She was asking guys to pay for downright hostility!

A couple of guys walked down the street going the other way. The whore called out to them softly, and they didn't glance her way. Captain Gringo noticed they didn't glance toward the hotel entrance either. He decided to write them off as a couple of guys heading for the cantina.

He was about to go back to the bed and warm his chilled hide when he heard the soft snick of a key turning ever so gently in a lock. *His* lock!

He moved quietly on the balls of his bare feet, heart pounding as he cursed himself for leaving the gun under the mattress a million miles away on the far side of the door. He knew the door hinges were on his side. He flattened against the wall just as the door began to open, slowly and ever so quietly. The party on the other side wasn't packing a light. So they were both playing kitty cat and Captain Gringo had at least the advantage of eyes accustomed to the dark and a knowledge of the layout. He knew where he was. The other probably thought he was in the bed. From there on, things went rapidly downhill. The other probably had the only gun in the game.

Captain Gringo tensed to spring as the mysterious intruder moved into the room. He could see only that it was somebody a lot shorter than himself, and probably alone. To make sure of this, he let the intruder clear the door, then slammed it shut as he dove forward. He crashed into the dark figure and his momentum carried them both over to and across the empty bed, with Captain Gringo on top and groping for wrists and/or weapons as they crashed down together. The whatever gasped in surprise and fear as he got the right wrist and twisted it up into the small of his victim's

25

back, using his superior weight to pin whomsoever down. He got his other hand against the nape of a neck and shoved his victim's face into the mattress as, at the same time, he became aware that it seemed to be wearing a skirt and that his nude pelvis had the other's hips pinned against the edge of the bed with its knees on the rug and one round hemisphere of buttock on either side of his semi-erection.

He growled, *"Quién es?"* as the obviously female derriere gripped his growing interest between cloth-covered trembling fanny muscles. She answered, face buried in the mattress, "Have you gone mad, Señor? It is I, Vanessa."

He had no idea who on earth Vanessa might be, but he allowed her to raise her head from the mattress enough to breathe freely and speak more clearly. So naturally she said something dumb like, "Let me go. You are hurting me."

The hard-on between her cheeks didn't seem to bother her all that much, so he stayed put but eased off the pressure on her elbow as he said, "I'm pleased to meet you, Vanessa. But I don't remember ringing for room service."

"I was afraid you might be cold, Señor. I only came for to see if I could make you more comfortable."

"With a passkey, in your bare feet? How come you didn't knock?"

"Please get off me, Señor. I did not wish for to disturb other guests and, well, people say wicked things about a woman who knocks on a man's door late at night. I thought, if you were already asleep, I would simply put the extra covers I brought over you and tiptoe away without disturbing you."

He moved a naked foot over toward the door and, sure enough, his toes felt the blankets on the rug where she'd dropped them. The new angle to his hips felt interesting as hell, too. She had a really nice little rump and his raging erection was lined up just right, if it hadn't been for all those fucking clothes she had on. He could feel she had no pantaloons on.

He moved his free hand down to hoist her smooth taffeta skirting as he smiled and said, "Well, as long as you came to comfort me, I wouldn't want to send you away frustrated."

As he felt the bareness of her thighs with his own naked legs she gasped and protested, "Oh, Señor, I only came for to lay a blanket over you. What kind of a woman do you think I am?"

26

He replied, "That's what I'm trying to find out. So far, I like what I feel."

She struggled, not really too hard, as he got the skirting out from between them, and his turgid member popped into the moistness between her smooth, trembling thighs. He shoved the cloth above her waistline and caressed her firm but feminine rump as he moved his hand down to guide it to glory. She said, "This is most rude of you, Señor. I never came here for to be raped."

He laughed and said, "You don't have to be so formal, Vanessa. You can call me Ricardo. We both know you're not being raped."

Then he had it in position, and as he thrust home with a sigh of pleasure she gasped and bleated, "Oh, *Madre de Dios!* What are you *doing* to me if that is not rape?"

"Let's call it common courtesy, *querida*. I can see you needed some comforting, too. Your little box is hot and hungry. How long has it been since you've had some of this, *muchachita?*"

She sobbed, face down against the mattress, and thrust her tail bone up to grind it into his belly hairs as she moaned, "Oh, far too long, you lovely brute! Don't tease me with your questions. Fuck me hard and deep!"

That seemed the most reasonable suggestion he'd heard all evening, so he did his best to oblige. He was already hot as a pistol, so he tried to hold back a bit, not wanting to leave her up in the air by coming too quickly. But apparently that was impossible. Vanessa chewed a mouthful of linen as she hissed like a mountain lion in heat and contracted on his questing shaft with repeated orgasms until, in less than three minutes, he exploded inside her with a pyrotechnic climax of his own.

She said, "Oh, I felt that. Is it all over so soon, alas?"

He said, "*Querida*, we are just getting started. I haven't had anything this nice for a month of Sundays and if you weren't ready to meet your maker you never should have started this."

She giggled girlishly as he rolled off, turned her on her back, and undressed her, kissing her naked flesh as he exposed it to the cool night air. As his own had been, up to a minute ago, Vanessa's slightly moist skin was covered with goosebumps to be soothed with warm lips. He nibbled a turgid nipple as he slid the last of her clothing out of the way

27

and cupped her warm mons in his palm. She spread her thighs and crooned, "Oh, stop teasing and *do* it again, my great German bull."

He mounted her and started to enjoy a nice old-fashioned rutting before that sank in. Vanessa, whoever the hell she was, made love like a sex-starved mink and kissed like the intake of a blast furnace. He'd told the dried-up old land-lady he was a German, now that he thought about it. So Vanessa had to be her chambermaid, maybe her daughter, and just what in the hell had he started? If the old bat who owned the place found out how he'd responded to extra blankets she might act sort of frantic. A guy down here had to remember that Hispanics took a pretty narrow view on country matters. There were only supposed to be two kinds of Latin girls. Whores and madonnas. A lot of chambermaids put out, but only on the very sneaky Q.T.

He started to ask her if anyone downstairs knew she was up here with him, but Vanessa wrapped her legs around him and sobbed, "Don't talk. Screw me. I go crazy so nice when you pound me hard!"

He was feeling crazy so nice, himself, so what the hell. The fat was in the fire and he'd worry about the landlady later. Vanessa's firm breasts were moist and slippery now, as she slithered them back and forth against his heaving chest and, below the waist, she was moving up to meet him like a Arabian belly dancer in love. Her kissing was more French. She was great at that, too. As he felt her already tight vaginal muscles contracting in another orgasm she managed to some-how get her tongue almost deep enough to make him gag. He sucked it perversely as he fired a shot heard round the bed as deep as he could get inside her. He collapsed atop her, trying for a well-earned rest, but she kept moving, pulsating with insatiable orgasmic desire, and even with no effort on his part, it felt like he was pounding her hot and heavy, so what the hell, in a little while he was.

The next time he came, he gasped, "Hey, time out for a smoke at least."

"You are not pleased with my body anymore?"

"Your body is just great. My body is about to melt into the mattress. Just give me a chance to get my second wind, *querida*. You don't have to leave right away, do you?"

"No, I can stay the night if you wish for it, my Ricardo."

"I wish for it. You won't get in trouble downstairs?"

"No. I will tell you a secret now. Nobody else knows I am here. I confess I am a wicked girl. I was hoping you would, ah, trifle with me."

"Confession is good for the soul and I'm going to trifle you dog style in a minute. But let's share a smoke, first. You do smoke, don't you?"

She laughed archly and said, "You smoke what you like and I will smoke what I like."

He didn't get it until he stretched an arm out to fumble a cigar and a light from his shirt draped over a nearby chair. That was when he felt her long hair dragging across his overheated belly and as he lit up, back braced against a pillow, Vanessa took his limp shaft between her moist lips and began to "smoke" it.

He lit his Havana Perfecto and took a luxurious drag as he held the match for a moment, gazing fondly down at the woman crouched broadside to him on her knees as she bobbed her head over his supine lap. The little flickering flame was kind to the ivory perfection of her firm nude body. He still had only a hazy idea what she might look like, after exploring her so thoroughly by feel in the dark. So he stared with interest at the profile of the face he'd been kissing hell out of under the cloak of night. Vanessa was Frenching him with enthusiasm and hence didn't glance his way as he studied her by matchlight. So, mercifully, she never caught the look of utter dismay in his eyes as he recognized her.

Vanessa wasn't a young chambermaid working for the old bat who ran the place. Vanessa *was* the old bat who ran the place!

The match burned his fingers and he shook it out, but not before he'd seen the gray streaks in her hair and the little lines that Time's cruel shark had bitten into her once pretty little face. He didn't know whether to laugh or cry as he lay there, being sucked off by a woman old enough to be his mother. But he knew he didn't want her to stop, so what the hell.

He lay in the dark, breathing funny as he smoked his cigar and she smoked him. The sudden surprise had cooled him off a bit and, of course, he'd been partly satisfied to begin with. So it took her longer than usual to erect his monument to Venus to its usual heroic height.

It felt sort of weird as he lolled there like a jaded pasha, enjoying the contrasting pleasures of tobacco and oral sex.

29

Once the light was out, Vanessa reverted to the harem cutie he'd been playing with in his imagination. Sort of. On the other hand, knowing now that she was an older, albeit salty widow added something to the spice of carefree sex.

In the darkness, Vanessa was saying, "Oh, I have it nice and hard now. But my little pussy is so jealous. She is feeling most left out."

He reached out to snuff the cigar in an end table ashtray before he groped for her derriere in the darkness and soothed, "We wouldn't want anyone to feel left out."

Vanessa gasped in startled pleasure as she realized what the position he was moving them into might mean. She kissed the head of what she held in her hand and purred, "Oh, I was willing to get on top, but if you are really *that* considerate . . ." and then she almost shouted, "Oh, *Jésus, Maria y José!*" as he got two fingers in her and began to tongue her clit. She responded in kind by inhaling him to the root as they went sixty-nine, and he could tell she wanted to finish that way this time, so he decided he might as well. It was no more revolting to kiss a friendly twat than those pursed steel-trap lips he remembered shuddering at the first time he'd seen them!

After they'd enjoyed one another that way, and tried it dog style as a change of pace, they naturally wound up old-fashioned in each other's arms and it only seemed polite to kiss the old bat while she was sobbing about coming some more. It was funny, but with the lights out, her lips did feel as soft and passionate as many a younger girl's, and it did feel as if she was pretty when they lay quietly together in the lovely afterglow. It was no wonder the poor old bat went around looking so grim. The still healthy woman was starved for sex . . . or maybe more.

The next time he suggested a smoke she lay quietly with her head on his shoulder and one thigh across his, toying with the hair on his chest with her free hand. As he lit the cigar she ducked her head, kissing his collarbone, and said, "I wish you would tell me when you are going to strike a match. I am ashamed for you to see me like this."

He ran his own free hand over her soft, smooth skin and soothed, "There's nothing I could see in the light that I don't like pretty well in the dark, Vanessa."

She sighed and said, "You are just being gallant. I know

what I look like today. Would you believe me if I told you I was once considered a beautiful woman, Ricardo?"

"You're still beautiful," he lied, and for some reason that made the poor old broad start to cry. He didn't comment as he felt a tear run off her cheek onto his chest. She got a few more out of her system before she said, "Thank you, my *caballero*. I wanted you so badly. I knew the moment I saw you that you were the kind of lover I need. But I was so afraid you would just be another big naughty boy. I feel so abased when a man I seduce has less tact than you about my, well, age. I wish there was a word less ugly than age. But there is nothing else wrong with me."

He caressed her and said, "Hell, there's nothing at all wrong with you. We all have to get older, sooner or later. I think you worry too much about it, Vanessa. What the hell, you can't be much older than maybe thirty-nine or forty, right?"

"Oh, my God, you're such a gallant liar, and I needed that. If you must know, I am nearly sixty."

"I didn't have to know, and I don't believe you," he fibbed kindly. Then he kissed the part in her hair to add, "Let's forget about birthdays. I have no complaints to register about tonight. I needed you a lot more than you needed me, kitten."

She giggled and said, "I know. I felt so awkward, coming in, not knowing how I was going to approach you. And then you leaped on me like a beast and tore my clothes off. It was too good to be true."

He chuckled back at her and held her closer as he took a drag of smoke. She began to walk her fingers shyly down his belly as she said, "Downstairs, when we were talking about your room earlier, I could see you were a most lusty man. I was happily married for many years to a lusty man. So I can tell when a man needs it. I was so foolish when I flustered around up here before. I wanted so for you to take me in your arms, but of course I knew you thought I was just a silly old woman."

He said, "As a matter of fact, I noticed what a nice shape you had and I was feeling pretty silly, too. It was all I could do not to make a pass at you the moment I found myself alone with you."

"Oh, Ricardo, is that the truth?"

31

It wasn't, but he figured he owed it to her. He said, "Yes, if you hadn't made a play for me, I'd have made one for you. But let's not worry about it. Now that we've gotten past the awkward stages, we can just enjoy each other."

"Oh, I am so happy, Ricardo. Are you really going to stay here with me?"

"I paid a month in advance, didn't I?"

"Yes. But now I will have to give you back your money. It would not be right if I kept it. Only wicked women take money from the man they are sleeping with and——"

"Hey, back up," he cut in. "I'm not paying you for your body, doll. I only rented the room! I could see right away you were a woman to be respected."

That made her cry some more. Then she said, "The angels must have sent you to me, Ricardo. Would you believe I have not had any sex for over a year?"

"That sounds reasonable. Uh, how long have you been a widow?"

"Oh, my poor husband died many years ago. But, as you may have guessed, I am a woman of strong passions. I am afraid this has made me act the fool on more than one occasion. You see, I know I should look for a man closer to my own age, but . . ."

He grimaced and cut in with, "I understand." She didn't have to explain why she liked younger studs. Not many teenagers could keep up with old Vanessa as a steady bedmate. He liked his women hot and horny, but it was probably just as well he wasn't really intending to stay any backbreaking full month!

She said, "The last time I made a fool of myself like this I swore it would never happen again. I knew what you'd be like in bed the moment I saw you, but you younger men can be so cruel."

"Anyone who was ever cruel to you was too stupid for you to worry your pretty little head about, *querida*."

"Oh, my God, if only I could believe your beautiful lies. But others have used and abused me, Ricardo. If you could know the way it stabs a woman to the heart to be jeered at in the cold light of dawn."

He got rid of the second smoke and soothed, "Nobody's going to abuse you, *querida*, but, speaking of using, that's not a milk churn you've started playing with down there."

She laughed in girlish delight as he rolled aboard her

32

again and as he settled into the saddle she coyly mocked, "Haven't you had enough of this old worn-out shoe?"

He thrust into her and as she bit down hard with her love-slicked flesh he growled, "It'll be worn out by the time I get through with it!"

But this time they made love like friends instead of acrobats and now that he'd gotten used to the idea, he was starting to like old Vanessa. He couldn't think of any improvements he wanted to make that counted in the dark, and this solved another problem. His hideout was not only a safe one. It offered all the comforts of home! He didn't even have to ask, when, after they'd finished another round, Vanessa suggested a midnight snack.

He had no idea, as they finally dropped off to sleep in each other's sated arms, that he'd never get to spend another night with her.

4

The dirty sons of bitches who'd laid out the military presidio on the far side of town had known what they were doing.

Since leaving the States to escape a hanging, Captain Gringo had tangled with a mixed bag of military skills, or the lack thereof. Some Latin American officers he'd met had been nothing more than bush-league bandits. Others had been as good as anything West Point or Saint Cyr L'Ecole could turn out. A lot had been trained at The Point or Saint Cyr. The old Spanish aristocracy of Colombia tended to be pure white. Snobbish Castilian white at that. In his travels Captain Gringo had noticed that Costa Rica, Colombia, and other places where pure-blooded Europeans had remained in power tended to be run on more "civilized" lines. This was not "proof" of white superiority by any means. Nobody who'd fought Apache or seen the Aztec, Toltec, or Maya ruins in Mexico could put the American Indian down as an idiot. The apparent superiority of the pure Hispanic communities was a matter of education. The original Indian cultures had been wiped out with bell, book, and candle, leaving a sullen, ignorant, second-class imitation of a Spanish field worker to take over when the old Spanish Empire fell apart in most of these countries. But the white Creoles had hung on in the highlands of Colombia and while they were conservative and living in the past, their past was the Baroque era, when people built elaborate fortifications.

The first thing Captain Gringo noticed about the presidio he had to get into was that they'd made it tough to get anywhere near it without being seen by the guards on the

walls. There was no moat. It was too dry up here for that, but they'd ringed the presidio with open ground. The locals used some of it for a park, but no trees or bushes grew within three hundred yards, or easy rifle range, of the walls.

The clever sneak who'd designed the layout had obviously assumed there was little chance a modern army with heavy guns would ever make it all the way up here to the highlands, so the presidio was designed to stand off moody local peons, as it had, in fact, during the recent riots and revolution. Nobody had taken a military installation from General Reyes. General Reyes had kept his men in the places he already held until both the other sides ran out of steam, then simply marched out to grab the rest of the country. So the presidio wasn't the usual mass of angled walls and jutting bastions that made it so hard for an attacking army and so easy for a single infiltrator. The bastards had a high screening wall all around the outer perimeter. You couldn't see a single roof top on the other side, so there was no way to judge the interior layout from out here. Just that big blank, staring, stupid vertical wall. You couldn't even piss against it without crossing open grass the length of a football field. No sally ports. No drainage ditch running out from under the wall like Ethan Allen had used so coyly at Ticonderoga that night in '75. The only way in or out seemed to be via the stout gates with a sentry box on either side. The goddamned sentries were wide awake in well-fitting uniforms, too.

Captain Gringo started to circle in what he hoped would look, at a distance, like a casual stroll. The rest of the town had spread out around the presidio, stopped by the deadline on all sides, of course. So there was a natural ring of tree-shaded walks, storefronts, and smaller plazas all around that featureless wall and its apron of open ground.

As he rounded a corner, out of sight of the main gate now, he spotted a boy herding a small flock of sheep on the forbidden lawn. Captain Gringo perked up. Maybe they weren't as strict about walking on the grass as he'd thought.

Then he spotted the rifleman on the wall above, keeping a casual eye on the kid with the sheep. The young shepherd wasn't trespassing. He was a military contractor. His job was to keep the killing ground around the walls as neatly mowed as a golf course. The grassy flats all around had been graded perfectly level, so even at night there'd be no shadows out there.

Captain Gringo stopped near a lamppost to scratch a light for a smoke. He glanced up casually and noted the lamp above was burning, even though it was a bright sunny morning. He grimaced as he lit his cigar, staring ahead. Yeah, they'd installed streetlamps all around the deadline. Burning twenty-four hours a day. Anybody trying to sneak up to the walls after dark would be outlined sharp as a black bull's-eye, and the night guards' rifles would be zeroed in for the range. Snuffing out a streetlamp would be no big deal, but that wouldn't work, either. Anybody smart enough to illuminate their night perimeter would have standing orders about lights winking out too.

He was nearing a sidewalk cantina, fronting on the paved path he was on. On a sudden impulse, Captain Gringo stepped over to a green metal table and sat down. The two guys trailing him at a hundred yards hadn't expected him to do that. So he spotted them as they ducked into a doorway back the way he'd just come.

Captain Gringo had spotted tails before, so he didn't wave or offer any other hint he'd noticed. He moved his head casually back the way it had been pointed before he sat down and went on calmly smoking until a girl in a flouncy skirt came out to take his order. He asked for gin. He would have asked for the usual *cerveza* of the knock-around guy south of the border, but he'd changed into the wool suit and tie that went with his cover and since she could see he was a gringo, she might as well think he was a big spender who drank European.

The hairs on the back of his neck started marching up and down in quick step as he forced himself to sit there, his back exposed to whatever, as if he hadn't spotted them. They'd been wearing suits and gringo hats. But he hadn't gotten a good look at their features. So, okay, who the fuck were they? Police? That made no sense. If the new regime was aware he was in town, why would they be tailing him? Why not just pick him up, or try to?

His right hand started feeling its way toward the .38 under his jacket. He ordered it to stay put and muttered, "Easy, now. They had the drop on you before you spotted them. If they were out to nail you, you'd have been nailed by now. Let's just eat this apple a bite at a time."

The girl came back with his drink and waited expectantly. He smiled up at her and gave her a large bill. She

murmured, "Does El Señor have something smaller? It is early. I am not sure we can make change for this."

He said, "Keep the change. I was wondering if you could do me a favor."

The girl looked dubious and replied, "A favor, Señor? I am not ungrateful, but I am not a wicked woman either."

"Anyone can see that," he lied, adding, "The favor I ask is quite proper. But we may as well keep it our little secret. I want you to find me a mirror. The smallest one that you have around here. Just bring it out and place it face down on the table, like my change, and keep the change. Is that too complicated to remember?"

Apparently it was. She frowned down at him and stammered, "A mirror? El Señor wishes for a mirror, here at this table?"

"Yes, I'm very vain. Wait, it's a joke. I'm waiting here to meet a friend who really is sort of silly about his appearance and . . ."

"Ah, I understand." She nodded and walked away, muttering to herself about gringo *locos.* He thought it sounded pretty crazy, too, but it wasn't as funny to him.

A million years went by and he'd finished half the gin when the girl came back with a conspiratorial smile and a little square shard of mirror glass. He thanked her, and as soon as he was alone at the table again he stood the mirror on edge against his glass and adjusted it until he had a view of the path behind him. Considering all the trouble he'd just gone to, there wasn't much to see. The kid was still mowing the grass with the sheep back there. Nothing was moving on the tree-shaded walk.

Then he spotted a head sticking out of the same doorwas and as it ducked back in, he could almost hear someone say, "He's still sitting there."

Okay, they weren't going to move in just yet. What the hell *were* they planning? It would be siesta time in an hour or so. It was too cool up in Bogotá to really need the siesta, but old habits were hard to break and everyone who spoke Spanish around here was going to hole up until at least three in the afternoon anyway. There was no law saying the streets had to be cleared at high noon. The police would probably be home enjoying a siesta too and . . . That might be it. The guys back there obviously were not working for the ruling junta. They might find it more convenient to knock a guy off while

37

the ruling junta wasn't looking. A guy alone in an alley during *la siesta* could be as alone as if it were midnight. Maybe more so. Latins were night people. But along about, say, 1:00 P.M. the streets of most Latin towns were more deserted than New York's at 4:00 A.M.

Okay, he'd get back to Vanessa's before *la siesta* and have a good lay instead of a fight and . . . That was not a very good idea. If they weren't planning to jump him as soon as the streets cleared, they might be tailing him to see where he was holed up. They couldn't have tailed him from the friendly widow's nieghborhood. In the first place, he'd made sure he was alone before he ever checked in with Vanessa. In the second, he'd left her via a back alleyway and done some cutting and backtracking before leaving her *barrio*. He'd bought new clothes at a store in another *barrio* and left from there via a rear exit. So they'd spotted him within the past hour and . . . now what?

Captain Gringo decided to find out. He finished his drink and cupped the mirror in the same hand he was smoking with as he rose from the table and strolled on. He made sure he was in the shade of a pepper tree before he tried his rearview mirror. It worked. All he had to do was raise the cigar occasionally and make sure the sun didn't hit the glass. The two men tailing him passed the cantina he'd stopped at and kept going. Another break. They hadn't spoken to the waitress, so they couldn't know about the mirror cupped in his mitt.

They were pretty green at the game in other ways. He would have been amused at the way they skulked from doorway to doorway if he hadn't learned the hard way that the game was played for keeps down here.

He'd intended to circle the presidio all the way. But that was out for now. Even bush leaguers could guess he was casing the fortress if they watched him doing it! Figuring out who he was and what he was up to could be their game. It was possible they were local security agents, after all, if they'd simply spotted an obvious stranger near a military installation and had decided to keep an eye on him. So the first thing he had to do was to get the hell away from the presidio.

Captain Gringo turned a corner and did just that. He strolled off down a residential street, and two blocks later the bastards were still tailing him.

It took some doing. The street was narrow and the walk on one side was even more so. The walls of the courtyard houses came right to the walk in a solid line of polychrome stucco and there were no shade trees. The sun was almost straight up in a cloudless bowl of cobalt blue. He'd have been able to spot anything larger than a lizard five blocks behind him in that narrow, dusty slot. But they kept trying. They sort of slid along the stucco from one doorway to another, and the doorways were at least fifty feet apart.

Captain Gringo opened the front of his jacket to free his gun for action if need be. It was not yet officially siesta time, but they were getting there, and he passed few people on the side street. He found himself alone on a long bowling alley stretch and tensed for action as he checked with the mirror. But they weren't moving in for a kill. He couldn't see where they could expect a better opening. Following him wasn't going to get them anywhere, since he wasn't going anywhere until he knew what the sons of bitches wanted!

He came to another corner and casually strolled around it, as if he had any idea where he was. He found a door niche and stood inside it, drawing his .38 as he glanced up and down the brightly lit and absolutely deserted narrow street. He dropped the cigar and snuffed it out with his foot as he pocketed the mirror. Then he waited.

The Ice Ages came and went. Man discovered the wheel and built a mess of pyramids. Then, shortly after Columbus discovered America, Captain Gringo heard the grate of shoe leather on stone and stopped breathing. The '49ers were heading west when the two men came around the corner, saw him there, and froze in place with sick grins as Captain Gringo smiled at them above the muzzle of his unwavering .38 and said, "*Buenos días,* motherfuckers. What's this all about?"

Now, while it was two to one, prudent men seldom attempt to draw on a man who has the drop on them. So, while Captain Gringo was ready for it, he was surprised to see one of them go for the shoulder holster under his blue serge jacket. His astonishment at the other's dumb move didn't throw his aim off as he fired. The tall American's round took the would-be assassin under the heart and slammed him dead to the dusty pavement as Captain Gringo covered the other and snapped, "Freeze, you stupid bastard!"

The other mysterious shadow might have intended to.

His hands came up to shoulder height in a gesture of resignation. But then he jerked like a puppet on a string as another gunshot echoed in the narrow street! Then he fell face forward to land dead at Captain Gringo's feet with a blossom of red spreading between his shoulder blades!

Captain Gringo muttered, "What the hell?" as he realized he had most definitely not fired that second shot. Then a voice called from around the corner, "*Achtung*, Walker, do not fire! I am on your side!"

Captain Gringo took that under advisement as he watched and waited, gun leveled, until a small, dapper figure came around the corner, wearing a coffee brown suit, a derby to match, and of all things to be unexpected, walking a bicycle by its handlebars. If the little guy in the derby had been the one who'd just back-shot one of these other guys, he had put his weapon away.

Derby Hat said, "We must away from here be moving, *nicht wahr*? Come, on *mein* handlebars you will sit and I will us pedal to safety."

"Who are you and what in the hell is going on?"

"I will upon the way explain. Let us out of here get! This place in no time will with police be crawling. Are you coming or not?"

Captain Gringo saw the little guy had forked one leg over the bike frame and was scowling at him from above a ferocious Kaiser Wilhelm waxed mustache that matched the handlebars pretty well. The American holstered his still-hot gun and stepped over to hook his rump over the chrome bars, back to the other as he muttered. "This is sure silly."

The little guy in the derby grunted them forward and started to pedal furiously. Captain Gringo felt like an idiot perched like a bird on the handlebars, but he had to concede a point as, somewhere behind them, he heard a distant police whistle and the closer sound of some woman screaming. Not looking back, he asked, "Do you think we were spotted? It won't be hard to describe two grown men riding double on a kid's bike, you know."

His mysterious fellow gunman replied, puffing some with effort, "*Ist* not a child's machine. *Ist* a very good German racing bike and I have often been observed on it, *mein* exercise taking. I don't think anyone saw us. We are almost to *mein* place in any case. You will of course there have to spend the siesta. Even if the police were not for a murderer

looking, a big blond gringo on the streets during the siesta would attention attract, *nicht wahr?*"

"I can see we agree on some things. You knew my name. I have you down as a German agent. Correct me if I'm wrong."

The other said, "Of course. Have you forgotten us so soon? During the revolution you and your friend Gaston were of service to *Der Kaiser*."

"Bullshit. We worked with some Germans because they were in the same fix the rest of us white folks were back then. It was let's-kill-the-gringo time and, like it or not, you squareheads qualify as gringos down here."

"No matter. Whatever your motives, you and Gaston were of some service to German Intelligence and now I intend to repay you. Needless to say, you are now aware you were being followed back there, *nicht wahr?*"

"Yeah, I've been meaning to ask you why you shot that guy. I had him cold and he might have been able to speak up for himself if we'd let him."

"*Nein.* There was not time, once you had fired the first shot. I was, as you can guess, following them. But they had a backup a few blocks away. I thought it would save time if we simply liquidated the whole team and were on our way. I can tell you anything they could have."

"I wish you would. Who were they working for, General Reyes?"

"Worse. They were agents for El Araño, the head of Colombian Military Intelligence."

"I think I heard about him the last time I passed through. He's supposed to be pretty dangerous."

"*Ach,* you Anglo-Saxons and your love of understatement."

"Okay, so if the ruling junta had me spotted, why didn't they move in? They have Gaston in the presidio. So why pussyfoot around? And while we're on the subject of pussyfooting, where do you Germans fit in? And don't hand me any more shit about young Kaiser Bill's love of humanity. I've been following his career since he took over. A guy who'd fire Bismarck as a softy doesn't strike me as a natural do-gooder!"

"*Ach,* so much you talk and so hard I have to pedal. How much do you weigh? Don't answer. I don't want to know. I told you I would all explain when we got to my place

and we are almost there, if I don't die from huffing-puffing!"

Captain Gringo shrugged and shut up. He had no choice. Whatever this little guy's game was, it beat hanging around back there waiting to be arrested. The derby and silly mustache didn't fool him. He'd seen the way the little bastard aimed a gun. He was trying to be taken for a humorous, harmless little fop. Maybe even a sissy. Despite the mustache, the German agent seemed a bit effeminate as well as short. What the hell was that stink he had on? He was sweating in the hot sun, and when the wind was right it smelled like a whorehouse towel back there. A raunchy mixture of hot crotch and French perfume. Captain Gringo knew European men wore more in the way of aftershave lotion than Americans, but this little guy overdid it. The accent was plastered on pretty heavy, too. He'd crossed swords with German agents before. Most of them had spoken pretty good Spanish as well as English. The little guy threw in a lot of *nicht wahrs* and *achs*, like a music hall comic trying to sound like a German. Would a real German do that?

He almost lost his balance and spilled them as Derby Hat whipped around a corner he hadn't expected and coasted to a stop near a breezeway break in the walls. He told Captain Gringo, "Get off, we are here." So the tall American did so.

The German led the way in, wheeling the bike. The breezeway led into a small, cool, well-manicured patio with a pink stucco house wrapped around it. Captain Gringo asked, "Is this whole place yours?" and the German said, *"Ja,* privacy in my kind of business I need. I have a cleaning crew in twice a week, but we are here completely alone and, as you see, nobody knows you are here."

The weird little German leaned the bike against a tree and ushered him into a beamed drawing room that opened on the patio. A pair of big black vicious-looking Dobermans eyed him thoughtfully from where they sat, like cast-iron statues, near the cold hearth of a baronial fireplace. Captain Gringo said, "Hi, dogs," and the German said, "They will pay you no attention, since they see you are an invited guest."

"Yeah? What if I was an uninvited guest?"

"They would kill you, of course. They are not pets. They are trained German soldiers. But sit and allow me to intro-

duce *mein*self. *Ich heiss—ach,* I mean, I'm called Max. Last names, as you know, are unimportant in this business."

As he took a seat on the leather sofa, Captain Gringo grinned and asked, "Is Max your real first name?"

The German laughed, took off the derby, revealing close-cropped blond hair, and replied, "Of course not, but one must to some name answer. Sit quietly and let the hounds get used to you. I will us some refreshments fix."

Captain Gringo leaned back but eyed the two silent Dobermans warily as he lit a smoke and tried to relax. They were breathing, so you could tell they were real. He wondered how Max had trained them so well.

The German puttered at a sideboard for a few moments before coming to join him on the sofa with a silver tray holding glasses, a soda syphon, and a bottle of Glengorm. As he built his own highball he asked, "Scotch, Max? I thought you guys were sore at the British!"

Max shrugged and said, *"Der Kaiser'*s grandmother is Queen Victoria. We only wish our place in the sun beside the British. We do not reject the finer things of Anglo-Saxon culture."

"Yeah, I noticed the Spandau is a pretty good copy of the Anglo-American Maxim gun. But let's get to where *I* fit into the Kaiser's plans these days. What made you butt into my tussle with El Araño's agents back there, Max?"

Max built another, stronger drink as he replied, "Two reasons. As I said, you and your friend, Gaston Verrier, worked with German agents at a time the last government was planning to seize all foreign property in Colombia, including ours."

"That was a side issue and you know it. Get to the good part."

"Very well. Let us say that in our own march to empire we Germans have learned well the British game of fishing in troubled waters. Like everyone else, we have no idea what the new ruling junta's policies will be. As you know, Krupp-Siemans has important mining properties here in the Andes."

"Meaning you figure to keep the new government so busy with other problems that they won't have time to get around to nationalizing any German holdings, eh?"

"Exactly so. General Reyes, we think, is a man we can

43

deal with. He is neither for nor against outside interests developing the mines in this country. He is an old-fashioned Spanish don who only wants, as you Americans say, his cut?"

"So why are you trying to screw him up by helping outlaws like me?"

"*Ach,* so much you talk and so little you listen! General Reyes *ist* not holding your friend in the presidio. General Reyes leaves such matters to El Araño. And El Araño *ist* to us an unknown quality! Not even the officers of Colombia we have on our payroll can tell us what El Araño is planning next. It makes *Der Kaiser* nervous to have wild cards in his poker game with the British. *Ist* better they be dealt out of the game, *nicht wahr?*"

"Maybe. It seems to me you blew a chance just now to get in good with El Araño. You knew he had me under observation. Didn't it occur to you to help them in your capacity as an agent of a friendly government?"

Max shook his head and said, "We are not dealing with such a dried-and-cut officer in El Araño. Surely you see he was up to something more than the usual security precautions? Arresting you is not his game."

"What is his game then?"

"*Donner und blitzen,* I don't know! That is why I think we should keep you alive until we find out. I helped you throw them off your trail. Now they will have to look for you some more."

"Meanwhile, other German agents will be watching to see where they look?"

"Exactly. They must be expecting you to contact somebody. If we can find out who, we will have certain advantages. Fishing in troubled waters works best when one knows where to cast the bait, eh?"

Captain Gringo shrugged and took a swallow of his Scotch and soda before he said, "I had no intention of looking up any old rebels. The only guy up here I want to see is Gaston, and they already have him. I don't suppose you guys would be up to helping me bust him out of that presidio, huh?"

Max laughed and said, "That would be troubling the waters indeed. I will be frank. I have already *mein* neck stuck out for you more than my orders called for. But why not wait and see what we shall see? You are safe here. Even if they

found out you were here, I have diplomatic immunity. So make yourself at home. Are you comfortable?"

Captain Gringo shrugged and said, "Sure. Considering the alternatives."

"You don't find it too warm in here? Why don't you take off your coat? When in Rome, one must observe the customs, and it is siesta time, *ja?*"

The tall American shook his head and said, "I'm fine. It never gets really hot up here in the highlands and, as a matter of fact, it's pretty cool in here."

Max stood up and said, "Suit yourself. I am going to slip into something more comfortable. Maybe I will take a little nap. Would you care to join me?"

"Uh, I guess I could use forty winks, if you, uh, have a spare bedroom."

Max frowned and said, "Of course I don't have a spare bedroom. I am a spy, not an innkeeper. What's the matter, are you afraid I snore?"

"You snore all you like. I'm not really tired, anyway."

Max shrugged and sort of flounced out of the room. Captain Gringo poured another stiff one as he glanced over at the watchful dogs by the fireplace and muttered, "Oboy! Like the girl said in *Alice in Wonderland*, things get curiouser and curiouser, don't they?"

The dogs didn't answer, so Captain Gringo was left to decide on his own how he'd deal with little Max if the guy turned out to be a fairy. He knew the German was a killer. He knew it would be suicide to do any flouncing out on his own right now. Between them, they'd just put two Colombian agents on the ground. The streets would be crawling with avenging patrols. It wouldn't be safe to go out on the streets again, if then, until the siesta was over and, better yet, the sun went down.

Max came back in, walking barefoot in a wraparound fancy cloth robe. It wasn't a particularly feminine robe, but Max had it fastened from the right, like a girl's. Max rejoined him on the sofa, tucking his bare shins and feet up under the robe to say, "There now, that's better."

Captain Gringo didn't answer as Max built another heroic drink. His old Legion buddy, Gaston, had admitted to having been *"practique"* about sex a few times at lonely outposts. Captain Gringo had just never been able to get excited about boys.

He was a live-and-let-live guy and too sure of his own manhood to have to go around beating pansies up to prove he didn't have a secret yen for them. But Max was making him nervous as hell. It was one thing to gently tell a queer you met in a bar that you weren't the kind of lad he was looking for. But Max was backed up with a gun and two killer dogs and, worse yet, he couldn't afford to offend the little bastard.

He tried to steer the conversation back to El Araño and the dark deeds of derring-do they'd been talking about. But Max was staring owlishly at him and didn't seem interested. Captain Gringo said something about Gaston and Max said, "Screw Gaston. And, by the way, have you, ever?"

"Hey, Gaston's a guy, Max!"

"So you keep telling me. But I must say you're going to an awful lot of trouble for a platonic relationship." Then Max giggled and added, "Of course, Plato also favored other kinds of friendships, *nicht wahr?* We all know how the Greek hoplites solved their sexual problems on the march through enemy territory. You can tell me. I, too, am an old soldier."

Captain Gringo managed not to grimace as he met the German's gaze and said flatly, "I'd rather pull my pud. I guess I'm just an old-fashioned boy."

Max was staring wistfully down in the general direction of the big Yank's lap and there were little beads of sweat above the silly mustache. Max was younger-looking than he'd first taken him for, or maybe he was one of those little guys with a glandular problem. He'd have been a nice-looking little guy without the Kaiser Bill and Heidelberg haircut. He wasn't too short to get a girl. But Captain Gringo didn't think this was the time to bring that up.

Max finished the first drink and started on another. Captain Gringo resisted an impulse to tell him he was putting it away pretty well, too. The German seemed to be trying to get up his courage with booze. But courage to do what? He'd just shot a man in cold blood, cold sober.

Max said, "I am making you uneasy, *ja?*" and the American lied when he replied, "No, why should I be nervous? Are you packing a gun inside that bathrobe, old buddy?"

Max laughed and the voice got even higher as the German said, "Maybe I will let you see what I have under my

robe. If we are to work together it might be better to get the sexual tension out of the way, here and now. Why don't you take off your clothes, Dick? I am really dying to make love to you!"

Captain Gringo took a sip of his own drink and said, "Gee, I wish you wouldn't, Max. Uh, I don't know how to put this delicately, but ..."

"Do you find me so unattractive? I have made love to men better-looking than you, you know!"

"I'm sure you have," he soothed. "I'm sure I'm passing up a great opportunity, Max. But you see, I'm sort of, well, let's call it shy."

Max swallowed some more Scotch, without the soda, and said, "I, too, was shy about such matters when I first went to work for *Der Kaiser*. But a secret agent has enough worries. We *Ubermenschen* do not live by the mundane rules of bourgeois society. We are free to live and love as we please, or as we must. Shall I confess something to you, Dick? The first man who had me was a Turkish officer who had me as a prisoner in his power. I did not like him. I hated him. He was old and bald and greasy fat. But to save myself, I was forced to give in to his lusts. And, in the end, shall I tell you something even stranger, in the end I began to enjoy it!"

"Yeah, I've heard some guys enjoy it in the end. But I'll pass for now."

Max giggled and said, *"Ach,* such a naughty you are, *mein* innocent with the knowing eyes. Next you will tell me you have never in the end of any *mädchen* put it, *ja?"*

"If a *mädchen* means a girl, I'll plead no-contest. But let's get off the subject, Max."

"Why, am I an erection giving you? But you are right. It *ist* to talk about it without doing it a silly thing. So why don't we just do it, and then we will more comfortable with each other be, and can make serious plans about serious matters, *ja?"*

"Thanks, but no thanks. I'm just not interested, Max. I'd like to help you out, as a friend, but I couldn't get it up for you with a block and tackle. I've had this conversation before and I've heard all your arguments. The idea just doesn't interest me. You're wasting your time."

Max rose a trifle unsteadily and said, "You are just being shy. We both know very well that if I presented my body to you, you would not be able to resist your natural desires!"

"Hey, Max, I don't even *try* to resist my *natural* desires, but . . ."

And then he muttered, "Aw, shit," as Max peeled off the robe, moved over to the sofa again, and got on hands and knees to present a round pink rump to him expectantly.

Captain Gringo couldn't think of a single thing to say as he stared blankly at the pink little asshole winking at him at point-blank range. Then he put his glass down, stood up, and unbuttoned his fly as Max giggled like a schoolgirl, watching him over one bare shoulder.

Captain Gringo got one knee on the sofa, positioned his sudden erection between the German agent's quivering buttocks, and thrust home as Max gasped, "Oh, so much of you there *ist!*"

As Captain Gringo started screwing and undressing at the same time in his upright dog-style position, he asked, "Max, do you mind if I ask you something?"

"Anything, *Liebling*. Just don't stop."

"Well, I was wondering why the hell you wear that false mustache when you're trying to seduce a guy. It would have saved us a hell of a lot of time if I'd known all along that you were a woman!"

Max laughed and answered, *"Mein Gott,* I forgot I had it on! You mean you thought . . . *Ach, du Lieber!* No wonder you were talking about putting it in *mein* rear. But, *Gott* be thanked, I see you found the right place after all!"

Captain Gringo got rid of the last of his upper clothing as he said, "Yeah, and it's nice as hell. Let's turn you over and do this right."

So Max rolled over on her back to allow him to mount her properly, with his pants down around his booted ankles, but what the hell, that could wait. She was mannishly enough built to pass for a small, dapper male on the street, but female enough, from the chin down, for anyone on a sofa. As he settled into the saddle of her pale pink thighs and felt her little cupcake breasts against him, he started to kiss her, but said, "For God's sake, can't we take off that fucking mustache?"

She moaned with desire and said, "Later, it is on me stuck with spirit gum and I must with alcohol remove it. Kiss me, Dick, I'm almost there!"

He was, too, so he kissed her as they both climaxed in each other's arms. She kissed as good as she screwed, but it

sure felt stupid with that waxed mustache above her moist Frenching lips!

He laughed down at her as they came up for air. Her eyes glowed with still unslaked desire as she asked uncertainly, "What's wrong, *mein* tiger? Why have you stopped? Why are you so funny looking at me?"

He said, "I haven't stopped. Like John Paul Jones said, I've just begun to fuck. But I'm not the one that's funny-looking. It's just hit me that I don't ever have to worry about turning swishy. I find it hard enough to kiss somebody wearing a mustache even when it's a pretty girl!"

Max moved her pelvis teasingly as she looked relieved and said, "*Ach, mein* poor innocent, before I have finished with you I shall teach you all the forbidden pleasures of bizarre sex. Let me arouse you again with my lips. Let me up, I wish to swallow you like a pythoness!"

He said, "Well, all right, but goddamnit, you're going to have to peel off that mustache!"

Meanwhile, over at the presidio, an aide came in to Colonel Maldonado's office wearing a somber expression. He said, "They just brought Gomez and Robles from the Calle de Mariposas, my Colonel. They had both been shot at close range. Gomez from the front and Robles from the back. The bodies are over in the infirmary, if you wish for to see them."

El Araño looked disgusted and asked, "Why would I wish to see them? I knew what they looked like before they behaved so stupidly. Notify their families and make the usual arrangements for a military funeral. One may suppose even an idiot deserves a military funeral, eh?"

The aide nodded but said, "Forgive me, my Colonel, I assumed you would wish for to examine the bodies for clues."

"Clues? Why do we need clues? I know who killed them. The police informant working as a waitress just a few yards from our gate has already made her report. The morons were following Captain Gringo, against my orders."

"The waitress identified the killer, my Colonel?"

"Bah, the *chica* has no idea what happened. She only says a tall gringo bought a mirror from her. Do I have to draw you a picture, too?"

The aide didn't answer. El Araño sighed and said, "Look, the *Americano* was over there, scouting this installa-

49

tion, when he stopped at the cantina. He got the mirror from the girl to keep an eye on his rearview. It's an old trick, but it usually works."

"Ahah! And naturally, when the gringo left, the girl saw Gomez and Robles following him and . . ."

"Will you just shut up and listen, Lieutenant? The waitress did not notice anyone following the gringo. She wasn't supposed to notice anyone on his tail. She just reported an odd incident and the rest falls into place as soon as one thinks about it. The two security men must have spotted Captain Gringo and, unaware they were to completely ignore him, trailed him to find out what he was up to. The rest you know. The *Americano* spotted them and killed them, as I'd assumed he would."

El Araño turned and stabbed his map viciously with a blue pin before he added, "So, we know he was here long enough to kill two incompetents. And now . . . Now we don't know where the big bastard is!"

The aide cleared his throat with a smug expression and said, "Forgive me, my Colonel, but they did not leave the scene completely unobserved."

"They? What is this they? Do you mean Captain Gringo was not alone?"

It felt so good to be one-up on El Araño that the aide almost hugged himself as he explained. "An elderly woman from the Calle de Mariposas was seated at her window grill when they went by. I don't know why old women sit at window grills all day, but you know how they are and . . ."

"I had a grandmother, goddamn your eyes, get to the point!"

"She saw two men on a bicycle."

"I beg your pardon?"

"It is true, my Colonel. She thought it most curious, too. That is why she came forward, even though she did not see the killing. She says she heard distant shots at a time the street was deserted. She watched. It must be boring to stare out at nothing during *la siesta*. But this time she was not disappointed in her vigil. Two grown men tore past her, riding double on a bicycle. She says a very large man was perched on the handlebars while a very small man pedaled. They were both wearing suits and had Nordic features. When she said the little one was wearing a derby, one of my men says he thinks he knows who it is. There's this little runt from

the German legation, a military attaché or something and . . ."

But Maldonado had turned his back and was sticking another pin in his map. The aide looked hopeful and asked, "Ah, you know him, my Colonel?"

El Araño chuckled and said, "Yes, I have been keeping an eye on her for some time."

"*Her*, my Colonel? The description I was about to finish includes a wax mustache."

Maldonado nodded and said, "I know. It makes her look like a little fairy. But that is not *our* problem. Make a note of this latest location on Captain Gringo, it's the house of the British agent. I don't want any of our men within two blocks of it."

The aide took out his notebook and took the liberty of stepping around his superior's desk to write down the street intersection nearest the latest pin as he muttered, "Forgive me, my Colonel, but someone is mistaken. My people say this little, ah, whatever in the derby is working out of the *German* legation."

Maldonado said, "She is. The British planted her there some time ago. You know how the Queen and the Kaiser have been fighting over the last scraps on the map lately. One of these days they're going to have a lovely war. But that is not Colombia's problem. We'll let *El Tío Sam* do any fighting for this hemisphere, since he thinks he owns it in any case."

Maldonado turned back from his map with a pleased look as he added, "You did well, Lieutenant. I confess there are advantages to *nepotismo*. Your father had a brain when we served together. It is nice to see the condition seems to run in your family."

The aide smiled back uncertainly. The same father who'd gotten him the job had warned him about El Araño's sardonic sense of humor. He said, "My Colonel is too kind. I really have no idea what on earth is going on! First you tell me a little German on a bike is a woman, and then you tell me she is a British spy. Now she and Captain Gringo are . . . what?"

"Probably screwing each other to death," said Maldonado. "The woman is a notorious sex maniac in addition to her other talents. She's almost as dangerous as the *Americano*. So make sure nobody disturbs them in their love nest."

51

The aide knew better than to ask El Araño directly what in the hell he was up to. But he couldn't help asking, "Does my Colonel think British Intelligence is working with Captain Gringo in this . . . whatever?"

Maldonado shook his head and replied, "No. The girl who calls herself Max knows that he pulled some chestnuts out of the fire for the Kaiser during our recent, ah, reorganization of the government. Her mission is probably to find out why he came back to Bogotá and if the Germans are involved in it."

"Are the Germans involved in whatever he is up to, my Colonel?"

"Of course not. He thinks he's here to rescue his comrade Verrier. The German government couldn't care less. They have more serious matters to worry about."

"I know about the vital minerals they've been mining at a good profit to us, my Colonel. But why should British Intelligence concern itself in the affairs of those two soldiers of fortune?"

Maldonado said, "What indeed, once La Señorita Max establishes that Germany is not involved? As I see her plan, Max will offer German help to Captain Gringo and go along with him until it's clear that her superiors have nothing to worry about and then . . ."

Maldonado's eyes narrowed thoughtfully. Then he smiled thinly and said, "It pays to chat with junior officers after all. But we'd better get back to work. Carry on, Lieutenant. I fear I have some serious planning to do."

The aide left and El Araño sat down at his desk. He picked up a pencil and began to doodle as he considered the ramifications of this latest development in an already complicated plan. Then he picked up the desk phone and called up a field agent on the other side of town.

He said, "*Número Cinco,* we have a problem. Our pawn is in danger." He explained the situation and added, "That British nymphomaniac has a short attention span as well as a most unprofessional itchy trigger finger. We have to get him out of there, *muy pronto!*"

The field agent replied, "I know the house and the woman's evil reputation, my Colonel. But why would British Intelligence wish for to harm him once they find out he is not of any interest to them?"

Maldonado said, "British Intelligence wouldn't hurt him.

Max will kill him when she's through with him. I don't know if she's worried about her reputation in England or just vicious, but she's done it before. She uses men like toilet paper. We've got to get him out of there before she flushes him down the drain."

5

The siesta ended, as all good things must, so Captain Gringo rolled off Max and sat up when he heard the sound of an ox-drawn cart going by outside. Max smiled wistfully up at him, her hands clasped behind her short blond hair, and asked, "Are you already tired of me, *mein* tiger?"

He tweaked a nipple playfully as he smiled down at her and said, "No. You're a lot prettier without the mustache and I was just getting my second wind. But let's save some for later. I've really got to find out where they have Gaston locked up."

"*Ist* still light outside. Wait until dark. Lie down and let me get on top this time."

He shook his head and got to his feet, muttering, "I used to have some clothes around here someplace. I've been thinking about the timing. They know we know they've found the bodies and so forth. They'll expect me to come pussyfooting around after dark. That's why I feel it's safer now, with the streets crowded. Everyone is out and the shops will be open. The best time for me to circle the presidio again will be during the *paseo* time, just before and after sundown. I'll look like just another stud trying to pick up a *muchacha* and . . ."

Then Max was up on her feet, too, and plastered against him in the nude as she warned, "You pick up any *muchachas* and I will your heart cut out!"

He held her against his own naked flesh, and they sure fit nicely, considering how short she stood in her bare feet.

He slid his hands down to cup her little buttocks as he laughed and said, "I wouldn't be able to do much for another

woman if I found one right now. Damn, you're pretty without that dumb mustache!"

She stood on her tiptoes and teased with her blond pubic hair as she said, "I wish to come with you."

He said, "It's too dangerous. For one thing, two, uh, guys draw twice as much attention as one. For another thing, a lot of people know you here in Bogotá. But, hopefully, I'm mostly a strange face."

She slid her hand down between them and purred, *"Ach,* I didn't mean I wanted to come with you to the *paseo.* I meant I wanted to come with you here!"

He started to protest, but what the hell, it was early yet, and she was sliding his semi-erection between her wet vaginal lips in a hell of an interesting way. He took a step back toward the sofa, but Max resisted, spreading her thighs a bit as she braced her feet on the rug. She said, "Stay here. Do it here. We have not done it standing up, yet."

He laughed and said, "Okay, but hadn't we better find a wall to lean you against?"

"Nein. That would be cheating."

He laughed again and braced his own legs apart to lower his center of gravity as she tried to work it in for him, standing tiptoe with her own knees between his now. He shook his head and said, "Honey, it won't work. One of us is too short. Too tight, too. There's just no way I can get inside you with your legs together like that."

She said, "Hold on *mein* fanny good," as she wrapped her free arm around his neck and suddenly hopped up to fork a thigh around his waist from either side, guiding his shaft with the other hand. He staggered a step, recovered his balance, and marveled, "Kee-rist!" as Max slid on like a soft, tight boot filled with whipped cream.

He had a hell of a time staying on his feet as Max started bouncing with enthusiasm. He knew that if he let her rollicking rump slip from his grasp it would ruin them both. It was fun for the first few moments, but as he felt his own orgasm threatening, he tottered over to a big overstuffed chair to brace her tail bone against the leather back. It gave him the leverage to lean into her with his own harder thrusts and Max sobbed, *"Ach, jah,* even better!"

Then she let go without warning and fell backward to hang head down with her head and shoulders on the seat

cushion and her spine hooked over the chair back, presenting him with an astounding view as well as a fantastic angle of attack. He had to stand on his own toes and grab the chair back on either side of her pale hips to keep it in and, even so, it was bent the wrong way as he fired off his cannon.

He knew she was almost there and that he couldn't keep it in that way. So he grabbed one of her thighs and rolled her hips, still up on the chair back, until she was face down, laughing, with her breasts on the seat cushion and her sassy rump aimed at the ceiling, legs hanging down on either side of his thighs. She gasped, "*Ach,* such ingenuity, *und* even deeper!" and then she moaned and started chewing the edge of the leather seat as he shoved her over the peak with his semi-sated but polite tool.

By the time she came, he was naturally aroused again, but his legs were killing him. He grabbed her by either hip bone and, still inside her, lifted her off the chair and lowered her to the rug, face down, to finish with some push-ups. She liked it that way, too. In fact, he couldn't think of a position she didn't like it in, and some they'd tried that afternoon had been pretty strange. She didn't resist when he rolled her on her back to finish more romantically, albeit on the hard floor. He asked if he was hurting her as his heavy weight slammed down against her upthrust pubic bones. The floor under her tail bone offered no cushioning to them as they slammed each other passionately. She said she loved it. So he let himself go until, again, all good things had to come to an end.

The next time he tried to put his clothes on, Max let him. Even she had had enough, for now. But she promised, or warned him, that she expected more of the same as soon as he came back.

As he sat on the sofa, getting his breath back and checking the chambers of his .38, Max cuddled naked beside him and asked how he thought he'd ever get inside the presidio, even if he found out where they were holding his friend Gaston.

He grimaced and said, "That's going to be a bitch, all right. I was wondering if somebody from your legation has a friendly contact with the French Consulate here in Bogotá."

Max wrinkled her nose and said, "*Ach,* since the French *und* British ganged up on *Der Kaiser* over Suez, we stiffly speak to one another at formal dinners only. But why do you

want the French in this, *mein Lieber?* What could they do about your friend Gaston?"

"Gaston's wanted by a dozen governments. If any banana republic gets him, he's dead. But the French may have a seniority situation, since he started his business in these parts by deserting the Legion in Mexico when Juarez started winning. If we could get an understanding Frenchman to put in a claim for him, get him out of the effing presidio . . ."

Max shrugged and said, "You have nothing to offer France, do you?"

"No. I was hoping you wouldn't ask that. But look, the French wouldn't just shoot Gaston. They'd want to take him alive to Devil's Island, and a lot of things can happen between here and Devil's Island. Do you think you could work something out with the French agents you know in town?"

Max looked dubious and then she said, "Any French secret agents who know me at all know me as a German agent. They would suspect a crossed double, *nicht wahr?* But I am not the only friend you have in German Intelligence, Dick. Who was that officer who helped you during the revolution? The one who got you the guns and ammunition in exchange for certain favors to that German mining company?"

Captain Gringo started to answer. Then he said, "Gee, it's right on the tip of my tongue, but I forget the bastard's name. It was one of those unpronounceable Von things."

"Von Dreihausen, Von Stettin, Von Rodenau?"

"Could have been any of 'em. It'll come back to me in a while. I've got too much on my mind to remember dumb names. I'd rather work through you, anyhow. I don't think the officer over there that I dealt with liked me very much. It was one of those revolutions making strange bedfellows things."

Then he kissed her and added, "Speaking of strange bedfellows, leave a light in the window for me, doll. I've got to go, but when I come back I'm going to show you a couple of positions *I* just remembered."

He got to his feet and the naked girl walked to the door with him. He kissed her again and she giggled when he fingered her. But as he turned away, Max raised the little whore pistol she'd been holding palmed since she'd slipped it out of its hiding place while he dressed. As the tall American

crossed the patio, Max raised the muzzle and trained the sights on his broad back.

Then she lowered it with a puzzled frown. She was almost sure she could safely report that the notorious Captain Gringo was simply a gun thug operating on his own and that none of the major powers was involved in whatever he was up to. But what on earth *was* he up to? He *said* he was only here to rescue his friend. But Max was good, too. She'd spotted it when he'd gone suddenly vague about his German contacts here in Bogotá. Was it possible he suspected her of not being a true German? Her superior, Greystoke of British Intelligence, had often warned her about laying on too thick an accent. He'd warned her about Captain Gringo, too. The big American had worked with and against Great Britain in the past and Greystoke respected him as more than a drifting soldier of fortune.

As her afternoon lover vanished from sight, Max smiled to herself and murmured, "He does have a lovely cock, and it's my duty to the Queen to get all I can out of him before he's eliminated from the Great Game. We'll just wait and see. He has to come back, and it's not like he'll ever leave again, alive."

6

Captain Gringo went to a barbershop on a busy street near the presidio. He didn't need a haircut that badly, but he asked for a trim. A guy could hear a lot in a neighborhood barbershop. He could hold his gun cocked and ready in his lap under the barber cloth, too, as he watched the doorway in the mirror.

There were plenty of Europeans in the capital in the first place and a lot of the natives were pure Castilian in the second, so he didn't get the usual double-take from the Colombians lounging in the shop. His own Spanish was pretty good by now. So, while he was ready to tell them he was a Swede if anyone commented on his accent, nobody did.

The barber was pretty good and the others seemed relaxed and friendly as they gossiped back and forth. Nobody said anything about dead guys on the pavement a few blocks away. So he and Max had been right. The men they'd shot had been secret agents. That El Araño guy he kept hearing about was pretty good. No obvious dragnet. No noisy house-to-house rough stuff. Just bag the stiffs and lay low for a break, eh?

That meant there'd be other plainclothesmen strolling the *paseo* in a little while, pretending to ogle the girls as they kept an eye peeled for anything unusual. So how the fuck was he going to seem usual? His biggest problem since he'd become a soldier of fortune in the Bananalands was that he didn't look usual to a Latin American. He'd have never become Captain Gringo if some *mestizo* wasn't always coming up to him and saying something dumb like, "Hey, Gringo, why are you looking at my sister?"

59

The guys in the shop were talking about the *paseo*. The barber must have had him down as a foreigner after all, because he asked him if he knew the custom. Captain Gringo nodded and said he did. He didn't elaborate. He thought himself that *El Paseo* was an idea they could use in the States. It sure beat the Victorian games people played back home.

In almost every Hispanic community the *paseo* was run along the same lines. Along about sundown, all the young guys and gals put on their best duds and told their mammas they were going for a stroll. Then the guys circled the square one way and the gals circled the other way, so that they kept sort of bumping into one another, face to face. A guy got to size a dame up a few times as they circled in opposite directions. After you met the same pair of eyes a couple of times it seemed only natural to smile on the next passing and, what the hell, after you'd smiled at a gal a few times it seemed only natural to say hello and so forth until you both noticed it was getting sort of late and wouldn't it be a good idea if you walked her home, and, as long as you're walking her home, why not stop for a drink along the way, and if you weren't going to make it that way you weren't going to make it at all.

The nicest part about *El Paseo* was its delicacy. Most of the promenaders struck out, but even homely people got to have the fun of flirting and nobody was made to feel the fool. The ugly girl was simply not approached, although she could imagine that nice boy she'd smiled at was just shy. The guy who got turned down politely could tell himself she was a nervous virgin, too. It sure beat sidling up to an American girl on a streetcar and getting thrown off as a masher.

But Captain Gringo knew he couldn't walk the *paseo* that evening. It was too risky. Even if he wasn't spotted by the law, he'd gotten into more than one scuffle with a jealous punk that way in the past. A guy didn't have to wink at a pretty girl to draw the attention of a jealous would-be lover if she decided to wink at him and, for some reason, dames winked at Captain Gringo a lot.

He left the barbershop and fell in behind a quartet of men headed in the direction he was going, trying to blend in with them. He stopped on the corner when he came to the strip around the presidio. The *paseo* had sort of started. A few eager kids were already promenading, but it was early yet. He lit a cigar to give himself an excuse for standing there

as he glanced around. He spotted a sign down the way. It was an upstairs Chinese restaurant. Better yet, they had a balcony overlooking the street. He grinned and decided he wanted some pork lo mein.

He climbed the steps to find the place just opening for the evening. He told the pretty little Chinese waitress that he'd like to eat out on the balcony. She led him to a table and took his order. He ordered a pot of tea and a lot of food. He wasn't really that hungry, but he meant to take his time eating and sipping as he watched from his vantage point. He could see he wasn't very noticeable up here under the awning to anyone passing below. But he had a bird's-eye view of everything down there.

As he waited in the gloaming light he stared over at the forbidding walls of the presidio. As he'd hoped, he could now see the red roof tiles of the buildings inside.

Big deal. The barracks and so forth were built around a central open square. It looked sort of like a German *Kaserne* layout. He knew the Germans had a lot of influence in this part of South America. Some Fritz engineer might have helped them lay the joint out once. There was no way to tell which of those buildings Gaston was in. They'd probably have him in the guardhouse. Okay, so which was the guardhouse? Probably near the main gate. That was where you'd find the provost marshal on most posts.

The girl brought his tea. He poured himself a cup as he muttered, "Wait, remember Fort Mason in Frisco? The fucking provost marshal's office was way the hell *away* from the main gate!"

He sipped the tea with a frown. Guessing at it from here was no good. He had to know. And even after he knew, how in the hell was he going to get in, and, if he did get in, how the hell was he going to get out with Gaston? They wouldn't have the little Frenchman in a guest room. If they hadn't locked him up in something solid as hell, Gaston would have gotten out by now. The ex-legionaire was a born escape artist.

The sky was going purple over the mountains to the east now and the walk below was filling up. The always-lit streetlamps glowed kindly on the bare shoulders of the *señoritas* and at this altitude the shoulders would have been covered if the *señoritas* hadn't wanted them to be seen. Some of the local talent wasn't bad, either. More blondes and redheads

than usual, up here in the white Spanish country. But he reminded himself that wasn't why he'd come here. He had *two* women already expecting him home early. One of them was going to be disappointed as hell.

That was something to think about, so he did so as he nibbled at the noodles the waitress placed before him in a big steaming pile. He knew he'd be safe at Vanessa's hotel, and, while she wasn't as young as Max, she was as good, and less demanding, in bed. On the other hand, old Vanessa couldn't do anything about Gaston. She didn't even know about Gaston.

Max was waiting for him, too, and Max had connections here in town. So it seemed obvious enough where he should hole up for the night. Or did it? There was something funny about Max, and it wasn't just her mustache. The accent didn't ring true. And why the hell had a German agent tried to pump him about the officers at her German headquarters? Wouldn't she have known about the deal he'd made with the German military attaché just a few weeks back?

He shrugged it off and decided, "What the hell, may as well play along with her for now. She's good in a firefight, which is more *très* than poor old Vanessa can say."

As he ate, watching the crowd below, Captain Gringo became aware of another customer inside. The damned waitress was leading him out on the damned balcony. Captain Gringo moved his chair slightly to get his back more to the doorway as the Chinese girl seated the other early diner. As she stepped inside, Gaston Verrier said, "Well, well, great minds do run in the same channels, my old and rare!"

Captain Gringo swiveled, astonished, and as he met the sardonic smile of the dapper little older man seated at the other table he gasped, "Gastón, you're supposed to be over there, locked up behind those fucking walls!"

Gaston rose and moved his own chair over to join his younger friend as he said, *"Mais non, au contraire,* it is you they told me the new junta had locked up over there! I see we both had the same idea about watching for a main chance from this *très* droll observation post, *hein?"*

Captain Gringo felt a slight lump in his throat as he said, "Wait a minute, you got away clean after all, and then you came back here to stick your neck out for me?"

Gaston shrugged and said, *"Oui,* I must be getting senile. I would not have expected you to take such a chance for me.

But this is most odd, don't you agree? I assume you got a message from me, telling you I had been captured and to save yourself, *hein?*"

"Just about. How did you know that?"

"That was the kind of message I received as I was about to board a tramp in Barranquilla. I got those Americans safely out, as we planned, and I was going to rejoin you in Buenaventura when some mysterious stranger dropped a note over my transom. *Très* intriguing, *non?* As you Americans say, what *le* fuck is going on?"

The waitress came with Gaston's tea, saw he'd moved over to the other table, and placed it before him sans comment. As she moved away, the little Frenchman eyed her rear view with approval and observed, *"Très formidable.* It is not true what they say about Chinese women, by the way."

Captain Gringo said, "Forget her ass. I think we'd better haul our own asses out of here, on the double."

"But why? I have not eaten yet."

"Screw eating. Don't you see we've been set up? We both got out one jump ahead of the new takeover. So what did the bastards do? They sent us both the same message to lure us back up here where they could get their hands on us!"

Gaston said, "I insist on a full stomach before I proceed with this nonsense. I don't know why or who, but the game is more subtle than that. Consider, my old and rare. To confuse us with false messages, somebody had to know where we both were, true?"

"Sure. But the messages must have been meant to lure us into a trap."

"Mais non, we were already on Colombian soil when they contacted us. They could have arrested you in Buenaventura and me in Barranquilla if that was their game."

"I can see that. So, what's the game?"

"I have no idea. Let's eat. I think better on a full stomach."

Meanwhile, as the two bewildered adventurers had dinner near the presidio, El Araño and a pair of picked men had left the presidio to visit Max. As they moved in, Colonel Maldonado asked one of his agents, "Are you sure about those dogs?"

The agent grinned and replied, "Yes, my Colonel. As I told you, the blond slut is overconfident as to her security. She leaves her door unlocked, trusting to the viciousness of

63

her pets and, in truth, no child in the neighborhood will go near her gate. She forgot the dogs knew her cleaning people, and I was accepted, along with Tico, here, when I simply entered with the peons. The rest was simple. We thought to bring along some liver scraps. After we had entered a few times to search her quarters as you ordered, Tico had one of them sitting up to beg. They have become most tame, and since you are with us . . ."

Maldonado said, "I understand, you have done well. Isn't it odd how one advantage often leads to another? I never thought, when I began a routine security operation against a double agent, how handy it might come in to be able to enter her house at will. But be careful, *muchachos*. The dogs may be friendly. The woman is armed and dangerous."

The three men came to the spy's entryway and the agent called Tico hissed softly. One of the big Dobermans came to the patio entrance, wagging its short tail. Tico fed it some raw liver and patted its muzzle, whispering, "This one's the least friendly of the pair. The other must be sleeping."

Colonel Maldonado drew his service revolver and said, "Let's move in. You boys keep the dogs off me and I'll cover you."

They moved quietly across the patio, with the dog following, wagging its tail. Maldonado tried the first door he came to. It was unlocked. He opened it and stepped into the living room. He sniffed and muttered, "Jesus, it smells like somebody's been fucking in here. Which way's the bedroom?"

One of the agents pointed with his chin. El Araño led the way. He knew the big American had been spotted leaving, so when he heard the sounds of a woman in orgasm on the other side of the door panels he frowned, puzzled. Who the hell was the nymphomaniac entertaining now? Nobody else had come in since he'd put the house under observation. Whoever the poor bastard was, he was done for. There was no other way.

Maldonado tried the knob with his free hand. It turned. He opened the door a crack and froze, slack-jawed.

The pale blond Max lay on her back in the middle of a fourposter, arms and legs wrapped around the big jet-black dog that was rutting with her, stretched out atop her like a man as it slobbered, its muzzle against her open gasping mouth. That dog's tail was wagging, too. He had a lot to be

happy about. Maldonado gagged at the obscene spectacle as he raised the gun in his hand. The woman's eyes were closed as she rolled her cropped head from side to side, crooning endearments to the animal in her arms as it humped excitedly. But, even in the throes of its lust, the big Doberman sensed the intrusion and growled, trying to withdraw from his mistress. Max held on tightly and pleaded, "No, Beasty-Weasty, Mommy isn't through! Make Mommy come like a good doggy!"

And then Maldonado retched and opened fire from the doorway.

The Doberman yipped and leaped off as a bullet slammed into its ribs. Max sat up and gasped, "Oh!" as a bullet smashed into her little left breast and slammed her back against the rumpled linens. Maldonado put two more bullets into her twitching naked flesh and then as the dog came around the bed, drooling blood and snarling at him, he blew its head half off and dropped it at the foot of the bed, its big red penis still engorged.

He heard a shot behind him and whirled to see Tico had shot the other dog, whose friendliness to strangers had certain limits. The other agent looked into the bedroom and gasped, "Madre de Dios! You said she was crazy, my Colonel!"

El Araño shuddered and said, "Vámanos, muchachos. It does not matter what she was now. Let's get out of here before that big Americano comes back."

As they scurried out, Maldonado recovered his poise, and when he saw they had gotten in and out unobserved, save for the army lookout on the roof across the street, he felt pleased enough with himself to chuckle and muse aloud, "I wonder what Captain Gringo would have done had he caught her flagrante delicto with such an unusual rival."

7

Captain Gringo stopped Gaston in front of the blonde's entryway and said, "You'd better wait here. She's got a couple of oversized mutts she'd better introduce you to herself."

Gaston shrugged as he looked up at the stars and said, "I am in no hurry. I am not sure I ought to be here. Germans have made me *très* nervous since 1870. They owe me a war with better odds on the French side."

Captain Gringo eased inside, watching out for the dogs. It was just light enough to see by in the patio, and neither Doberman seemed to be out to chew his leg off, so he walked over to the house. The living room door was open. The room inside was dark. He started to strike a light, but then he saw the light from the hallway beyond and called out, "Hey, Max?" as he walked toward it.

He stopped as he spotted the Doberman dead in the hallway. He drew his gun and stepped over it. The light was coming from a room he'd never been in. He stepped over to the doorway and looked in. Then he sobbed, "Oh, no!"

Max lay dead across the bed. He didn't have to feel her pulse. Nobody had ever looked so dead. He glanced down at the dead dog near the foot of her bed and muttered, "You tried, old boy. They caught all three of you napping, huh?"

Then he turned and hurried outside. He grabbed Gaston on the fly and as they headed down the street the Frenchman protested, "Where are we going in such a hurry, you long-legged gorilla of mine?"

The American said, "They got Max. I found her riddled

66

like a sieve. If we don't go somewhere, *muy pronto*, they'll get us!"

Gaston started walking faster, but after they'd whipped around a couple of corners he glanced back and said, "Wait, let us not be the chickens with our heads cut off. Before we run ourselves into the ground, would it not be better to consider whether anyone is chasing us?"

"For Chrissake, Gaston, I told you the girl was a secret agent who helped me. Isn't it obvious what happened?"

"Mais non, it is *très* weird! If the executioners were after you, why did they leave after shooting the wrong person?"

Captain Gringo started to tell him he was full of it. Then he frowned and said, "You're right. I walked in like a big-ass bird with a hard-on. If the place had been staked out, we'd both be dead by now!"

"Spoken like a lad who's beginning to use his noodle, as you Yankee Doodles say. The girl was a secret agent, a *très* dangerous trade. Any number of people might have killed a German spy for any number of reasons. I know that I, for one, might have volunteered for the job, despite your grotesque views on trusting *Les Boches.*"

"Hell, I never said I trusted her. I was hoping she'd help me get you out of jail."

"Très bien, but since I was never *in* jail we can forget about that part. I have no more idea than yourself about her recent demise, but I don't see how the local government could have been in on it. From what you've told me of her, they already knew she worked for the Germans. Besides, gunmen with the local law in their pockets do not hit and run. They don't have to. Don't you see what this might mean?"

"No. Not a fucking thing about this whole deal makes any sense at all."

Gaston slowed down and looked back to make sure they were alone on the dark street before he said, "Nobody in the Colombian government knows anything about what's going on, so it could not have been a police trap. Even if I was wrong about that, and some species of a mad policeman went to so much trouble to lure us back here, they just, how you say, blew up a perfect chance to trap you once again."

Captain Gringo nodded and said, "I'll buy that. So it reads two ways. Max might have been killed by an enemy of her own. She shot people a lot and spies aren't very popular

anyway. On the other hand, if it was the same people who tricked us into coming back here, they might not have had the balls to hang around if they were spies, too!"

"Ahah! Who do you think we're dealing with—Grey-stoke of British Intelligence again?"

"Maybe. Up to now he's always hired us or tried to kill us by this late in the game. Whoever it is, and whatever they want, it didn't work. We ran into each other before either of us could be sucked deeper into this mess. So now there's nothing to keep us here and I suggest we get the fuck out!"

Gaston laughed and said, "Lead on, MacDuff, my old and rare. We have guns and enough money to last us a month or so and, of course, we have each other, you sweet young thing. But tell me, do we just keep walking, or is there some goal to this relentless march of yours?"

Captain Gringo said, "It's early yet. It's pretty obvious the cops aren't out in force after us. We could leg it back to a hotel I know and hole up for the night. Then we could scout the railroad depot in the cold gray light and if the coast is clear . . ."

"You are losing me," Gaston cut in, adding, "I do not like this hotel of yours. If you know where it is, who is to say who else knows about it?"

Captain Gringo started to explain the precautions he'd taken leaving the widow's shabby little hotel in a *barrio* where he was unknown. Then he smiled sheepishly and said, "Yeah, I told the people there I was a German, and a German agent was tailing me to find out why. I don't want to risk getting old Vanessa in trouble, anyway. But if they have the railroad depot staked out . . ."

Cutting in again, Gaston said, "The longer we give them to plan, the more certain we can be that they'll get around to that sooner or later. You and I are both supposed to be lurking around the presidio, for some reason. We would be, if we had not met by chance. The *paseo* is just getting interesting back there. I, too, have a hotel room here in town. They may have both under observation. They don't know that we know about the dead girl either, since they did not see fit to hang about there after they killed her. So, all in all, I consider a bee line for a choo choo the best possible move. Don't you?"

Captain Gringo agreed and together they legged it across town to the railroad depot. Fortunately the main drag was

well illuminated, so fortunately they both spotted the blue uniforms from a block away.

Captain Gringo hauled Gaston back around the corner and sighed, "Shit. Have you any other great ideas?"

Gaston shrugged and said, "A *très* impressive military cordon around the depot. Perhaps a bit obvious?"

"Look, it doesn't matter if those troopers are after us or somebody else. We sure as hell can't walk through them now that a couple of government agents have been shot here in town."

"How do you know the men you and Max killed were working for the military here?"

"Hah, this time I've got you. They had to be government agents. The government wouldn't have covered up their killings if they'd been anyone else. El Araño may or may not know about Max. But he has to know about his own people. I'm hoping he'll think some unreconstructed rebels left over from the recent riots did his boys in. That cordon around the depot smells like counter-guerrilla stuff. Don't nobody leave town until we ask some questions and all that shit."

Gaston nodded and said, "In that case, one can only suggest we don't leave town. At least, not via that obvious exit. I don't know how we contact the rebel mule skinners I used the last time I wanted to vacate quietly with those refugees. Everyone we worked with before has crawled under the rug to wait for better days. But at least I know the way to the north coast via the overland route through the mountain passes. I suggest we hole up somewhere, and in the morning . . ."

But Captain Gringo had him by the arm again and was heading back to a side street he knew that circled the depot. He said, "Nuts to that. I all but turned myself inside out looking for Vanessa's place and the sons of bitches still caught up with me. There's no place here in Bogotá that we can be sure of."

"Agreed, but in that case where do you suggest we hide?"

"Nowhere. It's a nice night. Let's just start walking."

"But, Dick, we can't just wander around Bogotá all night. In a few hours people will start wondering about two strangers on their street and if we meet a police patrol . . ."

"Knock it off. Who said anything about walking around town all night? Bogotá's not that big. I know the way through

the *favelas* to the north and you know the north trail to Barranquilla. We can be out on the open road long before it's late enough to matter."

Gaston fell in step with him but protested, "Dick, the north road is not exactly a road. More like a goat path over hill and dale. Make that a lot of hills, with rocks and snow and *banditos* full of *coca*. We have not had time to chat, but the last time I headed that way I had to shoot a few truculent Inca types. I was riding a fast mule, too. All in all, I feel a certain hesitancy in strolling into certain villages on foot with nothing but a lousy pistol and you, lovely as you are."

The tall American smiled thinly and said, "Okay, so it's the devil we know against a very spooky devil here that we don't. Let's just put some space between us and whatever. We'll play it by ear after that."

Gaston sighed and said, "I see no other choice, but, Dick, you play so noisy by ear."

"That reminds me. We've got to pick up some heavier weapons along the way. Maybe some shotguns, or better yet, a machine gun."

"Merde alors. That's what I meant."

8

It took them less than two hours to clear the outskirts of the capital. They settled into the easy mile-eating pace of the seasoned soldier, although Gaston, as usual, kept bitching.

The barely visible countryside of the *alto plano* was farmland where it was flat and looked like rolling prairie where it wasn't. The thin night air was downright cold now, and the stars looked close enough to reach up and gather. From time to time a nightbird neither of them knew sounded off with a whimpering lonely cry. The irrigation water in the roadside ditches smelled like stale human shit. That was probably what was in it. A line of telegraph or telephone poles followed the road, its overhead wires humming in the night wind off the mountains, invisible to the east. From time to time they noticed a distant light, off across the fields. But there were few farmsteads. Like most Latins, the Colombian peons tended to cluster in huddled villages rather than live spread out like Americans and northern European farmers.

Gaston was saying, "The last time I passed through here I cut those thrice-accursed wires."

Captain Gringo said, "You were lucky. That was dumb. They probably had too many other things to worry about in the middle of a revolution."

"What are you talking about, Dick? One cannot afford to have the enemy talking back and forth about one, *hein?* There are at least a dozen military outposts between here and the north coast. They are all connected with Bogotá by wire."

"That's why it was dumb of you to cut the wires. Look

71

around you. Do you see anybody staring at us? Cut a fucking wire and within minutes some C.Q. back at the Bogotá presidio will be waking up the brass and sticking pins in the map. How far apart are these outposts, the usual day's ride?"

"*Oui,* one may safely assume their patrol areas overlap. Why?"

"Why? We're on foot, you asshole! Ten minutes after the line goes dead in any outpost some son of a bitch will be blowing boots-and-saddles. You want to outrun cavalry patrols in open country, be my guest, but do it far away from yours truly! How far are we from those salt flats you were telling me about earlier?"

Gaston thought and said, "I am not certain. I have passed no landmarks I remember in this distressing darkness. But the Great Salt Desert starts a good thirty miles north of the capital. So we don't have to worry about hitting it tonight."

Captain Gringo frowned and said, "The hell we don't. It should be staring us right in the face about dawn."

"*Merde alors,* you expect me to walk thirty miles in less than one night?"

"Shit, a good soldier can cover fifty from dusk to dawn if he keeps his feet moving and his mouth shut. I thought they soldiered in your old outfit, the French Foreign Legion."

"Perhaps they did. It was so long ago I don't remember. Listen, Dick, we have to get out of these street clothes and aboard some horses. Even with mounts and canteens the Great Salt Desert is not a thing to be taken lightly. It is not your ordinary desert. It is pure table salt, covering hundreds of square miles. Our party was well mounted and we had plenty of water when I crossed it last. It was not a pleasant journey."

Captain Gringo thought before he said, "Hey, it's cool up here in the Andes and as I recall it rained a day or so after we split up."

Gaston said, "True. It drizzled one morning as we were crossing the salt flats. By noon the air was so dry we felt like mummies. The problem of this desert is not aridity. It is the salt. Salt absorbs moisture. It never stops absorbing moisture. There is not a bush or a blade of grass. There is not so much as a puddle of standing water between rains. When it is raining hard, you may see water in the low places. Pure pickle brine. Our native mule skinners kept us wisely to the

ridgeways. Dry salt is *très joligant* to walk on. Damp salt is fatal to the foot of man or beast."

"I get the picture. I chased some Apache across a desert once or twice. Are there any mining installations around the salt flats?"

"Our guides mentioned some we had to avoid. Why?"

"Somebody has to be digging that rock salt somewhere. Rock salt is a major export of this country. I was thinking of the Borax operations in my own deserts. They've got to have water tanks and mules around any salt diggings. Let's figure out where your guides told you not to go, and then head that way."

"Ah, when in doubt, march on the sound of the guns, *hein?* But would not they have military outposts guarding the salt mines, Dick?"

"I don't see why. Bandits raid gold and silver mines. I never heard of anyone robbing a salt mine. With any luck, we ought to find a peon work crew sitting on mules and water in some out-of-the-way nowheres-much. Do we bear to the left or the right when this road peters out? I can see it's already shrinking to little more than a wagon trace."

Gaston shrugged and said, "I am not certain. Our guides left the telegraph lines near a split we should come to in a few hours. I think they said the right fork was the main line to the coast."

"Then the wires to the left must lead somewhere else. If the country is dry to the north, that has to mean mining country. You notice something about that roadside ditch to your east, Gaston?"

"There is no roadside ditch now."

"That's what I mean. From the little I can see of it, we're in open range now. They probably graze cattle between the irrigated farmland and the desert ahead. Keep an eye peeled for El Toro. Some of these half-wild Spanish cattle get fresh as hell when they spot a human on foot."

Before Gaston could answer they both heard an odd sound coming up the road from behind them. Captain Gringo stopped and turned around, muttering, "What the hell?" as he listened to what sounded like a woodpecker trying to open a tin can.

Gaston cocked his head and decided, "Too little to be a railroad engine. Too big to be a clock. What does that leave us?"

Captain Gringo spotted the distant glow of two little

cat's eyes and marveled, "Holy Toledo. It's a horseless carriage!"

"An automobile?" blinked Gaston. "What the devil is an automobile doing up here, of all places?"

Captain Gringo said, "I don't know. But we'd better get the hell out of its path. The bugger has headlamps."

The two soldiers of fortune moved off the road at right angles, looking for cover. There wasn't any. The short dry grass just rolled on into the dark forever. Captain Gringo stopped and said, "Okay, let's just stand still here and act like fence posts or something. I can't see the road from here. So the road can't see us."

"Do you mind if I smoke?" teased Gaston.

Captain Gringo didn't answer. Gaston never shut up, but he knew how to freeze as well as any other old soldier when it was important.

They watched with interest as the horseless carriage putted closer. The tall American had been right about the range. The contraption was noisy enough and its two carbide lamps could be seen for miles in the open. But the rest was just a dark blur. They couldn't see how many passengers were aboard as it passed. Captain Gringo made a mental note of the headlamps' range as he watched the way they illuminated the roadway ahead of the vehicle. He wasn't totally unfamiliar with the critters since they'd been showing up here and there for the last few years. But a professional soldier had to keep abreast of newfangled notions and the art was newfangling like hell lately.

The noisy contraption moved on at a pretty good clip, considering, and as it faded into the darkness again he said, "That was interesting. Let's go. They didn't spot us."

As they moved back to the road and slogged on, Gaston said, "I rode in one of those things in Mexico City one time. My derriere still tingles, and the stench, *merde alors!* Why do you suppose they ever invented such a complicated way of getting from here to there, Dick?"

"They have some advantages if you can keep them running. You don't have to feed them when you're not using them, for one thing, and they don't get tired like a horse. That thing was moving faster than your average buckboard and this is a lousy road. They must have those new rubber tires. Did you gauge the range of those headlamps?"

"Of course. They can see about a pistol shot ahead of them at night. What of it?"

"Just thinking. It'll never make a tactical weapon. You can hear it long before they can see you. I was reading something about the German Army ordering some of those things. Can't figure out how they'd use them."

"Bah, *les Boches* are always testing new things. They are as bad as you Americans. Take it from an old soldier, my rosy-cheeked boy. War is a business of elephantine simplicity. It never really changes. The Great God Mars will always favor the bigger battalion and there will never be a real substitute for an infantry charge, pressed with *élan*."

"Against machine guns?"

"But of course. I know you are an enthusiast for automatic fire, Dick. But there are limits to what the machine gun can do. You shall see when the new young Kaiser gets the war he's been asking for of late. This time, France will be prepared. We shall show him what we think of his machine gun and other new toys. The flag of France will be flying over the *Unter den Linden* within six weeks."

Captain Gringo didn't answer. They'd had this argument before. Gaston was old enough to be his father and the skills he learned as a young man had served him well into middle age. But the last few years had been pissers. Captain Gringo was still a junior officer, or would have been if the U.S. Army hadn't stripped him of his first lieutenant's bars and sentenced him to hang. The military skills they'd taught him at The Point had been obsolescent when they sent him out to fight the last wild Indians. Now they were hopelessly out of date. The last ten years or so had seen more new inventions than the previous few hundred. Men still serving in his old army, who'd charged with muzzle loader in the Civil War, now had to bone up on the new Maxim and Browning machine guns by the light of the electric bulb in their quarters. Senior Navy men now walking the bridges of a dreadnought that could lob sixteen inchers at an enemy over the horizon could remember first engagements aboard sailing ships with wooden walls firing broadsides into one another at point-blank range. Every army now had field telephones and observation balloons. And he'd read in *Scientific American* that some silly son of a bitch was talking about some kind of horseless carriage that might someday fly, for Chrissake!

It was small wonder that older guys like Gaston clung to the past. The future looked sort of scary! But Captain Gringo was alive that night because he hadn't stopped growing when

he got out of West Point. A guy had to keep up with the times or they'd get him.

Gaston said, "*Regardez,* there seems to be a light ahead."

Captain Gringo said, "I see it. Looks like a window just off the roadway. Probably a roadside stop. Coaching inn or something."

"Do we stop for a drink or ease around it?"

"Neither. We move in closer and find out what the fuck it is before we decide anything."

The tall American didn't have to tell Gaston why they were walking on the grass beside the roadway instead of on the crunching gravel as they walked closer to the light ahead. As they approached within rifle range they could see it was indeed a roadside *posada.* The glow was from an open doorway spilling lamplight out on the dusty packed earth between the walls and the rutted roadway. As they got closer they could see two dimmer squares of illumination where red curtains hung across the bottle-glass windows on either side of the doorway.

There was more than that to see. Gaston blinked and said, "The automobile we saw before. It is parked just beyond the doorway!"

Captain Gringo led them in at a slant, putting the road and plenty of grass between them and the open doorway as they lined up on it for a look-see inside.

He stopped and hunkered down. Gaston joined him and together they stared morosely into the little *posada.* There was a bar against the far adobe wall. Two men stood at the bar with their backs to them. Both wore the blue of the Colombian Military Police. Gaston muttered, "*Merde,* I was dying for a drink, too."

"The night is young. Let's take a look at that horseless carriage."

They moved north of the *posada* and crossed over to the parked vehicle.

Gaston said, "I have met this beast before. It is a French Lenoir."

Captain Gringo muttered, "It looks like a sawed-off buckboard with the horses missing and, Jesus, look what's in the back!"

The Lenoir runabout was in fact little more than a flatbed wagon with the front half of an oversized baby buggy perched up front. But in the center of the flat deck behind

76

stood a steel post, and on a swivel atop the post sat a .30-30 Maxim machine gun!

A long ammo belt hung down to the wooden decking where the rest of it coiled like a rattlesnake. There were spare ammo boxes and drums of extra fuel in a rack behind the twin bucket seats. Captain Gringo grinned at Gaston and asked, "Do you know how to start this thing?"

Gaston said, *"Oui,* but are we not putting the cart before the horse, even though we need no horse? What about those soldiers in there?"

"Fuck 'em, let 'em get their own horseless carriage. This one's ours!"

"True. But they may not see it our way and you were the one who said we should not cut the wire, *hein?"*

"Yeah, when you're right you're right," growled Captain Gringo, drawing his .38 as he stepped into the shadow of the *posada's* corner near the Lenoir.

Gaston joined him, drawing his own revolver, and complained, "It would be quicker to nail them from the doorway, *non?"*

But the tall American shook his head and said, "Noisier, too. If this is a regular coach stop they could have a telephone inside."

"Modern science has its limitations, Dick. We could wipe out everybody, and then who would telephone whom?"

"Hey, there's no need to stage the last act of *Hamlet.* The innkeeper and his family are just innocent bystanders. Shooting women and children's not my style even when I'm mad at them. Relax, we've got plenty of time. It's not like we were going anywhere important tonight on our fucking feet!"

So they waited and it only took a million years until one of the uniformed men came out, either to take a leak or to get something from the vehicle. Captain Gringo stepped out of the shadows, gun leveled at the soldier's belt buckle, and softly said, *"Buenas noches.* If you're smart and want to go on breathing, *amigo,* you'll grab some stars and turn to stone!"

The soldier raised his hands wearily and murmured, "I have always been considered most intelligent, Señor. My wallet is in my hip pocket."

"To hell with your wallet. We want your motorcar. I want you to listen carefully before you answer. They call me Captain Gringo and if you've heard of me you know I'm a man of my word."

"I know who you are, Captain Gringo."

"Shut up. I haven't finished. I'm giving you my word that you and your comrade will come out of this alive and unharmed if you do just as I say. All bets are off if you try anything cute. Do you understand?"

"I am an old soldier, Captain Gringo. Soldiers do not get old by being cute."

"*Es verdad.* I want you to call your comrade out here. If he comes out shooting, you're both dead. I'll leave the dialogue up to you."

"We have your promise, Captain Gringo?"

"I said you did. What do you want me to do, sign it in blood? We haven't got all night. As a matter of fact, we have about ten seconds and then the egg hits the fan and we do it the hard way."

The captive sighed, then called out, "Hey, Ramon? I need a hand out here!"

There was a long pregnant pause. Then the other man came out, squinting into the darkness, with nothing but a bottle in his gun hand as he asked, "What do you mean, you need a hand? You want me to hold it for you while you piss? Hey, Chico, I'm not that kind of a boy."

Then he saw Captain Gringo and Gaston and froze, adding, "Oh, shit."

Captain Gringo waved his gun and told the two of them to get in the back. Then he hauled himself up to stand over them, holding the gun post as he covered them. He said, "Okay, Gaston. You're driving. Let's get out of here."

Gaston blinked and said, "I told you I knew how to start the engine. I said nothing about knowing how to drive one of these monsters, Dick."

"So start the fucking engine and learn! It's obvious you steer it with that tiller bar, isn't it?"

"*Oui,* but these other pedals and levers are *très* confusing. Let me see. There is something one should know about putting the gears in a certain position before one twists the starting crank."

Captain Gringo swore softly and said, "Get in the passenger seat." Then he pointed his muzzle at the captive he considered most reasonable and added, "You, start the engine and get us out of here, *muy pronto.* Gaston, you take his gun and keep an eye on his hands."

The old soldier didn't argue. He was smart enough to see the advantages of clearing the neighborhood before the *posa-*

da keeper became curious enough to come outside, too. The engine was already warm and started on the second crank with the gears in neutral. The soldier leaped in and threw them into gear and they were on their way. Nobody had had to tell the captive driver that they wanted to go north, away from the capital. But after they'd putted half a mile he asked them just where they thought they were going.

Captain Gringo yelled above the put-puts, "Where we want to go is not your problem. Where were you boys headed?"

The driver hesitated before he shrugged and said, "Well, it hardly matters now. We were on our way to the Arroyo Blanco salt mines with this gun car. El Araño expected you to try for mules and water there."

"I keep hearing about El Araño. He sounds pretty good. Did he mention us by name or was this just S.O.P. following a shoot-out in town?"

"*Por favor,* Señor, Colonel Maldonado does not take enlisted men into his confidences. Sometimes I don't think the officers know what he's up to, either."

"That's not the question I asked, *amigo.*"

"Look, let us not be grim with one another. I can tell you he is indeed after you and Señor Verrier here, without betraying secrets. After all, you both know who you are, too, no?"

Captain Gringo told him to keep driving and stood, legs braced, as he held the action of the machine gun with his free hand and considered these new developments. It seemed obvious now why they'd had a cordon around the railroad depot. Why hadn't they cordoned off the main country road out of town? Easy. It would have taken the whole army to seal off every lane leading out of town and El Araño had foreseen that anyone with half a brain could play hide-and-seek with infantry or even cavalry in the dark. So he'd sent these guys and probably others to race ahead and hold the bottlenecks. If the tricky colonel had thought of them needing mules and water to cross the desert, he was expecting them to cross the desert. Captain Gringo knew this gas buggy could get them across the wide open salt flats *muy pronto.* But the wires led beyond the desert and guys waiting on the far side could spot them coming for miles in daylight. Hell, they'd hear them for miles, even if they crossed the treacherous salt at night with their lights out!

Okay, there was no way El Araño could know this soon

that they'd stolen his horseless carriage cum machine-gun nest. If they drove like hell they might just get across the desert before . . . But that wouldn't work either. If the other side had thought to secure those mules at the salt mines on this side, they were already expecting them on the far side.

Gaston must have been thinking along the same lines. He kept turning in his front seat and asking where they were going. The American switched to English as he called down, "Later, damnit. I told these guys we were going to let them go alive."

Gaston said, "Oh," and shut up. The driver felt better, too. He spoke English, although he liked to keep some things to himself. He'd never know that Captain Gringo had hoped he'd understand. A desperate man might try anything. An old soldier who knew he was getting a break tended to behave himself.

They drove on for nearly an hour with the roadway getting rougher and the country around more rugged. The springy construction and rubber tires of the Lenoir allowed a speed that would have been suicidal in a regular buckboard at night. None of them knew, as later drivers would, the danger of outrunning one's headlight beams. So the driver just had time to spot the eye glows of a startled furry something in the ruts ahead before they'd run over it with a sickening crunch. He braked to a stop without thinking. Captain Gringo said, "I noticed. It was a wildcat. If it wasn't dead we'd be hearing about it now."

The driver started to throw the Lenoir in gear again. But Captain Gringo said, "Hold it. We must be fifteen or twenty kilometers from that *posada* by now. This is as good a place as any to say *Adios, muchachos.*"

"You promised us our lives, Señor."

"No problem. Just take off your uniforms and boots and leave them with us before you start walking."

"You are stranding us out here, in the middle of nowhere, stark naked, Señor?"

"Well, consider the alternatives and you'll see it's not so bad. You can keep your underwear. But let's get a move on, shall we?"

Grumbling and bitching about the cold as well as the indignity, the two soldiers undressed to their socks and union suits and Captain Gringo told them they were free to go. So they went, before he could change his mind.

Captain Gringo chuckled and waited until they were out

of earshot before he said, "Okay, Gaston, the engine's running. Slide over in the driver's seat and see if you learned anything."

"Maybe you had better drive, Dick. You're better at machinery than me."

"I know. I want you at the tiller in case I have to use this machine gun. Move over, damnit. I'm tired of standing up."

So Gaston did as he was told and Captain Gringo forked a leg over and joined him behind the curving dashboard in the other bucket seat. It was just as well he'd seated himself firmly; Gaston threw the Lenoir in gear and they flew backward, then stalled when he tromped the brakes.

Gaston muttered, *"Merde,"* as silence closed in around them. The tall American sighed and said, "Okay, I'll get out and crank, but for God's sake put it in neutral, huh?"

Gaston fumbled with the gear levers and said, "There, it is either in neutral or I am about to run over you," as Captain Gringo climbed down. The husky American started the warm engine on the first crank and climbed in as the Lenoir stood shuddering and complaining with an occasional backfire. Gaston said, "Here goes," and tried again. This time they rolled forward, albeit in a series of rabbit hops until the little Frenchman got the feel of things, or just got lucky. Captain Gringo said, "Slow down until you make sure you can steer this thing," and Gaston answered, "How, you species of imbecile? This creature has a mind of its own!"

The springs bounced them sickeningly as the horseless carriage ran off the road and across the open range at an angle. Fortunately, there was nothing much to hit out there and before they could find anything worth crashing into, Gaston had the tiller under control and was saying, *"Regardez!* I am a genius! I have never had a lesson and already I am *très formidable* at the steering of these things!"

Captain Gringo said, "Swell. See if you can get us back on the road, for Chrissake."

Gaston swung them in a tight circle that threatened to capsize them, and as his companion swore again, Gaston said, "Ahah, one learns with experience. A gentle hand on the reins is called for. But *regardez,* I can go right, I can go left, see?"

"Will you stop fucking around and get back on the road?"

Gaston laughed gleefully and hit the roadway at an

angle, bouncing over a rut with a Godawful jolt. As Captain Gringo saw they seemed, indeed, to be tearing up the roadway at an alarming clip, he said, "That's swell. Now slow down, for God's sake."

Gaston replied, "Poof, I have only learned to guide this ridiculous thing. The way one sets the rate of speed eludes me."

Captain Gringo leaned over and adjusted the throttle lever. Gaston said, "Spoilsport," as they dropped to about fifteen miles an hour. But he felt better about it, too, despite his delight with his new toy. He said, "We can outrun any mounted patrols with this adorable creature, Dick. But I was thinking about an ambush ahead, before we rid ourselves of those unwelcome guests."

Captain Gringo said, "Great minds run in the same channels. We're never going to make the north coast now. Every outpost between here and Barranquilla has been alerted by now. They're going to be sore as hell about this gas buggy, too. Those guys have a long hike ahead of them, but they'll get to a telephone long before we can get anywhere important."

"I agree. I would have shot them, but you Yankees are so sentimental. Unless we intend to drive around in circles until we run out of fuel we really should be considering some place to go, *hein?*"

"Yeah. Let's turn right at the next crossroads."

"Right, my old and rare? There is nothing over that way but the Andes. As a Frenchman, I am *très* pleased with the way M'sieu Lenoir's creation marches, but I doubt very much that it can climb mountains like the goat. And even if it could, there is nothing on the other side."

"Sure there is. The Colombian border is on the other side of the high Cordillera Oriental, right?"

Gaston gasped. *"Mais oui,* but now I know you are suffering from the altitude, Dick! Assuming we can get over the mountains, which we shall never manage aboard this thing, they drop off on the far side into unexplored jungle. A lot of unexplored jungle. Colombia's eastern lowlands extend at least four hundred miles, and when you get to your thrice-accursed border we would still be in the middle of the Amazonian rain forest!"

"So what? You just said it was unexplored. If it's unexplored, nobody lives there."

"Nobody civilized, you mean. The jungle is not uninhab-

ited. Some of the tribes on the far slope are cannibals. Others, more delicate, merely cut off one's head and shrink it. Even armed with a machine gun, the country over there can be dangerous to one's health."

"So what do you want to do, hang around up here until we meet some other guys with machine guns?"

"Hmm, since you put it that way, perhaps we should start watching for a road to the east, *non?*"

9

M'sieu Etienne Lenoir had designed his horseless carriages for the paved streets of Paris. So they were already stretching their luck trying to run at over 8,000 feet. Even with the fuel mixture as rich as possible, the engine was complaining bitterly about the thin air when dawn found them tooling up some sort of leftover Inca road between steep alpine slopes. They, of course, had no idea where they were, but since all roads had to lead somewhere, and since the one they'd found ran more or less east, they'd been following it for some time before the sun came up to reveal the desolate grandeur all around them.

The country would have been okay on a postcard sent from the Alps. It didn't offer much but rocky scenery and no cover at all if anyone was scouting them from the ridges all around. But at least there were no telephone poles. So who could be expecting them?

As the sun rose higher Captain Gringo suddenly said, "Shit," and Gaston asked why. They'd been chilled to the bone, even with the stolen uniforms over the pants and shirts they'd been wearing, and Gaston welcomed the sun as an end to their discomfort. But the tall American pointed up at the sky with his chin and said, "We're trending south, not east, damn it! We've been driving all night in a circle!"

Gaston said, *"Mais non,* we are most definitely in the mountains. Listen to the way that engine coughs for breath. Besides, we keep rising, *non?"*

"Okay, so we're off the *alto plano,* but we still must have circled south of Bogotá by now. These damned mountains have a north-south grain to them. We've got to get across them, not follow them."

84

"That sounds most reasonable, my old and rare, but what do you want me to do about it? Do you see any triple-titted passes over there to our left?"

"No. But you're right about this road still climbing. It may lead to a pass somewhere south of where we intended to cross over."

"And if it does not?"

"Beats me. We'll just have to follow this road until we run out of fuel or it starts downhill again. If there's not a main route over the sierra we may spot a footpath or something. We sure can't go back down to *alto plano* again."

"Why not? They'd hardly expect to find us *south* of Bogotá, would they?"

"Not until somebody noticed a couple of funny-looking guys in ill-fitting uniforms and a motorcar. There's no way out, down that way. I looked at the fucking map before I headed north, damnit."

Gaston thought before he nodded with a sigh and said, "Ah, *oui,* the mountains do run together at the south end of the plain like the bottom of the sack, now that you mention it. *Le Bon Dieu* did not lay out these Andes with much consideration for weary travelers."

The road they were following wound around a gentle bend, trending even farther to the south, and as Captain Gringo spotted something far ahead he said, "Slow down and look innocent." Then he climbed back to the mounted machine gun and stood behind it as they overtook the party up the road.

It was a column of about thirty ragged, dusty men and women on foot with a corporal's squad of mounted troopers herding them. The armed guards rode at intervals beside the obvious prisoners. Gaston called back, "What is our story if those soldiers question us, Dick?" and Captain Gringo said, "I'll handle that part. You just drive by. Fast, if they don't ask us to stop."

Gaston shoved his throttle forward and, although the engine coughed and sputtered, they picked up speed. Naturally, the mounted troopers heard them and looked back, surprised. Captain Gringo stood at the Maxim and waved nonchalantly as the guards herded the ragged peons off the road and sat their mounts, bemused, on the grassy verge. A couple waved back with their rifles and one of them with stripes on his sleeves shouted something. But then they were past the column and it was too late to reply. But the tall

American shouted back, "Up your ass!" as if he'd answered whatever with something sensible.

As they left the unusual development behind, Gaston called back, "If those are rebel prisoners, we would seem to be headed toward the prison camp those troopers were marching them to, *non?*"

Captain Gringo answered, "I think you're right. Slow down again and keep your eyes peeled. This bastard road might dead-end against some mountain outpost."

The engine wheezed and Gaston replied, "I have little choice. Now that it is warming up, the air grows even thinner. I don't know how much higher she will take us."

The road wound up a bit more, then leveled off and began to descend to the south-southeast. Captain Gringo shouted, "Hold it. I think this is the end of the line."

Gaston braked to a stop in the middle of the road, but said, *"Oui,* one can see this diabolic road is taking us back to the *alto plano*. But we have to go *somewhere*. Those damned troopers are right behind us. They will be coming around the bend back there any minute, now."

The tall American pointed up the slope to the east with his chin and said, "Looks like a sort of footpath zigzagging up between the boulders over that way. See how it leads to that saddleback between the peaks up there?"

Gaston shrugged and said, "It may be a pass over the sierra. But that's a two-mile climb, Dick. Those troopers would get here long before we could reach the top. And even if we found some cover up there, what about this motorcar? We can't take it with us and I see no big wet rock to hide it under."

"Yeah, you're right. We could probably get away, but this Lenoir would make a neat map coordinate once they reported it abandoned here."

"Oui, so what do we do, Dick?"

"We make sure they don't report it, of course! Turn around and head back to meet them. I don't want anybody connecting the next few minutes to that path over the ridge to the east!"

Gaston grinned wolfishly but bitched, of course, as he threw the Lenoir in gear and made a U turn. They met the column again just around the next bend. The leader of the troopers swore when his horse spooked at the tinny rattle of their engine. He waved his free hand to halt them as he

fought to control his mount. Gaston just drove into them as Captain Gringo opened up with the machine gun.

The tall American manning the Maxim traversed from his right to his left, aiming just above the heads of the screaming prisoners as they scattered in all directions. The mounted troopers' midsections were at just the right level as he spread his lethal fan of hot lead. So he emptied all eight saddles before anyone on the other side had any idea what was going on! All but one of the troopers hit the dust dead or dying and unconscious. As one struggled to rise, a quick-thinking female captive picked up a rock in both hands and smashed his head. As he collapsed in a gory heap at her bare feet, she looked up at the tall American behind the smoking Maxim with a mingled expression of resignation and hope.

He called out, "Everybody calm. It's over, *amigos!* We are not Colombian *soldados*. I think we may be on the same side."

As the others began to recover their wits and balance, the girl who'd finished off the trooper brushed her dusty hair from her dusty face as she came closer and said, "You are on our side, Señor, if you came straight out of Hell! We are all that is left of the Blue Brigade and they were marching us to who knows what doom! I am called La Diablilla. My gallant father was our leader before he was betrayed to the betrayers who stole our revolution out from under us."

A bearded *mestizo* who'd just helped himself to one of the downed trooper's guns and ammo stepped up beside Diablilla and said, "Hey, I know you, *hombre!* You are the Yanqui they call Captain Gringo. Do you not remember me? Pancho?"

Captain Gringo frowned down and said, "Wait a minute. The last time we met, you were in uniform. We tangled with those *banditos* down in the lowlands, more or less on the same side. But you didn't know I was Captain Gringo then, right?"

"Es verdad, it was ages ago, before the revolution. Our sergeant later figured out who you were, but it did not matter, since we had joined the rebels by then."

Pancho slung the captured rifle from his shoulder with a bitter little smile as he added, "How was I to know we'd picked the losing side? We were young and foolish six weeks ago." Then he turned to the girl and told her, "He's all right, *muchachita*. You just saw how good he is with that machine

gun, and they say he is immortal. I vote we make him our new leader. God knows we need one, now."

Diablilla beamed up at the American standing on the flatbed and for the first time Captain Gringo noticed she was quite pretty, given a face wash and a comb run through that tangled, dusty mop. She said, "Attention, all of you. Pancho has nominated Captain Gringo to lead us out of here, and I, La Diablilla, daughter of El Diablo Azul, second the motion!"

There was a chorus of agreement and someone shouted, "Viva Captain Gringo!" The American turned and glanced at Gaston, who shrugged and said, "You and your big mouth. Now look what you've gotten us into, Dick."

10

As it turned out, the bread he'd cast on the waters hadn't been such a bad move after all. They didn't have to carry the machine gun and ammo themselves, for one thing. For another, one of the other men in the band knew the area and so he saved them from following Captain Gringo's first chosen path over the ridge into another valley that ended in a blind alley.

They left the stolen Lenoir with the dead troopers. They killed and disarmed it, too, by shooting the tires and fuel tank full of holes. Diablilla wanted to burn it. But he told her someone might see the rising smoke. They took the horses, of course. The man who said he knew the way over the sierra said the horses could make it partway at least.

So Captain Gringo put Diablilla, the machine gun and its ammo, and the other five women in the party aboard the purloined mounts and led Gaston and the other men on foot as he followed the volunteer guide.

The horses made it over the higher pass the guide led them to, five or six miles farther south. On the far side they found a mountain stream and refilled the eight canteens of the dead troopers and the larger canvas water bag they'd taken from the horseless carriage. One of Captain Gringo's first direct orders to his new recruits was to husband the food and water they were packing. It was true they were high among cool mountains with summer snow visible on peaks all around them. But deserts were not the only places man and beast could suffer thirst. Horses needed far more water than humans to begin with and the thin dry air sucked moisture from one's lungs like blotting paper. His own lips had started

to crack and his mouth tasted like the bottom of a bird cage as he panted on the up-slopes.

They found themselves on another winding trail leading south-southwest between grassy alpine slopes. There was no sign of human habitation as far as one could see, but wherever the trail ran uphill for a stretch Captain Gringo noticed a cairn of stones set beside the trail on the crest of the rise. He asked the guide what they meant. The guide said he didn't know. But Diablilla, sitting sidesaddle on her mount just behind him, had overheard the exchange and called down, "The Quechuas have been leaving a stone at the top of each climb since the days of the Incas."

"Quechuas?"

"Indians. The ones you strangers and even ignorant Colombians keep calling Incas. The Inca was the Sun King of the Quechua Empire. Nobody else was an Inca." She grimaced and added, "The Brothers Pizarro were not too interested in such distinctions. They only wanted the Inca's gold and emeralds. The survivors of the conquest were enslaved and told to put on pantaloons and be in church Sunday morning sharp, as Spanish subjects. The history of the native peoples has never interested His Most Catholic Majesty or the many so-called liberators we've had since."

Captain Gringo shot her a curious glance. She'd washed up and combed her hair, back at that brook. She was even prettier than he'd first thought. But while her high cheekbones and dark almond eyes hinted at a dash of Indian blood, she was obviously mostly Castilian. Nobody but a Castilian aristocrat, or a Hispanic bullfighter of any background, ever held their head like that.

But he was more interested in where they were going than he was in the story of Diablilla's life. So he asked the guide about the trail.

The peon shrugged and said, "I have never been all the way to the town of Gueppi myself, Señor, but I know they pack mail to Gueppi along this trail."

Captain Gringo frowned and said, "Gueppi? Where the hell is Gueppi? I never heard of it. It doesn't even sound Spanish."

Again the guide was stuck for an answer and again La Diablilla supplied it. She said, "The name is Indian. Gueppi is the last outpost of Colombia on the headwaters of the Rio Putumayo."

Captain Gringo consulted the rough mental map of the

country that he'd memorized and gasped, "Jesus, that's way the hell south! Isn't the Putumayo on the borderline between Colombia and Peru?"

Diablilla nodded and said, "Yes, it runs down into the jungle lowlands to join the Solimees and the main Amazon."

"Hell, that's no good. I was hoping to hit the headwaters of the north-bound Orinoco. We want to get back to the damned Caribbean."

"The plans of myself and these others are flexible, Captain Gringo. We most obviously cannot go back to Bogotá now. I have heard one can reach the Orinoco from the Amazon, via a swampy water passage in the low country. Even if one can't, do we have much choice?"

Gaston had been walking well to the rear, flirting with one of the other women. When he heard his tall friend's tone of voice he abandoned her to her own devices and moved forward to ask the leaders what was up.

Captain Gringo explained and Gaston shrugged and said, "What does it matter? We shall all wind up with our shrunken heads on poles in any case."

He smiled up at Diablilla and added, "Since you are the Indian expert, M'selle, forget the way back to civilization and let us discuss the *très* distressing customs of such Indians as we might meet before we get there."

Diablilla said, "We shall descend to the rain forests a bit south of the main Jivaro tribes' usual haunts, but they have been severely harassed by the savage *flagelados* of late. They could be anywhere."

Captain Gringo knew the Jivaro were Indian headhunters. The *flagelados* were a new one on him. So he said, "The scourged ones? What are these *flagelados,* some sort of self-torture tribe?"

Diablilla laughed and said, "No. They are supposed to be Christians from Brazil. They come in all colors, but in your country they would be called white trash. Their nickname indicates the esteem the Brazilians hold them in. When they meet an Indian in the rain forests they tend to rape or kill, depending on the Indian's sex. Although, even in such matters, *Los Flagelados* tend to be mercurial. Sometimes they kill women or rape men. They are desperate men, with uncultivated tastes, even for Brazilians."

"We've met the type in other places, Diablilla. But what are these wild *banditos* doing out in the jungle?"

91

"Some work as rubber tappers. Others are just outlaws, attracted into Brazil's wild west by the rubber boom."

Captain Gringo didn't ask about the rubber boom. He'd already heard about it, although he'd had no idea it was causing Indian trouble all over the Amazon Basin. The new bicycle craze and the demand for rubber insulation on the electric wires that seemed to be spreading like spiderwebs across the whole civilized world had launched a demand for latex that poor old Charles Goodyear, who'd found out how to use the stuff, had never lived to see. That Lenoir motorcar they'd abandoned on the other side of the mountains had worn far heavier tires than any bike, and of course even horse-drawn carriages were starting to run on rubber these days.

Gaston broke in on his chain of thought by saying, "I am getting my bearings now, Dick. It's not so bad. If we can make it to Manaus, on the Amazon, we can hop a freighter out. Manaus is almost in the center of the continent, yet it may as well be on the sea. Ocean-going ships steam in and out of Manaus, and you will like it. It's the wildest town this side of Singapore."

"Hmm, Diablilla, here, tells me there's a way north to the Orinoco through the river maze."

"Bah, what is the point? I just told you Manaus is a seaport. Ships leave Manaus bound for every part of the world. I vote for the line of the bee. We have yet to see the green hell of Amazonia and I am already *très fatigué* of it."

Captain Gringo didn't answer. He'd spotted a higher than usual stone cairn on the rise ahead and held up his hand to halt the column as he hissed the guide to a sudden stop. The guide turned to ask, "What is it, Señor?" and Captain Gringo said, "I thought I saw movement up there. Keep everybody here while I scout over the rise."

Gaston fell in beside the taller American as he legged it up the rest of the slope, drawing his .38. Gaston did the same as he whispered, "What do you think you saw, Dick?"

Captain Gringo replied, "Not sure. Just a blur of something sort of reddish brown behind that cairn and moving away. If somebody spotted us and lit off down the far slope, he'll be in plain sight for miles. So we should know in a minute."

They lined up with the cairn and used it for cover as they reached the crest. Captain Gringo peeked around one side of the rock pile as Gaston did the same on the other.

A few yards down the far side, out in the open alpine meadow and under a vast empty vault of sky, a dusky old Indian herdsman, naked from the waist down, was fucking one of the big brown shaggy beasts he was supposed to be grazing. He held his sweetheart fast with a fistful of her rump hair grasped in each hand as he humped her from behind, standing up. Captain Gringo grimaced and said, "Jesus, that's disgusting," and Gaston answered, *"Mais non,* it's a llama. I understand they're better than sheep for one who indulges in such hobbies. What do you think we should do, now? Assuming we do not wish to join the party, we have women with us and they may have delicate feelings."

"Yeah, you're right. He's going to have to knock it off until we pass by."

Captain Gringo stepped from cover and walked down the slope toward the beastialist, calling out, "Hey, *amigo,* can I talk to you for a second?"

The herdsman stared owlishly at him but went right on shoving it to the llama as she swung her camel-like head and, chewing her cud, gazed at the approaching American. Captain Gringo said, "Listen, I don't want to spoil your fun, but we've got some women with us and, what the hell, it's not like you haven't got plenty of time."

The herdsman said something in his Indian dialect and went on screwing his big pet. Gaston joined the American and observed, "He's been chewing coca. I don't think he cares about our delicate feelings."

Captain Gringo glanced back up the slope. The crest was empty, thank God, but he knew the curious Diablilla would be wondering what was keeping them. Gaston said, "He's not going to stop. Coca does that to one's sex drive. The silly creature probably does that day and night. Hmm, I wonder if *she* enjoys it."

Captain Gringo growled, "Okay, enough is enough," and stepped over to take the herdsman by one elbow with his free hand. The coked-up peon yelled and took a swing at him as he hauled him off the llama's rump. So Captain Gringo hit him on the head with his pistol barrel and knocked him senseless to the ground. As the semi-nude idiot lay on his back with an erection aimed at the sky, Captain Gringo stepped over to the poncho he'd dropped in the grass nearby, picked it up, and threw it over him. The llama stared back at him reproachfully as she walked away sedately, her moist, pink, surprisingly human-looking vagina winking at them

from between two vast shaggy buttocks. Gaston raised an eyebrow and said, "Hmm, this may well have been a most fortunate encounter, Dick."

"Goddamnit, this is no time to think about sex."

"*Merde,* there are six women with us and I have not really tried one of them, yet! There are other things one can use a llama for. I have noticed the way our stolen horses are breathing. I see ten . . . no, eleven llamas grazing *très* tamely about us. They are no good as saddle mounts, but they are reasonable pack animals. They are natives to this high country and require less nursing than even a mule. What do you say, Dick?"

Captain Gringo glanced down at the unconscious herdsman and replied, "Well, it's sort of shitty to rob this guy, even if he did act sort of weird just now."

"Look, we can leave him the horses as a more than fair exchange, *hein?* One supposes he will notice the difference when he comes to and tries to make love to a mare. But one can always sell a horse for more than a llama. Eight horses should make him rich. Who knows, he may be able to afford a woman, or even a boy, *non?*"

Captain Gringo nodded and said, "Makes sense. That guide back there, Nuñez, says we have to go higher before we can go lower. Let's get the others and make the switch."

11

The sunset caught them high in the Andes, leading the stolen llamas over frost-shattered scree between scattered patches of snow. They'd only taken four of the herdsman's charges, leaving all eight cavalry mounts in exchange. But the female in heat had followed, despite occasional rocks tossed to discourage her, and Gaston kept needling Captain Gringo that she liked him. An amorous llama was the least of his worries as the shadows lengthened around them. He and Gaston were warmly dressed, albeit hardly well enough to play Eskimo in the chill night air. The captives they'd rescued were wearing only cotton rags. They'd taken eight blankets from the saddle rolls of the slain troopers, of course, but eight blankets weren't going to do thirty people much good once the sun went down.

Diablilla must have been thinking along the same lines as he walked beside her. She hadn't complained about having to go the rest of the way on foot. Diablilla knew her high country and had agreed the llamas had been a good notion. She said, "We must find a sheltered place for to build a fire, Captain Gringo."

"I agree, but call me Dick. I've been looking for some boulders or something. We have two problems with a fire up here. The wind will blow the heat away from us unless we find a backstop, and a night fire in the open can be seen for miles, even when you don't build it on a mountaintop."

Diablilla nodded and pointed up a boulder-strewn arroyo running at almost right angles to the trail. She said, "I have never been here, but I know a bit about the old Quechua ways. In places along this trail one can see where the Inca ordered steps cut in the rocks."

"Is that who carved those boulders flat back there a couple of miles? I thought maybe the old Spaniards did it."

"Bah, they never looked at a rock unless they thought there was gold under it! Almost all these high trails were Inca post roads. Those who came later just used them and, as you see, wore them out a bit. But, as I was about to say, the ancient Inca empire was well organized. They built rest stops for their travelers at convenient places along the old road network. That arroyo over there offers the only permanent water supply for several kilometers around. There should be at least the ruins of an old waystation, no?"

Captain Gringo raised his hand to halt the column, but as he stared up along the jumble of house-sized boulders he frowned and said, "I don't see anything in the way of walls, Diablilla. Come to think of it, I don't see any water either, and we could use some."

She laughed and said, "Silly, one does not see water running over the rocks, when it has not been raining or snowing. The steady trickle is always under the rocks. Come, I will show you."

Leaving the others in Gaston's charge, he followed her across and upslope at an angle that took them to the long wavy line of rounded granite boulders paving the apparent dry wash. She led him down the gentle slope into the jumble of big dusty rocks. Then she paused, resting one hand on a waist-high boulder, and said, "Listen."

He did so, cocking his head to one side. He could hear the liquid gurgle of running water, as if someone had left a tap on in the cellar. He nodded and said, "Yeah, it sounds like a fair-sized babbling brook. But how the hell do we get at it?"

She said, "We can't, from here. It would take dynamite to blast these boulders out of the way. But let us explore farther. If there is anywhere a passing traveler can get down to the water, the ancient Quechua engineers would have found it."

She started up the arroyo, leaping lightly from boulder to boulder on her bare feet. The view as he followed was interesting as hell. She flashed well-turned sturdy limbs as the loose skirt flapped flirtatiously. She leaned forward as she climbed the slope, her nicely rounded derriere aimed much like the llama's had been presented to its human abuser, or maybe amuser, back down the mountain. He wondered if she had anything on under that skirt, and what she'd say if he

caught up with her and shoved it to her dog style. He doubted like hell she'd chew a cud, so he decided to pass on the idea, even though it was teasing as hell to catch a flash of thigh now and again without knowing just what lay above and beyond. He was glad it was getting harder to see by the minute.

"You know Goddamn well what's up under that skirt," he warned himself, adding a mental note to behave. The rebel band had accepted him as a natural leader, but he knew at least some of the other men had noticed this kid's ass by now and Spanish-speaking guys took their jealousy more than seriously. They tended to go nuts when another guy aced them out.

Diablilla suddenly vanished like the imp she was named after, as if she'd read his mind and wanted no part in his sexual fantasies. He blinked and muttered, "What the hell?" as he heard her laughing somewhere.

He hopped from boulder to boulder and then stopped short, grinning in surprise as he saw the girl again. She was down in a hollow the size and shape of an old Greek theater. His first thought was that some freak natural event had formed the crater. Then he saw the stone steps she'd scampered down and that the ground around the little pool she stood beside was paved with cobblestones. There were fluted mossy stone channelways leading up and down slope from the circular pool. As he moved down to join her, he spotted the foundations of what looked like housing around the evenly sloping banks of the depression. He nodded down at her and said, "Somebody went to a hell of a lot of work here."

She sighed and said, "I know, but they had a lot of time. This place could have started as a natural low stretch where one could get to the running water from the surface. The Quechuas stationed here to aid passing packers and messengers on the road below must have simply started moving rocks, one at a time, until this was the result."

She pointed at a wall nearby and added sadly, "They never finished. Quechua ruins don't fall down once they have been built for the ages. This waystation was abandoned about the time of the Spanish Conquest. I doubt if anyone has ever been here since."

"It sure offers a great campsite, Diablilla. But how come you know so much about Indians? You sure don't look Indian, meaning no disrespect."

She smiled bitterly and replied, "My late father liked to

97

say he was descended from El Aquilar, a noted Spanish general who in turn claimed second cousinhood to the Inca himself. But you are right, I am a *blanca,* or so I considered myself until they classified everyone who did not agree with the government as an animal to be exterminated. Despite his dramatics, my father was a university professor before he took up politics. He was a noted anthropologist. As a child I accompanied him and my late mother on field trips. I probably know more about the native cultures in these parts than the sadly abused natives. They make such terrible Spanish peasants and, of course, one can hardly consider them Indians any more."

Captain Gringo saw she was sort of cut up inside and resisted the impulse to console her by putting a hand on her shoulder. He didn't know how she'd take it. The sky above them was purple and the hollow was filled with a soft romantic light from the glowing peaks around them. He broke the spell by saying, "Why don't you look around for some firewood here? I'll go get the others," and she looked disappointed when she agreed.

12

The sun was setting in Bogotá, too, when the telephone on Colonel Maldonado's desk rang. El Araño picked up the receiver to answer. It was his superior, General Reyes, and the President for Life did not sound happy as he asked, "All bullshit aside, Maldonado, what in God's name are you up to?"

"I am serving yourself and Colombia to the best of my limited powers, my General."

"Hey, don't fence around with me, *muchacho!* I've been getting reports all day about that crazy Captain Gringo and his little French partner. Do you know what the bastards have done now?"

"*Sí* my General. I, too, have been keeping tabs on their somewhat overdramatic escape to the southeast. At the moment, hopefully, they are crossing the Orientes with the machine gun and a band of dangerous outlaws we are well rid of."

"So I hear. You know I generally give you a pretty free hand, Maldonado, but this time your web spinning is making me very nervous. First you lure those maniacs back up here after I thought we'd seen the last of them. Then you as much as hand them guns and followers, and every time some of our guys start to close in, you countermand the orders. Damnit, *muchacho*, they've killed a mess of our followers and wrecked an expensive automobile and——"

"The few deaths were unfortunate," El Araño cut in. "But, as someone said on another desperate occasion, to make an omelet, one may have to break an occasional egg. We would have lost far more than a dozen people in a border war with our Brazilian neighbors, no?"

"Border war? With Brazil? What in the devil are you talking about? We just wrapped up a fucking revolution! I'm in no shape to have a war with Brazil or anybody else, goddamnit!"

"I am aware of that, my General. So are the goddamned cocky Brazilians. You are aware, of course, that our eastern jungle frontiers have been invaded by Brazilian adventurers?"

The general hesitated before he replied. "I've heard the complaints from over there beyond the mountains. I've passed them on to the Brazilian Embassy. They claim they're as shocked as we are and that they have no control over their rubber barons."

El Araño smiled thinly and said, "I know what they say. They are still shipping rubber stolen from Colombian trees out of Manaus. Our jungle outposts are still getting hit by desperate Indians who can't tell one of us from a slave-raiding *flagelado*. I, too, have mentioned the matter to my opposite Brazilian number. He literally smirked as he told me there was little he could do about the situation. You are aware, of course, that the Brazilian army has been sharing in the rubber boom via a certain amount of rather open bribery?"

General Reyes growled and said, "If it's that serious, I can authorize a military sweep of the jungles on our side of the border, Colonel. How big an operation would it take to clean the pests down there out?"

El Araño said, "It would probably cost us many men in snakebite and Indian arrows alone. It would also get us into a war with Brazil at a rather awkward time. That is why I have sent in Captain Gringo."

There was a long, stunned silence. Then General Reyes said, "Wait a minute. Are you telling me that that crazy *Americano* has gone to work for us?"

The crafty Maldonado chuckled dryly and answered, "You might say that, although he doesn't know it. We have gotten his services at a bargain, my General. He and the Frenchman usually ask at least a thousand U.S. dollars a month for such services and, of course, we are paying nothing for the platoon of guerrillas I managed to supply him with, either.

"They should be hitting the rubber country in a few days now. I am looking forward to my next conversation with that smug military attaché from the Brazilian Embassy. I intend to

listen with grave respect as he tells me his tale of woe. Then, of course, I am going to look the son of a bitch straight in the eye as I explain, alas, that there is nothing I can do about it. After all, if Brazil is not able to control her bandits, how can Colombia be expected to control her own, eh?"

General Reyes sounded somewhat relieved but still dubious as he asked, "How do you know this Captain Gringo will tangle with the *flagelados?* What if he joins them?"

El Araño said, "An outsider would have more chance joining the head-hunting Jivaro. The Indians are just savages. *Los Flagelados* and the rubber barons they work for are totally dedicated bastards! Trust me, my General. I know this Captain Gringo and the crazy little Legion deserter he runs with. They are hard and desperate men. But I have found them to be decent enough enemies in the past. The kids I allowed to escape with them are from the old Blue Brigade. Another band of rather quixotic types I was not, alas, able to recruit for our side. Altogether, I feel I have handed Brazil a problem we are well rid of, and the bastards had it coming."

Mollified for the moment, General Reyes said, "Well, I would rather the Brazilians killed our unruly idealists than us. It is hard to convince the world of my sincere desire for peace and stability if I have to keep putting people against the wall. I suppose they'll cause some grief to the other side, but are you sure it will be enough, Colonel?"

El Araño said, "Captain Gringo has been more than enough everywhere he's been so far. He doesn't have to wipe out every trespasser inside our border. I doubt very much that he'd be able to. But I have high hopes for him making enough noise to discourage further invasions for a time. After all, they have more than enough rubber growing on the other side of the border, and they may find it less noisy to search for it in their own backyard."

"I'm beginning to like this Captain Gringo, after all. Have you done anything to, uh, encourage trouble with the rubber barons?"

"No, my General. Once our own domesticated guerrillas make it over the mountains they will be on a mission of vengeance on their own. One may say I have rather skillfully herded a wild bull into the china shop and what happens from now on should be most interesting."

"Yes, but what if they kill our bull? Those rubber barons and their *flagelados* are supposed to be tough, too."

Maldonado shrugged and answered, "That will be unfortunate, my General, but what the hell, we got our bull cheap, and we certainly don't want him, alive or dead, in our china shop!"

13

The hollow in the rocks was a literal life-saver. By the time the Andean sky had turned to star-spangled India ink the temperature had plummeted a good sixty degrees. But the thinly clad fugitives were out of the wind around the long-lost Inca oases and knew enough to build a circle of small campfires close to the rock walls instead of one or two big ones where you could roast one side of you and freeze the other. They were above timberline, but the woody roots of alpine brush and the torn-out turf of the thickly matted grass all around offered a smoky slow-burning fuel. As Captain Gringo looked back down from the stone steps he'd climbed, the hollow sort of resembled a corner of Hell with the rising smoke plumes illuminated blood-red from below. He knew nobody more than a mile away could see the glow from their pit, so what the hell. They'd be at a warmer altitude this time tomorrow night.

As he legged it across the rocks to relieve Gaston he heard a Christ-awful bleating somewhere in the night. He called out to Gaston and when the Frenchman rose from the lee of the boulder he'd been sheltering behind, the American asked him, "What's that noise out there?"

Gaston laughed and said, "It's our lovesick llama. She can't reach us over the rocks and the four others we tethered out there to graze can offer her no consolation for her condition. It was your cruel idea to choose four other females!"

"Jesus, she sounds like she's dying. I wonder how far that sound carries."

The llama called again. It sounded like the bray of a donkey mixed with the bleating of a sheep and the squeal of a

pig caught under a fence. Gaston said, "At least as far as a Swiss can yodel, and they yodel from one Alp to another. I have never understood why. Are you expecting company, Dick?"

"I hope not. But we are just off a trail and this is no time to shout about it!"

"*Eh bien,* in that case we have two choices. We shall either have to shoot the foolish creature or put her out of her misery."

"Aren't you being redundant?"

"*Mais non,* shooting her would put her out of her misery by killing her. Screwing her would put her out of her misery, and leave her *très* grateful!"

"Glugh! You can't be serious. Who the hell would want to fuck an animal?"

Gaston shrugged and said, "When one considers some of the women I have picked up in my time, the difference is not as great as it might seem. What about you and that hairy beast you had in Panama. She looked like a monkey with a rose in her hair, remember?"

Captain Gringo chuckled and said, "Come on, she wasn't that bad."

"She wasn't that good, either. How about that six-foot voodoo queen who liked you so much? She was black as the ace of spades and slicked her hide with palm oil, remember?"

Captain Gringo remembered. He said, "Voodoo was the least of her skills. Cut it out, you randy old goat. You're giving me a hard-on. Do you want to go back to the fire and catch forty or do you want to stand out here in the wind talking dirty? Give me that fucking poncho. It's cold up here."

Gaston chuckled and slipped the blue military poncho he'd been wearing off. He handed it to the American, along with his rifle. As Captain Gringo slipped the still-warm poncho over his head, Gaston said, "I thought you'd want the Maxim we've been packing up here, Dick."

Captain Gringo shook his head and said, "Not for sentry duty in the dark. This Winchester's the weapon for in-fighting. Machine guns are only better when you have a mess of targets lined up. Too clumsy for man-to-man stuff."

Gaston said, "Well, you're the machine-gun expert," as he started to move away. Captain Gringo asked where he was going and the Frenchman said, "To answer a call of nature,"

and the American nodded and hunkered down behind the boulder. Having those girls along was becoming a bother. There weren't enough to go around, so nobody could sleep with them. But they make taking a crap a delicate matter on the trail. He hadn't seen one of the girls take a leak all day, but he knew they all must have by now. The idea of La Diablilla squatting behind a rock sent a twitch through his groin again, damnit. He felt pretty disgusted with himself. It hadn't been *that* long since he'd been with a woman. Gaston had told him once that his problems were no doubt aggravated by his Puritan upbringing. Most professional soldiers and sailors masturbated often, with enthusiasm, and, as Gaston said, the nice thing about masturbation was that one did not have to look one's best. But the tall New England Yankee didn't like it. It made him feel stupid. So Gaston was right that he'd screw almost anybody first.

The crotch of his pants seemed tighter than usual as he crouched in the lee of the boulder, trying not to think about sex. But there wasn't much else to think about, damnit!

The moon had risen, oddly shrunken but ever so bright in the thin mountain air. He could see well down the slope to the chalky trail below. The wind was soft, despite the cold bite of its teeth, and the night was so still he was sure he'd hear any hoofbeats if anyone was dumb enough to be moving about at night at this altitude.

There was little point in planning beyond the following day's march, which promised to be much like the one they'd just completed, save for feeling safer and getting to go downhill by noon. He'd been through a few jungles by now. He knew that you didn't plan a jungle trip. It just happened to you. You never knew what lay beyond a fallen log until you got to it. The Colombian rebels with them knew little more about the country they'd be marching in to than he did. So what the hell, they'd take it as it came. All they had to know was that if they made it to Manaus alive they could hop a tramp steamer out.

Gaston had been to Manaus years ago. He'd said it was one wild town. A sort of degenerate Paris, shoved up the Amazon to serve the get-rich-quick adventurers who either wandered out of the surrounding jungle with plunder or left their bones in the jungle to slowly molder in the constant damp heat. Gaston had said the women of Manaus were wild as hell, and that they came in all sizes, shapes, and colors. He'd mentioned a Polish virgin of thirteen who'd been im-

ported all the way from Warsaw by an enterprising Brazilian whoremonger. He'd said he'd had the famous Tiger Lady, a Eurasian lady who danced naked, painted with black stripes on her tawny yellow body.

Somewhere in the night that goddam llama bleated again. He turned his head but couldn't spot her. He grimaced as he thought of the oddly human snatch he'd spotted earlier. It was sort of weird, when you thought about it. The Tiger Lady tried to look like an animal to excite her customers. The fucking llama *was* an animal, with a human snatch, and, damnit, the idea was sort of intriguing. He wondered if it would feel like there was a woman tucked inside that big shaggy brown beast, and if it would be thrilling or disgusting to find out.

"Jesus, maybe you'd better jerk off," he told himself, as he realized he had a raging erection now. The llama burbled and bawled like she was calling to him. He considered his options. He could just tough it out. He could beat his meat. He could mosey over and find out what all the sheepherder jokes were really about. Nobody would ever know, no matter what he decided. Sure, he'd feel stupid as hell, but who was the lovesick llama going to tell?

He decided he wasn't really that hard up. Then he wondered just how you went about it. Did you just walk up behind it and stick it on, or did the stupid critter require some foreplay? He laughed to himself as he pictured himself saying, "Easy, honey. I'll stop if you tell me I'm hurting you."

He remembered the old joke about the sheepherder counting his herd and saying, "One, two, three, good morning, darling, five, six . . ." It didn't sound as dumb, once you reconsidered what it would be like to spend a whole summer on a mountain with no women around. What the hell, it wasn't as if anybody or anything was likely to be hurt. Guys pulled all sorts of shitty tricks on women to get in their pantaloons, and left a lot of them crying and feeling used and abused. Was that any nobler than, well, sort of petting a pet more than society approved?

"I think I'm more curious than in love," he decided. He knew that a lot of the trouble men—and probably women—got into was simple curiosity. Nobody wanted to take a dwarf home to Mother, but a lot of people wondered what it would be like with a dwarf, a tattooed lady, or whatever. He

remembered how oddly exciting it had been to kiss Max with that dumb waxed mustache pasted to her lip, and the way those tribal markings on that black girl had felt as he explored her curves with his hands that time. He knew he'd never miss either sudden surprise again. But they had been sort of interesting. He'd never really been tempted by another man. But he'd often wished a couple of homosexuals would let him watch, just to see what the hell they did. He wished, right now, that somebody would screw that llama and give him a full report on what it felt like. Was it really like having a woman in a fur coat, or was it different, maybe better?

He heard someone moving over the rocks and stood up, holding the rifle trained that way, under his poncho. He called out quietly, *"Quién es?"* and a soft female voice replied, "It is I, Diablilla."

The girl came over to join him by the big boulder, shivering as the cold hit her. She said, "I wished for to speak with you about Pancho."

"Is he giving you trouble?"

"Yes and no. Brrr, it is freezing up here away from the fire, no?"

He put down the rifle and said, "Here, get inside this poncho with me. There's plenty of room."

Diablilla hesitated. Then she laughed and moved over to him. He raised the poncho and dropped it over her, pulling her close as he got the center opening around both their necks. Naturally, this put her smack against him, face to face, and he could feel that the nipples of her otherwise soft breasts were turgid, probably from the cold. She murmured, "Oh, this feels much warmer, but is it proper? What if someone were to see us like this?"

"They'd think we were friends. What's going on with Pancho? Do you want me to speak with him, Diablilla?"

She said, "I don't know. It is a delicate matter. You see, he thinks it wrong that I am not any man's *adelita*. He says every woman in a rebel band should be someone's *adelita*. He says it is an old guerrilla custom."

Captain Gringo smiled thinly, putting an arm around her more or less automatically to make a warmer bundle of them. He said, "Well, in most of the bands I've fought with, the leaders at least had *adelitas*. When your father led the brigade, I guess it never came up. But Pancho has a point. Girls are sort of useless to a guerrilla band unless they're

107

carrying some man's ammo and attending his needs. I take it Pancho has volunteered to be your *soldado* if you will be his *adelita?*"

She shuddered against him and said, "Yes, and I don't want to carry his ammo and cook his food. I think I did a bad thing. You may be cross with me if I tell you what I told Pancho."

"Let's find out. What did you tell him?"

"Well, you see, the other girls have all said they would be *adelitas* for the new men they now find themselves marching with. When our old brigade was shot up, they lost their men and . . ."

"Get to the point, Diablilla."

"I told Pancho you had already asked me to be your *adelita.*"

"Oboy! How did Pancho take that?"

She shrugged, and it felt sort of interesting to both of them, as she replied, "He said it was a good idea but that in that case I should not tell you he had approached me. He said you might be angry if you thought another man had trifled with your woman. I am not sure what Pancho meant when he said you *Americanos* are surprisingly discreet about such matters."

Captain Gringo sighed. He knew that most Latins claimed their bedroom privileges rather dramatically with a lot of "He who touches my woman shall die!" bullshit. He told the girl, "Okay, I'll act possessive in the future. None of the other men are likely to trifle with the boss *adelita.*"

Then, since they were pressed face to face anyway, he pulled her even closer and kissed her. She started to respond, then drew back as far as the hole in the poncho would let her, and gasped, "Señor! What is the meaning of this unseemly behavior?"

They were still plastered together and if she couldn't feel his erection against her soft warm belly she was dead from the waist down. He said, "I thought you wanted to be my *adelita.*"

"I do. I will tend your fire, carry your ammunition, and clean your guns. If you are wounded, I will nurse you. But does an *adelita* have to behave like a wicked woman for her *soldado,* too?"

He closed his eyes and muttered, "Swell. I get the pick of the litter, and she's a schoolgirl!"

He realized Diablilla was the victim of a false romantic

108

impression. *"Adelita"* was a generic term for the camp followers of the rebel trade south of Laredo. It was sort of a girl's name and sort of a pun, since in Spanish slang the untranslatable term meant something like "Small female with ambitions to improve her station in life." The tough little hard-eyed girls who trudged in the wake of rebel armies had been glorified in song and legend. But in real life, Señorita Adelita was more a tramp than a Joan of Arc. It was time someone explained the facts of life to Diablilla.

So he did, putting it as gently as possible that when it got down to the bare bones, a guy could always carry his own ammo if that was all he wanted. He said, "A *soldado* has enough on his plate without two mouths to feed and two targets to worry about, *querida*. Most modern armies frown on the idea of female camp followers. The only real advantage, for a guerrilla leader, is that it cuts down on desertion in his ranks and avoids a lot of rape if your guys have their own women along."

"But, Dick, none of the *adelitas* I know are married to their *soldados!*"

"What can I tell you, kitten? It's a rough business. Look, we'll drop you off somewhere and, what the hell, nobody's looking for you in particular. Wait until the dust of this last revolution settles a bit and you can go back to school or whatever."

She started to cry. He said, "Oh, for God's sake," and patted her under the poncho to comfort her. She said, "I have no home anymore. I want for to be a rebel. I have dedicated my life to the cause!"

"Yeah, it is sort of fun to play soldier. But that's all you've been doing, Diablilla. Sure, I saw you hit that trooper with a rock and I know you have a ferocious nickname, but you're too soft and, well, too nice to make a real guerrilla, kid."

"How dare you accuse me of being an amateur! Are you saying that to be a real rebel, a girl has to be vile?"

"Not vile. What Gaston calls *practique*. This game is for keeps, and the only thing a real soldier worries about is staying alive. You can't be too delicate about what you eat or how often you take a bath. A female fighter who's more worried about her virtue than survival has no place in such rough company. Many an *adelita* has helped her cause by seducing an enemy. I've never heard of anyone winning by yelling rape."

109

Diablilla considered as she remembered a song about a brave girl. Then she shuddered and said, "Would I have to be vile with everyone on my side?"

"No. Of course not. No *adelita* gives herself to anyone but her *soldado,* unless its to help him."

"Very well, but you will have to teach me how. I have never been vile before."

"Are you saying you're a virgin, for God's sake? I mean, I knew you were a good girl, but this is ridiculous!"

"I do not understand you, Dick. How could I be a good girl if I was not a virgin? But you have convinced me that I must be a complete *adelita.* So how do we start?"

That was a good question. He wasn't sure he wanted the responsibility. She was cute as a button and he was horny as hell, but, Jesus, a virgin?

On the other hand, if she went on talking this way he'd wind up having trouble with Pancho or some other guy with less delicate feelings. He knew Hispanics respected a friend's woman more than many Anglo-Saxons. A Spanish-speaking enemy would rape your mother and delight in taunting you with it. But unlike certain church-going New Englanders he could mention, they never even winked at a *compañero's* girl behind his back.

He rolled them toward the boulder until her back was against it with him leaning on her as he kissed her again. He tongued her this time, and she was breathing fast when they came up for air. She said, "Oh, that was very vile, but I think I liked it."

So he did it again, running his left hand down her trembling flank to gather a handful of cotton skirting and hitch it up as he rubbed his body against hers. When he got her skirts up around her hips, he found, as he'd suspected, that she wore nothing under them. She flinched and hissed but didn't turn away from his kiss as he moved his hand between her legs and cupped her warm furry *mons* on his palm. He let her get used to it for a moment. Then, as he felt her trembling less, he slid two fingers into her wet warmth and began to stroke her off. She started moving from side to side as if to avoid what he was doing, but he had her pinned pretty well, albeit not hard enough to frighten her, and she began to respond to his petting. But she turned her head to one side and, as he kissed her earlobe, she gasped, "Oh, that feels so strange. But I don't think you are really being vile. Those are your fingers, no?"

110

He whispered, "Easy does it, we've got all night," and then began to tongue her ear. She giggled and said, "You are tickling me all over, and, *Madre de Dios!* Are you trying to drive me mad?"

He was, but he didn't say so. She was moving her hips to meet his manual dexterity now, and for a virgin she moved pretty well. Her legs stiffened as she stood on tiptoe, aiming her pelvis to receive him. A less experienced lover would have broken the spell by a clumsy move about now, but the tall American had met up with virgins before, albeit not as often as Queen Victoria would have one believe, so he knew enough to make her come at least once before he got down to serious business.

It was easy. She suddenly turned her head to kiss him full on the lips, and this time she tongued him as he slid his fingers to the knuckles up inside her, massaging her clit with the web of his thumb. He felt her clamp down as she sobbed, kissing him wildly. He left his hand in place as she slowly came down from a long teasing orgasm and then, before she could cool off, he unbuckled everything with his other hand and let his gun belt and trousers fall anywhere they wanted to. He got his bent naked knees between her bare legs and used the fingers he already had in her as a sort of shoehorn to guide his quivering erection in place. As he withdrew his hand and thrust seriously into her she hissed again and said, "Oh, no, not that!" But it was that and it only took a few good thrusts before she was bumping and grinding against him, while saying she felt so ashamed.

They were leaning against the boulder at an angle, but standing sex has certain limitations. So he reached down and pulled one of her knees up until he had it at the level of her breasts, hooked over one wrist as he braced his palm against the rough granite. She gasped, "Oh, it's so deep!" and he said, "Yeah," and did the same to the other leg, holding her higher and spread wide against the rock as he came, touching bottom.

She was rolling her head from side to side against the rock as she moaned mingled protests and demands for more. So he kept moving until his own desires returned. This didn't take long with a beautiful girl having repeated orgasms while she rode him like a witch on a broomstick. But the position was tiring. So, now that he had her convinced, he pulled her from the boulder and peeled the poncho off them to spread it on the flat surface they'd been standing on. As she asked him

what they were doing, he lowered her to the poncho and began to undress them both completely. She said, "Dick, it's freezing up here!" but he said, "I'll be your blanket," and mounted her again in the usual and more romantic position. She laughed and wrapped her arms and legs around him as she said, "Oh, I like this blanket. But tell me, am I really your vile *adelita,* now?"

He didn't answer. He was enjoying her too much for one thing, and for another he had no idea how he was going to end this thing he'd most obviously started.

Meanwhile, far up the slope, Gaston's own experiment was going better than he'd expected. The friendly llama smelled a bit more like a camel than any lady he'd ever done this with before, but her warm contractions were fantastic as he clung to her rump hairs, humping with enthusiasm. The randy little Frenchman had started this as a lark, more to satisfy his curiosity than from any real desire. He hadn't expected the llama to be so cooperative, and had been quite prepared to give it up as a poor idea. But when she'd responded to his first casual petting by presenting her rump to him, it had seemed common courtesy to help the poor thing out with a finger and, once he'd delved her surprisingly human interior, what had followed had seemed inevitable.

"This is ridiculous. I seem to be coming." Gaston frowned as the llama wriggled her big rump against him and bleated softly. Her wet opening opened and closed around his shaft and he grinned and said, "You, too, *mon chérie?*" The gentle animal couldn't talk, but it didn't have to. Gaston had experienced too many female orgasms to have to be told he was making her very happy, and the very insanity tititlated him more than the sane part of his mind approved of. Gaston closed his eyes and groaned, *"Merde alors!* This is good!" as he exploded in her wet, warm interior.

He clung to her hide, gasping for breath, as she went on milking his shaft with her vaginal muscles, as if chewing a cud at both ends. He laughed and said, "Enough, *chérie,* one would not wish to make a habit of such bestial behavior."

The llama didn't answer. Gaston realized this was one girl who'd never discuss his lovemaking with her friends. He laughed and said, "Well, as long as you like me so much, maybe one more time, *hein?*"

14

They ditched the incriminating military uniforms the next day.

The llamas had to be abandoned when they descended to the elfin fog forests on the far slope. So Gaston's sweetheart and the other four were left to fend for themselves on the higher pastures, and the packing got more serious. But they were moving downhill as they took turns packing the Maxim and ammo. Pancho suggested leaving behind the canteens, but Captain Gringo vetoed the idea. It was true they'd find water everywhere in the rain forests, but how much of it would be fit to drink was up for grabs. He said, "Nobody drinks water they haven't boiled at least twenty minutes. We've got enough to worry about without the jungle trots."

Despite the lower altitude, the upper reaches of the fog forest were cold as hell. Everyone was chilled to the bone by the constant gray mist all around. For, in truth, they were still high and descending through the cloud ceiling that hung over the vast jungle basin of Amazonia. The growth along the trail was spooky. The trees that grew this high were gnarled and stunted visitors from some other planet, reaching clawlike limbs out to snatch at hats and skirts when you weren't looking. Everything from slimy boulders to twisted trunks was covered with fuzzy green moss. Long gray beards hung dripping from the leafless trees killed by lightning. It was sobering to note how many trees up here in the cloud had caught a bolt of Jove's fire. Yet even dead wood shared the same spinach green of the mist-nourished moss.

Diablilla marched rather smugly at Captain Gringo's side, with a belt of machine-gun ammo proudly draped over one shoulder. The ponchos had all been rolled to carry, since

113

the mist penetrated every fold of cloth and walking in wet wool was asking for pneumonia. Gaston and Captain Gringo knew more about lowland jungle running than most of the highland natives they were leading. So there'd been a little griping about unusual orders.

But the two adventurers had insisted. They knew that as the greatest killer in a desert was the unexpected flash-flood, one of the unexpected dangers of the jungle was the common cold. People expected jungles to be hot, and they were, a lot of the time. That was why pneumonia claimed so many lives among jungle dwellers. It was impossible to tear-ass through the jungle in an overcoat. So people with damp, naked skin tended to get sudden chills when the temperature dropped. It never got really cold in a jungle, but sixty degrees is cold enough to make one shiver like hell under damp cloth.

It took them the better part of a day to descend through the fog belt. But by late afternoon they'd gotten down to what the natives called *La Montaña*. High rolling country covered with quinine and other trees one associates with the South American jungle, or, to give it its Brazilian name, the *selva*.

Selva, which means forest in Portuguese, was actually a better description than the East Indian term, jungle. The Amazonian rain forest is not a thick tangle, save near the edges of a river or a clearing. Under the high tree canopy it's too shaded for thick growth at ground level. So while they had to hack their way through places where a fallen forest giant had exposed the red soil to sunlight and a growth spurt, it was more like walking through a vast pillar-filled cathedral, in this case with a sloping floor. They could only see occasional patches of the gray sky high above, and it was dank and gloomy at ground level all through the day.

But after they'd been slogging down the slope through the *selva* a few hours it was obviously getting darker. Pancho, who was packing the Maxim, asked Captain Gringo what they were going to do about it.

The tall American had been keeping an eye on Pancho. But the ex-soldier hadn't seemed particularly upset about his relationship with Diablilla, and the erstwhile virgin had been acting rather obvious about her newfound worldliness. He'd caught her talking to one of the other girls that morning, both of them grinning his way, as Diablilla made a measuring motion with her hands that there was no possible mistake about them meaning.

114

He told Pancho, "You're right. We'd better start think-ing about a campsite. You're an old campaigner, Pancho. Where do you think we ought to set up."

The bearded *mestizo* looked pleased and said, "Well, near water sounds good in the high country. Down here it could be dangerous, no?"

"Yeah, caymen and anacondas make me nervous, too. Any open clearing would be choked with brush. On the other hand, a fire in the open under these trees could be seen a long way between the trunks."

Pancho said, "We passed a place a few minutes ago that I considered. Perhaps we shall come to another soon."

"Perhaps we won't. It'll be dark in another couple of hours. Let's move back to your choice, Pancho. Give me that gun and take the point."

Pancho grinned boyishly and said, "Hey, you are the kind of leader I like, Captain Gringo!" as he handed over the Maxim and pointed back up the slope to add, "Remember that wall of second growth a quarter kilometer back? If we built our fires between tree boles and the brush . . ."

"Good thinking. Nobody chasing us down-slope could slip up on us through the brush without making noise. Nobody farther down knows we're here, and if they don't see our fires, they won't know we're here some more."

So Pancho led them back to his chosen campground, strutting a bit, but what the hell, he'd earned it. Unlike many officers, Captain Gringo liked to lead men who didn't have to be burped. No leader can do all the thinking for everyone. Most soldiers think pretty well for themselves, if they're encouraged. Captain Gringo owed his life to a Negro private in the old Tenth Cav who'd had a hell of a good idea one night in Apache country.

Some of the others grumbled that they were backtrack-ing, but Gaston had caught on and backed Pancho with a string of curses, adding, "The point of this operation is not to get anywhere in a hurry, my children. It is to get there alive, *hein?*"

So the camp was set up where Pancho had suggested as a long line of small night fires tucked against the wall of uphill brush. Captain Gringo left his part-Indian followers alone as they laid small Indian fires screened from prying eyes by buttress roots and fallen logs. The way you found out if a recruit was an idiot was to let him show you by making a

115

mistake before it really mattered. So far, he'd yet to see these guys and the handful of girls in a real emergency. But they'd lived through a revolution and seemed to be shaping up.

Meanwhile, as Diablilla built their own fire near the spread-out poncho she'd decided was theirs, he set up the machine gun on a fallen log. It had no tripod mount and the water jacket made it heavy and clumsy to fire offhand. He took out his jackknife, opened the screwdriver blade, and opened the petcock to drain the jacket. Pancho, who'd been a soldier and seemed eager to learn, strolled over to ask him what he was doing. Captain Gringo said, "Water weighs eight pounds a gallon. If I have to fire this gun from the hip, I'd rather not have to lift that much."

"Ah, I heard about the way the famous Captain Gringo fires a machine gun like a carbine. But they told us the water is for to cool the barrel, no?"

"It is, if you're firing steady in a siege situation. I've found these guns can take a little dry firing in short bursts."

"What if a long burst is needed?"

"It very seldom is, Pancho. I don't think the modern manuals we read have machine-gunning down to a science yet. Someday I'll bet they make all these things air-cooled. I'd like to see more weight in a thicker barrel and forget this horseshit with a water-filled tin can around it. I just explained about the weight. There are other problems Señor Maxim didn't think about when he designed this toy. You can't always get water, and when you can, it can freeze. Maxim builds these things to hose a steady stream of lead, like the old Gatling gun. Think what you could do with a lighter weapon, made more like a rifle and fired in quick bursts. You don't need more than six or eight rounds at a crack to discourage hell out of anybody coming at you. I've found the other side has a tougher time locating your position, too."

Pancho shrugged and said, "Well, you are the machine-gun expert," and moved away. Captain Gringo watched him out of one corner of his eye. If Pancho lined up one of the other girls, the problem was over. But Diablilla had said something about the other women in the band having chosen new *soldados*, hadn't she?

He finished with the gun and stood up, putting the knife away. As he started to walk off, Diablilla called, "Where are you going, *querido?*" and he said, "Down the slope aways. I want to see if anyone can spot a fire from farther down."

He turned his back and left the campsite. It was quite

116

dark now. He had to watch his step. The leaves rotted away soon on the red soil, but freshly fallen ones were slippery as banana peels, and there were other things a guy could step on in the dark, like bushmasters or other poison snakes. Fortunately, army ants didn't march at night. They made camp, too.

Mosquitoes didn't. He slapped the side of his neck and got one. Mosquitoes weren't really much worse in the jungles down here than they'd been in the backyard on a New England summer's eve, but he didn't enjoy them anywhere. He'd met that old Spanish doctor in Panama who kept saying mosquitoes carried Yellow Jack. Nobody else believed him, but Captain Gringo had an open mind on Yellow Jack. He'd had it once, and he didn't want to go through that again. They said a guy was immune to jungle fevers once he'd lived through a bout. But they'd lied to him about Santa Claus, too.

Diablilla called his name and he stopped and turned. It was damned near pitch-dark and he couldn't see any fires. It looked like they were safe for at least one more night. One night at a time was the way you lived your life down here.

Diablilla's form was a ghostly blur as she caught up with him. She said, "I brought the poncho, my *toro*."

"Yeah? How come? Don't you want to sleep by the fire?"

She laughed and said, "Of course I wish for to *sleep* by the fire, but how can we make love up there among the others, eh?"

He grinned and said, "You're on, but it's sort of early, isn't it?"

"Early? I have been wanting to feel you inside me all day! Come, make me your vile woman some more. We can eat and sleep later."

So they spread the poncho on the ground and undressed to resume her education. Considering how late in life she'd started, there seemed little he could teach her. She'd never known the girl could get on top, but when he suggested it she responded with enthusiasm. As she lowered herself on to him she gasped, "Oh, I feel like a little chicken roasting on a spit! Am I being vile enough for you, my *soldado?*"

"Yeah, I've never had it so vile. Jesus, if only I could get you in a hotel room where we could go at it right . . ."

She bounced happily and replied, "I, too, think this would be nicer on a soft mattress. Is it true that wicked

117

people do this in front of mirrors with the lights on? That sounds very vile."

"I know. Would you like to do it, Diablilla?"

"Oh, yes. It is most pleasant, doing terrible things with you. It is very odd, but I do not feel ashamed when we do vile things together. I have always heard this is a fate worse than death. Yet I have never felt so alive! Do you think I have become a wicked person, Dick?"

He propped himself up on one elbow to kiss her and fondle her bobbing breasts as he assured her, "You're not being wicked. You're being a woman."

"*Si*, but the Church says that Our Lord does not approve of people doing this, *querido*."

"Maybe. Do you think Our Lord made us, Diablilla?"

"*Si*, it says so in the Bible."

"All right, if He made us, He made us the way we are below the waists, right?"

"Of course, and I am most grateful for the way He made you, Dick!"

"I owe Him, too. You've got a lovely little box. So listen, why would anybody go to all the trouble of giving us such complicated organs if we weren't supposed to *do* anything with them?"

She started breathing faster as she gasped, "Oh, I like what we are doing with them, Dick. I think I am, how you say, going again?"

He rolled her over on her back and began to pound her as he growled, "You're not going, doll, you're coming," and she moaned, "Either way, I love it!"

15

The Indians were there at dawn. Captain Gringo was sleeping, fully dressed, on the poncho with Diablilla up near their fire, when the girl nudged him awake and murmured, "Dick, don't move too suddenly. Don't say anything. Just sit up naturally. Let me do the talking."

He rubbed his face and sat up on the poncho, still wondering what the hell she was talking about. Then he spotted the trio of naked, long-haired youths standing with their backs to the wall of brush across the way. Their privates were dangling naked in the morning breeze but each wore a string belt with a little bark quiver of tufted darts. Each held a blowgun taller than he was. Captain Gringo glanced down the line and saw nobody else was awake yet. He kept his voice down as he asked the girl, "If you can talk to them, ask them what they want and warn them that I'm going to call down the line. If anybody else wakes up unexpectedly we could have a nasty accident."

Diablilla nodded and called out softly in a liquid bird-song language. One of the Indians nodded gravely and burbled back at her. She said, "We are in luck. They are Jivaro."

"That's luck? The Jivaro are the ones who shoot you full of poison darts and shrink your head, right?"

Diablilla smiled and said, "I'll explain later. Wake the others and make sure nobody does anything silly. These boys are nervous."

"*They're* nervous? Okay, keep them chatting friendly and if I get a dart in my back I'll probably never speak to you again."

It wasn't much of a joke, but Diablilla passed it on to the

Jivaro and they seemed to think it was pretty funny. It was odd to hear a headhunter laugh like anyone else.

Captain Gringo nudged Gaston awake at the next poncho. He knew Gaston never leaped before he looked. He told the Frenchman, "Company for breakfast, I hope. Pass it on and make sure nobody acts unfriendly or frightened."

Gaston sat up yawning, spotted the Jivaro, and muttered, "*Merde alors*. I have seen pictures of that breed. They are Jivaro headhunters!"

"So Diablilla tells me. She can speak their dialect so she must know something we don't know, unless she's one hell of an actress."

He moved back to hunker down beside the girl as Diablilla said something in Jivaro. One of the youths put his blowgun down and gingerly came forward to accept the small paper packet Diablilla held out to him. He squatted near the edge of the poncho, opened his small gift, and tasted. Then he grinned happily and called out to his friends. They grinned too as, down the line, somebody sat up and sobbed, "*Madre de Dios!*" before Gaston could silence him.

The Jivaro ignored the byplay since they'd obviously found themselves among friendly people. Captain Gringo asked about the gift and she replied, "Salt. It's the one thing they value more than anything else."

"Hmm, this far from the sea, it figures there'd be a shortage of salt. Tell them there's more where that came from. But I'm missing something, doll. These guys are Jivaro headhunters and those are blowguns they're packing, right?"

The three Jivaro began to share the salt, eating it like sugar candy, as Diablilla said, "I have met Jivaro before, with my poor father. They are headhunters, it is true. But people misunderstand their motives. The Jivaro only take and shrink the heads of their *enemies*. The shrunken head is not a war trophy. It is for the protection of the victor and his family against the ghost of the man he had to kill. They believe that the ghosts of the dead live in the heads of dead enemies, so if one shrinks the head, one shrinks the ghost. If one sews up all the openings and guards the head well, the ghost, even a little ghost, cannot get out to haunt one."

"Sympathetic magic, huh? What about those weapons?"

"Those are not weapons of war, Dick. They use the darts for to hunt small game. If a Jivaro wishes for to kill you, he uses his bow or machete like anyone else. You can see these

boys are not out for to fight anyone. They are hunting monkeys and birds."

"Well, there goes another illusion. Since you're still alive, you must know what you're talking about. I thought you were crazy when you said they were friendly, but I'm beginning to believe you. Look at 'em go for that salt."

Diablilla smiled fondly at the desperate-looking trio and said, "The Jivaro are one of the friendliest tribes in the lowlands, if one understands their ways."

"And if you don't understand them?"

"Well, we did see some shrunken heads that looked like they may have once been white men when my father and I last visited some Jivaro. The story of their ferocity is not completely a myth, Dick. They are good fighters, if they feel you are not their friend."

"Hey, give 'em some more salt. If we can get them to guide us through to some landing where we can beg, borrow or steal a boat . . ."

But Diablilla put a hand on his sleeve to silence him as he said, "No. That is what I mean by misunterstandings in the past, Dick. The very first rule you must know in dealing with the Jivaro is, do not ever ask a Jivaro to do anything!"

"Not even if you ask politely?"

"That could be even worse. If you yell a demand at a Jivaro warrior he may think you are joking and just laugh. But, you see, they are very gentle people among themselves. So the tribal elders never shout orders. They just suggest politely that a younger follower do something. These boys would surely do anything we asked them to, within reason. They are trained to obey their elders, but . . ."

"Right, the elders would resent it like hell and gently suggest somebody shrink our heads a lot. I'm glad you came along, doll. Aside from the reasons we discussed last night. I'm beginning to see there's more to making friends in this neck of the woods than I thought. A lot of missionaries who wound up dead could have used someone like you to chat with the natives for them."

The youth she'd given the salt to chirped at Diablilla, and when she answered, he shook his head in an agitated manner and kept pointing to the southeast as if it was an awfully shitty place.

Captain Gringo listened to the odd lingo, trying to follow the drift. He was pretty good at picking up on odd

dialects. He'd been one of the few officers or men in the ol
Indian fighting army who'd bothered to ask their India
scouts to teach them a few words of Pueblo or Apach
Knowing the difference had once saved his ass, and o
another occasion it had prevented a needless atrocity whe
he'd been ordered to "pacify" the wrong Indians.

But Jivaro obviously was not related to either Uto-Azte
nor Na-dene. It sounded like it had been made up aboard
roller coaster. It went up to falsetto tweets and dropped t
guttural grunts. He knew Diablilla was cold sober, but if he'
just come in, he'd have thought she was drunk from th
expression on her pretty face as she and the Indian chatte
He knew each lingo had its own gestures and facial expre
sions that went with the words and that she'd fallen into the
automatically. Along with what she'd already told them,
was small wonder everyone thought the Jivaro were prett
weird. They looked and sounded weird as hell.

The three Indians suddenly took off without ceremony
As they vanished into the jungle gloom like silent ghost
Diablilla turned to Captain Gringo and the others to say
"Those boys said we should avoid Gueppi and stay awa
from any riverbanks until we work our way far east."

"Any particular reason, or are we talking about mor
odd native customs?"

"They said there are *flagelado* slave raiders hunting u
and down the rivers. They have steam launches and repeatin
rifles. Those boys are from a band that was driven far sout
of their usual hunting grounds by others just as bad. They sa
they are afraid to go farther south, but that their wise me
think they are safe enough for now in this part of th
selva."

He pursed his lips and said, "I can see why the India
are afraid to go near the water, but we're not Indians. S
what the hell."

Diablilla shook her head and explained, "The Jivaro sa
being a *mestizo* or even a *blanco* is not much help. T
raiders are taking everyone they meet."

"Hey, that'll be the fucking day! Did they tell you wh
all this flesh peddling is about, Diablilla?"

"They were a bit confused, but I think I was able to p
it all together from what they told me. The *flagelados* a
working for big rubber companies. They need latex tapper
A lot of latex tappers. The price of crude rubber has climbe
to an all-time high on the world market. But one only gets

little latex from each tree, and the wild rubber trees stand widely spaced in the *selva*. The Jivaro told me the raiders have even seized Colombian troopers and put them to work. I think they have something else in mind in chasing Jivaro. It is of course impossible to hold a male Indian captive very long in his own *selva*, but the Jivaro girls are very pretty and the houses of ill-repute in Manaus pay well for exotic imports. The new rich rubber barons find it exciting to be vile with something different."

Captain Gringo grimaced and said, "They sound like keen guys." He looked up at Gaston, who'd drifted over to join them, and asked, "Still want to go to Manaus?"

The dapper little Frenchman shrugged and replied, *"Oui,* it may be amusing at the House of a Thousand Variations these days. We are on the wild frontier here, Dick. Conditions will be more civilized farther to the east. Manaus has an opera house and police force in addition to its wide-open wickedness. A certain amount of public order is required if only because it's good for business. Nobody will attack us on the streets of the jungle metropolis. At least, not on the well-lit streets."

The American nodded thoughtfully and said, "Yeah, I remember Nuevo Laredo on a Saturday night. Hey, Nuñez?"

The rebel who'd guided them over the mountains came closer and Captain Gringo said, "We have to work our way east to civilization the hard way. The Indians tell us Gueppi and the river may be a bad move. Any other ideas?"

Nuñez said, "No, Señor. I was getting lost in any case once we left the trail in the fog forests. I have never been this far east. I have never heard of traveling through the *selvas* away from the riverbanks. I am not sure this is possible."

Captain Gringo waved expansively at the cathedral gloom around them and said, "It has to be. The Indians do it all the time. You just keep walking between the trees. How far due east would you figure Manaus could be?"

Nuñez said he had no idea. Gaston said, "I make it a little under a thousand miles, Dick."

"A thousand *what?* Jesus, Gaston, that's one hell of a walk!"

"Oui, I tend to agree. That is why sensible people use steam boats in Amazonia, my overactive lad. In addition to being *très fatigué,* have you considered we have no compass?"

Captain Gringo glanced upward as he realized he'd been

123

about to say something dumb about navigating by the sun. H[e]
said, "Well, the land slopes to the east," and Gaston replie[d]
"Only for a little ways. We shall soon be walking in circles o[n]
dead-flat terrain. We'll be out of food in another day or s[o]
and please do not tell me we can live off the country. Game [is]
sparse in Amazonia. That is why the Indians must shoot bir[ds]
and monkeys out of the trees. We have as many mouths t[o]
feed as the average Indian band and they barely manag[e]
despite being raised in this confusion!"

The American thought and decided. "Okay, we're goin[g]
to split the difference. We'll work our way east of this wa[ter]
zone and then cut over to some settlement or other and se[e]
about something that can float us down to Manaus." H[e]
turned to Diablilla and asked, "Did the Jivaro tell you wh[at]
settlement the slave raiders are working out of?"

She said, "They don't visit towns, so they don't know th[e]
names of any, but I was able to learn that the *flagelados* a[re]
most active along the Rio Putumayo and that they raid as f[ar]
north as the headwaters of La Caqueta."

He frowned and said, "Hey, aren't we *south* of l[a]
Caqueta?"

"Yes, Dick. That was why the Jivaro warned us to b[e]
careful."

16

Captain Gringo had known they were in trouble. He hadn't known how much trouble they were in until they stopped for a noon break farther to the east. The going hadn't been too tough, but everyone had wet feet and damp clothes and there was no way to dry out in the sunless depths of the *selva*. If they didn't catch pneumonia that night, they faced jungle rot in a few more days. The parched corn and jerked beef they'd taken from the Colombian troopers' saddlebags was getting moldy and there hadn't been all that much to begin with. Pancho came over to ask if they could light fires. Captain Gringo told him not to. There was a slight breeze from the north, left by the trade winds dragging their bellies along the canopy overhead. The smell of smoke traveled far in damp air and would contrast sharply with the normal rain forest smell of mold and rotting vegetation.

Pancho wandered off, grumbling. There was a lot of that going around now that they'd lost the inspiration of hot pursuit. Captain Gringo knew there'd be more to come if he didn't shape up and lead them someplace that sounded sensible.

Gaston must have been thinking along the same lines. He waited until Diablilla went off with one of the other girls to take a discreet crap in the woods before he moved over to his taller sidekick and hunkered down to say, "We are carrying a lot of extra baggage, Dick. When are we to lighten the load?"

Captain Gringo didn't ask him what he meant. Save for the eight men who'd armed themselves with the dead troopers' rifles the ragtag band was a large, discouraged gang of

125

ragged, helpless fugitives. They had six women, eight ponchos, and damned near no food to share among two dozen men.

Gaston read his hesitation correctly and urged, "Come on, Dick. We owe them nothing. We saved them from captivity and got them out this far. What can they expect from us, eggs in their *cerveza?*"

"We can't ditch them. Aside from it being sort of shitty Diablilla and the ones with guns wouldn't like it."

"Have you asked them? Diablilla will do as you say Pancho is a born survivor. Nuñez, Quico, and a couple of others who were quick to arm themselves and move in on the women are men who think well on their feet, too. The others are just peons and a burden. A smaller, well-armed party could move faster and take on anybody we might meet. Even then, it could be a tight squeak. Have you any idea how awkward it would be to attempt to load all those people in one canoe, if we got lucky?"

"Look, Gaston, I know you're right. I just can't abandon kids in this green hell. If they didn't starve to death, the damned slavers would catch them and put them to work tapping rubber trees. The guys, I mean. The *flagelados* would probably rape the girls."

Gaston shrugged and said, "Tapping rubber is no more distressing than being shot against a wall. As to the *adelitas* none of them are convent girls. The *flagelados* won't have to rape them. They admire tough men with guns, *hein?*"

"Look, I said you were right. But there has to be a better way. We don't have to worry about it right now, do we?"

"*Mais non,* we can worry about it ten minutes from now if you wish. But let us come up with something soon. This would be a tough trek for legged-up soldiers. These barefoot children do not move fast enough for important destinations and I, for one, grow weary of this casual strolling through the countryside."

Diablilla and the other girl came back. They were not alone. An older Jivaro was walking between them, carrying machete. Captain Gringo whistled for attention and called out, "Everybody stay calm like I told you before. Just go on about your whatever and pretend you don't see him."

Gaston nudged him and murmured, "Don't you mean see *them?* We are being covered from all sides, Dick."

"Yeah, I spotted that guy ducking behind that tree, too

ut the girls were out among them alone just now. I think
iey're just being cautious. The old gent looks like a chief."

His guess was correct. Diablilla brought the old Indian
ver to them and as they all hunkered down she explained,
This is the *casique* of our earlier Jivaro's band, Dick. He
ells me his scouts have spotted a gang of *flagelados* headed
iis way. He says he is going back to his own hideout and he
aggested we might like to come along."

"Suggested, eh? Didn't you tell me a suggestion is an
rder from a Jivaro chief?"

She said, "I feel he is sincere, Dick. Those others
eported we were friendly and gave them salt. He knows all
hites are not *flagelados* and of course he knows we have
ins. Jivaro are shy but pragmatic. They seldom invite
rangers to visit them. But I told him we don't like slavers,
ther, and he suggested that our guns and his hideout might
aake a good match."

"Yeah? How do we know he isn't trying to lure us into a
ap and steal our guns?"

"Oh, Dick, how silly you talk. He does not have to lure
s into the *selva* for to rob us. We are already in the *selva* and
irrounded by his warriors. Besides, they don't know how to
se modern guns. The only guns some few Jivaro have are
d trade muskets and they don't trust them. The powder
on spoils in this constant dampness and the guns keep
owing up when they will fire. I don't know if this is because
ey are cheaply made or poorly cared for. This *casique* says
has no guns."

The chief nudged the girl politely and said something
se. She nodded and translated, "He says he has something
teresting to show us at his camp, too."

"Ask him what it is."

She did, and after a long discussion in bird she looked
izzled and said, "He says he was hoping we could tell him.
e says his warriors captured a creature they can't under-
and. He says it looks like a human being, but that it is
ilder than any monkey. They have been trying to decide
hether to tame it or eat it. It is obviously not a person, but
e women feel sorry for it and say it looks too much like a
rson for to eat."

The American glanced at Gaston. The Frenchman
rugged and said, "Don't look at me. I have never heard of
ild apes in Latin America, and in any case these Indians

127

would know every animal that belonged in the *selva*. Perhap
some species of African ape escaped from some zoo o
circus? I think they have a zoo in Manaus."

The American nodded and said, "Well, we may as wel
give it a shot. We can't stay here if raiders are moving ou
way. Tell the old boy we accept his invitation, Diablilla."

The girl did so, and the *casique* grinned and handec
Captain Gringo a greasy lump of what looked like black
board chalk. He looked at it dubiously and the girl said, "H
likes you. He has given you a lump of precious rock salt. Licl
it and hand it back to him."

Captain Gringo kept his face neutral to hide the gree
taste in his mouth. He could see the lump of rock salt ha
been slobbered over by other tongues. But what the hell, he'
shared a spit-slicked peace pipe with Apache in his time. H
gingerly licked the piece of rock salt, rubbed his tummy, an
said, "Yum yum," before handing it back. The old ma
grinned with delight and imitated the motion before tuckin
the salt in with his poison darts. Then he rose and walke
away without further comment. Diablilla said, "We are sup
posed to follow him."

So they did. It wasn't easy. Captain Gringo could hav
walked that fast with little trouble, but the others trailin
behind him cursed and stumbled as the Indians led them at
mile-eating clip between the trees.

The guerrilla band was strung out and some had falle
behind completely within a few miles, but the guys packin
the machine gun managed to stay in sight and he noticed on
of the Jivaro warriors had moved in to help by packing on
of the ammo cases. The Jivaro were shorter than the white o
even *mestizo* Colombians, but they were sturdy little runt
with muscular brown legs. They seemed to move with n
effort, even though Captain Gringo was starting to sweat a bi
now.

As he'd expected, they led him to an area where the tree
had been leveled, either by a storm or slash-and-burn agricul
ture a while back, so the undergrowth had grown up rank an
tangled. The chief ahead walked into what seemed a soli
green wall and vanished silently. Captain Gringo saw, as h
followed, that they'd hacked a twisted path through the brus
and what looked like monstrous lettuce armed with thorns.

As the fugitive party wound through single file, the tra
suddenly opened on a clearing the size of a baseball diamon
The bright red earth had been cleared and packed down b

bare feet. A circle of thatched huts surrounded the village plaza. No smoke rose from any of the huts. The Jivaro knew about the way you spot a hideout at a distance, too.

As the rebels stumbled out into the open space and clustered dubiously around Captain Gringo, some naked little potbellied kids ran out to laugh and caper around them. The Indians in the huts stayed put but peeked out with shy grins. Some of the girls weren't bad.

By no stretch of the imagination could a Jivaro maiden be considered beautiful by a white man's standards. They were oddly built with thick waists and swaybacks. Their faces were moon-shaped and sort of funny-looking even if they'd had eyebrows. Yet there was an appealing childish cuteness to the younger ones. Their skins were smooth as peaches and the same color. Their small, firm breasts stood proudly at attention as if someone had pasted a grown woman's tits on a little girl. The juvenile effect was enhanced by the absolute lack of pubic hair between their chubby reddish tan thighs. This detail was apparent at a glance because all any of them wore, if that, was a string around the waist. Both male and female Jivaro wore their long hair in bangs. For headhunters they all smiled a lot and he'd never seen such perfect teeth.

As the chief orated an introduction for them to his people, some of the older Jivaro came shyly out for a closer look. In Spanish, Captain Gringo called out casually, "All right, all you men, I can't tell you not to peek, but for God's sake keep your hands off these girls. Remember, we're guests and these guys are tougher than they might look."

There was a muttering murmur of agreement. Then, apparently inspired by the sound of a white man's lingo, a pale figure exploded out of one of the huts and ran toward them as a shorter, darker Jivaro girl followed with an exasperated expression.

It was a white woman. Or, rather, a white girl of about seventeen or eighteen. She had long blond hair, period. She wasn't wearing a stitch, and as she got closer she suddenly became aware of this and tried to cover her breasts and blond pubic thatch with her hands. Since she only had two hands, she didn't quite make it.

She settled for dropping to her knees, thighs together, hands over her breasts, at the feet of the bemused Captain Gringo. She was blushing beet-red as she sobbed in English, "Oh, thank God you've come at last! I have been a captive of these cannibals for weeks!"

The old chief was saying something to Diablilla. The brunette stared down at the blonde in dawning understanding as she translated, "This is the mysterious creature they were telling us about, Dick."

"For God's sake, couldn't they see she's a *girl?*"

"Apparently they've been debating that. Do you speak Spanish, Señorita?"

The naked blonde at their feet looked up blankly. She was awfully pretty, despite her tears and dirty face. She asked in English, "Beg pardon?" and Diablilla told Captain Gringo in Spanish, "There's part of your answer. The Jivaro know there are other people in the world beside themselves, but every Christian they've ever met spoke Spanish or the related Portuguese. Some Jivaro know a little of those tongues. This poor girl's language must sound like utter gibberish to them. The unusual color of her hair and eyes didn't help, either."

Captain Gringo leaned down to help the blonde to her feet, but she sobbed, "No, I'm naked. They won't give me any clothes to wear. Oh, God, don't any of you speak English?"

Captain Gringo said, "I do, miss. Who are you and how did you wind up here?"

She looked relieved as she answered, "Oh, thank God you're a white man! I'm Susan Reynolds from Salt Lake City, Utah. I was with a party of Mormon missionaries when we were attacked by Indians. I don't know what happened to the others. I was bathing in a brook near our camp when the shooting started. I crouched in the bushes and watched as they looted and burned at a distance. Then, when someone seemed to be coming toward me, I ran away into the jungle."

"So nobody stripped you? You ran off in your birthday suit, Susan?"

"Yes, I was afraid to go back for my clothing. I must have run and run for ages and then these other Indians caught me. I screamed and tried to get away, but they just tweeted at me like birds and then they tied me up and brought me here. You have to get me out of here! You have no idea what horrors I have witnessed. They have human heads in the huts. Little tiny black heads, shrunk like dried apples and hanging by the hair. They are terribly immoral, too."

"Uh, have any of them, well, been immoral with you?"

"No. That's the only outrage I haven't been subjected to. The children tease me and everybody laughs at me. Every

130

time I've tried to get away they slap me and put me back inside."

He held up a hand to silence her and turned to the Spanish-speaking Diablilla and the chief. He said, "The old gent was telling us the truth, as he sees it. It seems to be a case of mutual misunderstanding. She's a perfectly rational white missionary who thought she was about to go in the pot. I can see how her actions must have convinced them she was sort of nutty. Can you explain to the chief?"

As Diablilla twittered at the Jivaro, Captain Gringo took off his shirt and handed it to the blonde, saying, "Here, put this on. It's going to be okay, Susan. These aren't the guys who attacked your party. I suspect they were outlaws rather than Indians if they had guns. These headhunters were trying to help you, but you've about convinced them they caught a critter."

The Mormon girl put on the shirt with a grateful sigh, but complained, "My legs will still show if I stand up."

"Hey, let's not get silly! I'm not about to take my pants off for you, and besides, we all saw anything you might want to hide."

She blushed again and hung her head as she allowed him to help her to her feet. She was right about the shirt. It only hung down to her mid-thighs and she had nice legs indeed.

Diablilla said, "The *casique* says he is glad you have tamed her. He says she has been a great bother and that you can be vile with her if you wish. But I, Diablilla, will carve out both your hearts if I catch you doing any such thing!"

He was glad the blushing missionary didn't speak Spanish as he answered, "Take it easy, *querida*. I've already got a sweetheart, remember?" Then, in English, he told Susan, "Listen sharp. I think you're out of the woods. Stay close to me. But don't act like we're in love. The pretty brunette is a good kid but inclined to be possessive and I saw her kill a guy one time."

"Why sir, whatever are you suggesting? I'll have you know I'm a good girl!"

He imagined she would be good, at that. "Okay," he said, "keep a stiff upper lip and let's have no more sudden moves you don't clear with us first." He pointed at Gaston and added, "This is M'sieu Verrier. He speaks English too, sort of. If he tells you to do anything, don't argue."

In Spanish, Gaston asked, "Anything, Dick?" and Captain Gringo answered in the same lingo, "Keep your pants

131

buttoned, you wise ass. The Indians find her yelling tedious, and she's a yeller if I ever saw one."

Gaston smiled at the blonde and said, "Enchanted, Miss Reynolds." Then he turned back to Captain Gringo and added, *"Eh bien,* we have reached the secret castle and rescued the maiden from the dragons. What comes next on the menu? Do we ask them to show us their collection of heads, get drunk with them, start a football pool, or what?"

Captain Gringo asked, "Diablilla?" and the Colombian girl said, "The *casique* says he will have some huts and hammocks ready for us soon. Meanwhile, we should probably just find some shade and stay out of their way, no?"

He nodded, looked around, and called out, "All right, gang. Let's all stick together. We'll head over there to the shady side of the clearing and take a break. If anybody comes near you, offer them a smoke. Otherwise, leave them the hell alone."

His rebels and the "rescued" girl followed him into the strip of shade afforded by one brushy wall's angle against the slanting afternoon sun. The sky above, even in the open, was a dazzling misty white rather than blue. Unfiltered by the forest canopy, the light through the overhead cloud cover was uncomfortably warm in the open, and Captain Gringo knew you could get a nasty sunburn through the mist. As they hunkered down together he asked Susan how she'd managed not to do that. She said, "They made me stay inside. Every time I left the hut they were holding me in, the women in charge of me dragged me back."

"They might have saved you a nasty burn. They probably knew they were doing it. Even Indians get sunburned if they stay out in it long enough. We're damned near to the Equator."

Two little kids came over, leading a pet armadillo on a string. They all admired it, and Diablilla told them it was swell. Hanging around an Indian village could get pretty tedious. The other Jivaro, having accepted them, went on about their business as the afternoon began to drag. The men squatted on their muscular haunches making darts and weaving cage traps. The women nursed babies or made *chichi,* according to Gaston, who knew most disgusting native customs in these parts. He said the two girls chewing starchy roots nearby and spitting the results into calabash bowls were preparing the mildly alcoholic native beer called *chichi* by the riverboat crowd. Gaston said it tasted like malt liquor. Cap-

tain Gringo didn't want to hear how he knew. The two girls looked healthy and he supposed their saliva was no worse in beer than it would have been in a French kiss, but the idea of drinking fermented starch and human spit just didn't appeal to him very much.

Another Jivaro woman came over and squatted near Susan Reynolds with a puzzled smile. She said something in Jivaro and Diablilla translated, saying, "She says she is glad the señorita has recovered from her madness. She says she was very worried about her." Captain Gringo told Susan in English.

Susan turned her face aside and said, "Tell her I hate her. She's one of the girls who kept me in that hut with all the shrunken heads."

Captain Gringo nodded thoughtfully and said, "Yeah, I'd forgotten you were supposed to be a Christian missionary. I guess the Prince of Peace would have hated her, too, huh?"

Susan looked stricken and then she sighed and said, "That was a cruel thrust, Dick. But I guess I had it coming. I'm *trying* to remember why my friends and I came down here, but it isn't easy. What should I do?"

"I'm not sure. Instincts are usually safe to follow, if you're a reasonably nice kid. I think she'd settle for a smile."

Susan looked timidly on her erstwhile captor. Then she suddenly leaned forward, took the surprised Indian girl by the shoulders, and kissed her on the cheek. The delighted little Jivaro girl laughed and wrapped her arms around Susan, saying something in her own language. Diablilla translated, "She says it makes her heart soar to have a new friend. She says the cheap blonde made a lousy pet."

Captain Gringo chuckled and translated a cleaned-up version as the Indian girl leaped to her feet and scampered off to get something. Then he added, "You're doing fine, Susan. That didn't hurt, did it?"

The blonde laughed and said, "No, as a matter of fact, I haven't felt so good in weeks! Now that I understand, I can see they weren't as nasty as I thought. But there's still a lot of work for missionaries here, Dick. They have absolutely no morals. You can see how shameless they are about their bodies, and at night, oh, Lord, the way they carry on in the huts, right in front of everyone!"

"Everybody has morals, honey. They just don't agree on

what morals are. I don't know Jivaro rules, but I once had an Apache point out how sinful we whites were. He tortured prisoners and had two wives, but as I was taking him back to the reservation he asked me if it was true that we had little children working in cotton mills back East. Clothes don't make much sense in a jungle when you study on it. I feel just fine without my shirt and I'd probably feel better without pants if I wasn't a product of our own culture."

"Oh, even if one accepts the nudity, Dick, they still seem pretty nasty. I've seen grown men mistreating little girls and . . ."

"Now just back up and try that again, Susan," he cut in, adding, "You saw a Jivaro making love to a girl. Period."

"No, ravaging a child, damnit! Give me credit for having eyesight. I tell you I've seen them doing terrible things to girls as young as six or eight!"

"Well, leaving aside the fact that they look pretty young at any age, you're forgetting something. You say none of them abused you sexually, right?"

She nodded and he continued, "Okay, if they're not in the habit of raping helpless captives, what are the odds on them taking a Jivaro girl against her will with her parents within earshot?"

"It's still dirty and disgusting. Don't tell me you approve of child-molesting, too?"

"It's not for me to approve or disapprove, Susan. I'm not a Jivaro. If they like to start younger than we do, that's their business, not ours. Who knows, maybe the kids like sex. Most people do."

Diablilla had been trying to follow the conversation without much luck. She nudged Captain Gringo from the other side and asked, "Are you two flirting?"

He laughed and said, "No, she was telling me she doesn't approve of being vile."

"Why talk about it at all in that case? I'll bet she would like to be vile with you, but I shall be most cross with her if she tries to take you away from me. You must tell her you are my *soldado*, Dick."

He patted Diablilla's shoulder and said not to worry. The awkward three-way conversation was abruptly ended by the old chief coming over with a worried look. He tweeted and grunted at Diablilla and she told Captain Gringo, "He says his scouts have spotted *flagelados*, many *flagelados*, headed this way. He thinks they may have cut our trail."

134

Captain Gringo nodded and was still thinking when the girl Susan had kissed came back with a big bowl of something sloppy for them. That helped him make his mind up in a hurry. He called to Gaston and said, "Round up the guys with guns and let's take a hike. I'll carry the machine gun. Everyone else should be safe here if we do it right the first time."

17

It was still light but would soon be dark as the long line of slave-raiding *flagelados* moved abreast through the *selva*. Their leader, a big mulatto with an ugly scar down one cheek, smiled thinly as he spotted another scuff mark in the forest duff. He didn't know who they were trailing. It didn't matter. El Cicatrizo's forty men were hard-eyed jungle runners armed with twelve-gauge pump guns in addition to their pistols and machetes. El Cicatrizo made it twenty to thirty people they were trailing and at least a couple of them seemed to be women. That was nice. He and his men hadn't had any women since they'd raided that last village a week ago, and while rank had its privileges, a man gets tired of buggering a youthful follower. A couple of the people the slavers were trailing wore shoes. So they weren't Indians. That was good, too. El Patrón didn't like them to bring back wild Indios, although an Indio would do if they couldn't catch anyone else. The bunch ahead were doubtless Colombian peons. The best kind of slaves. If a man spoke Spanish it was a simple matter to put him to work, no?

El Cicatrizo stepped around a huge mahogany bole and stopped thoughtfully. A wall of second growth lay in sight up ahead. He hoped the damned peons fleeing from him hadn't run into that brush. It was a bother digging people out of bushes with machetes. It could be mildly dangerous, too.

A lieutenant moved over to him and said, "It's getting late, Chief. The boys are a little worried about meeting a Jivaro in the dark."

El Cicatrizo spat and answered, "I spit in the mother's milk of any fucking Indian. We outnumber any band we might meet, even without our shotguns. Besides, no Indian

left all those footprints we've been following. They are peons, I tell you."

"Sí, I, too, can read sign. But why are they running? One can see they moved through here in a great hurry. We have not raided this deep into Colombian territory before. Could somebody else be after them?"

El Cicatrizo shrugged and said, "Who cares? We will make them tap rubber for El Patrón, too. These ahead of us could be smugglers running from the Colombian border guards. On the other hand, they may have heard we are recruiting in the neighborhood. That missionary camp we hit a few weeks back is not far from here. Word may have gotten around. I have told you boys to be quiet and watch your smoke, but does anybody ever listen? Let's move in on those bushes. I want to get them before dark, whoever they are."

So the skirmish line edged closer, guns trained on the wall of greenery. A shallow gully running at right angles to their advance made a natural fire line. El Cicatrizo held up his hand and called out, "Form on my flank, *muchachos*. Take cover here and let us see about that thicket before we move in closer. Gomez, Silva, you two scout forward, and be careful, eh?"

As two men moved cautiously forward, the burly El Cicatrizo hunkered down in the gully, shotgun across his knees. The men beyond did the same. It was what Captain Gringo had been expecting them to do when he'd spotted the gully earlier. He, of course, was off to their flank, behind a fallen log with the Maxim. Gaston and the eight riflemen with them lay flat behind other cover flanking the slavers.

As the *flagelados* lined up so considerately, he whispered to Gaston, "See if you can pick off the scouts. Are you all set?"

Gaston said, *"Mais oui,"* and might have said more if it hadn't gotten so noisy all of a sudden as the husky American rose from behind his log, machine gun braced on his hip, and opened fire!

The cathedral-like *selva* echoed with the insane woodpecker rattle of his spitting Maxim and the screams of dying men as he hosed hot lead the length of the gully. A shotgun blossomed orange at him, but he ignored it. He'd chosen his position with care, and knew that he was out of shotgun range. The same could not be said for his returning fire. A machine gun shot as far as a rifle, albeit not as accurately. Accuracy was not much of a problem when you threw

137

enough rounds into a target, so he gave them a full belt of .30-30 before the Maxim fell silent and left him standing with his ears ringing in a cloud of drifting blue smoke. He saw no movement among the bodies lined up in the gully. Off to his left he heard the flat crack of a rifle and the duller roar of Gaston's pistol. Whatever they were up to was their problem. He lowered the hot Maxim to the log and inserted the end of a fresh belt before he stepped over the log, dragging the belt behind him as he advanced with the machine gun muzzle leading the way.

He rolled El Cicatrizo over with his foot. The big mulatto still looked surprised. Captain Gringo didn't see what all the mystery was about. Anybody with six rounds in him was *supposed* to be dead.

As he moved down the line he saw some of the others were in better or worse shape. None of them were ever going to bother anybody again. He'd put at least three rounds in every one of them and one guy had taken maybe eight. It was hard to judge, with half his head blown away like so.

Gaston came in at an angle to join him, calling out, "We got both the scouts. One is still breathing, with considerable effort. I told Pancho you might wish to discuss his unseemly past before we finished him. So Pancho is watching him."

Captain Gringo saw Quico and some of the others coming over to the gully. He called out. "Hey, Quico. Take over here and gather up all the weapons, ammo, and anything else we can use. I think the Blue Brigade is back in business. We've even got guns for the girls, now."

Then he asked Gaston to lead him to the wounded prisoner.

They found Pancho seated on a log, discussing the joys of Hell with the groaning *flagelado* who lay at his feet with a bullet in his guts.

Pancho looked up and said, "His name is Silva. He's a Brazilian motherfucker and he says he does not wish for to die. Is that not amusing?"

Captain Gringo told Pancho to shove over and took a seat on the log to quietly study the dying *flagelado*. Silva was a Creole with a gold ring in one ear and a shaven head that belonged on a baboon. He had a gold tooth he kept baring in pain as he complained to his mother, God, and a couple of saints about the way he'd been treated. Captain Gringo had a hard time following until he got used to the accent. Silva

138

spoke the mixture of bad Spanish and bad Portuguese that made up the lingua franca of Amazonia.

Portuguese spelling was a lot different from Spanish but the spoken words were not that different. Speakers fluent in one could understand the other about as well as an English-speaking Texan could savvy a broad Scottish brogue. Portuguese had a sort of French accent and he missed some words, but it wasn't hard to see that *Senhor* meant *Señor* or that *San* and *São* both meant Saint.

Captain Gringo nudged the wounded *flagelado* with his booted toe and said, "Enough of this bullshit. Where did you guys get those neat American shotguns?"

Silva sobbed and said, "That hurt, damn your eyes! Have you no pity, Senhor?"

"For a wounded man-eating tiger, maybe. For an animal that preys on its own kind? You have to be joshing us. You were going to tell us about those Browning pumpers, remember?"

Silva said something dumb about needing medical attention. Captain Gringo kicked him harder and snapped, "I'll give you something for your pain, you prick. I'll give you another bullet in your knee cap. And if that doesn't put you in a conversational mood I might get unpleasant."

Silva whimpered, *"São Cristavo!* I think I am dying!"

"Think, hell. Of course you're dying. We're all dying, sooner or later. What we're talking about is how *comfortable* it's going to be. You didn't get all those repeating shotguns from those missionaries. You had too many of them. Who outfitted you? Who are you working for?"

"Please, Senhor, I have a woman at the plantation. Dom Luis will kill her if he learns I talked."

"Listen, it will be our little secret, see? Who's this Dom Luis, a rubber baron?"

"A rubber *emperor,* Senhor. Don't tell me you have never heard of Dom Luis Do Putumayo?"

"No, but you were just about to tell us all about him, right?"

"You promise not to tell on me? You promise to do something for this pain, Senhor?"

Captain Gringo did, so Silva spilled his guts. Rather literally, toward the end. His story was disjointed and rambling. Captain Gringo had to make him repeat a lot of words he didn't understand. He had to keep kicking the semicon-

139

scious slaver to keep his mind from wandering, and the results were sort of messy. But, with Gaston helping with some of the more French-sounding words, they got as much as Silva knew out of him, and Captain Gringo was already condensing it to the shorter version he'd tell the others as they compared notes and planned their strategy. Then, when Silva started repeating himself and reminding Captain Gringo that he'd promised to do something for the pain, the tall American nodded and rose from his seat. He placed the instep of his boot on Silva's throat and tromped hard, crushing the windpipe like a cockroach, with a sickening crunch. Then he said, "Let's go. Pancho, send one of the guys back to the Indian camp for a salvage detail. It'll be dark soon and I don't want to leave a single round of ammo behind out here. We're going to need every round if that guy was serious about the army this Dom Luis has."

Pancho shuddered as he looked down at the dead man and said, "I am sure he spoke most sincerely, Señor. Do you always finish them off like that? I was expecting you to shoot him in the head."

Captain Gringo shrugged and said. "Old Infantry trick. I just told you we need all the ammunition, didn't I?"

18

The war council in the Jivaro camp that night was sort of weird as well as awfully complicated. Captain Gringo met with the tribal elders, Gaston, Diablilla, the natural leaders of his band, and the blonde Susan Reynolds in the chief's hut. The pleasant old gent had a line of little black shrunken heads hanging from his smoke-stained ridge-pole just above them, and while Captain Gringo was too polite to ask, some of the heads looked like they'd once been attached to white men. The beards and mustaches gave a grotesque touch to the tiny serene faces with the lips and eyelids neatly sewn shut as they dangled just above his own eye level, facing the others around the little smudge fire. It was funny how large living heads looked in the flickering light.

As he repeated what the dying slaver had told him in Spanish, Diablilla twitted at the Jivaro, and Susan, of course, looked blank, trying to follow. It was surprising that her church had sent her into a solidly Catholic part of the world not speaking a word of any language she was likely to hear. But the idea of Mormon headhunters was sort of dumb in the first place, when you thought about it. The Catholics had spent centuries trying to make Christians out of everyone in these parts. So anybody who was still holding out had to be a hard sell.

The old padres had been allowed pretty rough methods of conversion by the Inquisition. Any tribes who'd held out against the fire and sword of the conquest were going to be rough to convert via brotherly love in English. But that was Susan's problem. Or, rather, it had been, before her party had gone out of business. He waited until he'd told it all to his Spanish-speaking followers before he turned to her and said,

141

"I'm sorry, honey. But your freinds are all dead. Those guys we chopped up out there were the raiders who hit your camp. They work for a big rubber guy called Dom Luis. He calls himself Dom Luis Do Putumayo, like he owns the headwaters of the Putumayo. I guess he thinks he does."

Susan gasped. "I can't believe that! We knew Dom Luis! He struck me as a perfect gentleman of the old school."

"No kidding? When and where did you meet Dom Luis, Susan?"

"At his plantation, down the river. The steamboat from Manaus dropped us off there. He has a regular little town at his landing on the Putumayo. He was ever so gracious. He entertained us for a few days, told us all about the tribes we might meet and so forth, and tried to talk our leaders out of going farther upstream. He warned us the country was dangerous."

"Yeah, he probably didn't want you to see too much of it. What happened then?"

"Oh, Dom Luis loaned us some canoes and ordered some of his men to paddle and guide us up this way. I don't see how they could have intended any treachery, Dick. I know at least two of our native porters were killed in the raid on our camp. I watched them die. They *worked* for Dom Luis!"

"Yeah, so did the *flagelados* who massacred your party. There might have been a mixup. More than likely, the porters he sent with you were just innocent peons. Everybody living under the Tsar is not a Cossack, and it's not like Dom Luis is short of help. He's got his slavers combing the country for new recruits."

"I can't believe that of Dom Luis, Dick. He seemed like such a nice man. There must be some mistake. Maybe he doesn't know what his roughnecks are doing when he isn't watching them."

"He knows, doll. Dom Luis is a Brazilian. He's added a big chunk of Colombian territory to his rubber empire in the last few months. And let's not say something dumb about him being confused about the borderline. He started with a land grant from Brazil, so his plantation has to be on the map, and the map says it's just inside the Brazilian border. A guy who invades other countries on his own must feel pretty smug and powerful. He knows they just had a revolution in Colombia. The Colombian military is weak and divided. Patroling the jungle down here is the least of their worries. So he's just

started grabbing. He's issued spanking new modern weapons to his own private army and he has enough men to make hash out of any little patrols Colombia will be in shape to send for a while."

"But, Dick, that's out-and-out robbery! Won't the Colombians eventually do something about it?"

"Sure, in a year or more. Meanwhile the price of rubber is booming and you can ship a lot of latex in a year. I suppose, in time, if he can't beat or bribe the whole Colombian army, he'll have to pull in his horns a bit. But what the hell, they can't hit his headquarters on the Brazilian side of the line without getting into a war with Brazil, and they won't be ready for that in Bogotá in the foreseeable future. Brazil could eat Colombia for breakfast and Bogotá knows it. Old Dom Luis must think he has it made. Did you get a good look at his spread while you were visiting there?"

Susan nodded and said, "Oh, yes, I told you he was ever so hospitable. He has a huge baronial house on a hill back from his private township near the landing. He took us for a ride around his holdings on his little narrow-gauge railroad. He seemed very proud of his railroad. It runs for miles through the jungle, and the Shay locomotive he had shipped up the river was gilded with gold paint. He had what he said was his family coat of arms painted on the tender."

"Sounds like a neat toy. Did they have the train armed?"

"Armed? Oh, now that you mention it, there were some Gatling guns on the tender and caboose. Dom Luis said he was on guard against wild Indians."

"As well he should be. How do the tracks run? Is it a single loop or a network of track through the *selva*, Susan?"

She thought and said, "I honestly can't say. We went in a sort of circle. A big one. There were other tracks branching off, now that you mention it. But it was hard to see anything. We spent most of the time chugging through thick forest. I'm a little confused about rubber plantations, Dick. We hardly saw any rubber trees at all. Dom Luis speaks very refined English and he was pointing out the different trees to us. He seems to know them all. Quinine, mahogany, balsa, and others I can't recall. How can you gather enough rubber to matter if the rubber trees are scattered about like that, Dick?"

"You walk a lot. The British have been planting regular rubber plantations in the Far East lately. Brazilian rubber is gathered from wild native trees. Why wait for a tree to grow

143

when you can get some slob to hunt a really big one down for you? Those other spur tracks you saw must lead to widely spaced tappers' camps deep in the *selva*. The tappers are sent out with their tools and buckets and told not to come back until they fill them. The way I understand it, a tapper covers a beat of maybe twenty square miles or so, staggering from tree to tree and sleeping under them at night. He taps them going one way. Gathers the latex on his way back. They smoke and bale the latex at the central camp and then the choo-choo comes to pick it up and deliver it to the landing."

"Brrr, it sounds like a hard life for the poor tappers. How much do you suppose Dom Luis has to pay a man to work like that, Dick?"

"It is a hard life. That's why nobody wants to do it unless they get paid a lot. I don't think Dom Luis pays them anything. He needs the money for his gold choo-choo and private army. His slaves get maybe enough food to keep them on their feet and a chance to go on living. It's the going rate on the rubber frontier."

"That's awful, Dick! Why don't the poor slaves run away?"

"Where? Damned few slaves have ever run away, Susan. People who keep slaves don't make it easy for them to do that. You spent some time alone in the *selva*, naked and unarmed. Would you care for another shot at it if you knew that there was a warm meal waiting for you if you just came back with the latex, or a good beating if you got caught again by the *flagelados* before you starved or got killed by a snake or an Indian?"

She shuddered and said, "It's frightening either way. But I think I'd take my chances with the jungle. Wouldn't you?"

"Probably. Educated people don't make good slaves. They know there's another world somewhere for them to get to. That's why Dom Luis acted so polite to you missionaries instead of handing you some buckets. The Indians and *mestizos* he's been recruiting are simple people who've already gotten used to being abused. They've lived close to the bone all their lives as it is. Being forced to work for Dom Luis can't be much fun, even for a subsistence peon, or they wouldn't run from his slavers. But, once he has them in his power, they probably settle down and just do as they're told. The good workers probably get a pat on the head and an extra rum ration. If they're very good indeed he may let them

have a night with a slave girl every once in awhile. That's how slavery works, Susan. A few modest comforts and a smile instead of a scowl from the man who holds your life in his hands. Most people are sheep, even working in a bank back home. As long as Dom Luis either kills or makes gunmen out of the few tough guys his recruiters bring in, he hasn't got much to worry about."

"Oh, that's terrible, Dick. What can we do to help?"

"We have to supply the bastard with more troublemakers than he can handle, of course. These boys and girls with me might look like ordinary peons, but I doubt if they'd tap rubber, free, for *me!*"

"I see. You and your Blue Brigade will attack the plantation and free the slaves of Dom Luis, right?"

"Wrong. My gang is pretty tough, and now we have them all armed to the teeth. But Dom Luis has a whole private army and, when he misses the patrol we just cut up, they'll be expecting trouble. You don't hit a larger enemy force on their own ground with a dozen fighters, Susan. The smartest thing we could do would be to go around them."

"But, Dick, you just said you wanted to make trouble for the slavers."

"Year, I know what I said. I never said it was smart."

Gaston had been listening, quietly for Gaston. He said soberly, "I am not a fan of this mysterious Dom Luis, Dick. But I liked the idea of going around him better. The disgusting rubber man has never done anything to us that warrants the risk of our lives."

"Come on, Gaston. They wiped out Susan's friends and just attacked us!"

"*Mais non*, it is *we* who attacked *them*, remember? They were not after us personally. They only sought to improve the lives of these primitives. As to vengeance for the loss of the missionaries, Silva confessed to us that the band we wiped out was indeed the guilty gang. We are ahead, for once, my old and rare! We are almost out of Colombian territory. We are armed and formidable. Thanks to the contents of a few *flagelado* pockets, we even have drinking money to go around. I vote we march on by. This Dom Luis has no idea we are in his thrice-accursed jungle, *hein?*"

"Yeah, that gives us a nice edge, doesn't it?"

"*Merde alors!* You have not been listening! We will soon be over the border. We are not wanted on Brazilian soil! Not, that is, at the moment. But have you considered the dim view

Brazil would take if we were to announce our entry into their fair country by attacking a powerful Brazilian planter who knows enough people in Rio to obtain vast land grants?"

Captain Gringo nodded and replied, "Yeah, we've agreed I'm being stupid. But the son of a bitch is more than a slaver, Gaston. He's a two-faced out-and-out killer! Don't you see what he did to those missionaries? He played Mr. Innocent and treated them like guests, for the record. Then he sent hired guns after them to wipe them out, along with some of his own people."

"I agree he sounds like a most tiresome ogre, Dick. But the world is full of them. How can one man hope to rid the world of all its ogres in one lifetime?"

"He can't. But he can wipe out the ogres he meets. Light one little candle and all that crap. We've been in a lot of fights together, Gaston. Most of the time, we've simply been fighting to stay alive, and some of the guys we've had to fight had to be nicer guys than this Dom Luis. The kids with us picked up the gun to fight for a better world. Are we all going to just walk away from a fight that might really mean something?"

Gaston sighed and said, "I would, if I could, but I have seen that look in your eye before." He turned to Susan and added, "He thinks he is on a crusade. I think it must have something to do with the books you blond Protestant types read. The nice thing about receiving one's early religion in a dead language is that less of it seems to rub off on one, *hein?*"

Susan smiled at Captain Gringo adoringly and said, "I think he's just wonderful."

Across the hut, Diablilla turned from the Jivaro chief and asked in Spanish, "Is that girl talking dirty to you, Dick?"

Captain Gringo called back, "No, we're talking about the rubber slavers." But as he made eye contact with the young blonde, he wasn't sure whether he was telling the truth to his *adelita* or not.

He got Diablilla to translate for him as he attempted to explain his plans to the Jivaro. It gave her something to think about, but the Jivaro didn't seem too taken with the idea of wiping out a colony of Brazilians. The old chief explained that he was a peaceful gent. Captain Gringo pointed up at the heads dangling from the ridge-pole and asked how such a peaceful gent had accumulated such a collection.

146

Diablilla warned, "Do not press the matter, Dick. I told you they do not like to take orders. I can tell you how those men lost their heads. They bothered the *casique*. Or he *thought* they were bothering him. Jivaro do not make such fine distinctions as we."

"Jesus, do you mean they can turn on someone just for the hell of it?"

"No, although their motives may seem unpredictable to their victims. You saw how they took in and cared for this girl they found lost in the *selva*. You saw how easy it was to make friends with them. Some of the earlier visitors you now see the remains of were not so lucky."

"They made some dumb move, huh?"

"Who knows? They may have simply been in the vicinity when some member of the tribe took sick or was bitten by a bushmaster. You see, Dick, these Jivaro do not believe in accidents. Any misfortune, to a Jivaro, must be the result of a hostile act by someone. Someone who wishes them harm."

"You mean if a Jivaro stubs his toe it's witchcraft?"

"Of course. *He* did not mean to stub his toe, did he? They understand open hostility, naturally. They knew those slavers were out to do them harm and they are most pleased with you for what you did to them. I think I have them convinced that this Dom Luis is their enemy and that they should blame him for any misfortunes in the near future. But let us hope no child comes down with a fever while we are among them. Forget trying to recruit them to our cause, Dick. They don't understand, and it could be playing with fire to press them further. I have already had some difficulty explaining to them why you and the men with you did not bring back any heads for to shrink."

"Hell, they're welcome to them if they want the heads."

"You still do not understand, Dick. No Jivaro has any use for the head of an enemy another man kills. The *casique* says you and the men who helped you fight the *flagelados* should sleep apart from the rest of us tonight. He says his people are frightened of the ghosts that may be following you."

"Oboy! Purification rites. I ran into that among North American Indians a while back. I guess we'd better not be vile until we do something about appeasing the spirits. But can't they settle for something easier? I've no idea how the hell you shrink a head. I don't think I want to know."

Diablilla spoke to the Jivaro. A man older than the chief

threw some powdered tobacco in the fire to excuse himself to the spooks before he answered her in some detail. She told Captain Gringo, "They say they are not ignorant people and that they know our customs are not the same as theirs. But he says you'd better do *something*. I think so, too, if we intend to stay here much longer."

The American thought, remembered a book he'd read, and said, "Okay, tell them the ghosts of Christians are different. Tell them that iron is big medicine to us and that I took all the iron weapons away from the dead men. I have all their iron and their ghosts will be afraid of me now."

She tried it and it seemed to work. It made no sense, but it sounded as logical to him as shrinking a dead man's head. She said, "They say our customs are our own business, but that they'd prefer you to sleep alone anyway. The ghosts might try to give someone else a bad dream if they can't get inside your head tonight."

He nodded and said, "That sounds fair." Then, grateful that Susan didn't understand Spanish, he added, "I was sort of looking forward to trying it in a hammock with you, *querida.* But we'd better not press our luck."

Gaston, who of course had been following the conversation with interest, chimed in, "In my opinion we are pressing our luck to stay here at all. Do you think they would try to stop us if we left before bedtime, Diablilla?"

She replied, "No but they might feel insulted. They have already been erecting new thatch and hanging hammocks for our party. They say they wish for to get drunk with us before we all turn in. If we were to leave and disappoint them . . ."

"No problem," Captain Gringo cut in. "It's too dark to travel and God knows where other *flagelado* gangs may be camped out there. We're safer here with Jivaro scouts out around us to pass the word along if anybody important is headed our way. What's this getting drunk business, Diablilla?"

"Combined hospitality and magic. They know the alcohol in their *chichi* does crazy things to one's head. They don't know why. They think it is a gift from the spirit world, since they often have visions when they are drunk. They always get drunk with guests. It is fun, and they know they must remain sober around possible enemies."

Gaston laughed and said, "In that case, let us not be rude, *hein?* The stuff is not bad, Dick. Hardly even an ordinary wine, but when in Rome . . ."

148

Captain Gringo shot a warning look around at Pancho, Nuñez, and the others as he said softly, "Listen, *muchachos,* if you've paid any attention at all, you know what thin ice we're skating on. Pass the word that nobody refuses a drink, but that they're to spill as much as they can and swallow as little as possible. If a drunken Indian gets out of line, let it pass. If any of our people takes a swing or makes a pass at an Indian I'll shoot first and ask why later."

Pancho nodded and said, "We can hold our liquor, Señor. I will tell the others to nurse their drinks and pass out as soon as possible, eh?"

"Good thinking. Better make sure all the guns are set on safe, too. Tell the *adelitas* nobody expects them to out-and-out give in to any youthful high-jinks, but to fend off passes gently. Diablilla, what are the odds on a drunken Jivaro trying to rape one of you girls?"

Diablilla looked reproachfully at Susan and said, "They never raped that flashy blonde, did they? I don't think that will be much of a problem, Dick. These wild tribes are most casual about sex. It is considered proper for any man to ask any woman but his mother-in-law to sleep with him. But they do not get excited if she says no. They just ask someone else. I am sure we girls can handle it."

So Captain Gringo said the party sounded like a good idea, and the old chief leaped lightly to his feet and led them all outside, laughing boyishly as he shouted to the others.

A central bonfire had been started in the plaza and the idea seemed to be that anybody who didn't feel like dancing should sit in the circle around the fire. So Captain Gringo hunkered down between Diablilla and Susan, with Gaston on Susan's far side. There were some disturbing-looking monkeys roasting on spits over the coals. Calabash bowls were being passed around the circle. He asked Diablilla what the form was and she said anybody who was hungry should help themselves to some roast monkey and that anybody who wanted to be polite should take a slug of *chichi.*

He decided he wasn't hungry enough to eat anybody that looked like a toasted baby in a fur coat. Meanwhile the calabash bowls were getting closer. Each Indian in turn took a big swallow before passing it on with a grin. Some of the grins looked sort of ominous in the flickering red light. Other Indians behind them had formed a circle to shuffle sideways around the plaza. It was a pretty boring-looking dance. They kept time by grunting in unison as they shuffled in unison. He

wondered what they'd think of the waltz. He decided not to show them. As the guests of honor they were already getting more attention than he really felt any need for.

The bowl reached Diablilla. She'd visited the Jivaro before and didn't hesitate as she raised the bowl to her lips, took a ladylike sip, and passed it on to him. He raised it gingerly to his face. It smelled like stale beer with a lot of malt in it. He repressed a shudder and took a mouthful experimentally. It tasted like sweet malty beer, so what the hell. Was it any worse to drink booze prepared with clean girl's teeth than it was to drink wine a lot of unwashed feet had been stomping in? The best cheese was rotten milk, when you thought about it. So why think about it, if it tasted okay?

He passed the bowl to Susan, who was kneeling in his shirt to hide her thighs despite the darkness. She said, "Oh, I couldn't!" and he said, "Sure you could, and you'd better. It's not as bad as I thought, Susan. Just pretend it's regular beer."

"Heavens, I can't drink beer! There's alcohol in it!"

"Not that much. You'd have to swill a quart of it to feel anything."

"That's not the point, Dick. My church forbids alcohol, tobacco, and coffee."

"Sounds like a fun religion. Pretend it's tea, then."

"We don't drink tea, either. The Prophet Joseph teaches us that it's wrong to take artificial stimulants into our sacred bodies!"

"He sounds like a lot of laughs. Drink your damned beer, babe! That's a command from the Prophet Dick Walker and you can quote me at the Pearly Gates someday. You're liable to get there at a later date if you do as I say. These guys smear artificial stimulants on their darts and arrows, too! So this is no time to be a wet blanket! Come on, damnit, they're watching you!"

Susan shuddered, closed her eyes, and took a swallow. As she passed the bowl on to Gaston, she said, "Oh, that wasn't so bad. I was expecting something more, well, exciting. Do you suppose I'm drunk now?"

He chuckled and said, "No. You'd have to put away an awful lot of that stuff to feel it."

"It tasted rather refreshing. What does it feel like to be drunk and abandoned to the temptations of Satan, Dick?"

"Beats me. Usually, by the time I've gotten drunk enough to do anything all that interesting, I've just wanted to lie down and sleep it off."

"Really? I've always been taught that one sip of Demon Rum can lead straight to ruination. How do you account for all the drunken brawling and sinful behavior if it's only supposed to make you sleepy, Dick?"

He said, "I guess you have to start out feeling ornery to begin with. I've never seen a really decent cuss get fighting-mean on liquor. It just brings out the devil that's already in you."

Gaston nudged her and said, "If M'selle would permit me, I have a raging thirst and a certain curiosity about my own devils."

Susan handed the bowl to him, but not before she'd taken another, rather heroic gulp. She repressed a belch and said, "I was thirsty, too, and the Prophet teaches that if one sins once, one may as well sin twice, for there is no evading the All-Seeing Eye and it marks the fall of the sparrow. Amen."

Gaston took a swallow and passed it on. Another bowl was following the first around the circle faster than the dancers shuffled. Captain Gringo took a swig and passed it on sans comment as he eyed the roast monkeys dubiously. He knew he really ought to put something in his gut if this was going to be an all-night beer bust. But some of the others had torn off bits and pieces to nibble now, and the only thing more gruesome than a monkey roasting whole on a spit was a mutilated monkey doing the same thing. He remembered he had some parched corn and jerky in his roll, over by the guns. The last time he'd looked, it had been covered with a sort of gray fuzz, but at least it didn't have tiny hands. He'd wait until things settled down a bit and fetch it. He wanted Susan to eat something, too. Diablilla and Gaston were used to alcohol. He didn't know what effect even weak booze might have on a what . . . virgin?

He chuckled to himself as he wondered if virgin was the right word for a novice drinker. He wondered why he found that so funny. Then he wondered if the blonde was the other kind of virgin and why that seemed so funny, too. Then he frowned and warned Gaston, "Watch it. This *chichi* has more of a kick to it than I thought."

Gaston said, *"Oui,* the sweetness masks the alcoholic

151

content. Sherry wine can sneak up on one the same way. But never fear, my old and rare, I can drink a Russian under the table."

"I'm not worried about you. Keep your eyes on the other folks in our party. Some of the Indians are already sloshed and it's early yet."

The dancers had been passing *chichi* around and some of them were smoking funny cigars that looked like cornhusk tamales and smelled like burning hemp. They were dancing faster now, although, like every American Indian dance he'd ever seen, the choreography was pretty uninteresting. They seemed to think shuffling one step one way and two steps the other was inventive as hell, though, because it made them giggle a lot.

Diablilla nudged him and passed him the Indian cigar going around in the wake of that last bowl. She was exhaling through her nose with a dreamy look in her eyes as he took it from her. As he took a polite puff, Diablilla murmured, "God, I'd like to suck your cock."

He choked and inhaled more than he'd intended before passing the smoke on to Susan without thinking. Then he blinked in surprise as the cannabis hit him and said, "You'd better pass on that, Susan, it's marijuana."

But the missionary had already inhaled a deep drag, coughed, and was saying, "Wheeee, so it is! What's marijuana, Dick? I thought it was tobacco."

He said, "It's not tobacco, it's dope," and she looked relieved and took another puff before passing it on to Gaston. He frowned and asked, "Weren't you listening?" and Susan said, "Yes, you said it wasn't tobacco. The Prophet never said anything about marijuana in the Book of Mormon, so it must be all right. Ye shall name and gather the fruits of the earth and have dominion over something or other. Amen."

He shrugged and turned back to tell Diablilla to take her hand out of his lap, for Chrissake. She said, "I wish for to be vile," and he said, "Later. I think they've gotten over their first fear of ghosts and in a little while we'll be able to slip away and tear off a quickie."

"I do not wish for to fuck later. I wish for to fuck right now. What is the matter with you? Have you forsaken me for that blond pig? You men are all alike. You get a girl to be vile with you and then you want another."

"Knock it off. I told you she's a Bible-thumping missionary and, even if she wasn't, you're my *adelita*."

"Prove it. Be vile with me in front of her."

"Jesus Christ, you're hopped up. What's the matter with all of you? Neither the booze nor the smokes are all that powerful. I hardly feel a thing."

Then he reached out, tore an arm off a monkey, and began to gnaw it like a chicken leg. He was hungry as hell all of a sudden, and it tasted better than he'd expected. Sort of like veal with a pork aftertaste.

Someone got their signals mixed and now bowls of *chichi* and cornhusk reefers were being passed around both ways. Diablilla passed him a smoke, he took a cautious drag and handed it to Susan, who, in the meantime, had gotten one going the other way. She put both in her mouth before he could stop her and inhaled deeply as he muttered, "You're going to damage your lungs." Her lungs looked pretty good as she leaned back in his loose shirt, expanding her chest. She smiled owlishly and said, "Oh, hello," as she handed him both smokes. He sat confused, with one in each hand, and said, "I think one of these is supposed to be going the other way." But Diablilla took them both away from him and said, "I can do anything she can do, and better. Watch this."

Then Diablilla put a tip in each of her nostrils and inhaled furiously. For some reason it struck him funny as hell, and as he laughed she did it some more. Then he took them away from her and passed them in opposite directions, saying, "Come on, quit kidding around." He might have known Susan would stuff hers up her nose before passing it to Gaston, who handed it on to the Indian on the other side of him sans comment and received a bowl of *chichi* in return. Captain Gringo reached for more monkey. He was okay, he was sure, but feeling sort of lightheaded and hungry as a bitch wolf. When Diablilla put her head in his lap, it didn't seem as embarrassing as he knew it should have. She fumbled at his fly and then she snuggled down and went to sleep. He was a little disappointed. He had a raging hard-on now. But he decided it was just as well. He remembered it wasn't polite to screw in public. He'd forgotten the reason.

Susan didn't seem to notice Diablilla's actions. She'd been staring up thoughtfully at the dancers. Suddenly she muttered, "You call that dancing?" and then she was on her feet and doing a cakewalk around the fire.

The Indians loved it. They laughed like hell. Captain Gringo laughed, too. For a missionary, she gave a pretty good imitation of a saucy music hall gal. They'd have raided the

153

show in Frisco or even Paris, though. The cakewalk was a daring dance wearing a flounced skirt and tights. Susan only had his shirt on, and as her long bare legs flashed in the red firelight you could sure see she had nothing on under it. The Indians had already seen her bare-bottomed. So had everyone else, come to think of it, but Pancho and some of the other guys were clapping their hands to keep time for her as they shouted *"Olé!"* and other things he didn't think he'd ever translate for the American girl if she asked.

She didn't ask. Born and raised more soberly than even the average Victorian miss of her generation, Susan was like a kid in a candy store, or maybe a runaway convent girl, as she forgot her inhibitions for the moment. A couple of Jivaro girls broke out of the dance line and tried to cakewalk behind her, squealing with delight. They were both stark naked, of course, and now that a guy had had time to settle his nerves, they looked a lot nicer and a lot nakeder in the sensual flickering light. One of them kicked too high and fell on her rump with a laugh. An equally naked Indian nearby rolled over on her and proceeded to screw hell out of her with no further ceremony. Captain Gringo looked over at Gaston and muttered, "Jesus, how do we cool things down?"

"Merde alors, who wants to? This is turning out to be a better party than one might have anticipated, *non?"*

"Yeah, but we can't let our guys start an orgy with these natives."

"Why not, if the natives are friendly? Relax, Dick, our people are heavier than the Indians and it takes more to affect them. Besides, I have been watching and the *muchachos* have been nursing their refreshments."

Captain Gringo pointed across to Quico, holding a young Jivaro girl in his lap, and growled, "Like hell. Look at Quico!"

"I see him. She's pretty, in a droll way. What is the problem? She sat down in Quico's lap. He did not sit in hers. If any of her tribesmen did not approve, they would have said so by now, *non?"*

"How could they? The whole tribe seems to be drunk as a skunk."

"Oui, they have little tolerance for drugs or liquor. Perhaps this is just as well, when one has only limited quantities at one's command, *hein?"*

"Oh, shit, you're not listening either. Before they started

154

this brawl they handed us a whole mess of taboos, remember?"

"*Oui.* Obviously they have forgotten them, along with any other rules of the house they may have had. *Regardez,* is that not a boy buggering a boy, over there in the shadows?"

"That's their problem. They're both Indians. I can see they're getting too sloshed to give a damn about ghosts and stuff, but they're going to remember them in the morning, and everyone's likely to have one hell of a hangover. I think we'd better get our crew together and retreat gracefully to some empty huts."

Gaston shrugged and suggested, "Wait a few minutes. It could be as dangerous to offend their hospitality as it might be to abuse their sisters."

Before the American could answer, Susan Reynolds was shaking him by the bare shoulder. She said, "Hey, let's dance. I'm lonesome."

He hesitated. Then he gently lowered Diablilla's head from his lap to her crossed arms and left her there, face down, as he rose. At least he saw a way to keep Susan from flashing her blond snatch at everybody. He took her lightly in his arms and began to waltz her around the fire. She giggled and said, "Oh, nice. 'The Blue Danube' has always been my favorite."

Since the only music was the rhythmic grunts and clapped hands all around them, she was either kidding or she'd been smoking some more.

The outer dance ring had broken into trios and quartets of Jivaro, sort of staggering in step with locked arms. At least half of them were on the ground, either out like lights, coupled in casual sexual embrace, or, in one embarrassing case, jerking off.

As he tried to whirl her past without comment, Susan asked, "Why do men do that, Dick? I've noticed a lot of that since I've been here among these Indians. When they're not abusing one another they seem to be abusing themselves."

"Yeah, well, they don't have an opera house or library. Let's sort of move out of the way. The party seems to be getting rough."

He waltzed her to the edge of the clearing and let go of her. It wasn't just to spare her feelings. He had some feeling of his own to worry about. He was naked above the waist and all too aware that she was naked everywhere under the thin

155

cotton shirt he'd given her. Her nipples against his chest as they'd fooled around hadn't done a thing for his erection and he'd been worried about her feeling it. She tended to dance pretty close, for a missionary.

She took his hand calmly and said, "Well, we could sit this dance out, if there was a place to sit." Then she giggled and said, "Oh, I know this hut. I have a hammock inside. Lesh go sit in my hammock, huh?"

He eyed her dubiously. She was tight as a tick. He looked over to where Diablilla lay by the fire. Gaston was seated beside her, quietly smoking marijuana. He knew Diablilla was safe. But was anyone else around here?

Susan was tugging at him. He let her lead him into the thatched hut. It was pretty dark, but he could see enough to observe she'd been right about the shrunken heads hanging from the rafters. The quickly erectable Jivaro roofs of thatch were held up by saplings driven into the earth. Four hammocks of hand-spun wild cotton hung around near the outer walls of interwoven twigs. Susan said, "This one's mine," and leaped into it, exposing her bare behind as she did so. She rolled over, the shirttails up around her waist and her long shapely calves dangling over the edge as she added, "Come and sit by my side if you love me, like the song says. Do you love me, Dick? The cowboy loved the girl in the Red River Valley and you sure look like a cowboy to me."

He remained standing over her as he said, "I know you're feeling gaga, but try to listen anyway. I'm a soldier of fortune, a bum. Love is just another dirty word to guys in my business. No offense, but . . ."

"Oh, hell, let's just fuck platonically then."

He blinked and gasped, "I beg you pardon, Miss Missionary?"

"Whash the matter? Don't you like to fuck, Cowboy?"

"It's always been one of my favorite hobbies, but for a girl who doesn't smoke or chew . . ."

"Oh, you Gentiles always think we Latter-Day Saints are some sort of fanatic Puritan sect, don't you? I'd forgotten."

"Hey, that's not all you've forgotten, doll. I tried to read the Book of Mormon one time. Couldn't really get into it, but I do know you kids have the same Ten Commandments as the rest of us."

She giggled and said, "We break them as often as the rest of you, too."

"Even missionaries?"

"I know, I'm being awful. But for some reason, tonight it doesn't seem to bother me. What are you waiting for, Dick? I haven't had sex since our camp was raided and I'm really hurting!"

He started to climb into the hammock. Then he grinned and started to unbuckle his belt as he said, "Hell, I thought you were a damned virgin."

She laughed and said, "The Prophet Joseph teaches that all virgins shall be damned indeed. The body is the fleshy temple given to us by the Lord. Amen. Thou shalt not defile it with artificial stimulants. Neither shalt thou abuse it by jerking off."

He dropped his pants and said, "Amen!" as he climbed into the swaying hammock with her. He fought for balance on his knees, gripping the rope edges on either side of her as she hooked one calf over either side, presenting her open thighs to him as she unbuttoned the shirt demurely. He gingerly lowered himself and as his turgid shaft touched the blond fuzz, she took it in one hand, murmured, "Oh, nice," and guided it in for him.

He realized as she hissed and arched her spine to meet his thrusts that she hadn't been nearly as drunk as she'd been pretending. That made it even better. He'd set her straight that this was to be no more than good clean fun, and, since she seemed so surprisingly pragmatic, he'd be able to explain about Diablilla without the usual tears and recriminations. He knew he'd get plenty of those from Diablilla if he wasn't careful! But they could sort out the details later. Right now, it was time for a good healthy orgasm with a beautiful woman who obviously wanted the same.

So he gave her one, and then, since the crazy sway-backed position in the hammock was ruining his spine, he suggested they try it another way. She said she was game for anything that didn't hurt.

He climbed out and lay her crossways on the cotton strings with her tail bone and heels hooked on one side rope at the level of his hips. He stepped in and re-entered her at the new angle as she gazed up at him in wonder with the other rope against the nape of her neck. She gasped, "Oh, whee! It certainly feels deep that way!"

"Am I hurting you?"

"No. I said it felt deep. I never said I didn't *like* it deep. Try swinging me, it feels deliciously wild."

So he did, and it did. Considering it was the second time,

157

it made for a fast as well as novel orgasm. Susan climaxed easily, too. And he wondered why that sort of bothered him.

It wasn't that she'd turned out to be more earthy than he'd imagined. Susan was, in fact, the sort of woman men always said they were looking for. A healthy, uncomplicated broad who just plain loved to screw and went at it as casually as any man. She didn't say silly things about loving him and when he got around to telling her about Diablilla being his *adelita,* and what that meant, she just said, "We'll have to be careful then. But don't worry, I've handled jealous girls before. Let's try something new."

She rolled over and lay face down, her legs dangling and her spine arched by the sag of the hammock to present her pale derriere at an astounding angle. He started to put it into her from behind and she murmured, over the other side, "Shove it up my rear. It's fun that way, too."

He hesitated. Then he saw she'd run her hand under the side rope and was fingering herself. He nodded, got his wet shaft into position, and gingerly entered her tight pink anus as she hissed and said, "Oh, that's lovely. Swing the hammock, will you?"

He did, and it felt good as well as strange. The strangest thing was the conversational way she went at it, as if she was sharing a meal with him. He put a palm on each buttock and as he moved in and out, enjoying the unusual view, he said, "You sure are full of surprises, for a girl who bitched about the way the Indians carried on, doll."

She said, "A little faster, please. I was hysterical when you met me, Dick. I kept expecting them to rape me, and, despite the way I seem to be shocking you, I *am* particular who I do this with. Besides, they really are rather disgusting little creatures. They don't just indulge in normal sex. They seem to be bisexual child molesters and you have to admit that an old man doing, well, this, to a little boy is a bit much."

"It's okay if we're the same size and opposite sexes, huh?"

"You kind of like it, don't you?"

"As much as you do. But, no shit, were you this friendly with those other missionaries coming up the river to save souls?"

"Not with the other girls in our party. One has to draw the line somewhere. Perhaps I should explain about our

mission, Dick. You seem to have the idea I was with a lot of dried-up old prudes."

"Not any more."

"Our temple doesn't send out the usual lifelong missionaries. Every young man and woman of our sect is supposed to donate two years of his or her life to missionary work. After that, we return to the Great Salt Lake and resume our regular lives. The elders feel that youthful enthusiasm helps in doing good among the unbelievers."

He felt he was coming and muttered, "God knows you've got youthful enthusiasm, and you're doing me a lot of good. Do you want to turn over and finish right?"

"No, wait, I'm almost there and . . . Faster, Dick! I'm coming! Shove it all the way and let me feel you gushing in my bowels!"

He sighed, "Glugh!" but closed his eyes and fired his weapon despite her unromantic reminder where it was. As he leaned against her, letting it subside in her contracting, pulsing rectum she sighed and murmured, "Oh, that felt naughty. Let me up. This damned hammock is a bother. Let's do it right, on the ground."

"I think I can. Let me see if I can find something to wipe off on."

But she dropped to the ground at his feet, opened herself to him on her back, and said, "Don't worry about that. Give it to me while I'm still hot."

He dropped to his hands and knees to mount her frontally, but observed, "Doesn't it bother you that I'm sort of shitty?"

She answered by wrapping her arms and legs around him and pulling him into her. So he guessed it didn't. Her armpits smelled rank and gamy, too, and he could tell she hadn't bathed since she'd been with the Jivaro. It was sort of disgusting and sort of exciting. In her own way, the pale American blonde was more earthy and primitive than either the Indians, or his *mestizo* companions, male and female. He knew she liked her sex hot and smelly, too, and the hard-packed dirt under her rollicking rump didn't faze her a bit as she bounced to meet his thrusts, kissing him now for what he suddenly realized was the first time.

The cannabis had affected his drive, and while he had no trouble keeping it up, it was starting to turn into work now. He found himself wishing this was the softer, sweeter little Diablilla. He knew that he could just tear it off and go to

159

sleep with Diablilla. The memory of Diablilla's totally different body seemed to inspire him and he laughed at his own contrariness as he felt the firmer, bigger blonde responding to his faster lovemaking. She moaned, "Oh, here it comes again!" and he lied, "Me too," and faked an orgasm of his own as she stiffened and sobbed, "Enough! I can't take any more tonight!"

He stopped, withdrew, and helped her to her feet, asking, "Shall we return to the party?"

She said, "You go. I have to lie down. That stuff we've been smoking has had a strange effect on me and all of a sudden I feel faint."

Then, without further discussion, Susan flopped into the hammock, rolled over, and started to snore.

Bemused, Captain Gringo put his pants and boots back on, hitched his gun belt in place, and muttered, "There goes my last illusion. She snores like a man, too!"

Then he laughed and went outside.

The fire was still glowing in the center of the camp. He'd noticed it had gotten sort of quiet. The dancing had stopped, and dimly visible forms lay scattered about in the faint glow. Some of them were just dead to the world. Others were screwing casually around the fire. He spotted a naked Indian throwing the blocks to one of the *adelitas* from his guerrilla band, and though she didn't seem to mind at all, Captain Gringo looked quickly around for her *soldado*. He was a guy named José and he was sort of big and wild-eyed most of the time. Then he saw there was apparently no problem. José was nearby, staring dreamy-eyed down at the Jivaro girl he'd mounted, closer to the fire. The girl was about twelve and seemed to be enjoying the novelty as much as José, so what the hell.

But Captain Gringo hadn't counted on his people rutting with the Indians and so he looked around for Gaston and Diablilla with renewed concern. He didn't see Gaston. Diablilla lay where he'd left her, snoozing off her refreshments. As he hunkered down beside her, Diablilla rolled over on her back, looked blearily up at him, and said, "Oh, there you are. Where were you just now? I thought you had deserted me, but every time I try to get up my legs act funny."

He said, "I went to take a leak. We'd better find a hammock for you, kid. You can't sleep out here on the ground. The fire will be dead in a while and you'll catch a chill."

As he started to lift her, Diablilla sniffed and muttered, "Bastard. You have been vile. I can smell it. Who's codfish shop have you been in to, eh?"

"Yours," he lied, adding, "Don't you remember? You said you wanted to, before, so we did. I guess you were drunker than I thought."

He picked her up and started to carry her as far from Susan's hut as he could manage. She snuggled in his arms and muttered dreamily, "You should have awakened me, *querida*. I don't remember being vile tonight, and it's not fair." She sniffed again and said, "Oh, my, we *were* vile, weren't we? I did not know I needed a bath that badly. My poor baby, I have made you smell like pussy all over."

He said, "Hey, I like the way pussy smells, remember? Here's a hut we might be able to use for the night. It seems to be empty."

"Can we be vile some more, Dick?"

He started to say no. Then he reconsidered. There was only one way she was going to buy his story, once she sobered up. He had to get her just as raunchy.

He ducked inside and stood with her in his arms, trying to adjust his eyes to the gloom. He saw one of the hammocks was occupied by a couple who seemed to like each other a lot. He carried Diablilla to an empty one, lowered her into it, and removed his pants and boots again. He hung his gun belt over a crossbeam and climbed in with Diablilla. She was still half stoned, but she'd had the presence of mind to raise her skirts around her waist and, like Susan, she'd hooked a knee over each side rope. It seemed an instinctive reflex for any woman in a hammock.

He lowered himself into her, surprised he still had an erection capable of entering anything that tight. Diablilla said, "Oh, that feels good, but I feel sort of dry for a girl who has just been vile, *querido*. How do you account for this?"

He got it all the way in, luxuriating at the new feeling as he soothed. "It's that stuff you smoked. My mouth feels dry, too. It feels better now, doesn't it?"

She moved her hips, intrigued by the advantage the ropes under her knees gave her, and said, "Ah, I am starting to feel wet for you, again, my *toro*. Are you sure you do not mind the way I smell tonight? I seem to be most fishy and . . . you did not do anything vile to my back door, did you? *Madre de dios*, we smell like farting herrings left too long in a warm place!"

161

"Your warm place is fantastic. Do you want to talk about it all night or do you want to enjoy it?"

She replied by offering her undivided concentration as well as her soft little body to his guilt-excited thrusts. And after she'd come, fast, he knew he was in the clear. For now. He'd worry about how Susan was going to come out of her own haze in the morning, when the morning got there.

His own slaked lust, despite the novelty, made it take him much longer than usual. But, fortunately, Diablilla took this for inspired lovemaking as he drove her over the peak three times before he came anywhere near joining her. The constant stroking in her between-times throbbing afterglows drove the little Colombian crazy and she was letting the whole world know it. As she literally screamed she was coming, a dry voice from the other side of the hut observed, "Can't you two keep it down a bit, Dick? This child with me speaks a little Spanish and she says her Jivaro boyfriend is inclined to be possessive."

"Gaston, is that you?"

"*Mais non,* it is the Tsar of all the Russians. Fortunately, this nubile wench's boyfriend was *très* unconscious when last we observed him, but you two are making enough noise to wake the dead."

Diablilla had shut up, embarrassed, the minute she heard Gaston's voice. But she whispered, "We shall be quietly vile. But are you saying you are being vile with a Jivaro, Gaston?"

"Of course she is a Jivaro. How many kinds of Indians does M'selle think there are around here? I told you we were being discreet, *hein?*"

They weren't being discreet enough. The Jivaro girl was tittering and carrying on as Gaston's hammock creaked, groaned, and threatened to break free of its poles, or split, or both. It put a decided cramp in Captain Gringo's own style. He was already having enough trouble keeping it up. It seemed to bother Diablilla, too. She'd stopped cooperating and, in a hammock, if you don't get some cooperation you're not going anywhere.

He told the girl to hang in there and eased himself over the side to have a word or two in English with Gaston. As he approached the other swinging love nest and got a better view of its contents, he blinked and said, "Jesus H. Christ, I knew you were a dirty old man, but I didn't know you liked boys!"

Gaston was on his back with his Jivaro sex partner

astride him, bouncing like a kid on a bed. Come to think of it, it was a kid on a bed. Gaston said, "Snide me no snide, my old and rare. I assure you I am enjoying a *très* pleasant old-fashioned rutting with a female of the species, whatever her species may be."

"If that's a girl, how come she has no tits?"

"You Yankees and your constant preoccupation with secondary sex organs. I brought her in to *screw* her, not to *milk* her, *hein?*"

"Oh, shit, Gaston, that's a *baby* you're banging! She can't be nine years old!"

"I do not ask ladies for birth certificates. If they are big enough, they are old enough, and, if you will observe more justly, I am not banging her. She is banging me, and most enthusiastically, might I add? Leave me to my small pleasures, my old and rare. I am almost there again and I am not an exhibitionist."

Captain Gringo stood bemused and undecided as the little Jivaro girl grinned roguishly at him and bobbed up and down on Gaston's old but massive tool. If this was child abuse, which it had to be under the law, the child didn't seem to feel abused and there wasn't any law for hundreds of miles.

Curious despite himself, Captain Gringo marveled, "Jesus, is she really taking it all?" and Gaston closed his eyes and muttered, *"Oui,* and I am coming, so go away. You can have her later, Dick. I am not selfish, but let me finish with no further distractions, *hein?"*

Captain Gringo went back over to his own hammock. Diablilla asked, "Is it as bad as I thought?" and he answered, "Worse," but he didn't go into it. He remained on his feet and took a smoke from the pocket of his pants hanging over the hammock rope. Then he realized he'd light things up if he struck a match and Diablilla had enough to worry about. So he passed up the smoke.

There were some disgusting noises from across the hut and then it got silent for a time until Gaston sighed and said, "That was *très* amusing. We can talk, now, Dick. My amorous *amie* seems to want to go out and play."

Captain Gringo moved over again and saw Gaston was alone in the hammock, grinning like a shit-eating dog. He said, "You ought to be shot. Like those other dirty old goats who hang around schoolyards with bags of candy."

"Merde alors, I told you she has a boyfriend, and he is

163

bigger than me. Where did you think she picked up her Spanish? She's been putting out for guests since she was six."

"Glugh. I didn't think that was possible."

"Well, to get in a six-year-old, one must be hung a bit more modestly than you or even me. But who broke her in and with what is not our problem. She screws like a mink and I assure you she likes a well-hung *hombre*."

Gaston laughed and added, "It was rather droll, observing what seemed to be a little girl on a seesaw as I felt myself inside what was most obviously a woman of experience. Those contractions, ooh la la!"

"Okay, forget that. I've got another girl for you."

"Really? I thought you and Diablilla were quite satisfied with your arrangement, but if you need any help with her . . ."

"Shut up, I'm not talking about my *adelita*. I want you to get over to Susan Reynolds' hut and make friends with her before Diablilla cuts us both up with a rusty knife."

"*Sacre!* You wish for me to attempt the seduction of a missionary?"

"You'll find it's not as hard as it sounds. She just surprised hell out of me, and I want out. Go over and console her when she wakes up hungry. I think she's a nymphomaniac, but she's a nice uncomplicated lay and, uh, she likes variety."

Gaston laughed and said, "I thought I was finished for the evening, but your words of cheer inspire me to new heights. Are you sure she will accept a father figure, Dick?"

"She'd probably screw her father if she could get at him. Don't ask *me* what she wants, goddamnit. Get your horny ass over there and find out what she wants for yourself!"

Gaston rolled out of the hammock, picked up his clothes and gun, then decided he'd save time by just carrying them as he crossed the clearing in the dark.

Captain Gringo chuckled and went back to rejoin Diablilla. She was sound asleep. The combination of soft liquor and drugs, plus hard sex, had knocked her out for the night.

He knew two in a hammock made for great screwing and lousy sleeping. So he climbed in another hammock, naked, and settled down to catch a few winks of his own. He felt he'd more than earned them.

He was too keyed up to sleep. His body was tired, but

his brain was racing with plans and other worries as he lay there, listening to the small night noises that could mean anything. He had to get his people out of here before they wore out their welcome with the unpredictable headhunters. He had to figure out how he intended to take on the private army of Dom Luis with his smaller band. He had to do wonders and eat cucumbers, too. He knew he was wasting brain cells planning tactics against objectives he'd never scouted. It made more sense to just go around the rubber baron's empire. It made more sense, right now, to *sleep*, for Chrissake. He couldn't shoot any bad guys or screw any more bad girls tonight. Everybody else around him seemed to have packed it in for the night.

He was wrong. He snapped alert as he heard someone enter the hut. He didn't say anything. It was doubtless some poor Indian who belonged here. He might be in the guy's bunk. But what the hell, there were others. So he lay doggo. The Jivaro could figure out how to tell him, if he wanted him to move.

The moon had risen and was shedding her pale rays through the woven basketwork wall nearby. So the face that peered over the edge of the deep hammock at him was dappled silver and black by light and shadow. It was a round little face with bangs and a bright smile. He saw it was an Indian kid and wondered if it was the one Gaston had been fooling with.

A small brown hand came over the side to explore his naked body and he decided it had to be. In Spanish, he muttered, "Get away, kid, you bother me."

He or she giggled and replied in Jivaro. He asked, "Don't you savvy Spanish?" and was answered with more grunts and tweets. Ergo it was yet another Jivaro kid. As it grasped his limp shaft and began to play with it he saw it was also another juvenile delinquent.

He started to push the hand away, saying, "Hey, have a heart. I've already had two grown women tonight and you're not my type!"

Then, as the little Jivaro giggled and sprang into the hammock with him, he fended off the naked flesh with his hands, felt a small warm groin cupped in his palm, and added, "Well, not exactly my type. At least you're a girl!"

The little Jivaro was built like a boy above the waist and had no hair between her skinny kid thighs. As she spread them above his lap and wriggled against the hand shielding

an experienced grown woman, cheating on a husband asleep in the next room. Come to think of it, she might have a husband sleeping in the next room. Or hut, at least. He could tell she hadn't had another man that night. But she'd sure had others in her tiny time. A lot of others. If he closed his eyes it was impossible to imagine he was actually rutting with a child. If he opened them and ran his hands over her little form, it was obvious he was and the mixture of desire and shame was doing funny things to his used and abused shaft. He wanted to come and knew he really shouldn't. You couldn't go all the way with a little kid, could you?

You could. The naughty little Jivaro started moving faster and wilder as her drum-tight love muscles responded to the throbbing of his excited erection and she purred down at him like a kitten as he exploded wetly inside her and she felt it. His coming got her going and she was breathing hard between her tightly clenched teeth when she, too, experienced a long shuddering orgasm of her own and collapsed against him. He held her against his own heaving flesh. It felt weird as hell. Her head only came to his chest and it felt like he was holding a child on his lap, save for the fact he was inside her lap as it milked him with teasing spasms.

He muttered, "Well, there's a mystery cleared up. I always wondered how old you had to be to come. I was a late starter next to you, honey!"

He remembered that time, back in Connecticut, when Ernie Matherson told him what fuck meant and how the "big boys" jerked off. They'd both been six or eight and Ernie wasn't quite sure how you did it. He said his nine-year-old sister knew about jerking off and fucking, so they'd gone over to Ernie's house to ask her about it. What the hell had that girl's name been? Oh, yeah, Ernestine. The Mathersons had moved out West the next summer and been massacred by the Sioux, he'd later heard.

He held the little Indian girl and wondered why his homesick eyes were misting like that as he thought back to those golden Indian summer days and how pretty Ernestine Matherson had been at nine. Nothing had happened, of course. They'd found Ernie's sister alone and asked her to tell them about fucking, so she had, in the innocent, detached way kids talked about all the mysteries the grown-ups never let them in on. Ernie had suggested the three of them experiment with fucking, but Ernestine had said she didn't want to take her pantaloons off because she'd heard it was

167

wrong to take one's pantaloons off in front of boys. So they'
decided to go down to the corner and find some other kid
for a game of kick-the-can, and for years he'd wondered wha
it would have been like to do it at six or eight.

"Ernestine would have liked it," he decided, adding, "
wonder if she ever got any. She'd been eleven or s
when the Sioux killed her."

The other little wild Indian must have thought he wa
muttering at her and began to indicate by wriggles an
gestures that she wanted him to get on top.

He said, "Hell, no way, I'm over six feet and you can't b
more than four."

But she kept trying and when she detached herself an
snuggled down into the groove between him and the ham
mock wall he thought and then decided there was only on
way it would work without wrecking her.

He climbed out, took her thin legs by the ankles, an
swiveled her broadside as she softly laughed. He could see sh
knew it that way, too, as she propped her tiny fanny on th
side rope facing him and spread her shapely little legs. H
took one of her ankles in each hand and held them high as h
moved in closer. The little Indian reached between her brow
thighs to guide him in again. Then she locked her ankle
around his neck as he started to swing her in the hammock
Standing up. He'd just done this with Susan across th
clearing, but what a difference!

There were limitations, after all, to how far a grown ma
could go with an immature child, however precocious. Th
girl had learned to accept a full-sized shaft's cross-sectiona
dimensions but she still had some growing to do, lengthwise
and he hit bottom, hard, with every swing. He started to eas
off, not wanting to hurt her. But she indicated she wasn'
getting hurt. She loved it. So what the hell, it felt sort of lik
he was stubbing his toe on soft warm velvet, but if she coul
take it, he could, so they both did, and she came twice ahea
of him.

When he finally managed himself, he gasped, "I don'
know where that came from, kid, but there sure ain't any
more where it came from. You three crazy dames have wrung
me out like a dishrag."

Diablilla stirred in her sleep and murmured, "What did
you say, Dick?"

He froze, still throbbing inside the little Indian as he

soothed, "Go back to sleep, *querida*. I just had to, ah, take a leak."

"Come back to bed, *querido*, I'm lonesome."

He gingerly withdrew from the silently smiling mischief-maker and moved over to pat Diablilla back to sleep. She took his hand in hers and kissed it dreamily before her soft breathing told him she'd dozed off again.

He turned around to see if she could have seen anything. The other hammock was fairly visible in the dappled moonlight. But the naughty Jivaro girl was gone. He sighed with relief and moved over to it. He flopped in, weakly, and this time when he closed his eyes he fell asleep.

It seemed no time at all and he was having a very confusing and very dirty dream when he woke up again to find Diablilla standing over him in the dim gray light of dawn. She said, "It's morning, *querida*."

He said, "I noticed. Why are you playing with my prick, Diablilla?"

"I like your prick, and I think we have time to sneak a quickie before the others wake up. Don't you want to be vile this morning?"

In Spanish he said, "Of course." In English, he muttered, "God give me strength."

19

Considering their reputation, the Jivaro seemed more interested in making love than war. So Captain Gringo decided they'd better keep it that way and haul ass before the unpredictable little headhunters changed their minds.

As he led the guerrilla band through the jungle shadows he noticed Susan was walking close to Gaston. He and the Frenchman hadn't taken time to compare notes, but he figured if the missionary gal hadn't accepted Gaston's advances they wouldn't be acting so friendly right now. He didn't have to ask if Gaston had made advances.

Diablilla walked at his side, just ahead of the men packing the machine gun. He knew she'd come in handy if they encountered any more wild tribesmen. The old Jivaro chief had said there were no other Jivaro in the area, but he wouldn't have that collection of shrunken heads if every other tribe had diplomatic relations with the Jivaro, and the way the slave raiders were stirring things up in the *selva*, a lot of tribes might not be where they were supposed to be these days.

They crossed the small side stream Susan said her missionary party had been camped beside when they were jumped. There were no signs of her old campsite or missing companions, dead or alive. They'd crossed at another ford apparently. Or the ravenous jungle life had simply absorbed the pathetic remnants. People were always telling bullshit stories about finding skeletons in the jungle. But you seldom saw so much as a monkey bone, even though they had to be dying all around all the time. The calcium-starved red laterite soil sucked bones into it like ice melting in the constant moisture. Prowling ants and beetles took care of anything

softer, fast. Paper, leather, cloth, or flesh just vanished. Metal rusted away in little more time. So the kids the *flagelados* had murdered hadn't even left a stink to remember them by.

The rebel who'd led them over the mountains had no idea where they were, either, by this time. Captain Gringo had Nuñez out on point anyway. This wasn't just to spare the guide's feelings. Somebody had to take the point. He had Pancho out on the left flank and José was scouting to the right. They had orders not to stray too far. He knew where he was going, sort of, thanks to the crude map the Jivaro had drawn for him in the dust back there. But the Indians were hazy on some details. So he only had a general idea where the infamous Dom Luis and, more important, his jungle runners might be hanging out. His own people had enough to worry about without running into an ambush. Most of them had seemed to think he was crazy when he'd outlined his plans to them before leaving the Jivaro. But when he'd said he was open to suggestions, not even Gaston had offered anything better than simply skipping the whole deal and trying to work around the rubber baron's empire.

But, aside from being cowardly, as he'd pointed out, bypassing the vast holdings of Dom Luis meant one hell of a detour and, in the end, might lead them from the frying pan to the fire. The Indians had said there were other Brazilian adventurers encroaching on Colombian territory now. Some seemed to be nicer guys, which would be easy, and others were said to be as bad, which took some doing. At least, as he'd explained, they knew what they faced if they bored on down the Putumayo drainage. A two-faced murdering son of a bitch, but a known quality. Why go out of the way to meet the devil you didn't know when the shortest way led through the devil you did?

They camped in the *selva* that night. He allowed small smudge fires to keep the bugs at bay and rousted everybody up well before dawn. It wasn't easy for him, either. Diablilla had insisted on a lot of vile. He noticed Gaston was walking sort of funny, too. But the two girls just looked sort of like Mona Lisa as they rested their thighs by walking with them a lot closer together.

He missed José during the noon break. Pancho and Quico suggested looking for him. But Captain Gringo swallowed the Jivaro smoked parrot he was trying to get down and vetoed the suggestion. He said, "We can't stay here that long. He'll either catch up or he won't."

171

"But, Señor, what if he is lost or down with snake-bite?"

"He should have hollered. Look, I know this seems hard, guys, but you ran away to be *soldados* and those are the breaks. Nobody ever told you this would be an easy life. If you can help a *compañero* without endangering the greater number, swell. If you can't, tough titty. José was pretty drunk at the Jivaro camp and last night he was doing pretty good with a gourd of *chichi*, now that I think of it. Do you guys think he might have stumbled off drunk?"

Pancho said, "Anything is possible. But José means well."

"Well isn't good enough. Finish your meal and smoke if you've got 'em. We're pushing on in ten, and if he doesn't make it he doesn't make it."

They went to join their own *adelitas*. Gaston ambled over, hunkered down, and asked, "Is it wise to push them so, Dick? They're starting to bitch more than soldiers usually do."

"I noticed. That's what makes it so nice leading an army down here. Give a Latin cornhusker a big hat and a gun and he starts thinking he's a general. They'll be okay in a firefight. They have no choice."

"Have you considered that José may have deserted, Dick?"

"First thing I thought of. He knows at least one Jivaro girl back there that likes him a lot. I didn't think I'd better remind our guys of that option. Captain Bligh had the same problem getting his crew away from Tahiti, remember?"

"A little before my time, but I know the story. Do you think José will get away with going native?"

"No. Diablilla has been explaining Jivaro to me. He'll be okay until some Jivaro gets a boil on his neck or a kid drowns in a creek. But once the elders start trying to decide who bewitched them, guess who they'll probably pick as first choice? I doubt if we'll ever see that poor asshole again. But, if we do, we'll be able to recognize him by his mustache. Some of those shrunken heads had neat mustaches."

Then he glanced up at the tree canopy high above and added, "Let's move it out. If we time it right, we should make it to Dom Luis do Putumayo's steamboat landing before sundown."

172

20

They timed it right. There was still perhaps an hour of daylight left when Captain Gringo's launch hit a two-log *balsa* in a sluggish backwater of the tea-colored Rio Putumayo, upstream from the headquarters of Dom Luis, albeit well within the territory he claimed as his own. They knew this because Nuñez, out on point, had spotted one of the rubber baron's patroling guards before the guard had spotted Nuñez, and as he'd died, they'd gotten some information out of him.

Unfortunately, not enough, and hence the experiment with the *balsa*. Gaston wasn't enthusiastic about the experiment as he stood in the shallows with his taller friend. Gaston was naked to the waist and Captain Gringo had taken his shirt back from Susan, which seemed fair when you thought about it, but not the main reason for the American to want to make himself more presentable. Gaston said, "Listen to me, Dick. I have backed you in many a mad venture, but this time you have most definitely cracked under the strain. Going in alone is madness. Going in with only a pistol and one rifle is even crazier. If you won't take me with you, won't you at least take the machine gun?"

Captain Gringo shook his head and replied. "That would really be whacky. I'm on an espionage mission, not a one-man war. Who the hell's going to believe my story if I come wandering out of the bushes with a fucking Maxim? I'm supposed to be the only survivor of a party jumped by Jivaro in the first place and the pricks down the river saw those Mormon missionaries in the second. They might buy me as one of the guys from Salt Lake. It was a couple of weeks back that the Mormons passed through, and we all look alike

to them, too. But Susan's friends most definitely did not come up the river with a machine gun."

"True. The Mormons were not attacked by Jivaro either. They were *flagelados*."

"You know that, I know that, Dom Luis knows that. I'm about to prove to him that his two-faced act worked just the way he expected it to. No survivor of Susan's party would walk right into his lair like a big-ass bird unless he was too stupid to wonder what primitive Indians were doing with rapid-fire pump guns, right? When we first found Susan she still thought Indians had attacked her party. So it'll seem natural that I, or rather the poor Bible thumper I'm supposed to be, saw things the same way."

He climbed on the *balsa* with his long pole, laid the Colombian army rifle across the logs, and added, "Come on, push me off, damnit. Then go back and keep the rest of our gang quiet and out of sight till you hear from me."

"What if we don't hear from you, my old and rare?"

"Give me twenty-four, then run like hell and do what you can to get them to Manaus. It'll mean Dom Luis is too smart for us, as well as too big."

Gaston was still cursing as he helped Captain Gringo move the clumsy *balsa* into the current. The standing American started poling without looking back. The Putumayo was shallow this far upstream, but too deep to touch bottom as he got out on open water. So the *balsa* started drifting sideways. But what the hell, he was going that way anyway.

The current took him around the bend between thick green walls of rank growth and he soon spotted the gray tin roofing of a fair-sized river settlement ahead. He was feeling for the bottom with the pole, aware he was coming down the wrong bank, when he saw a dugout coming to meet him. The paddlers were Indians. The guy scowling at him from the bow of the dugout was a *flagelado*. The shotgun in his hands was American.

Captain Gringo called, "Help! Don't let me drift back into that terrible jungle!" as the canoe approached. The gunman in the bow grinned crookedly and called back, "Have no fear, *muchacho*. Nobody passes the landing of Dom Luis without giving us an accounting!"

The dugout pulled alongside and Captain Gringo caught the line they tossed him. As the canoe towed him across, the man in the bow was too far forward for much conversation,

174

so the wary American studied the approaching landing. He was supposed to have been here before. Susan had coached him (and reproached him), but with an advance idea of the layout, it was going to take some acting to convince them he was a simple good old Utah boy too dumb to be running through the *selva* without a leash.

A little teapot Amazon steamboat was tied up at the dock jutting out from shore. The banks were blood-red and lined with quite a crowd of curious onlookers. He saw most of them seemed simple peons. But there was a sprinkling of swaggering armed *flagelados*. So the next few minutes would be dicey indeed. Nobody seemed to be pointing a gun his way. He figured they figured they didn't have to. He was in no position to scare them as much as they scared him.

A more civilized-looking fat man in a white Panama suit stood on the dock as they towed him up to it. Captain Gringo hoped Susan's description had been a good one as he waved and called out, "Dom Luis, thank God I made it back here!"

The Brazilian rubber baron's fat sly face wore an expression of polite wariness as the *balsa* bumped against the pilings and Captain Gringo leaped over to join him on the dock. As the American held out his free hand, the fat man took it, but said, with a puzzled smile, "Do I know you, Senhor?"

"I'm Reynolds, Mission of the Latter Day Saints. Don't you remembe me? We passed through here just a few weeks ago, although I must say it feels like a million years. Good Lord, if you knew what I'd been through out there!"

"My *casa* is your *casa,* Senhor. Come, we shall talk about it over food and other refreshments, eh?"

The gunman from the canoe nudged him and growled, "You will leave your guns with me, Senhor."

Captain Gringo handed him the rifle with a hurt look and started to unbuckle his gun belt. But Dom Luis snapped, "Do not be rude, Pessoa. I have just made Senhor Reynolds welcome."

Pessoa nodded and stepped back a pace. But he didn't offer the rifle back. Captain Gringo shrugged and followed the fat man up the path to the imposing albeit jerry-built mansion on a rise dominating the landing.

As they walked, Dom Luis said casually, "Reynolds, Reynolds, there was a blond girl named Reynolds in your party, no?"

Captain Gringo put a slight sob in his voice as he answered, "My sister, Susan. I don't know if she's dead or worse off."

"There is something worse off than dead, Senhor?"

"Of course. The Indians may have her. You see, we were jumped by wild Indians a few days after we left you. I got away. I don't think any of the others did. God, if you knew what I've been through, alone in the jungle all this time, living on monkey and parrot and . . ."

"Easy, Senhor. First we eat and drink and then we talk, eh?"

Captain Gringo knew why he displayed so little interest, but it meant Dom Luis was overconfident as well as a lousy actor. The oily prick was so used to this game he'd forgotten the subtle lines. No really innocent white man would have dismissed the excited babblings of a survivor popping out of the *selva*. Human beings would have wanted to hear all about it back there on the dock. Things were looking up. The cocky sons of bitches seemed to be buying his story simply because it didn't seem possible to them that anyone else could be half so smart.

He knew Dom Luis had no intention of letting him leave this place alive. He'd ordered the missionaries killed to keep the Brazilian authorities downstream in the dark about just where he was and what he was doing up here along the border. This polite bullshit was intended merely to extract such information from him as they might find useful. Okay, he'd better make them think he knew lots of interesting fairy tales, like the dame in the Arabian Nights, right?

As Dom Luis led him up on the veranda and clapped his pudgy hands for the servants, Captain Gringo said, "I saw some other people those Indians must have attacked. There were bodies all over the place. At least fifty of them. It was awful. They were bloated and . . ."

Dom Luis whirled and cut in, "You saw some of my men dead out there in the *selva*, Senhor?"

"I don't know who they were, Dom Luis, but they certainly had been killed. I didn't get too close. The smell was awful and I was afraid of the Indians."

Dom Luis ushered him to a seat at the table on the wrap-around veranda before he answered, "Yes, the Jivaro and Colorados in the area are said to be most savage. These dead men you say you saw in the *selva* . . . could you guide a party of my men back to the place, Senhor Reynolds?"

Captain Gringo looked around as if trying to get his bearings and then he said, "I'm not sure. I remember you took us for a train ride around your holdings when we were here before, but I'm afraid I may be turned around."

He pointed due east, away from the setting sun, and said, "That way is north, right?"

Dom Luis repressed a smirk and answered, "You are turned around indeed. How on earth did you ever find your way back here?"

"I didn't know I was anywhere near your place. I guess I wandered in big circles until I came to a river. I found a raft on the bank and pushed off. I figured the current had to take me somewhere, and anywhere was an improvement! The rest you know. I *might* be able to find those dead men again, starting from here. I think I could find our camp, and the other party was hit fairly near it. Do you have any idea who they might have been, Dom Luis?"

"Yes, they worked for me. Tell me, did you notice if their heads were missing?"

"Gee, I didn't look that close, but, no, I don't think so. I remember one man's face. It looked awful. But if I saw his face . . ."

"Quite so, they were hit by Colorado Indians. That explains them being caught unawares. They were scouting Jivaro. We didn't know any others were that close."

A pretty Negress came out with a tray of refreshments. Dom Luis seemed unaware that she was also stark naked. But as the girl put down her tray, nipples swaying in time with her graceful movements, the rubber baron rose and said, "Forgive me, Senhor Reynolds, but we do not have much light left. Let us walk around the veranda together, eh?"

Captain Gringo had hoped he'd say that. He got up to follow as the pudgy Brazilian led him around the big frame house, saying, "Try to think back to the last time you were here. It is too late, of course, to mount a patrol into the *selva*, but if you could offer some suggestions about the directions, my boys and I could plan tonight more intelligently."

So Captain Gringo cased the layout as the Brazilian made small talk. The American now had a mental map of the steamboat landing and everything between it and the house. He spotted a tin shack with a tall tin funnel like a riverboat and casually said, "Oh, that's where you refine the rubber or something, right?"

Dom Luis shot him a curious look and replied, "One

177

does not refine rubber, Senhor. One smokes it into bales by holding a stick dipped in latex over a fire. Don't you remember? I thought I showed you through that powerhouse over there. I remember your poor sister commenting on my having electricity with some surprise."

Captain Gringo was surprised, too. He'd asked Susan not to leave anything out and the silly cunt had forgotten to tell him they had a generating plant! He shrugged and said, "I'm afraid I wasn't paying much attention. As you may recall, I was fighting a bout of malaria the last time I came through here."

"Ah, I was wondering how I'd forgotten a man your size. You must have been one of those who stayed behind when I took most of your companions on a tour of my holdings."

"Yes, my sister said she enjoyed the train ride. How far into the jungle do your tracks run, Dom Luis?"

"About fifteen of your American miles. That is the siding, over there, where your unfortunate friends boarded my train."

Captain Gringo stared due west at the little switch-yard behind the main house. A single spur line ran past to the generating plant and beyond to the river. He'd missed the track in the tall grass, coming up from the landing. The layout was falling into place in his mind now. He nodded and said, "I don't see any railroad cars or that gold engine, Dom Luis."

The rubber baron chuckled and said, "Ah, you remember that, eh? Everyone remembers my pretty little locomotive. Some find my tastes a bit gaudy. But I ask you, what is money for, if not to enjoy it, eh?"

"It's your money, Dom Luis. I guess this rubber boom has made a lot of people rich, right?"

Dom Luis shrugged and said, "One has to be in the right place at the right time. Unfortunately, the wild rubber trees grow far apart. It takes organization to show a profit, even with cheap help. But we manage."

Captain Gringo repressed a sarcastic answer. He knew how cheap indeed Dom Luis was about his labor force. But he was supposed to be a dumb missionary.

They completely circled the house on the veranda and as Dom Luis led him back to the table Captain Gringo said, "I know where I am now. I'm pretty sure I can lead your recovery party, Dom Luis."

The rubber baron frowned and answered, "Recovery

178

party? Oh, yes, of course we must see to a decent burial for my poor employees. But then we shall dispose of any nearby Indians with far less formality. The savages must be taught a lesson. I do not permit trespassers on my land, even when they don't murder my help."

The Negress had gone back inside, but Captain Gringo spotted her peeking out at them through the window, over Dom Luis's shoulder. The girl caught his eye and gestured urgently, but he had no idea what the hell she wanted.

Dom Luis pointed at the sandwiches and the pitcher on the table and said, "Help yourself, my young friend. If you will forgive me for not joining you, I have already eaten and, as you see, I have a weight problem."

Captain Gringo nodded thanks and picked up a sandwich. The pitcher looked like it was full of watered milk and smelled like rum. He asked what it was and Dom Luis said, "Rum and coconut water, of course. Unfortunately, even if you boil it, the local water leaves much to be desired."

Captain Gringo was hot and thirsty. So the drink looked as good to him as it sounded. But he remembered, just in time, and said, "I'm sorry, Dom Luis, but as a Mormon I can't drink alcohol."

"That's revolting." The rubber baron frowned. "Everybody drinks a little here in the *selva!*" Then he remembered his manners and said, "I'm sorry, I forgot you were a missionary. I will have them prepare you a pitcher of pure coconut water before we tuck you in for the night. You will of course be staying in the master bedroom."

Captain Gringo said, "I wouldn't want to put anyone to so much trouble," but the oily Dom Luis insisted. "I shall hear no more about it. I have so few guests up here on the Putumayo. It is my pleasure to make them feel most welcome."

There was an odd glitter in the Brazilian's eyes as he purred on about how much he liked to be nice to people. Captain Gringo knew how nice he'd been to Susan's party. But he doubted they'd gun him here in the house. Apparently Dom Luis had at least a few decent people down by the landing, and of course the crew aboard the steamer didn't work for him at all.

He asked about the steamer, explaining he was anxious to book passage down the river. Dom Luis soothed, "You have plenty of time for that. The boat will not leave until we finish loading her. That will take two days. At the moment

179

my train is out at the far end of the line and won't be back until about this time tomorrow evening with half a cargo. It will take at least another day on another spur to gather all we need. One must learn to bide one's time down here, my North American friend. The heat can kill you if you move too fast. In any case, I find it difficult to recruit good help these days."

Again Captain Gringo bit his tongue. He knew that while the fat tub of lard rested his big ass in the shade of this veranda a lot of poor slaves were working hard indeed for him. And, speaking of slaves, where had that pretty black girl gone, and what the hell had she been waving at him about?

She hadn't been making obscene gestures, so, despite her costume, that hadn't been it. She'd looked more scared than lusty. This fat slob probably got all the sex action around here anyway.

They made small talk for a time and then, as the sun went down and the fireflies came out, Dom Luis excused himself with something about seeing the captain of the riverboat. He clapped his hands again and another servant girl, this one a naked Oriental, came out to lead the American to his quarters. As she switched on the lights he saw the Edison bulb was mounted in a revolving electric ceiling fan above a big brass bed. This was grand luxe indeed and he said so, in Spanish. The Oriental girl understood well enough to shrug and say something about Dom Luis being *"muy simpático"* but he didn't think her heart was in it.

It was too early to turn in. But he knew Dom Luis expected a guy who'd been lost for weeks in the *selva* to act pretty bushed. So, while he had no intention of staying the night, he decided he'd better go through the motions.

He undressed and hung his clothes and gun belt over the head rails of the bed, enjoying the cool breeze from the fan as he sat on the clean linen sheets. He saw they had indeed left a big pitcher of coconut water on the nearby dresser. He cursed Brigham Young as he thought back to the rum he'd missed on the veranda. But at least the stuff would be wet.

His bare heel felt something cold under the bed. It was a chamberpot. That reminded him that he had to pee, so he did. He could see he was a bit dehydrated as he put an inch of very yellow urine in the bottom of the pot before stepping over to the dresser for a drink. He poured some of the pitcher's contents into the thick glass tumbler beside it. He raised the glass to his lips. A bell rang inside his head. He normally didn't sniff

his drinks too carefully, but he normally didn't stay as a house-guest with a known murderer, either.

It wasn't coconut water. He had no idea what it was, but he'd drunk a lot of coconut water in his time and this wasn't it. It didn't smell like any poison he knew. It hardly had any smell at all. Just a sort of juicy vegetable odor with a vaguely familiar whiff to it around the edges. He knew it would look funny if he didn't drink anything at all after coming in from the *selva* with his tale of woe. So he poured the contents of the glass in the chamberpot, hoping his piss would disguise the skimmed milk appearance for now.

He put the glass down and started to shove the pot under the bed with his bare foot. Then he saw what was happening down there and marveled, "What the hell . . . ?"

The stuff he'd poured in the pot was turning to thick goo. As he watched, it seemed to get even tougher-looking. He grimaced and reached in his pants for his jackknife before he hunkered down, bare ass, to watch the interesting chemistry. He probed the rubbery scum with the blade of the knife. Then he nodded and said, "Of course. Alcohol is alkaline, so you can mix it with latex. Piss is acid, so it coagulates latex to crude rubber. But what the hell would possess anyone to drink latex and . . . son of a *bitch!*"

He rose, grim-faced, remembering where he was as he fought to control his temper. Dom Luis didn't just kill people. He killed them *dirty!* Human gastric juices were almost pure hydrochloric acid. The sappy latex, having no particular taste and lacking the "rubber" smell of vulcanization, would go down smooth enough. Then, when it hit one's stomach acids, lots of luck. An instant rubber ball you could neither digest nor throw up until you died, horribly, from what would look like some sort of jungle stomach upset to anyone curious enough to ask!

As he put the knife away, there was a soft knock on the door and when he called, *"Entrada,"* the black girl came in, looking like she'd have been blushing if she'd been able to.

He was stark naked, too. But what the hell, there was a lot of that going around. He nodded at her and asked, "Well?"

The girl licked her lips and said, "I am called Varginha. Dom Luis says I am to make you happy."

She passed him to get on the bed, roll over, and spread her chocolate thighs with a resigned sigh. But not before he'd spotted the fresh lash mark across her back.

It wasn't easy, but he stayed on his feet and kept from rising to the occasion as he said gently, "He did, huh? He must have odd views on your average missionary. What were you trying to tell me before, Varginha?"

The girl started to cry, but moved her hips teasingly and cupped her brown melon breasts up to him with her hands as she pleaded, "Don't you like me, Senhor? Dom Luis will be most cross if I fail to please you."

"I'll bet. Where is he right now, Varginha?"

"In his room, with La China. He told me to keep you company and, ah, keep you busy."

"Get me thirsty, too, I'll bet. Did he tell you what was in that pitcher, honey?"

The pretty Negress turned her face away with a shudder. He nodded and said, "Right. You did try to warn me, before they reminded you who you worked for with that whip. You're kind of in a spot, for a nice girl, aren't you?"

The black girl sat up, buried her face in her hands, and sobbed, "Oh, Senhor, I *was* a nice girl, once. They told me I was coming up the river for, to be a cook. But that was months ago, and if I told you half the horrors I have seen, you would never believe me."

"I believe you. Do you want out?"

"How, in God's name? Nobody leaves here alive. Just yesterday another white man came down the river, and I watched as Dom Luis entertained him out there on the veranda, as he was just entertaining you. They gave him latex and rum, too. He died horribly not two paces from where you were sitting when I tried to warn you."

"I told you I got your message and that we're friends, Varginha. Cut the blubbering and tell me what else you know about the man they killed. Did you get his name?"

"*Sí*, it was José Coronado, I think."

"Son of a bitch!"

"What is wrong? Do you know this José, Senhor?"

"I did. That oily slavemaster of yours knew all along who I was, if that deserter José got here ahead of me! Boy, Dom Luis is some cookie! He even kills people who come ratting to him on their friends!"

He stepped over to the head of the bed and started to dress. Varginha said, "Are you not going to make love to me, Senhor?"

"Maybe later. If we get out of here alive. Don't you have any clothes anywhere?"

"No, Senhor. Why? Is it possible you really mean to take me with you?"

"I can't leave you here. I guess basic black will have to do for now. If they don't find me dead in bed by midnight they'll swat you like a fly for failing."

He hitched on his gun belt, held out his left hand to her, and said, "Come on. Stick tight to me and keep your mouth shut."

Varginha raised his hand to her lips and kissed it as she rose from the bed, murmuring, "Oh, Mother of God, I thought I was meant to die in this terrible place!"

He said, "I told you to keep your mouth shut, so do it!" Then he switched out the light and opened the door a crack. The coast was clear. He drew his .38 and led the naked girl out into the dimly lit hallway.

They started down it toward the rear. She whispered, "There is a night guard walking the veranda, Senhor," and he hissed, "Gotcha. Shut up."

They were passing a door that stood a little ajar and funny sounds were coming from the room on the far side. Captain Gringo risked a peek. Then he blinked and took a closer look. What he saw looked impossible.

Dom Luis was fucking himself in a mirror.

The rubber baron stood, naked and pinkly obscene, facing a big standing mirror in the center of his room under another fan. As the baffled American watched, the Brazilian was thrusting his pelvis against that of his own image, gripping the edges of the mirror and grinning at himself like a shit-eating dog.

Then Captain Gringo spotted the tawny curves of the Oriental girl on the far side of the mirror. She stood bent over, with her buttocks against the back of the mirror and her hands braced on her knees. Dom Luis was putting it to her through a hole in the mirror! He liked pussy as much as the next man, but he obviously loved himself more than he had any right to. So he was trying for the best of both worlds. Screwing his own unlovely image while using the pretty girl's snatch as a surrogate for what he lacked himself.

Captain Gringo muttered, "Well, some guys collect stamps. Some guys have more unusual hobbies." Then he led Varginha on.

He stopped by the rear door and told her to be quiet. She was frozen with fear as he listened for the sound of footsteps on the planks outside. A million years later the

183

night guard passed the dark doorway and a second later he was laid low with a fractured skull. He'd been watching for an attack from the brooding darkness around the house, not from within it.

Captain Gringo led the Negress into the night, forcing her to run, not walk, for the nearest exit. They tore up the tracks until he was sure they weren't being followed. Then he slowed to a walk and said, "Okay, doll, I think we made it. Just take it easy and get your breath back. We've still got some walking to do."

Varginha stood beside him in the dark, panting for breath as he looked around in the dim light for someplace to sit down. He led her over to a mossy fallen log. They sat down together. Then she was wrapped around him, sobbing silly grateful things about his saving her and making it hard to remember he already had a girl back with the guerrilla band they were trying to reach.

That wasn't all she made hard as she suddenly slid off the log to kneel between his knees and fumble for his fly. He said, "Hey, take it easy, Varginha. I like you, too, but I have an *adelita* who's not going to like this very much."

Varginha had his erection in her hand, so it seemed silly to lie to her when she asked softly, "Don't you feel anything for me, Senhor?"

He said, "Yeah, but you have to understand . . ."

"Don't worry," she sighed in a hurt voice, "I was raised a servant. So I know my place." Then she proceeded to swallow him whole.

He said, "Hey, let's not waste it!" as he peeled off his shirt and pants, threw them on the ground behind her, and pushed Varginha on top of them to mount her properly.

As she wrapped her smooth dark arms and legs around him and felt his paler shaft enter her, she sobbed, "Oh, God, it has been so long since I have been like this with a friend."

He said, "I wish you hadn't brought that up, Varginha. Normally I'm a live-and-let-live guy, but that creepy Dom Luis is icky to think about when a guy has to take sloppy seconds."

She crooned, "I never gave myself like this to him. He is a nasty pervert with a tiny little thing."

"Oh, shit, you're getting me soft."

She arched her back and said, "I won't allow that. You don't understand. Why do you think I am so excited? He has

184

all of his harem frustrated half to death. Right now, poor China is taking it in the rear from that disgusting little monster and ..."

"Wait a minute. Are you saying he's only been in you via the back door?"

"Of course. He's not man enough to fill a woman this way."

So Captain Gringo filled her as best he knew how, and Varginha seemed to love every inch of it.

21

Dom Luis sat fully dressed on his veranda the next morning, smoking a cigar and scowling at the *honcho* of his *flagelado* army as the *mestizo* reluctantly reported, "Not a sign of the American and that damned Negress, *mí patrón.* We have scoured the *selva* in every direction, but . . ."

"Idioto!" Dom Luis cut in, pointing at the river as he added, "We sent the steamboat away with an excuse. But that José said the big Anglo has a gang with him and they know too much. If only one of them rafts down the river to report our, uh, enterprise to the authorities, I will have you all boiled in oil!"

Then he rose grandly as he heard the distant chuffing of a steam locomotive. He said, "The work train is coming in. I want you to make another sweep, farther out. As soon as they unload the rubber, take the train as far west as possible and have your men spread out from there, both north and south, understand?"

Then, without waiting for an answer, he walked around the veranda to await the work train. It sounded like it was coming fast. Could something be the matter? That deserter had said the guerrillas had a machine gun and they may have been raiding farther up the line. But if the train was under attack he'd have heard the rattle of its Gatling guns.

Dom Luis stood watching, puffing his smoke, as the gold-painted shay locomotive appeared between the trees on the far side of his big clearing. What in the hell did they think they were doing? It was moving too fast!

The main tracks ended just a few yards away, and if they ever intended to stop in time . . .

And then Dom Luis screamed in rage and terror as he saw the people leaping off the flatcars and fanning out as the locomotive kept coming and coming!

The shout brought other guards out as the rubber baron started running along the planks on his stubby legs. He yelled, "Guerrillas have our train!"

And then things got even more confusing as the forward Gatling gun on the gilded tender opened up, throwing hot lead down the track ahead of the ominously onrushing cowcatcher!

At the Gatling, Captain Gringo shouted down to Gaston in the cab at the controls, "That's enough, leave the throttle wide open and jump, for pete's sake!"

Gaston said, "I do not jump for Pete. I jump for Gaston!" as he dove out to land in the grass and roll ass over-tea-kettle, but pistol in hand as he rose.

Captain Gringo hosed the Gatling back and forth, raking the house as he cranked the handle of the old-fashioned but fast-firing weapon. He saw the portly Dom Luis go down as the stream of bullets chopped his legs out from under him. Then Captain Gringo, too, took a headlong dive from the tender as the cowcatcher slammed into the wooden bumper at the end of the tracks.

The bumper of heavy timbers had been designed to stop a slowly moving freight car at most. It didn't even slow the gilded shay locomotive down. As the heavy engine ploughed on through and across the back lawn of Dom Luis's mansion, the big American lay flat in the grass and kept his head down. It was well he did so. The shay crashed into the house and was somewhere in the middle of it when its momentum pooped out, it fell on its side, and the boiler blew.

They'd filled the firebox to overflowing with hardwood soaked in the inflammable stinky-smoking latex so there'd been a lot of pressure in that boiler. Sheet tin roofing was still fluttering down as Captain Gringo bounded to his feet and cut back to the tree line to flop down next to Pancho, Diablilla, and his Maxim machine gun.

It was timed close, but right. He'd just primed the weapon when a mob of bewildered *flagelados* appeared in the smoke around the ruins of the house. He didn't know what the hell they expected to find there, but most of them were waving guns and yelling a lot, so he adjusted his windage and opened up with the Maxim.

187

When he finished his first belt, there weren't as many of them on their feet and those who were seemed to be running in the general direction of the great Atlantic Ocean.

Captain Gringo put in another belt before he rose, bracing the gun on his hip, and called out, "Okay, advance in line of skirmish!"

The long, ragged line of guerrillas moved across to take and dominate the crest of the hill that had once held the mansion of Dom Luis and still overlooked the village down by the water.

Gaston fell in beside him and muttered, "Take the high ground, *hein?* I just counted Dom Luis among the parboiled. That Negress, Varginha, says her Chinese friend seems to have made it out the front door, doubtless running quite fast. She would be down there among the others we have yet to convince of the error of their ways. What do you suggest, plunging fire?"

Captain Gringo yelled, "Hold and cover down, gang! If that guy down the slope isn't waving his laundry at us, he wants a parley."

Captain Gringo and his comrades waited as a wary *flagelado* approached to within hailing distance, holding an undershirt on a stick. When the tall American asked what he wanted, the *flagelado* leader called back, "We would like for to know your terms, Senhor."

"I could ask, and get, unconfucking surrender, but I'm an easygoing guy. I'll give you *flagelados* one hour, repeat *one*. If you're all on your way down the Putumayo when I take over the landing, then fine. If I see one man who's ever owned a pop gun, he dies. Agreed?"

"Senhor, we need time to think about this. There are Jivaro along the riverbanks. They may be annoyed at us for any number of reasons."

"That's your problem. I'm annoyed at you, too. So are the peons you've been abusing for the late Dom Luis. I'd say your best chance of staying alive was out on the water. It's not a hell of a good chance, but what do you expect, a lollypop?"

"But, Senhor, be merciful. Aside from headhunting Indians, many of my companions are wanted, farther east for, ah, past misunderstandings with the Brazilian police. The bargain you drive is a hard one. One could deny it was a bargain at all."

"You think so? Okay, just stick around for an hour. *My*

188

people think I'm acting like a sissy. So I may have to execute any survivors with trimmings. Have you ever swallowed a latex cocktail, motherfucker?"

"No, thank you, Senhor. I was just leaving."

And so, less than an hour later, the surviving *desperados* were on their way down the Putumayo. None of them was going anywhere important, since Diablilla had spotted Jivaro scouts that morning. The Indians had signaled friendly intent toward Captain Gringo's group. But some interesting shrunken heads figured to appear on the local *selva* scene soon.

The slaves and peons they'd liberated of course went nuts and started a noisy fiesta. It went on all day and into the night and Gaston was trying to decide whether he wanted to get drunk, get laid, or both, when he found Captain Gringo seated alone on the dock.

He said, "Well, my old and rare, we seem to have done it. You look a bit down in the mouth for a victory celebration, though."

Captain Gringo shrugged and said, "I think we've created a monster. You look pretty weird, too. Where'd you get that fancy ruffled shirt?"

"You admire it, *hein?* The late Dom Luis's company store charged most outrageous prices, but what are prices to a man with a gun? I got a bargain on a new wardrobe for Susan, too. At the moment she seems intrigued with the festivities, but she asked me to find out when it would be possible for her to get back to civilization. One gathers the missionary life no longer holds her undivided attention."

Captain Gringo said, "That's the monster. The steamboat won't be back for a while and I don't think I can keep myself in the catbird seat much longer."

"*Sacre!* More muttering in the ranks? Point out the ringleaders and I, Gaston, will nip the mutiny in the bud. I am feeling, how you say, keyed up? For all the anticipation, we won *très* easily today, *non?*"

"Yeah, too easy. The scared rebel kids we rescued think they're the Golden Horde of the Great Khan, now. It's the first time they ever won big. So it's gone to their heads. We didn't lose a man and we took a whole private empire for them to call their own. The slaves and peons keep telling them they're heroic liberators. A mess of them want to join up with the so-called Blue Brigade."

"*Eh bien,* there are plenty of weapons for the new recruits. Aside from cases of machetes there are boxes and

189

boxes of ammo in the warehouse and company store. I thought you a trifle generous in allowing those gunmen who surrendered to keep one shotgun to a canoe, but they left more than enough behind. Assuming half the new recruits are worth the damn, we would seem to have the makings of a small army here. So what is the problem, my old and rare?"

"The here part. Diablilla, Pancho, and the others have started talking silly about liberating the whole upper Putumayo. The peons we freed say there are other shits like Dom Luis in the area. Diablilla wants to use this place as a base and fight a *guerra por libertad*. She's gotten cocky as hell."

"Ah, that is the trouble with cocking women. It gives them delusions of intelligence to share pillow conversation with a man who knows what he is doing. As the daughter of one general and the *adelita* of another, the child now thinks she knows all the answers."

Gaston lit a smoke with a sardonic smile before he added, "By the way, does Diablilla know about you and that astonishingly nubile Negress?"

"Varginha? Who the hell told you about that?"

"Ah, when one has eyes, who has to tell him what he sees in the eyes of any woman, *hein?* Your little slave girl has also found a most attractive dress and the last time I saw her she was trying to be discreet. But every time your name is mentioned, Varginha glows rather smugly, if you know what I mean."

"Oh, shit, I thought all I had to worry about was a civil war I can't hope to control."

"*Merde,* why try? *Le Bon Dieu* knows the rubber barons in these parts need a good lesson. Let our Blue Brigade loot and burn at will. They'll no doubt recruit more men each time they hit a layout like this one. I agree you've unleashed a monster, but it may be a benign growth, *hein?*"

Captain Gringo said, "I'm all for *libertad*, in moderation. But I can't lead an army that won't listen to me. I just told Diablilla I thought our next move should be down the river before some real army comes here to find out what all the noise is about. She said her boys can handle any fucking army and suggested we put it to a vote."

Gaston whistled and said, "Ah, you *have* lost control then. Democracy in action has no place on the battlefield. But look on the bright side, Dick. If they no longer feel they need

190

us, we owe them even less. I may have forgotten to mention this, but when the ruins of the late Dom Luis's house cooled down I took the liberty of searching for mementos of our social call. He had a wall safe and, despite the fact that the wall was no longer there, the money inside was untouched by the fire."

Gaston took a thick wad of bills from his pants pocket as he added, "I have not counted it yet. One must be discreet among one's fellow looters. But I feel sure we have the wherewithal for an interesting weekend in Manaus even after we book passage on a steamer out."

Captain Gringo didn't answer. Gaston waited a moment before he sighed and said, "Am I going to have to hit you on the head and drag you off again, you thirteen species of idiot? It was *très* thoughtful of you to rescue those ungrateful rebels. It was downright quixotic of you to save these other people from slavery or worse. Now it is time for us to look out for our own precious derrieres, damnit! Why are you hesitating? Don't you like your derriere?"

"I'm not hesitating. I'm thinking. I'm not dumb enough to fight for leadership. If they want to go on fighting on their own, fuck 'em. I wish them well, but it's their revolution and their problem. But we've got a couple of other derrieres to think of besides our own. We can't abandon Susan Reynolds and that other girl, Varginha, could be in danger if we leave her behind. Diablilla has a temper, and she's going to be mad as hell when we skip out on her. If she found out poor little Varginha and I had been, well, pals . . ."

"Ah, true. We shall have to take the big blonde and the pretty Negress with us. It should make for an interesting trip *avec* salt and pepper for seasoning, *hein?* We know Susan does not mind changing partners. So if your more recent conquest . . ."

"For God's sake, you old goat, who screws whom is the least of our problems? I figure the four of us, the machine gun, and a month's supply of provisions will fit in a dugout. I'm not worried about slipping away from here unobserved. I don't think the local Jivaro will attack us. But Manaus is a hell of a ways off and there's no telling who or what we might run in to between here and there."

Gaston chuckled fondly and said, *"Eh bien,* why worry? Knowing you, you will either shoot or fuck anybody interesting that we meet along the way."

191

THE BEST OF ADVENTURE
by RAMSAY THORNE

RENEGADE #1   (90-976, $1.95)

RENEGADE #2: BLOOD
                    RUNNER   (90-977, $1.95)

RENEGADE #3: FEAR
                    MERCHANT   (90-761, $1.95)

RENEGADE #4: DEATH
                    HUNTER   (90-902, $1.75)

RENEGADE #5: MACUMBA
                    KILLER   (90-234, $1.75)

RENEGADE #6: PANAMA
                    GUNNER   (90-235, $1.75)

RENEGADE #7: DEATH IN
                    HIGH PLACES (90-548, $1.75)

RENEGADE #8: OVER THE
                    ANDES
                    TO HELL   (90-549, $1.75)